This book is dedicated to horses and all the people who love them; and most especially to our horse, Solo.

JENNIFER GRAIS & MICHAEL GRAIS

CHRISTA'S LUCK

The story of a girl, her horse, and the last wild mustangs

Graisland Productions
Published by Ingram Sparks

Paperback edition ISBN: 978-0-9906053-0-0
Electronic edition ISBN: 978-0-9906053-1-7

Printed in the United States of America
Designed by Damonza, Inc
Text set in Carre Noir

ACKNOWLEDGMENTS

WE WROTE THIS novel over the course of many years while living in Topanga Canyon, CA, San Miguel de Allende, Mexico, Taos, New Mexico, and Sonoma, CA. Completing this project did not just take one village, it took many!

Thank you to all those who made this book a reality: Susan Page and Dorothy Wall for helping us to get our original ideas off the ground and down on the page. Lauren Bjorkman, Alexandra Sternhagen, and Todd Wynward for being best Taos critique group ever. Victoria Bright for a thorough and thoughtful copy-edit. Rhonda Stapleton and Laurie Weed for your editorial genius. Eric Elfman, your coaching and wonderful critique group was instrumental in helping us finish the novel.

And to the early readers, Sarah Sander, Jak Wonderly, and Betty Davis-Drewery, we offer you a deep thanks for your insights, enthusiasm, and horse wisdom. Patty Leitner, thank you for your plot commentary and for your ability to offer clarity with such kindness. We could not have survived the rewrites or the proofing without you. Dan Bach, thank you for your glorious proofing skills and sense of humor. Amanda Foulger, Delphine Demore, and Mari Tara, you kept us functioning with your healing power and wise counsel. Karen and Suzy Grais, we are grateful for your love and support.

Janet Hogue: Your notes proved invaluable at a crucial time, my sister. Joan Boyer, Judy Paulson, and Jean Dillon, my other dear sisters, thank you for knowing what did not belong and for helping us to discover what did belong. We love you. Kelly Ann Hogue, thank you for sharing your brilliant ideas for the opening of the book. To all my nieces and nephews for your inspiration... you are the best. And to my parents, Ann and Ervin Gross, who gifted our family with their stories around the dinner table... how I love to laugh with all of you!

Speaking of laughter, thank you Wendy Hanus for your sense of humor and enduring faith in me, and Renee Miller for showing me what loving a pony (and all horses) looked like from a tender young age. You will always be the coolest Pony Girl.

Jak Wonderly, your photography, original cover design and website design for Christa's Luck continues to inspire us. Thank you to you and Suzy Esterhaus for a magical photo-shoot with our horse, Solo in the golden September sun.

The Taos gang: Greg and Vanessa Moon; Bob Renwick and Sharron Tavernier, Gary and Sabine Cook...we cherish your friendship.

Our gratitude to Ginger Kathrens and Ann Evans of the Cloud Foundation, who gave us invaluable feedback regarding wild mustang behavior and inspired the idea for the final chapter.

And lastly, the deepest thanks to my husband, Michael, who shared his mighty pen with a novice writer and taught me about dialogue, about passion, and about persistence. Without him this novel, and my life, would have been a very different story.

A blessing on all horses for their generosity of spirit, heavenly beauty, and earthy integrity. And to our powerful horse, Solo, who carries, heals, and inspires us at every turn.

To all adults, teenagers, and children who feel like they are climbing a mountain and cannot see the peak; Never. Ever. Give. Up.

PROLOGUE

LOOKING BACK, I could have never known how the Lost Herd would change my life forever. All I knew during the winter of my thirteenth year was that I was worried sick for all of Nevada's wild horses. Even as the snow fell, helicopters were driving the mustangs from the mountains and chasing them into a corral with a gate that would lock behind them forever.

The thought of the horses being terrorized by the wings of a death chopper and running for their lives over miles of icy ground broke my heart. Once they were trapped in the holding pen, it was just a matter of time before they lost hope. I knew if we took away all their reasons for living, if we kept them imprisoned long enough, the fire would drain from their eyes...and everything I loved about them would be destroyed.

I wanted to save every last mustang from being captured. But as luck—or an incredible lack of luck–would have it, something so terrible, so unimaginable happened that in the end, I'd be the one who needed saving.

CHAPTER 1

THE BRIDLE JANGLED as I lifted it from the tack room and slung it over my shoulder. I shuffled down the barn aisle in my worn boots, dragging Lucky's saddle under my arm. Last night's gloomy dreams had brought me down pretty low, but the rosy predawn glow over the Sage Mountains lifted my spirits. No clouds, fog, or snow meant I'd be riding for the first time in months. A ride out on the trail would do me good.

Dad, my sister Sara and I usually rode out together every Saturday, but the brutal storms in February and March had grounded us. Even with all the bad weather the roundups went on as scheduled; a hundred more mustangs now stood in holding pens. I was almost fourteen and I'd never been to a roundup, which was fine by me. Just the thought of seeing wild horses in jail made me bite down on my jaw so hard I thought I'd break a tooth.

My gray pony watched me with liquid eyes and nickered as I set the saddle down. I pulled a quartered apple out of my pocket and offered it to him over the stall door. Apples were a rare treat and Lucky chewed until it turned to apple juice and dripped from the corners of his mouth. I couldn't help but laugh. His eyes sparkled back at me and I felt the rough edges of my sadness melt away.

With a tack box full of brushes in hand, I slipped into his

stall. He was a light shade of gray with a wavy tail that touched the ground, and a mane so thick I could barely run my fingers through it. Lucky exhaled and the air filled with his sweet apple breath. But there was more to him than sweetness. On our very first ride, he'd taken off with me across the fields. The wind had stung my eyes and I'd laughed so hard I thought I'd die of pure happiness. He was the toughest, smartest pony in Nevada and he didn't like rules any more than I did.

When he finished the apple, he nuzzled my chest right over my heart until it felt warm. Then he slipped his nose into the halter I held out for him.

"Maybe we'll see the Lost Herd today," I told Lucky. We'd seen some beautiful bands of mustangs out at Blue Ridge, but never the legendary Lost Herd. I'd know them when I saw them.

Lucky shook his neck and turned a patient eye on me, having heard this rant many times in the six years we'd been together.

I patted his neck. "Yeah, I know. First we have to find them." My grandmother had told me stories about the Lost herd since I was little, but I wanted to prove they were more than just a story.

I brushed Lucky's whole body with a currycomb, loosening all the dirt and shedding hair, and emptied the hair from the brush in giant clumps onto the floor. Then I went over him with a softer brush until his coat felt smooth.

At 14.1 hands tall, Lucky was big for a pony. My arms ached as I swung the heavy saddle up onto his back. "Think of it, Lucky. Not one member of that herd has ever been saddled." He craned his neck around and nipped at me as I tightened the cinch. I guess I shouldn't have told him about horses who have never been saddled. I soothed him as best I could by rubbing the inside of his ear until he tilted his head with pleasure. "Everyone from cowboys to gold miners have tried to round them up, but the Lost Herd has slipped through every trap, and then disappeared into the hills."

Sara strode into the barn in her skinny jeans, her face flushed with excitement. She glanced over her shoulder back toward the house. "Christa, Mom and Dad had a fight last night after you went to sleep."

I pretended I didn't hear her and continued to use a hoof pick to clean Lucky's feet. It wasn't like Mom and Dad to fight, but since Mom had gotten pregnant she could get kind of… emotional.

"Well, you're lucky you skipped breakfast. She was in a bad mood."

"So am I," I said. I knew where this was headed. I didn't want to give Sara any encouragement. Miss Drama Queen had a way of stirring up trouble.

Sara slipped into Star's stall and haltered her sleek black mare. "I'm just warning you. She's pissed about your algebra quiz."

"I got a 'C'. Big deal," I said. Why did Mom have to be a math teacher? If I got anything less than a B, she took it personally. Sara got around that problem by never getting less than an A. I didn't have a mathematical brain like they did. I led Lucky out of his stall.

Sara grabbed Star's lead rope and followed us like a magpie, flapping her beak. "She said you should be studying today and not riding."

"Maybe you should be saddling Star and not yapping," I said.

"For once we agree. Why would I want to talk to you anyway?" Sara tied Star to the hitching post and began to brush her coat furiously. Dust rose in clouds.

I waited a beat. "Because I'm so sweet."

"Right," she said sarcastically. "Like when you want something."

It may sound weird, but I loved the banter with Sara. It was our usual way of communicating. Sara talked too much, but she was cute in all the ways I wasn't. If we were horses, she'd be the racy, dark Thoroughbred, and I'd be the gritty sorrel. I got the red hair and pale skin with freckles. She got the arching eyebrows, curved cheekbones, and full lips. Since she'd turned fifteen she was a boy magnet. She was gorgeous and she knew it. In fact, her beauty was one of her favorite subjects.

"Your hair looks good," I said. I figured the day would go easier if she was in a good mood. I knew how to cheer her up.

"Exactly." Sara pointed the brush at me. "I'm having an incredible hair day and no one's going to see it. So I posted a pic on Facebook."

"Getting an early start. Great idea." I thought that was ridiculous, but whatever.

"Well, I'm not going to post a selfie after the ride…I'll have hat-head."

I nodded. "A disaster. If any of your friends saw you like that, it would ruin your image."

"At least I have an image."

That stung. Eighth grade sucked. I was known as the pony girl at school, which made me cool with some horse-crazy girls, but completely invisible to boys. Ever since my best friend Heather moved to Ohio over Christmas break, I hadn't had anyone to hang out with. I busied myself with Lucky's bridle.

"Oh, c'mon, don't pout. I didn't mean that, Christa."

"I know." Sara wasn't mean. She just liked to exaggerate, especially when it came to Mom. Or my faults. Or Dad. Or boys. Or her beauty. Or any combination of the above.

Sara laid her head dreamily on Star's flank. "I'm already in love with the baby. Can't you just picture her, curled up in Mom's belly like a giant peanut?"

"Yep." I settled myself in the saddle. "Do you think Mom will be okay this time?"

"I don't know. She's four and a half months"

Mom had lost her baby last time when she was five months along a few years ago. She plunged into a depression I didn't want to relive or remember. "I guess it's risky trying again at her age. She's kind of ancient."

"Thirty-nine is the new twenty-nine."

She'd probably just read that in a magazine or something. "Dad's waiting for us at the gate," I said, happy to change the subject.

"Yeah, just need to get my gloves in the barn."

Sara ran back down the barn aisle and then charged outside, holding my tack box in the air.

"You left this out. I'm not cleaning up after you anymore! You left piles of Lucky's shedding hair everywhere. You don't do anything you're supposed to, and I'm tired of covering for you!"

"I'll clean it up when we get back! It's just some hair." *What was her glitch today?*

"You know Dad's rules. I swear, I'm telling him."

"Go ahead!"

I turned away and urged Lucky toward the trail. I needed to get away from her. Ever since she'd become a sophomore she thought she knew everything. She was always bossing me around as if I didn't know about Dad's rules: "Order in the barn prevents accidents." But there hadn't been any accidents, so I wasn't worried. Besides, no one could clean up the barn like neat-freak Sara, so maybe she was better off doing it. It gave me more time to ride, and her more time to make everything look perfect and text her friends.

I'll admit there were things I forgot. Every once in a great while, I was known to oversleep while Sara rose faithfully at the crack of dawn and did all the feeding. By the time I showed up at the barn and tried to make myself useful, she'd sigh in exasperation and tell me I was just getting in the way. I was supposed to do the night feeding (on account of my late waking tendencies), throwing flakes of alfalfa and grass mix down to the stalls from the hayloft, but sometimes I got home late from a ride and Sara had already done it. It wasn't that I tried to screw up; I just got distracted. But I always kept the water troughs full and the stalls free of manure. Sara could complain all she wanted; I wasn't a complete slug.

I clucked at Lucky and he responded, trotting through feather light snow. The early morning air snapped with a dry cold that left my cheeks tingling. Lucky snorted and bucked as we wound up the path toward the gate. I halted him with a quick pull of the reins and a shift in my weight. "Mind your manners or we're turning back," I said in as stern a voice as I could muster. Being on his back again felt like heaven, and I could hardly blame him for being fresh after all the time off. "Good boy," I said once he'd settled.

Down below stood the faded red barn and our two-story yellow farmhouse with its wrap-around front porch. Mom's pottery studio stood off to the side of the house. It looked so cute down there, like a toy farm. Sweet and humble. We weren't like the ranchers in this area that had serious acreage. We didn't own cattle. Dad worked from home as an accountant and Mom taught at the community college in Albright, the next town over.

Beyond our little ranch stretched the valley, ten miles to the town of Spring Hills and five miles to Safeway. Everything down there appeared flat, safe and boring.

When I turned back to the trail, I felt a thrill of adventure. This path led right into the foothills of the Sage Mountains and out to the range. I took my first deep breath of the day and smiled. I'd choose the trail over town any day. I gave Lucky the reins and we continued up the hill.

The steady footfalls of Star's trot thumped up behind us. Sara pulled even with us just as we topped the hill. And there was Dad, leaning casually against the rusty pipe-corral gate, lighting up a cigarette while Eastwood, his golden Palomino, stood beside him saddled and ready to go. Our two dogs, Chico and Elvis, rushed up to greet us, tails wagging and bodies wriggling with joy. With their short-haired yellow coats, they wouldn't last long out in the cold. We never brought them along on the rides anyway.

I pulled Lucky to a halt. He stretched his neck down and touched noses with the dogs briefly.

Dad held the cigarette between his thumb and forefinger and inhaled with his eyes closed.

"You trying to start a fire, Dad?" I asked.

"Mom would kill you if she knew," Sara said.

He smiled apologetically. "I'm down to one a week." The words came out in a cloud of smoke. He looked at the cigarette like it had a secret message for him.

Dad smoked when he was upset about something. Maybe Sara hadn't been exaggerating for once about that fight she'd heard. I zipped my fleece up around my neck. There was a morning chill in the air. "Everything good with you, Dad?" I asked.

"Tax season. Everyone wants their returns done yesterday," he said.

I glanced over my shoulder toward Sara. "A nosy little bird told me Mom's on a rampage."

Sara shot me a death glare.

I thought I caught a spark of humor in Dad's eye, but he ducked his chin, and his face fell under the shadow of his hat. "Your Mom's got a stack of tests to grade and she's not feeling too good. How about we enjoy the day?" He rubbed his whiskered cheeks. Shaving wasn't his strong point.

"Yeah, let's go already," I said.

Sara's phone beeped with her stupid text alert. Lucky jumped. "Shut that thing off," I said. "Let's go!"

"I'm just gonna check it," Sara said. "Oh my God, it's Kim!" she giggled. Her fingers flew as she texted back.

Dad suppressed a smile and dropped his cigarette, grinding it out with the toe of his boot. He swung a leg over Eastwood and settled easily into the saddle. I couldn't imagine him without a horse. The only time he'd ever been without one was in college.

I watched Sara texting with disgust. When Sara goes to college, she'd probably marry some jock and forget all about Star, but I would never leave Lucky. I was going to be a vet. "If you're studying to be a vet, don't they have stables where you can keep your horse?" I asked.

Sara leaned back casually in the saddle and studied her phone. "You have to graduate from middle school first."

"Very funny," I said.

Dad cleared his throat. "Listen up, girls. The ice and snow should melt by noon, but this morning I want heads-up riding, especially on the hills. No racing, no fooling around, and–" he glanced at Sara, "no texting."

Sara pursed her lips and her jaw tightened. Then she slipped her phone back into her coat pocket.

"No texting and riding," I said, just to dig it in.

Dad opened the gate and Sara and I rode through side by side, falling into an easy rhythm born of hours riding together. Scrubby little piñon pines dotted the foothills, a dusting of snow on their branches. As we wound up the trail, the soothing smell of sage washed over me.

I loved the view from up here. The mountains extended to the horizon like an arrow, their granite crags glistening with snow. Turner's Peak, the highest point at 11,000 feet, looked like the face of an old man in profile with a big nose and chin.

Dad followed my gaze. "When all that snow up there melts,

we're gonna have floods in the washes and rivers running high and fast."

Sara and I exchanged glances. Dad liked to make a big thing of potential natural disasters.

"But not today," Sara said, grinning at me.

"Nope, not today," Dad said.

All I saw was blue sky, miles of freedom and the promise of wild horses. "We heading up to Blue Ridge? We might find the Marietta Herd there," I said.

"Don't set your sights too high," Dad said. "It's been awhile since we've seen any mustangs. The BLM's been awfully busy."

The BLM was short for Bureau of Land Management. The same people that were in charge of managing the trails and parks on public land were also in charge of managing our wild horses. Bad. The round-ups sickened me, but I didn't know how to stop them. I tried to push the thought of captured wild horses to the back of my mind and think about happier things. "Well, the Marietta Herd is still free."

Sara swallowed hard. "I didn't want to tell you, but I heard they got rounded up in March."

My stomach twisted into a tight fist, crushing the air out of my lungs. How many times had we seen that herd? Well, mostly just their butts and tails as they were running away, but still...I'd felt like I'd known them.

"They belong out at Blue Ridge, not in a corral," I said.

"I know," Sara agreed.

I had the sudden urge to chew off all my nails, but my gloves were in the way. Maybe I could gnaw my hand off. "Why can't they just let all of them run free?"

Dad tapped his reins against his leg. "It's complicated."

"Well, the horses aren't complicated, so it must be humans complicating things," I said.

Dad nodded.

That pissed me off. Why didn't he care? "Why do you act like it's no big deal?"

He coughed into his hand. "It's complicated," he said. Again.

"That's not an answer!" I said. "Why don't you try to fix it?

His eyes softened. "Christa, if there was something I could do, I would do it."

I couldn't believe how calm he was, as if none of this mattered. "If we keep on capturing them, how long will it be before there's no wild mustangs left on the range?"

Silence. I guess that was my answer–there wasn't one. But the longer Dad and Sara didn't say anything, the more frustrated and alone I felt.

I kicked Lucky into a trot and we took the lead. I needed something good to happen. I needed to know that something wild and beautiful could survive in this world, because I was losing hope fast. I leaned forward and whispered in Lucky's ear. "We have to find the Lost Herd today, or I will seriously die."

CHAPTER 2

FOR MOST OF the ride, I didn't speak. Lucky had been a handful, spooking at his shadow and every gust of wind. When Lucky danced sideways at a rabbit crossing the trail, Dad raised his eyebrow in my direction, but said nothing. I held Lucky back and we dropped into line behind Eastwood and Star. Lucky exhaled and pushed his nose into Star's rump. There were days he might get a swift kick for that, but not today. Star was the lead mare of the group. She could be bossy and moody, but for the most part, she was fair.

We halted at the edge of an icy slope. It looked like it was about fifty horse-steps worth of steep trail, which was enough to get into trouble. Dad's jaw tightened. "I'm not sure about this trail."

"It's fine, Dad," I said. Lucky and I had covered worse terrain than this. Besides, I wasn't going to sit around all day and wait for the ice to melt. Without waiting for his reply, I urged Lucky over the precipice. But I had underestimated the slick-factor. On the first step, Lucky's right hind leg slipped out from under him. He scrambled to get his footing, and then fell backward. I dipped in the saddle as his butt went down.

My heartbeat quickened and a spike of fear stabbed through me. Lucky braced his front legs, but the ice gave him nothing to hold onto. He was sliding down the hill on his haunches like a huge dog. Bad things could happen in a split second with horses. In a flash, I remembered how I'd fallen off Lucky and broke my collarbone. I'd ridden him all the way home in a haze of pain, hunched over his neck like a drunken cowboy.

"Christa!" Sara screamed. "Jump off!"

The grade was so steep, I only had to swing my leg over, tuck and roll, but I hesitated. Lucky's front hooves struck solid ground and his back legs came under him. He pulled himself up to standing. I let out a huge sigh of relief. We picked the rest of the way down one step at a time.

When we reached the bottom, Lucky shook the snow that clung to his haunches. I dismounted and ran a hand down his legs. "He's alright," I said to Dad and Sara, who had managed to safely navigate the icy hill.

I braced myself. Now I was going to hear from Dad about how I needed to be more careful. I was too impulsive. I needed to think before I acted. I didn't like hearing that speech. I was the way I was. Yeah, there were consequences. Sometimes it paid off for me, and sometimes it got me in trouble.

"You need to be more careful," Dad said, his face pinched with worry.

I knew it was coming, but it still stung. I hated to see him upset.

He adjusted his cowboy hat and rode Eastwood in a circle around me. "Lucky could've torn a tendon or broken a leg."

The last thing I wanted to do was hurt Lucky. For such big animals, they were fragile. "I know, I'm sorry. I was just in a hurry to get to Blue Ridge."

"Well, slow down," he said. He spoke quietly, but his words sank in. I lowered my head.

"You okay?" Sara asked.

"Yep," I said.

"At least you weren't hurt," Dad said as I mounted.

Sara leaned over and patted Lucky's neck. "You get extra points for skiing, Lucky," she whispered.

"Ha ha. I don't want to hear another word about it," I said. Star sniffed noses with Lucky and we moved on down the trail.

While Dad rode ahead, Sara made a complete recovery from my almost-tragic riding accident. She took the opportunity for some bonding time on the trail by filling me in on all her new friends. Apparently, Kim was her fave. "She's a junior. She just transferred from Albright. We're meeting a bunch of friends at Red's Diner later."

"Sounds like fun," I said. Sara was BFFs with juniors now. She'd crossed the line into the higher stratospheres of popularity.

"My best friend is in Ohio," I whispered under my breath.

Sara twisted in her saddle so I wouldn't miss a word. "Dylan's becoming a problem. I made the mistake of asking him to Sadie Hawkins and now he thinks we're going out."

"Uh-oh," I said. You could've teleported Lucky and me to some distant planet and I swear it would've taken Sara at least an hour to notice we were missing. "Asking him to a dance does seem like you're going out."

"I asked him as a friend.

"Well then, maybe he thinks you're going out as friends."

Sara huffed and turned her face away from me. "You don't get it."

When it came to boys, I guess logic was ridiculous. "Whatever," I said.

We climbed a rocky slope, and miracles of miracles, Sara stopped talking. For a moment, all was quiet except for the sound of horses breathing and the creak of saddle leather. The sun rose higher in the sky, warming my back and turning the snow to slush. I unzipped the collar of my fleece.

We topped the rise, and Dad fell back beside us. "The footing is safe now. Let's open them up."

Sagebrush drifted on a flat plain for as far as the eye could see. This was where we usually indulged in a race.

I caught Dad's eye. "Sure it's okay if I go fast now?"

He nodded.

Eastwood leapt forward into a gallop and all three of us were off, Lucky's shorter legs churning to keep up. The wind stung my eyes and the sagebrush blew past in a blur. Star ran neck and neck with Eastwood, and then she blasted ahead, her black tail flagged high, and her neck stretched long. That mare could run faster than the speed of light. If Lucky and I were going to win, we'd have to outsmart them.

The trail curved in a wide arch to the left and then straightened out by a lightning-struck juniper tree. That was our finish line. I swung Lucky off the beaten path and we cut across the desert at a high gallop. I could see Eastwood and Star round the bend, a yellow and black blur, and I leaned forward into Lucky's neck. "C'mon, faster!" I whispered in his ear.

He flung his hoofs out and leapt into a stride that would've made Sea Biscuit proud. We reached the tree just as Star and Eastwood rounded the bend. As we flashed across the finish line, I threw my arms up in the air. "We win!"

"No fair, you cheated!" Sara said and laughed. The horses pranced and blew through flared nostrils as we continued down the trail, three across.

I patted Lucky's neck. "Well, nobody can outrun Star without cheating."

"That's for sure," Dad said, shaking his head. "Nice riding, girls."

Sara could ride like she was built right into Star's back. I always admired her for that. But I sat a horse alright. Dad had plopped me in a saddle as soon as I was old enough to walk. Riding Lucky was as easy as breathing for me. "Well, Dad, we were taught by the best."

Dad seemed to puff up a bit from the compliment. "Let's celebrate Christa's win and take a break." He pulled Eastwood to a halt and threw us each a power bar and a bottle of water from his pack. We chewed in silence.

Dad squinted into the bright sun. "With weather like this, we could ride all the way to Gold Canyon."

Sara took on the hushed tone of a storyteller. "Gold Canyon... the legendary place of the Lost Herd, where Grandma's friend, Old Man Hutchinson, got caught in a storm." She winked at me. If Sara was trying to egg me on, it was working.

"What's so unbelievable about being caught in a blizzard?" I asked, stuffing the rest of the power bar into my mouth.

"I'm okay with the blizzard. It's the part where a black mare appears out of the swirling snow and leads Old Hutch to a cave— that's where Grandma lost me," Sara said.

Sara lacked imagination. That was always her problem. "Well, she didn't lose me," I said. "And when the storm passed, there was no sign of the herd except for a tangle of hoof prints in the snow near the cave." Just recounting the story ignited a blaze of desire to see the Lost Herd.

Dad shrugged. "Your Grandma tells a good story."

Grandma lived in Reno. She wasn't here to defend herself. Not fair. "Grandma's story is nothing compared to the other stories I've heard," I said.

Sara held one finger up in the air. "I know your favorite one— don't tell me–the black mare that galloped out of a lightning bolt during a storm?"

"Or the stallion that jumped from one side of Gold Canyon to the other, escaping from the cowboys that wanted to rope him," Dad said, grinning.

"Go ahead and laugh," I said, warming up to a real good rant. "Someday—"

Before I could say another word, Lucky pinned his ears, took the bit in his mouth, and trotted forcefully up the path. "Lucky! What's gotten into you?" I pulled on the left rein and brought him around hard in a circle. We'd reached a fork in the trail. One direction led up to Blue Ridge, the other swung in a loop back home. Usually when a horse wanted to run away with you, he pointed his nose toward the barn. But Lucky danced and tossed his head, fighting to go further down the trail. Then he stopped. He pricked his ears and trembled. I could feel his muscles tensing under my legs. My senses tingled. Was there an animal nearby? His nostrils worked. "What is it, boy?" I asked, peering into the sagebrush. "A bobcat?"

"Lucky's full of himself today," Sara said as she and Dad caught up.

I tried to act cool. "Yep. Are we going back home or up to Blue Ridge?" I asked, daring them to back down.

"I'm kind of ready to head back," Sara said, looking at her phone. "No cell reception."

At that exact moment, Lucky broke free again and veered sharply up the trail to Blue Ridge. This was not a proud moment for me. A rider should be in control of her horse at all times, but I knew Lucky well enough. It wasn't like him to act fresh this far into the ride. I trusted his instincts…I mean, Lucky could sense things well before I ever saw them, but still. If I didn't get him under control, Sara was never going to let me hear the end of it. I yanked on the left rein again and swung him back in another circle. "How about we head up to Blue Ridge?" I called to them. To my relief, they followed without comment.

I gave Lucky his head. He dashed up the curving switchback trail. As we crested the hill, he stopped and snorted. I followed his gaze.

And then I saw them.

Mustangs dotted the basin below, grazing on the first spring grasses of the valley. They weren't just a scraggly herd of mustangs either. I counted at least ten bands, each led by a stallion and mare, some with foals. If a wild horse lottery existed, we'd just won it. Something sprang alive in me, as if every cell of my body had a heart that had suddenly started beating. I had an instant desire to leave everything behind and run free with this herd.

Lucky dropped his head to search for grass, as if he could care less. A smile spread across my face. "Oh, Lucky, you're living up to your name today." I slid down from the saddle and wrapped my arms around his neck. "You clever pony." Lucky could pull some amazing stunts. Like, he could escape from his stall no matter what kind of latch we used to close it. And then when I'd find him grazing outside the barn in the morning, he'd look up and go back to grazing, like nothing was out of the ordinary.

"Did you know they were here, Lucky?" He nuzzled the toe of my boot and kept eating. "Okay, whatever. I guess I'll never know for sure," I said. "But I'm onto you." I looked out to the herd and my heart filled with such joy, it was like the goldfinch perched in the rabbit brush was singing just for me. I sank to my knees in wonder.

Dad and Sara joined us on the ridge. "What's up?" Dad asked.

I pointed.

"Whoa," Sara said.

Dad pulled out his field glasses.

"The Lost Herd," I said. I couldn't believe I'd forgot my binocs. Today of all days.

Dad focused the glasses. "Maybe." He spoke quietly as usual.

Sara looked skeptical. "How would we know?"

"There's no other herds this big left after all the roundups," I said.

"Figures you would know that," Sara said.

Several groups of horses grazed, their tails swishing flies. Occasionally a head shot up to smell the air.

"Will they run if they smell us?" Sara asked.

I scrambled back up onto Lucky. "We're too far away to spook them."

Without lowering the field glasses, Dad picked up the reins and nudged Eastwood a little closer to the edge of the ridge. "I count at least a hundred and fifty horses. There's no herd this big left in Nevada…"

He caught my gaze and held it. "Looks like the Lost Herd has just been found," he said.

"Grandma is gonna freak!" I threw my arms around Lucky's neck.

"The Lost Herd is real?" Sara pulled her cowboy hat off and combed her fingers through her silky hair. "Then those legends about them aren't true. They're not ghost horses."

Boy, could she miss the point! It was easy to see how a beautiful herd of wild mustangs could inspire legends, but I didn't want to waste my breath trying to explain. "I'd rather have them be real anyway. Just look at all of them down there," I whispered. "They're beautiful."

"They are," Sara conceded. For a second, I almost forgave her for teasing me about them.

Dad gripped the field glasses. "Looks like we've got something here. This must be the lead stallion and his band. All the other horses are making way for him."

I thought I saw a group of horses running, but my eyes couldn't quite make them out. "Dad! You're killing me." I stood up in the stirrups as if that might help, knowing full well it wouldn't.

Dad remained motionless, captivated by the Lost Herd. "In the legend, his name was Mesteño," Dad said.

"Mesteño means *mustang* and mustang means *untamed*. I Wikipedia-ed it a long time ago," I said.

"Nice," Sara said, grimacing.

I decided to torture her with another fun fact. "The Spanish brought them here."

"Fascinating," Sara said. "That was a million years ago. Mesteño is dead by now, unless of course he's a vampire and lives forever. "

I glared at her. "Of course, the stallion from the legend is gone, but another one has replaced him. And we can still call this one Mesteño. I'll know for sure after I get a look at him." I sighed. "*If* I ever get a look at him." I gazed longingly at Dad's field glasses. "Earth to Dad," I said. "C'mon, a minute ago you and Sara were joking about them."

Dad snapped out of his horse-induced coma and handed me the binocs with a starry-eyed grin. "You're gonna love this, Christa."

I scanned over the grassy plain below. Wild horses came into focus. Mares, yearlings, foals, and stallions of every color grazed together. The mustangs stood taller than Lucky, but only by a hand or so. Battle-scarred flanks, rounded muscles, hard hooves, and dramatically long manes set them apart from our horses. Wonder flooded through me and a tingle of nerves floated down my spine. "Look at all these bands."

Sara's ears pricked. "Boy bands? Now that would be something."

I laughed, but I couldn't help myself from stating the obvious. "No, horse bands. Families that live on their own."

"Thanks for the info," she said, sarcastically.

Dad took a swig of water from the canteen and spoke out of the side of his mouth, probably trying his best to ignore us. "Unless there's good water or grass available, then they come together like they are now."

I scanned the herd with the field glasses. "Where is the lead stallion?" I spotted a black mare that kept raising her head in the air. Whenever she did, it was as if all the other horses caught the same scent and lifted their heads up, too. The mustangs seemed as connected to each other as a flock of birds flying together.

I looked more closely at the dusky lead mare. Her mane fell in tangles almost down to the ground and her flanks held scars from at least one nasty fight. I'd never seen a mare this tough. Little hairs rose all the way down my arms. Could she be the black mare from the legend?

The mare led her band down to drink at the river. And then my breath caught in my throat. A red and white paint stallion broke from the cover of the dense brush along the water. He looked like a white horse that had been splattered with brownish-red paint. His long, white forelock fell over his eyes and his mane blew wildly as he pranced alongside his mares. The stallion had a narrow chest, thick mane and tail, and the most perfect curve to his neck. His muscles rippled under his coat with each stride and the space all around him seemed to crackle with energy.

"Dad, I see him. The stallion!"

"Let me see," Sara said, finally caving in to her curiosity.

"So now you're into them?" I gripped the field glasses tighter. My heart pounded like a crazy drum.

The stallion stood guard, looking out for his mares and all the other horses. Seeing his mane blow in the wind caused a knot of longing in my stomach. He was worthy of legend, his eyes alight with intelligence, his every raw movement a testament to the power of nature. "Mesteño," I whispered. In a world filled with computers, shopping malls, and math tests, I wondered how a stallion like Mesteño could still exist.

Sara's frustrated voice distracted me. "Christa, let me see."

I stalled. "In a minute."

Mesteño pawed the ground and wrestled with a young stallion, their manes and necks in a tangle. When Mesteño had his fill of the game, he spun and gave a final kick with his hind legs. The blow struck the haunches of the younger horse, which turned and galloped back to his buddies.

Mesteño trotted through the bands regally as if he were on patrol, sniffing noses with some horses and breaking up fights with others. No matter where he moved in the herd, he always seemed connected to his band of mares. He cantered back to the black mare's side and groomed her withers using his strong teeth. She stretched her neck out, as if she was getting her back scratched in just the right place. She looked like she was heavy with foal.

Sara grumbled something about my time being up, but I pretended not to hear. I knew there would be consequences for ignoring her—she had lots of ways to make my life miserable, but I couldn't tear my eyes away from the Lost Herd.

The black mare's head shot up and for a second she looked right at me, right through me. Did she have x-ray vision? My bones tingled. Did the instinct run so strong in her blood that she could see the real me?

In that moment, the spirit of a girl met the spirit of a wild mare. I named her Corazón, which means *heart* in Spanish. Something told me she had a lot of it. When she dropped my gaze,

I felt like I'd been released from a spell. Her nostrils flared and she looked out to the west hills.

The stallion stood rigidly, his eyes locked on Corazón. She stamped her foot. His skin twitched. Then the stallion wheeled toward the band, nipped at one of his mares, and the herd was in motion, the stallion behind them. We watched as they disappeared into the distance, and we stared after them a long time in silence.

Then I gave Sara the field glasses.

CHAPTER 3

THE DREAM TOOK me under. I stood watching from a ridge as all the mares and stallions of the Lost Herd galloped madly into a huge corral below. They were running away from a monstrous blue wave that rose from the desert, gaining speed as it swept toward us. Corazón caught my scent and snapped her head in my direction. Our eyes locked. Electric blue sadness loomed in her eyes as the blue wave roared like a hurricane. I was confused, scared, and didn't know what to do. The wave grew bigger and bigger until it blotted out the sun.

The last foal careened into the pen, and the metal gate slammed shut and locked. Slam! I wanted to run to the corral and let the horses out, but I couldn't budge. It felt like someone had poured cement in my boots as fear planted me to the spot. The wave tumbled, crashed, and groaned, a tsunami swallowing everything in its path.

Wind pummeled the desert as the first spray of water touched my face. An echoing boom roared in my ears. I looked up to see the wave curling like a python twenty stories high, ready to strike, right over my head. Mesteño gathered his herd into the far end of the corral and reared up, slashing the air with his hooves. All I could do was shield my eyes and scream.

The scream woke me up. I lay in bed shivering for a long time with the strange taste of rusted metal in my mouth– the taste of fear. My face was wet with tears and my heart thundered so fast I had to gasp for air. I looked around the bedroom at my horse models on the bookshelf, dirty clothes piled up on my desk chair, and a history book I was supposed to read poking out of my backpack. My bulletin board over the desk with its pictures of Lucky caught my eye. Just seeing his cute pony face calmed my nerves. I padded to the bathroom and splashed my face with water.

As I threw on my t-shirt and jeans, I glanced up at the poster over my bed of Wild Horse Annie. "I'm not you," I whispered to her sepia-colored picture. There she was, a strong, thin woman with a toothy smile sitting astride her horse. "I can't protect the mustangs like you did," I said. She just stared back at me. There was something in her eyes that made me feel like she was urging me to do something. "What can I do?" I asked, almost whining. Surprise—she didn't answer. Yep, I was talking to a poster of a woman who died in 1977.

I ran out to the barn before anybody came down for breakfast and found Lucky grazing on a dried bush near the corral. He must've slipped his lock again. I'd seen him in action during one of his stall busts. He used his upper lip to jiggle the lock and then slid the stall door open with his nose. A regular Houdini.

Lucky trotted to me with a sparkle in his eye. "Oh, Lucky. What am I gonna do with you?" I asked, rubbing his soft muzzle. "Just promise me you'll never run away." He nosed my pockets for a treat. I gave him a carrot. I wasn't above bribery.

After I tossed a flake of grass hay to Eastwood and Star, I saddled Lucky. I'd clean the stalls later. I mounted and we trotted up the hill. Sitting on Lucky's back and feeling the swing of his jaunty stride usually made me feel happy, but the image of Corazón's pleading stare lingered.

"I had a bad dream, Lucky," I said, as if he had any idea what I was talking about. I wound his mane around my hand. "Feels like something bad is about to happen."

Lucky darted sideways, spooking at a pine branch blowing in the wind. "You are not afraid of that tree," I laughed. "It's been standing there longer than you or me have been alive. Yep, right there in that same place." He snorted and tossed his head in the way he sometimes did before he bucked. "Don't go getting any ideas before we even get through the gate."

I tried to sit Lucky's bouncy trot and soak up the beauty around me, but I couldn't seem to shake the strange jumble of terror and sadness that lingered from the nightmare. When you live in the desert and start dreaming about tsunamis, it's not a great sign.

When the wind came up, it seemed to blow right through me. Normally I could handle any kind of wind Nevada could throw at me, but today I felt kind of wimpy. I turned back. We cantered the last stretch home, and then walked the rest of the way down the hill to the barn. By the time I pulled Lucky's saddle off, I was chilled to the bone.

I rubbed Lucky down and turned him out to pasture with Star and Eastwood. Sara had cleaned their stalls already and was sitting on the corral fence texting like mad. Her fingers flew over the keys in a blur.

Thanks for mucking the stalls," I said. "You beat me to it. At least I fed them this morning."

She glanced up and nodded. Clearly, she had more important things on her mind. Without stopping her text, she slid her eyes back to the phone and mouthed, *Dylan.*

"Wow," I said. Like I cared. Actually, I was starving.

When I entered the house, I heard Mom and Dad talking in the kitchen. "This Saturday there's going to be a roundup in Dixon," Dad said. "The BLM's going after the Towhee herd. It could be another—" He stopped when he saw me framed in the door. He cleared his throat and exchanged glances with Mom.

I steeled myself. I'd been avoiding it for years, but it was time to see a roundup. Not that it was the most daring move ever made in history or anything, but it was a place to start. Maybe I could learn something that would help the mustangs. "A roundup?" I asked. "I'm going."

Mom set a bowl of Cheerios down at the table. "Morning, Sweet Potato," she said. Her pixie haircut and delicate features made her look like an actress. Somehow, her red hair wasn't a tangled mess like mine. Oh yeah. That's because it was straight like Sara's. The thought that I was dropped at their door by a curly redheaded gypsy occurred to me. "You sure you want to do this?" Mom asked.

I nodded yes, but I noticed my foot tapping nervously as if I'd just pounded down a caramel frappuccino at Starbucks. I slipped into my chair at the table. "I'm as ready as I'll ever be."

Dad glanced up from his plate. "What changed your mind about seeing one?"

"It's just time." I didn't know how to set things right for the mustangs, but the girl in the dream who stood on the hill doing zilch? Well, that wasn't going to be me. Not anymore.

"I still don't think this is a good idea," Mom said. "The roundups are…well, it could upset you for a long time."

Sara bounced into the kitchen. She had freshened up since I'd seen her in the barn a few minutes before. Pink lip-gloss. Silky, shiny hair. A blue scarf tied in a French knot. Dark skinny jeans and sneakers. She looked like she'd walked out of a Gap ad. Whatever had happened with Dylan must've put her in a great mood. "What's this about a roundup?" she asked.

I tried to eat a spoonful of cereal, but the milk tasted sour. I pushed the bowl away. "It's this Saturday in Dixon. And you're going," I said.

Sara poured herself a splash of coffee followed by a half pint of cream and a mound of sugar. "Well, I can't let my little Sweet Potato down, now can I?"

I groaned. Sweet Potato was Mom's nickname for me. I always thought it was wishful thinking on Mom's part. But maybe I'd grow into it– I mean the sweet part. Mom and Dad had called Sara "Princess" since she was two, and God knows she'd grown into that.

"Promise me you're coming, Sara," I said. For some reason I really wanted her there.

Sara leaned against the counter with her hands wrapped around her coffee mug. "I'm hanging out with Kim on Saturday, but I can probably talk her into going." A dreamy look came over her face. "Kim lives next door to *James Miller*," she gushed.

We knew Mr. and Mrs. Miller from the horse show world. Their son, James, had led the Spring Hills' Cougars to the state championship and was officially the biggest hero ever to grace Albright County. Even I had to admit he was super cute. But he was in college now and safely out of Sara's reach. "Sara, stay focused. Swear on your life you'll be there."

She squirmed, but then met my eyes. "I swear."

"Pinkie swear," I commanded. Even after all these years, it was still our unbreakable law that a pinkie promise could not be ignored or forgotten.

"Okay, okay," she grumbled, linking her pinkie in mine.

I tried my most convincing Sweet Potato grin. "Well, it's settled then. We're all going."

When Saturday came, we piled into Dad's truck and drove through Spring Hills to get lunch, although my stomach was so tied up in knots I wasn't sure I could eat. Mom talked math with a teacher's assistant on her cell phone in the front seat, while Sara chatted non-stop about Kim, Dylan, the new Pink song, and what was happening in all the gossip mags with me in the back. I was thrilled. *Not.*

When Mom ended her call, she swung around to look at me, shocking me with her blue eyes. Were my eyes that intense? "You okay?" she asked.

"Yep," I said. "But I wish Grandma could be here."

Mom nodded. "She and Grandpa can't get away from the store just now."

She frowned. I know she missed them both. They ran a small jewelry store in Reno, which was only three hours away, but sometimes that seemed really far.

"Grandma went crazy when I told her about seeing the Lost Herd," I said.

Mom nodded. "You're the only one who ever believed her."

"I believed her!" Sara said, offended.

I looked at her in disbelief. She busied herself with her headphones, leaving me at Mom's mercy.

"Did you finish your homework?" Mom asked. I could see the crease between her eyebrows in the rearview mirror. "You need to get that math grade up."

Amazing how she could go from mustangs to mundane math. The fact was I wasn't done with all my homework yet. Somehow, I could go on to live a rich and fulfilling life even if I got a "C" in math, but she didn't need to know that.

Yep," I lied, hoping to shut her up. It worked.

Sara smirked. "Pinkie promise?" she whispered.

I wanted to growl but...score one for her. The girl was clever.

We drove past my school, the scene of my daily trials. Life might be more fun if I cared about what everyone else seemed to care about, but hmmm. Let's see...I wasn't outgoing (check). Not hot (check). Grades: boringly just above average (check). Hair:

frizzy. Clothes: barnyard chic (two checks). I was crushing it at Spring Hills Middle School.

I rested my head on the window as the entire town–the bank, the hardware store, and Red's Diner–slipped past, all renovated brick buildings from the Gold Rush days. It was kind of a stupid small town, but I forgave it for being stupid because it was surrounded by the range. We slipped through the drive-through at Dairy Queen for burgers and fries and then merged onto the highway.

"How much further?" I asked, getting restless and nervous.

"Enough time to go over some math problems," Sara said, grinning.

I scowled at her, which only made her laugh.

"Twenty minutes to Albright and then ten more or so to Towhee Ridge," Dad said. "The BLM is going after the Towhee herd today."

The BLM going after any herd was bad enough news, but then I remembered my dream. I stopped chewing and tried to swallow the fear rising in my throat. "Dad, could the BLM get the Lost Herd today? I mean, is it possible?"

Dad's eyes stayed on the road. "Anything's possible, but it's not likely. The BLM will go after the Towhee Herd as planned."

"But what if the Lost Herd happens to show up in the area. Wouldn't they be a better catch?"

Mom raised an eyebrow at me. "Stop worrying."

But I didn't stop worrying. In fact, my nervous thoughts only increased as we turned into an unpaved makeshift parking lot and Dad parked next to a BLM truck. I counted five cars. I guess the roundups weren't a spectator sport.

"Well, we're here," Dad said. "Let's get this over with."

We joined five other people on a high ridge overlooking the

sagebrush and grasslands...and a big corral. I swallowed hard. No horses or helicopters in sight.

Dad took out his ever-present 35 mm camera. As if I wanted to remember this day. He took a picture of Mom, Sara and me–I didn't smile–and then he turned to the desert, snapping away.

The wind gusted around us. Mom pulled an entire box of Kleenex out of her purse and held it out to me. "Put some in your pocket," she said.

"Mom! I'm not going to need those." Her fussing was making me more nervous.

She slipped the Kleenex back into her purse. "Might need some myself."

I noticed how pale she looked. "Maybe *you* shouldn't have come. You sure you're okay?" I asked placing my hands on Mom's belly.

"My stomach seems to be behaving," she said. "With me, it's not morning sickness, it's all-day sickness."

I thought I felt the baby move inside her under my hands. The baby was a welcome distraction from the roundup. "Have you decided on a name yet?" Mom and Dad had been debating between Hazel and Catherine.

"Hazel," Mom said.

Mom won.

I grinned. Mom was pretty good at talking Dad into things. "Good choice." I turned an ear to her tummy, trying to hear something. "C'mon Hazel, kick!"

"What a surprise, you're teaching her how to kick," Mom said, with a crooked smile. She tried to run her hand through my hair, but her fingers got caught in the tangles. She frowned and rummaged through her purse. "We need to get a comb through this."

"Someone here I need to impress?"

Mom sighed. "No."

I left her with comb poised in midair and wandered with Sara along the ridge. Dad stood talking to a rancher and a couple of women held signs that read, "Save Our Wild Mustangs." Some hipsters were filming with their iPhones, probably from Mom's college.

The sun went behind a cloud, making the empty pipe corral look even more forbidding. The dread and sadness from the tsunami nightmare washed over me. *Tell me this day wasn't going to get worse.*

Just when I was tempted to go impale myself on one of the fence posts, a tall girl with short dark hair ran up behind Sara and put her hands over her eyes. The smell of strawberry shampoo wafted through the air. "Guess who?" she asked.

"My favorite junior," Sara said.

Kim released her. "Good answer." Kim wore jeans, an unbuttoned sheepskin coat, and an aqua t-shirt that read *Instant Karma*. I envied her light brown skin, her cool style, and the air of confidence she projected.

"I am seriously so happy to see you, Kim," Sara said. "God, this is depressing."

I suddenly felt invisible. An ugly mess compared to these two. I tried to brush some of Lucky's gray hair off of my navy fleece. Mud crumbled from my cowboy boots with each step. And my hair! Maybe I should've let Mom tackle it. Quickly, I pulled a hair tie off my wrist and swept my mane back into a ponytail, but they were deep in conversation.

While Kim and Sara chatted on and on, a gangly boy shuffled up beside Kim. He jammed his hands into his pockets and looked down at his boots.

Sara cleared her throat. "Is this your brother?" She pulled me next to her without waiting for an answer. "This is my little sister."

Kim turned a hundred-watt smile on me. "Hi, I'm Kim

Rodriguez, and this ray of sunshine here is my little brother, Cisco."

Cisco yawned and stretched his arms over his head, avoiding eye contact. He couldn't have been much older than me. He had an angular face and chocolate brown eyes surrounded by thick lashes and the kind of long, lean muscles boys get from lifting bales of hay all year. I hated myself for noticing.

A wave of shyness crept over me. The fries I'd eaten felt like a giant glob of grease in my belly. Sara jabbed me in the rib with her elbow and I coughed out my name.

"Nice to meet you, Christa. I love your hair," Kim said warmly.

I bit my lip. "Seriously?" I asked.

"Totally. I love curly hair, it's so wild," Kim said.

Sara nodded. "Right? When you have straight hair, you want curly hair. That's what I tell her, but she never listens."

"You're both weird," I said, trying to pretend like it was every day that the performance art that was my hair received a compliment.

Cisco kicked a stone on the ground and looked like he wanted to disappear. Poor guy. Girls talking about hair was probably every boy's worst nightmare.

"This is gonna suck so bad today," I said.

"I know," Kim said. "But I can't believe you saw the Lost Herd. That is so cool." Her dark eyes bore into mine. "Were they awesome or what?"

Cisco snuck a curious glance my way.

"Yeah, they were," I said. "It feels like a million years ago already."

Kim's face darkened. "I hope they never end up here." She gestured to the holding pen.

I liked her.

Sara pulled Kim aside and started whispering about something, probably James Miller or Dylan, leaving me and Cisco standing there like two tree stumps.

Awkward silence.

My toes curled in my boots. "Are you, um, in high school? I asked.

"Yep," he said and spat tobacco on the ground.

Ew. Gross. "Tenth grade?"

He tipped his cowboy hat back. Then picked up a rock and studied it. "Ninth."

He was in high school. Only a grade older, but an impossible gulf. I didn't remember him from middle school. "What middle school did you go to?"

"Albright."

"I'm at Spring Hills." He was so shy—or maybe it was me. Boys. Always making girls do all the work in every conversation, as if we were born talking. "Do you ever say more than one word?"

I caught a glint of mischief in his eyes. "Maybe."

"Maybe when? Maybe today?"

He shrugged. "Maybe." I found myself liking the feeling his devilish grin gave me. A weird feeling.

A heavyset man pointed into the distance and a group of onlookers followed his gaze. "There's the helicopter," he said. "Looks like we've got ourselves a roundup."

The weird feeling disappeared. Dread replaced it.

CHAPTER 4

SARA YANKED ON my arm and waved to Kim and Cisco. "C'mon."

Me and monosyllabic, tobacco boy followed Sara and Kim through the sparse crowd. We found Mom and Dad standing with the Millers at the edge of the ridge. Mr. Miller clapped me on the shoulder with his big bear-like hand and congratulated me on seeing the Lost Herd.

Hopefully, we won't see them today," I said, scanning for the helicopter.

The sun glinted off a flash of metal in the sky and a cloud of dust rose in the distance, coming our way. The earth trembled slightly, sending a strange vibration up my legs. I choked back a surge of fear and steeled myself for the worst.

Mom grabbed my hand and squeezed tight.

A helicopter swept through the air. As it came closer, its propellers beat so loudly I covered my ears with my hands. A herd of wild mustangs galloped through the sagebrush. The chopper dipped lower and drove them mercilessly toward the empty corral. The rotors blasted like a hundred machine guns firing. Dirt rose in thick spirals from the horses' pounding hooves. The mustangs dripped sweat and their sides heaved. It looked more like a war than a roundup.

Sara filmed with her phone camera while Mom tried to shield me from the rush of wind. Dad lifted his camera and began snapping pictures. Other people clutched their phones, tweeting and texting.

My stomach heaved. "How long have they been running?"

Dad shook his head. "Could be hours." He pointed to the horizon. "The herd lives back in those foothills."

I bit my lip until I tasted blood. "This is wrong!" I adjusted the focus on the field glasses. One of the foals was limping. His eyes shone white with terror. Still, he ran frantically on three legs with his mother by his side. "I can't watch this," I said, lowering the field glasses. My heart trembled and shook. Cisco pulled his hat even lower and Kim swore under her breath.

"The stallion is the big gray in back," Dad said.

I dared to look again. Okay, there was the stallion. Yep, he was the gray alright. Not a red paint. I breathed a sigh of relief that it wasn't Mesteño, followed quickly by a stab of guilt. I didn't want any of the mustangs to suffer like this. Tears sprang to my eyes.

"He's trying to keep the herd away from the corral," Dad continued. He shook his head. "Smart guy, but it won't work. That chopper will outlast him."

Sure enough, the herd veered away from the corral. The force of the wind from the helicopter blasted their faces as it circled over them. This time the helicopter swung so low its runners nearly touched the backs of the exhausted horses. To them, it must've been like an iron predator, swooping down for the kill. The horses sprang away from the steel blades, bolting straight toward the corral. I felt a pang in my ribs. "It's not fair," I said again. Angrily, I wiped the tears from my cheeks. "I hate that helicopter," I growled.

Mom squeezed my hand tighter. "I know."

"Here's where they let the Judas horse lead them in," Dad said tersely.

"The what?" My stomach dropped into my toes. This was going from worse to bad, bad, bad.

"A horse tricks the mustangs and leads them right into the trap. He's been trained to run into the corral." Dad's eyes narrowed in a cold glare of disgust.

I glanced up in time to see the Bureau of Land Management employees release a horse. Their timing was perfect. The Judas horse slipped out right in front of the mustang's noses, fresh and running hard. The herd followed him right into the trap. At least forty horses raced into the enclosure. They skidded to a stop, but there wasn't room for a graceful halt. Many slammed into the iron-pipe corral while others reared and slashed the air, falling into each other.

"Oh my God!" I whispered, horrified.

Sara slipped in between Dad and me and clutched my sleeve.

A tiny foal went down on its back in the dust. My breathing hitched and caught in my throat. I wanted to turn away but I forced myself to watch. The gray stallion stood alone in a separate corral, his head hanging below his two front legs. He gasped for air. Men with long white sticks entered the corral and separated the other stallions from their bands.

"No!" I said. Sara gripped me around the waist like we were drowning. The stallions screamed and reared, calling for the mares. The mares whinnied back with terror in their eyes. Tears of rage streamed from my eyes. "They belong *together*," I said.

"Damn right they do," Kim muttered.

A vet entered a side pen and tended to the injured foal.

"What happens to them now?" Sara asked without letting go of me.

"The horses will be branded," Dad said. "Each herd carries a series of numbers and symbols on their necks so they can be identified."

"Like slaves or convicts," I said. Sara clutched my arm so tightly, the blood stopped flowing. I pried her fingers loose from her grip and rubbed my arm. "Then what happens to them?"

Cisco found his voice. "They turn some of them loose. Keep the rest in a holding pen and adopt out the ones they can."

I looked sharply at Cisco. How did he know so much about it? Mr. One Word was sure talking now.

"They don't adopt very many out," Kim laughed bitterly. "Not too many people can afford a horse these days. That's why we don't have one."

"So what happens to the ones that are left standing in the pen?" I almost shouted.

"Not sure," Cisco said. "They hold onto them…and some of them go to slaughter." He held my eyes, as if he was breaking some kind of big news to me. As if I didn't know. He was starting to really get under my skin. Even Wild Horse Annie thought it was okay for the old and sick horses to go to slaughter, although I wasn't sure I agreed with her. I looked out over the herd. "They shouldn't take any of these horses. They're all young and healthy." I set my jaw. "This doesn't make sense."

Cisco shrugged. He was down to zero words now. I tried to stay calm, but threads of sadness twisted inside me, leaving my stomach tight and making it hard to breathe.

Kim clenched and unclenched her fists like she was ready to take a swing at somebody. "They can't send all of them to slaughter. They've been rounding up a lot of herds."

I nodded. "Yeah, are we just going to hold them all prisoner?"

Mom hooked her arm through Dad's. "It must be expensive to feed them all. Why would they keep rounding them up if they can graze for free on the range?"

"Ranchers don't want to share the grasslands," Dad said.

"Is it really the cattle ranchers behind all of this?" I asked.

Dad nodded. "They must be putting pressure on the BLM."

His calmness annoyed me. I wanted someone to *do* something. Or at least explain the situation because this was making my brain spin like a tornado. "None of this makes sense," I said. We all looked out over the empty range full of grass and sagebrush. "There's enough land for the cattle *and* the mustangs," I said.

For a long minute, I listened to the gray stallion calling to his mares over the fences. I could hear his anguish. My thoughts whirled in a confused tangle. "Something strange is going on. Something we don't know," I said.

"You could be right, Christa," Mrs. Miller said.

Down in the not-so-okay corral, high, frightened whinnies erupted from the herd. Horses swirled and smashed into each other. The gray stallion took a run at the fence and leaped mightily, but could not clear the top rung. His front leg caught. He struggled, twisting and writhing until his leg came free. Without hesitation, he reared, trying to jump the fence again. All my sadness hardened into anger. Something inside me snapped. "Who's in charge here?" I asked.

Mr. Miller gestured down the hill to a portly man in a BLM uniform. "See that guy making the rounds? That's Bob Downs. He's the guy running the show."

The time for crying was over. "I've got some questions for him."

The Millers said a quick goodbye and slipped away. They probably sensed the tension. I was a ticking time bomb about to go off.

Mom exchanged a meaningful glance with Dad. "C'mon, let's get going. I've got loads of papers to grade."

My jaw tightened. "Does everyone stop caring about horses when they grow up?"

"It's not that we don't care, Christa. We just can't do anything about it," Mom said. "I knew this would upset you." She sighed wearily while Dad busied himself with his camera.

Being an adult was like a disease where you forgot about the important things in life or just gave up on them. "Why are you even taking pictures if you're not going to do anything with them, Dad?"

He let go of the camera and put a hand on my shoulder. "Don't take it out on me, Christa. I can post the pictures, but I can't stop this. Wish I could, but I can't."

Mom stared out to the horizon. "Life isn't always fair."

My heart sank. If they were powerless to do anything, then the roundups would keep happening. "Who's gonna look out for the mustangs?" I asked. I could feel my eyes blazing.

I caught Cisco looking at me. Somehow, his gaze steadied me, as if he understood how I was feeling.

"We need the next Wild Horse Annie," Kim said. She leaned into my ear and whispered, "Somebody who's pissed off enough to cause some trouble."

"I don't think I'll be filling her shoes anytime soon," I said.

Dad cleared his throat. "Looks like you're going to get your chance to meet the guy in charge, Christa. Here he comes."

A man in jeans and a button down shirt huffed his way up the hill. His considerable belly fell over his belt. By the time he reached us he was breathing heavily. "Hello, folks. I'm Bob Downs. I'm in charge of Herd Management for Albright County."

Not something to brag about, I thought. I studied his face. I guessed he was in his fifties–probably had a family of his own.

Dad took his outstretched hand and shook it. "Hello, Bob. I'm Harrison Cassidy. This is my wife, Claire, and my daughters, Christa and Sara."

"We're just taking in the old and the sick today," Bob said, tipping his hat to Mom. Sweat pooled on his forehead. He wiped his brow with a white cloth. "They'll starve out there if we don't look after them."

He was lying! I glanced down at the herd. "I see round bellies and thick coats, Mr. Downs. Not too many ribs showing." Blood hammered through my veins.

"Well, to be honest, Christa, there's just too many horses out there on the range."

My breath quickened. "Really?" I swept my arm out to the range. "Where are all of them? I don't see a population explosion of mustangs." I didn't usually talk like this to adults, but I couldn't stop myself. "Maybe they're doing fine without us."

I caught Cisco looking at me again with a surprised expression on his face. Or was it respect?

Bob's face reddened. "We're just doing our job, young lady. Don't you worry about the mustangs. We know what's best for them."

"Uh-huh," Dad said, squeezing my shoulder. "You might be able to cut some corners on vet bills if you didn't run the horses so hard. Those helicopters are flying awfully low and fast."

I loved Dad for saying that.

"And I heard there were some casualties at the last roundup," Cisco said. His eyes burned as he stared Bob Downs down.

"Casualties?" I asked.

Bob stumbled on his words. "Well, er—we didn't lose one horse today. Not like last week. You need experienced pilots out there, and that's what we're getting from now on." He rocked back on his heels.

"Oh my God," Sara said, covering her face with her hands.

I think that was the exact moment I gave up. I felt like a balloon that had just been popped. I was losing air and all hope with it. A kind of desperate determination gripped me. I looked Bob in the eye. "Why don't you just turn all of them loose?"

"Tell you what. Why don't you adopt one?" he asked with a cloying smile.

"*One*? What about the rest of them!" I pointed to the corrals swirling with horses.

Mom put her arm around my shoulder. "Let's go, sweetie. It's getting late."

I shook her arm off. "This is public land. Doesn't that mean it belongs to us?"

Bob Downs hooked his thumbs in the front pockets of his jeans. "Sure it does. We're a government agency, you know. We work for the people."

This guy acted like he was doing us all a service. My face flushed with heat. "Are you serious? Do you think this is what people want?" My voice rose in pitch like it does when I'm about to go over the edge. This was the sound of me losing control. I tried to steady myself, but I could feel tears threatening. "Our wild mustangs crowded into corrals–for what? What do you *do* with all of them?"

Mom touched Dad's arm and cleared her throat–her signal for us to get going. Dad nodded curtly to Bob Downs, grabbed my hand, and pulled Mom and me toward the truck.

Sara, Cisco, and Kim followed; each giving Downs a disgusted look as they passed by him. Bob's pasted-on smile never wavered. I knew I wasn't going to get any straight answers from him. Not today, anyway. But this cruelty had to stop. If no one else was going to fight for the wild horses, I would.

CHAPTER 5

WALKING THROUGH THE doors of Spring Hills Middle School was harder than ever on Monday. Seeing the roundup had changed everything. How could everyone go on flirting, texting and giggling in the halls as if nothing had happened? The problem was they hadn't seen what I'd seen. I was floating in a strange bubble that kept me distant from everyone. Even the smells in the hallway–sweat mixed with perfume, mingling with floor polish and the mats from gym–set my teeth grinding. I milled along with the others between classes like a giant herd of sheep, and fretted about my speech.

For the first time in my life, I didn't think speech class was stupid. Miracle of miracles, there was something I actually wanted to talk about. Maybe if my speech went well, I could get the class to text or email the BLM and get Bob Downs to sweat a little harder.

That's what I was thinking as I faced the class on Monday with my written speech in hand, the speech that I'd scribbled out the day before sitting on my bed under Wild Horse Annie's poster. I'll admit, I lifted some information from the Internet, but I knew her story. What I needed now was her courage.

The class consisted of four major cliques: the Jocks, the Hot Girls, the Hot Guys, and then my groups...the Whatev's and the Et Ceteras. No big deal. Everyone's expressions, moods, or looks meant nothing to me. I had this. At least that's what I told myself as I took the long walk to the front of the class. I wore my favorite pair of jeans that had some bling on the back pockets, cowboy boots and a "Pink" hooded sweatshirt.

When I arrived at the podium, Mrs. Myrtle looked at the clock and nodded. Time to speak. Butch Hansen, fullback, mumbled, "C'mon Pony Girl." Then he yawned theatrically.

And that's when my throat dried up.

I looked for a friendly face…Amy Whitehorse sat in the front row. She smiled shyly at me from under her dark, dyed-blue bangs. Anyone with "horse" in their name had to be okay, but Amy was one of the Et Ceteras, and we Et Ceteras didn't like to be seen together. Amy was a tiny, emo girl who hid behind her hair and her black clothes. She wore black converse shoes and a studded belt. She probably listened to depressing music and read poetry. I tried to remember if I'd even spoken to her outside of saying hello. I think she'd asked me about Lucky once. Yeah, the emotional girls could be pretty crazy about horses. My gaze flitted away from hers and I dropped my eyes into my notes.

"Wild Hoss, er, I mean, Horse Annie," I stuttered. A few boys chuckled.

"…became a hero in Nevada because she protracted, um, protected our wild mustangs from cruelty." When I swallowed, it felt like a mothball was jammed in my throat. "In 1961, she watched the cowboy roundups and was shocked to see stallions being roped from pick-up trucks, dragged, and then driven straight to the slaughterhouse."

This all came out in a big rush of words. Oh my God, slow down! My right knee began trembling and my cowboy boot knocked into the podium.

Butch Hanson snickered. "Did you forget your spurs at home?"

I wanted to say something smart back to him, I really did, but then I remembered why I was giving the speech. It was about the horses, not about me. When I thought of Mesteño, a tiny wave of courage broke through the wall of fear. I stood up taller. "Wild Horse Annie knew better than to try and talk to those cowboys," I said, looking Butch in the eye. "She took the fight straight to Congress."

"Cool," Amy whispered.

At least somebody was actually listening. That kept me from toppling over on my trembling knee. But then in the thick silence I heard a cough, and a few chairs scraping on the floor. All the sounds of restless disinterest.

My courage evaporated.

"After fighting Congress for ten years," I continued in a small voice, "she finally got a law passed that would limit the number of horses taken from the range. " I glanced at the clock. Oh, God. Not even one minute down. I needed to loosen up. It was like all my passion was trapped under a burning building. That's what fear of public speaking could do to a person. The good news was I had two and a half minutes to improve.

I noticed an empty desk in the back row. The image of Cisco popped into my mind. He slipped into the desk and nodded encouragingly. How ridiculous! But the idea cheered me up and gave me a small jolt of energy. I spoke clearly, loud enough to be heard in the back where Butch Hansen and the Jocks sat.

"But it didn't happen the way you might think...there's a pretty cool twist to this story," I said.

"I hope something cool happens soon," Butch whispered to Kaitlyn, one of the Hot Girls.

I raised my eyes from the paper. I was pissed, but something in Amy's smile calmed me.

"Everyone from Nevada knows about Wild Horse Annie. But

what you might not know is that she owes her success to us." I stepped out from behind the podium and paced back and forth in front of the class. "As in us kids."

My fantasy version of Cisco appeared again and nodded from the back row as if he couldn't wait to hear what I said next.

"She wasn't getting anywhere with the white-haired lawmakers. Congress was shutting her out. Not a big surprise to her, but then she noticed something that did take her by surprise. Of everyone she talked to, children were the most angry."

Butch scribbled in his notebook. He'd been passing notes to Kaitlyn since I started talking. If I could get him to listen, then the class would follow his lead. I walked down a row of desks, making eye contact with everybody.

When I reached Butch's desk I raised my voice. "So, Wild Horse Annie got the word out to as many kids as she could. And guess what?" I slammed my palm on his desk for emphasis. His pen flew to the floor.

"Thousands of children from *all around the world* wrote letters to the US Congress," I said right to Butch's startled face. "They cared that horses were being roped and dragged from pick-up trucks and then sent to slaughter. You heard me right–slaughter."

The class was suddenly silent.

"Kids like us from Europe and China and Japan cared that the great symbols of America's Wild West–the mustangs–were being mistreated. The post office delivered enormous bags of letters, enough to clog up the halls of Congress."

My passion had escaped from under the burning building. I stood tall and surveyed the room. My imaginary Cisco nodded proudly, then wiped a tear from his eye. Oh my God, Cisco, get a grip. I hoped I wasn't going to have to scrape him off the floor every time I gave a speech.

I snapped back to reality and caught Amy's eyes glimmering

with interest. Butch stopped staring at Kaitlyn long enough to look at me. Several of the girl Et Ceteras who were staring at Butch followed his gaze. Now they were all looking at me! I so had them. I strode down the aisle between desks and their eyes followed.

"In 1971, the Wild Free-Roaming Horse and Burro Act passed," I said. "It was created to protect and manage wild horses and burros on public lands. But over time, amendments have been made that reverse some of Wild Horse Annie's good work. If we're not careful, the horses will be treated even worse than they were before."

I only had one line of my speech left. "Maybe if kids could protect the wild herds once, they can do it again."

The class began squirming restlessly. I glanced at the clock. Lunch was in exactly five seconds and I hadn't gotten to the most important part. "I brought a sign-up sheet," I said, grabbing my paper from the podium. "Write your cell number here, if you want to text the BLM. "

The bell blasted and all twenty kids in the class shot up from their desks and scrambled out the door. "Wait!" I said with a sharp stab of disappointment as they streamed past me.

Amy approached and took the sign-up sheet to write down her number. "That was great," she said and hurried out the door.

I looked down at the sign up sheet with one number on it and shook my head. It didn't look like we were going to be storming the halls of Congress anytime soon.

Mrs. Myrtle stood up from her desk and peered at me through big glasses, her long neck protruding from a green pantsuit. She'd always looked more like a Mrs. Turtle than a Mrs. Myrtle. "Nice job on your speech," she said. Her right eye twitched. "But the classroom is no place for politics."

I gulped. From the frying pan into the fire! "Um, okay," I said. "Why not?"

She ignored my question and tapped her plastic fingernails on the desk. "I'll expect you to remember that."

"I'm sorry, Mrs. Myrtle, I didn't realize I was breaking any rules." There was no *sorry* in my tone of voice. There were lots of people in this town that sided with the ranchers, but I hadn't expected Mrs. Myrtle to be one of them.

"I don't think you really want to stir up trouble around here, do you?" Without waiting for my answer, she cleared some papers from her desk and swept out of the room, her heels clicking down the hallway.

That's exactly what I wanted to do. Stir up trouble. And lots of it.

CHAPTER 6

WHEN I ENTERED the lunchroom, Amy Whitehorse waved at me. Members of the Et Ceteras making contact? Unheard of, but it's not like the day could get any weirder. I sat down across from her.

"I liked your speech," she said.

"Thanks," I said. "I think I kind of lost everyone at the end."

"No worries. Everyone has A.D.D. at lunchtime," she said, brushing blue hair out of her face.

We watched a couple of the Hot Girls swish by in tight jeans, each holding a plate of salad they wouldn't eat. They sat at the popular table with the cutest guys in school. Lunch wasn't really about food.

"As if lunch is more exciting than wild mustangs," I said. The boy across from me wolfed down a slice of pizza dripping with grease. "Especially the lunch they serve here."

Amy grinned. "That's why I always bring mine."

"Me, too." I pulled my sad peanut butter and jelly sandwich out and took a bite.

We chewed politely in silence. "I think it's a good idea to text the BLM," Amy said, still staring at her cheese sandwich. "I know some other people who would, too."

Her reply took me by surprise. There weren't many people who cared about the wild horses enough to actually do anything. Even Sara didn't want to get involved. She'd refused to post anything on Facebook when I'd asked her. She said she just wanted to forget the whole thing.

"Well, thanks, Amy. That would be great," I said. "I need to get Bob Downs' attention!"

"I wish I was as passionate as you are." She leaned forward across the table. Her brown lashes blinked from under her bangs. "Is it true you saw the Lost Herd?" she whispered.

I tried to wipe the look of surprise off of my face. "Where did you hear that?"

"Cisco Rodriguez told me that someone in my grade named Christa had seen them."

Cisco! He and Amy were probably going out and here I was daydreaming about him right under her nose. How embarrassing.

Amy's eyes took on a dreamy glow. "You are so lucky. I've always wanted to see the Lost Herd."

"Yep." I waited a beat. "How do you know Cisco?" I asked casually.

"He's—"

"He's what?" I asked.

But before she could answer, Teresa from choir sat down next to Amy. They chatted about something as if I wasn't there. A second later, Amy stood up. "I have to go to rehearsal," she said, wrapping the other half of her sandwich and stuffing it in her bag. "You've got my number. Text me sometime."

I nodded, trying to act cool, but my heart raced. She seemed sweet. And it wasn't every day I made a friend.

When I got home, I found Sara sitting under the arching branches of our giant oak tree in the pasture, bent over her phone, of course. Lucky and Star grazed nearby. "Hey," I said as I plopped down next to her on the ground.

Sara's smile radiated with energy. She probably had a new crush. "What's up?" she asked. Her eyes slid back to her phone.

"Blew my speech today. I was going to get my class to text Bob Downs."

"Look. I'm on this Chinese zodiac website and your animal is the Snake." Sara held up her phone and showed me the picture of a creepy looking snake.

I didn't take the bait. Sara acted like she didn't even remember the roundup. "Maybe if we could get a bunch of signatures to Bob Downs, we could get him to stop the roundups," I said.

She didn't look up from her phone. "Snake is wise and intense with a tendency to be vain and hot-tempered," she said. She shook her head in mock disbelief. "Hot-tempered and intense? This can't be right."

I leaned over her shoulder and read the next sentence. "Yeah, but my tendency toward wisdom softens my temper," I said, getting angry.

Sara picked some grass and tossed it in the air. "I'm Rabbit, the luckiest of all signs. I am also talented, beautiful, and articulate." She paused and smiled. "Affectionate, yet shy. I seek peace throughout my life."

"And *I'm* the vain one?" I grabbed her phone before she could hide it and kept reading.

"Christa!"

"You're a good listener. Ha! Generally noted for your physical beauty. Duh. Others may call the Rabbit timid. They are rarely known to jump into any new situation."

I grinned. "Well, they sure got that part right."

Sara snatched her phone back and scowled at me.

I leaned back on my hands and looked up at the branches of the oak tree.

"Seriously, Sara. The roundups are cruel and I want to stop them. Now isn't the time to be timid."

Sara looked thoughtful. "I get it, but you can't stop the roundups."

She was just going to give up like everyone else. I gritted my teeth. "I have to try."

Lucky wandered over and nuzzled my hand, melting the knot of sadness inside. He could send rays of sunshine into the darkest corners of my heart. "You're better off not knowing about some of the bad things that happen in the world," I told Lucky, tugging on his forelock. He gave my boot a good sniff before returning to the spring weeds.

My mind snapped back to the roundup like a rubber band. "Try and focus, Sara. Why don't you want to post something about the roundup on your Facebook page? You have like 600 friends. You could get signatures from them. Or maybe you're too shy…"

"Nope, I'm too peace-seeking to be political." She flipped her silky hair back over her shoulder. "And you are way too serious." She threw some grass at me. "Lighten up."

"I wish I could." I took a deep breath and tried to be peace seeking, but grim visions of the roundup were flooding my brain. "I can't seem to shake the image of the gray stallion caught in the fence."

Sara winced. "I know. It was awful. But Mom and Dad are right. There's nothing we can do about it, so let's just move on."

I longed to see the Lost Herd so bad my heart hurt. "The Lost Herd has to stay free," I said.

"This is interesting." Sara was back staring at her phone again.

I groaned. "You're not even listening to me!"

"You'll like this, Christa—it's the Year of the Horse."

I wasn't sure what that meant, but shivers raced down my spine. "Really?" I was starting to like Chinese astrology. "If it's the

Year of the Horse, then anything is possible. I'm gonna email Bob Downs right now." I stood up.

"Well, good luck with that." She shoved her phone into her back pocket. "Look, Dad and I are leaving in an hour for Lamar Canyon."

That's right, her yearbook committee's field trip. Dad wanted to go so he could take pictures. Kim, Dylan and a bunch of her friends were going. "Okay, have fun, Rabbit. I'm sure you'll be extra articulate."

She stood up and brushed the grass off her skinny jeans. "Don't do anything stupid while I'm gone." She put a hand on my shoulder in a rare act of kindness. "And try to cheer up, Snake."

When she was gone, I wrote my email.

Dear Mr. Bob Downs,

I met you at the Towhee Ridge Roundup. I saw a lot of horses injured from the roundup and I don't think it's a fair way to treat the horses. It's your job to manage the herds, and I'm sure you're doing a great job, but why are they all disappearing? Weren't you just supposed to take the old and the sick? And I have a special request. Don't target the Lost Herd for your next helicopter gather. Please promise me you'll leave them alone. They've proved they're strong. They don't need us humans managing them.

Sincerely,

Christa Cassidy

I didn't think I could make a difference with one letter, but maybe if I bothered him enough over time I could get his attention. After sending the email, a text, and a snail mail letter to Bob

Downs, I finally got up the nerve to text Amy. I controlled myself and didn't ask her about Cisco. It was time to get my head out of the clouds, so I stayed on topic and told her I was hoping to find the Lost Herd.

Amy texted me back: *The tracks of 100 (more or less) wild mustangs turned up on Old Indian Trail in GC!*

Me: *gold canyon? omg! thank you for telling me! how did you hear about this?*

Amy: *I have some serious wild horse connections since we adopted a mustang.*

Me: *oh, that's so cool. do you ride?*

Amy: *not yet.*

Me: *okay. I will check it out and get back to you.*

Amy::-)

I felt a slight rush of blood to my head. My first text exchange with Amy had wildly exceeded my expectations.

Could the Lost Herd be back in Gold Canyon? The very thought of it set me on fire. It felt as if someone had dumped gunpowder into my chest and lit it with a match. I had to see those tracks with my own eyes. Gold Canyon wasn't more than a couple hours away from home.

I ran out to the barn and threw my arms around Lucky. "Get ready for a big day tomorrow. Bring all the luck you can carry. We're gonna need it."

CHAPTER 7

I SLIPPED INTO MY jeans and a t-shirt, pulled on my cowboy boots, and lumbered down the stairs. Mom had left a note on the fridge. She was in her studio and wanted to talk to me. I wondered what I'd done wrong this time. I packed a lunch and water for the day's ride to Gold Canyon. After I scarfed down a hard-boiled egg with some toast, I stumbled out into the darkness to face Mom.

Mom's studio stood apart from the house, kind of a tiny garden cottage. I opened the door. Red gingham curtains lined the small window, and shelves lined the walls. Her potter's wheel sat in the center of the room next to a large table filled with her bowls and mugs. I hadn't seen her out here in a while. It seemed she was always writing and grading tests these days.

She waved me inside and stood up from her chair with a hand on her back. Even with the ballooning curve of her belly, she moved with grace. Her fair skin set off her blue eyes, and her skin danced with the same freckles that seemed to weigh mine down.

She stoked the fire in the tiny wood stove and pulled another chair near its warmth. Sweet cedar scented the air. She glanced at the empty potter's wheel with longing. "I'm not throwing clay today," she said. "Too much to do, with your father gone..." She let her sentence trail off and sighed heavily, giving me the impression she was holding herself back from a pretty good rant.

I sat down. Mom seemed madder at Dad than at me. Well, whatever I'd done, I hoped it wasn't bad enough to keep me home for the day.

"How many times has Lucky gotten out this week?"

"Just once," I said.

"Well, it makes me nervous when he does that," she said. "I want you and your father to install a new lock for his stall door."

I groaned inwardly. She worried too much. "It's not a prison, Mom." I secretly liked Lucky to have his freedom.

"It's for his own protection. A horse can get himself hurt if he's out by himself at night—you know that. He gets to be free in the pasture all day."

I thought of the mountain lions or even coyotes that could try and make Lucky a meal and my gut twisted. "I'd never do anything to hurt Lucky."

Mom's hand instinctively flew to her belly and rested there. "At your age, you don't think bad things will ever happen to you… but sometimes they do. You can't afford to be careless."

She rested her hand on my shoulder. "I know you're excited about seeing the Lost Herd, and I don't blame you. But that doesn't mean you can shirk your chores around here."

She stood up and bent over her worktable and picked up a mobile she'd made for the baby. Eight ceramic angels danced in a circle. She studied it briefly before setting it down. "You left the barn a mess last night."

"But I was going to clean it up this morning."

She put her hands on her hips and stood tall. "Don't mess with the pregnant lady!"

Even though she was kind of being funny, I got the message.

She gestured toward the door. "Well, get to it then."

"So, I'm not in trouble? I can go see the mustangs?"

"You're going to do all of Sara's chores right now. I want that barn spotless and the horses fed by the time they get back from Lamar Canyon tonight."

"Okay, Mom." I rushed to the barn, fed the horses, and quickly swept the barn aisle before I saddled Lucky. I'd clean the stalls when I got home. We rode into the rising sun on the trail to Gold Canyon. There was no time to waste.

CHAPTER 8

THE SWEET SMELL of piñon pine tickled my nose as Lucky and I wound through the foothills. Most of the snow had melted, and I marveled at the gray winter world changing to green, one blade of grass at a time. The earth was shrugging off last night's freeze and it warmed to Lucky's footfalls, muffling his every step.

Sitting up on Lucky's back felt like home. I'd been allowed to ride out alone since I was eleven and I was almost fourteen now—my birthday was June first—so that added up to almost three years of riding solo. When it came to the trail, Lucky and I were old pros.

I thought back on the speech Dad had given me yesterday before he and Sara left. "Wild horses will run at the sight of you," he'd said, "but if you get close enough to startle them, they could turn on you. They've got big yellow teeth, jaws of steel, and hooves as hard as hammers."

He'd pushed back his cowboy hat and scratched his mussed-up brown hair. "I doubt you'll see the Lost Herd, but if you do, keep your distance."

His eyes had found mine and held my gaze. Things can get weird when the mares go into heat. The stallions will be in the mood for a fight. I wouldn't want you to get between Mesteño and his mares."

As if that was possible, but I hated to see Dad all worked up. I told him he had nothing to worry about. But as I rode down the trail with Lucky in the harsh light of day I wasn't quite so sure. Horses could be unpredictable and I had a way of finding trouble.

By the time we made it to the base of the hill leading to Crow's Nest, I had convinced myself there was nothing to be concerned about aside from whether or not Lucky would make it up this steep trail. Crow's Nest was what we called the high ridge that looked out over Gold Canyon and getting up there wasn't easy. Poor Lucky wound up the switchbacks that led to the summit, one foot in front of the other. When we reached the top, I took in the grand view of the canyon and the miles and miles of desert beyond, scanning for the Lost Herd.

The rocky hills were covered with chaparral, boulders and piñon trees. A crow whooshed across the canyon, but I didn't see anything at all with four legs and a tail. I followed the river as it wound its way through the valley floor, sparkling in the sun. The old Indian trail that followed the river appeared empty. Maybe I'd been too quick to believe in another story about the Lost Herd.

Then the wind gathered in a rush and came up from the West through the gully, drying the sweat that dripped down my back and raising the red dirt like a ghost. I felt, before I saw, the faintest trace of movement in the hills below. Anticipation fluttered in my chest…and then the blood pounded in my ears.

A wild ringing neigh sounded from the chaparral and a band of mustangs crashed through the underbrush. Manes and tails frisked in the wind. Black, yellow, white, spotted, gray, and buckskin horses trotted through the canyon. After all, true to the legend, this was their place. My heart fluttered and danced. We'd entered the magical kingdom of the Lost Herd.

Lucky's skin quivered and his nostrils worked. I slipped down from the saddle and steadied him with my voice until he settled a bit. Lucky wasn't the only one trembling. We were much closer to them than we'd been at Blue Ridge. My hands shook as I dug the field glasses out of my pack and peered through them.

A roan mare stood nursing her foal near three other mares. Lucky nickered, but quickly dropped his head to the spring grass. He was a gelding, not a stallion after all. Even the wild mares didn't interest him too much. I looked for Corazon and Mesteno but there was no sight of them.

Then, the air quivered with a stallion's bugle and Mesteño galloped into view, his ears swiveling this way and that. He moved with such fluid grace, I actually gasped. He thrust his nose high in the air, searching the wind for a scent–and then jerked his head in our direction. The wild stallion stood still as a statue, his eyes locked on us. Lucky's head snapped up and my breath froze in my chest. I hoped he could see Lucky and I were as harmless as the grass growing at his feet. But as it turned out, Mesteño had bigger things to deal with than Lucky and me.

A group of young stallions loped out of a ravine, led by a horse as red as my hair. The red horse pawed the ground and screamed a challenge. Every young stallion wanted to win a mare for himself. It would be like Cisco showing up at my school with a couple of his friends, trying to steal Cheryl the Cheerleader away from Jeremy the Jock. The red bachelor didn't stand a chance unless Cisco knew martial arts or something. You just never knew.

Mesteño snaked his mares away from the stallions and turned to face them, pawing the ground. I scanned for Corazón, but there was no sight of her.

Mesteño threw his head back and bugled. I held my breath as the young red stallion rocketed from the group of bachelors and charged at Mesteño. Mesteño met him with a flash of teeth and hooves and the two stallions twisted in the air. The bachelor wrestled away and backed into Mesteño's chest, kicking. After the second blow, I covered my face with my hands. Mesteño was getting pummeled! I looked up in time to see Mesteño dodge to the side and then hurl his body into the red horse. His teeth sunk into the young stallion's neck while his front hooves slashed. The bachelor squealed, tore himself free, and bolted away with the rest of the bachelors. Mesteño snorted and plunged after them, his ears flat back against his head, the whites of his eyes gleaming.

I cheered as Mesteño pursued the bachelors at a gallop, biting at their flanks. Only after he'd chased them halfway to Kansas did he stop and turn, ears pricked forward and head held high. Triumphantly, he cantered back to his mares. They batted their long lashes and looked sweet as sugar, as if they had no idea what all the fuss was about.

Shivers raced through me. Mesteño had defended his right to lead the Lost Herd, but something was missing. Where was Corazón? All the alarm bells in my head sounded. The lead mare should be with the herd. Had something happened to her?

Mesteño's band drifted into the cover of scrub that followed the river. It looked like they were headed somewhere else. I took hold of Lucky's bridle and mounted. We'd have to break a trail to the canyon floor if we were going to catch them. I knew one thing for sure. I wasn't leaving without seeing Corazón.

Lucky and I half-crept, half-slid down to the river. I gritted my teeth. Not easy riding, but if Lucky could handle going off-trail, I could, too. We doggedly followed the tracks left by the wild horses through dried-up washes, and then along trails leading to the uplands.

We were entering a meadow from the cover of the piñon when I spotted Mesteño's band grazing in the sun on the next hill. I wiped my sweaty brow with my sleeve as joy swept over me. Corazón had to be here.

Lucky lowered his head to the grass and I dismounted, dropping onto my belly. I had to get closer. I crawled until I could see the horses perfectly with the field glasses, and even smell their musky-sweet scent. *Be careful!* Dad's warning came back to me. I flattened myself in the grass and tried to lay still.

I searched for Corazón. Still no sign of her. Why wasn't she with her band?

I noticed an old swaybacked red roan with gray around his muzzle standing alone. Too old to be a bachelor. Maybe he'd gone solo. He seemed so patient and kind. I guess he was old enough that he no longer needed to fight for territory or mares. He stepped gently away from the other bachelor stallions when they approached. I wanted to rub his greying face and look into his clouded eyes. I bet he had a few stories to tell. Mesteño tolerated his presence in the band. It seemed the old guy had a special role looking out for the foals, the way he watched over them as they played. I named him *Grandfather*.

A peaceful feeling swept over me with the birds singing in the trees. I realized how tired I felt having woken so early this morning. The grass smelled sweet, and my head grew heavy. I glanced at Lucky grazing nearby. He was fine. Maybe I would lay my head down and rest my eyes for a second.

I hear the muffled footsteps of a horse approaching. It's a black mare. It's Corazón! I am so relieved to see her. She cautiously places one hoof down in front of the other. With each step she comes closer and my heart pounds faster. This is what I've always wanted... to be near a wild horse. Boom, boom, boom. My heart crashes in my chest. I realize this must be a dream. She's walking right up to me. She's reaching her nose out and now, strangely, I'm watching all of this from slightly above my body. She sniffs my head, brushing her muzzle against my

hair and exhaling sharply. Her breath is warm on my neck. It tickles.
I giggle and then, poof! I'm awake.

The birds were singing and my cheek was pressed to the grass just as it had been when I layed my head down, but something was different. I felt like someone was watching me. Slowly, I raised myself on my elbows. As I lifted my head, I found myself staring into the deep, black eyes of Corazón herself. This was no dream!

I froze, willing the mare to stay near, but she jumped back with a startled snort, her nostrils working and her eyes wild. I could only imagine what I'd looked like to her, laying on the ground with my tangle of red curls spread out on the meadow. Now that she'd gotten a close look at my face, I had the feeling she wasn't too impressed.

Corazón shifted her gaze from me to the tiny newborn foal at her side. Oh my God, Corazón was a mom! So that's where she'd been, hidden away someplace in the brush giving birth. The black filly wobbled along, testing her legs. She couldn't have been more than a few hours old. She looked so much like Corazon I decided to call her *Echo.*

Corazón took another step back and her skin twitched. She snorted menacingly. Echo looked up at her with wide, innocent eyes. With a sharp nudge from Corazón's muzzle, the filly whirled and ran back to join the other mares.

I thought Corazón was going to follow Echo, but then her alarmed and slightly curious gaze fell on me again. We locked eyes and the delicious feeling I'd had at Blue Ridge zinged through my bones. Corazón looked into me, through me. An electric wave of joy swept from my head to my toes. Her eye opened a hidden door inside, drawing me down a secret passage to another world. *Her* world. I couldn't have torn my gaze away if I'd tried. This mare was a mother…part of the earth, just as she was part of the wide sky and the wind, the rain and the snow. She belonged to this world as stone belonged to a mountain. My heart ached with love and shook with the power of the wild horses. I wanted to *be* her!

When she released my gaze I snapped back to reality. I was lying one foot away from Corazón. She could kick or trample me in an instant. What would Dad say if he could see this wild mustang standing next to me, eye to eye? His voice echoed in my ears. *I'd hate to see you get between Mesteño and his mares.*

A shrill neigh filled the air. Mesteño! My skin prickled and my heart slammed into overdrive. I needed to get out of here fast. I shouldn't have let Lucky wander off. *Where is he?* I glanced about helplessly.

Corazón answered Mesteño with a piercing whinny. She snorted and backed away, her hooves pawing the ground. Her eyes flashed dangerously. I stayed very still, not wanting the mare to think badly of me. Plus, there was power in those sharp hooves, and I knew a strike from her foreleg could be deadly.

Her wildness stole my breath. She whirled effortlessly, her mane swinging like waves around her head. She seemed to melt into the blue shadows cast by the rocks as she galloped down the slope back to Echo.

As soon as I could breathe, I stood up on shaky legs and whistled for Lucky. Much to my relief, he nickered and trotted faithfully from the cover of the piñon. I threw my arms around his neck and clung to him. "That was a close call," I whispered. "Thank you for being the best pony in the world."

CHAPTER 9

WHEN WE RETURNED to the barn, I rubbed Lucky down and threw hay for all three horses. Mom was going to be mad if I didn't get my chores done before dark like I'd promised. I forked the manure into the wheelbarrow until it was a heaping mound that I could barely push down the barn aisle. After I dumped it outside I bent down over my knees and caught my breath. Maybe I should've picked the manure in the morning when I'd had some energy. Too late to worry about that now.

While I worked, memories of the Lost Herd flashed through my mind. I was still reeling from my encounter with Corazón. In one glance, she had seen me...seen into me. And I had seen into her. Now I was linked to her so strongly, I felt as if I was bound to her forever. How could I explain that to anyone? Even Grandma might find that hard to understand.

In a rare but furiously productive effort, I threw Lucky's saddle, bridle, and brushes in the tack room and swept the barn aisle twice. I stopped once, caught by Lucky's sparkling eye and the sweep of forelock that fell over his thick white lashes. As he chewed his hay, he locked his eyes with mine and a wave of happiness bubbled up from my chest. We both knew we'd done well today.

By the time I finished my chores, exhaustion struck, leaving my limbs as heavy as tree trunks. I just had to feed the grain and I'd be done. I dragged my feet on the way to the grain shed, a pathetic little wooden hut badly in need of paint, located just a few steps from the barn. The rusty deadbolt nearly came off in my hands when I opened the lock. I kicked the big rock out from in front of the warped door, and the hinges groaned as the door swung open. Inside, the sweet smell of grain made me smile. This was Lucky's favorite thing in the world. Eastwood and Star got one scoop of grain and Lucky got a smaller scoop mixed with water.

My shoulders ached as I carried the buckets into the barn. The horses nickered and dug their noses in greedily when I poured the soaked grain into their feeders. I turned out the lights to the barn to the sound of horses chewing and blew Lucky a kiss. Then I beat a quick path back to the house.

The kitchen smelled of roasted chicken and potatoes, and my stomach rumbled. Sara stood at the counter chopping carrots for the salad and talking a mile a minute. When she saw me, she stopped and stared. It took a lot to shut Sara up. Maybe it was the wild look in my eyes or my frizzy hair that had done it. "How was the ride?" she asked.

"I saw them."

Sara's eyes widened. "Seriously? Get out!"

"Get the table set, dinner's ready," Mom said, as if eating with utensils was more important than the Lost Herd.

Dad strode in from his office. "Did I hear that right? You saw them?" he asked me.

"Yep."

His face spread into a wide grin of astonishment. He was speechless. I felt so proud that I took a bow. A low-blood-sugar moment.

Mom stopped bustling around the kitchen long enough to

give me a hug. "Congratulations, Christa," she said. "They really aren't just a story anymore."

"So, tell all," Sara said, her eyes sparkling.

It felt so good to have everyone's attention that I figured I'd draw it out. "After I get some food in me, I'm starving," I said and set the table at record speed.

We sat down and dished up the food. I ate two chicken legs before I began talking. I told most of the story: Mesteño's fight with the red stallion, the old horse I'd named Grandfather, and Corazón's newborn filly, Echo; but, I decided not to mention how close I'd come to Corazón.

When we were getting ready for bed and I'd heard a good earful from Sara about her trip (more Dylan drama), I couldn't hold out any longer. I told Sara. Not about the magical parts, just how Corazón had woken me. I'm not stupid.

"Wild horses don't approach people, even if they're asleep on the ground," she said. Her brain stored all kinds of knowledge that was irrefutable…but wrong.

I held her gaze. "It happened."

Sara climbed into bed. "Did it ever occur to you the whole thing with that mare was a dream? After all, you were *sleeping*."

I threw my pillow at her. "Doubter."

"Dreamer," she countered, throwing the pillow back.

I couldn't wait to see Corazón again. "You and Dad need to come with me tomorrow," I said. "You'll see."

"Let's get some sleep," Sara said. "Tomorrow will be here soon enough."

CHAPTER 10

THE NATIVE AMERICANS have a saying that the morning star sings at dawn to each of us that listens. When I woke the following morning, I strained my ears for the sound of stars, but all I heard was the wind.

My digital clock blinked 4:00 AM. The power must've gone out. Another blast of wind struck the house, whistling through cracks in the old wood. I slipped out of bed and crept to the window. Something felt strange, like the crackly feeling you get right before lightning strikes. A floodlight flashed on outside the barn and I heard Dad's voice. "Claire! Lucky's down. Call the vet!"

Lucky! Adrenaline sang in my blood. I threw on clothes and ran down the stairs, flying out the door to the barn. Somehow, Mom had beaten me there. She looked oddly out of place in the barn aisle, clutching her cell phone with a worried expression.

She caught me in her arms. "I couldn't sleep. I just had a bad feeling so I came out here to check on them. I found Lucky lying flat on the ground."

"Is he colicking?"

"Looks that way. I just called the vet."

I broke free of her grasp and ran to Lucky's stall. It was empty. Panic shot through me. "Where is he?"

Mom gestured outside. "In the pasture. That's where your father found him."

In the pasture? What was he doing out there? I could see my question echoed in Mom's eyes.

"I put him away last night, Mom. He must've gotten out again." Not waiting to hear her response, I rushed to the pasture.

Lucky lay on his side near the gate. He kicked and bit at his stomach as if there were snakes crawling around in there. Dad knelt by Lucky's head, pulling encouragingly on his lead rope and calling his name, trying to get him to stand up, but Lucky seemed not to notice.

A movement caught my eye. In a violent gust of wind, the door to the grain shed banged shut and then crept open, squeaking on rusty hinges. Oh, no. This couldn't be happening. I watched as Dad rose, walked to the door and closed it. Without a word, he jiggled the crusty deadbolt into place and kicked the rock in front of the warped door. Mom glanced my way then looked down at the ground.

My thoughts tossed, swirling wildly. "Dad, I closed it, I know I did."

"You have to learn to be more careful, Christa," he said.

"I'm trying!"

"Well, try harder." He scratched the back of his neck and sighed, as if he was only now realizing the depth of my stupidity. "What's done is done."

I flung myself onto Lucky's neck and tried to comfort him with my voice. He turned an eye my way. It was dull with pain. My breath felt trapped in the bottom of my lungs.

Dad took a cigarette out of his shirt pocket and put it in his mouth unlit. "Let's do what we can until the vet get's here. We need to get him up."

Sara appeared, wrapped in her blue bathrobe. "What's going on? What's Lucky doing out here?"

"I don't know!" I hissed in a low whisper, burying my head in Lucky's mane. "I put him in his stall last night, but he must've gotten out. You know how he is." I could hear the desperation in my voice.

Her eyes narrowed. "He got into the grain."

I felt my head sinking between my shoulders. "Yes, he did," I said through clenched teeth. "I know I closed the door, but he got it open."

Sara shivered, pulling the collar of her robe up around her neck. "Oh. My. God."

Mom touched Dad's arm gently. "Is there anything else we can do, Harrison?"

He lit his cigarette, inhaled quickly and blew the smoke over his shoulder. "We can fix the door to the grain shed."

I glanced at Dad, waiting for him to tell us how we could save Lucky. His ashen face said it all. My heart curled into a painful fist. I wanted to pull back time, to grab it and stop it from unraveling. I leaned in close to Lucky's nose. His gaze clouded. "Easy, boy. We'll make sure the vet fixes you right up." Lucky closed his eyes and groaned softly. I choked on my own breath. "No, Lucky. Don't give up." I hooked my fingers in his tousled mane. "I'm so sorry, Lucky. This is all my fault."

"Yeah, no kidding," Sara said.

I wondered if there was a crueler world than this one.

Mom grabbed Sara by the arm. "We'll talk about how this happened later. She needs you now."

Sara flashed me a dark look as she kneeled beside me, stroking Lucky's neck. "Easy, boy," she said.

Lucky continued to bite at his stomach. Sweat darkened his gray coat. When I held my ear to his side, I couldn't hear any gut sounds. It was as if things had stopped working inside. I prayed he would get up. If he kept rolling like this he could twist his gut. And if the grain swelling inside him and blocking his gut didn't kill him, twisting it like that could.

I pulled on the rope and shouted his name, begging him to get up, but he stayed down, nipping at his side. I glanced over my shoulder toward the driveway. Even out here in the middle of nowhere, you'd think a vet would show up when you needed him. Didn't he know what was at stake?

Just when I thought I couldn't wait another minute, Dr. Ferguson's blue Ford truck pulled up to the barn. He was a small-ish man with big hands and a clipped beard. He strode to Lucky's side, carrying a leather bag. I hoped he wasn't too late. He took Lucky's vitals, gaging his temperature and his pulse. "What have you done for him so far, Harrison?"

Dad cleared his throat. "I already gave him some Banamine. Thought that might relax his stomach and ease the pain. Doesn't seem to be helping him much."

Dr. Ferguson fished around in his bag and brought out a nee-dle and a clear glass bottle of liquid. "Well, let's give him some more and see if we can make him more comfortable. And then we need to get him on his feet."

Dad nodded.

Doc gave Lucky the medicine and then we tried to get him to stand, but he thrashed wildly with his hooves and bit at his sides. He made as if to get up, then got up, circled wildly and lay heav-ily back down on his right side. Dr. Ferguson poked and prodded Lucky's gut, his expression grim. "He's got a blockage here. I can tube him, but I think he needs more than I can offer him."

Shame flooded through me, drowning me. *What have I done?* I thought back to last night. I couldn't remember doing anything wrong. I couldn't help it if Lucky got out of his stall. I know I closed the door to the grain shed. But maybe, just *maybe* I hadn't put the rock in place or I hadn't slid the bolt properly. Then, Lucky could have nosed his way inside.

The sun began to rise and streaked the horizon with a dull shade of pink. Dr. Ferguson put a tube down Lucky's stomach and tried to flush the blockage. "That grain just blew up inside him. It's not moving. Gut may be twisted." He sighed and shook his head. "There's nothing more I can suggest unless we put Lucky in your trailer right now and get him to Reno for colic surgery."

Dad shook his head and met Dr. Ferguson's gaze. "Jim, we can't afford it."

Mom put an arm around Dad's waist. "Lucky's too old to be covered by insurance, Dr. Ferguson." She glanced at me. "Of course, we'd do anything we could for him."

The vet scratched the back of his neck. "There's no guarantee it would save his life anyhow."

No one spoke. The wind gusted, raising the dust in the pasture.

Dr. Ferguson cleared his throat. "Then I think the best thing we can do for Lucky is to get him out of pain."

Dad turned away. I watched his shoulders sag.

I jumped up. "What's happening?"

He shook his head. "Lucky's not gonna make it, honey," he whispered. "We can't save him."

The back of my throat stung. Panic clouded my vision. I looked at Mom through a blur of tears. She shook her head. "He's suffering."

"No." I sank to the ground by Lucky's side. With trembling fingers, I dragged my hands through his thick fur. I needed more time. Time to memorize the curve of his cheekbone, the way his eyelashes curled over his eyes, the way his nostrils flared when he breathed, the sound of his nicker when he greeted me each morning…too many things to name.

Dr. Ferguson withdrew a syringe from his bag. "I'm going to give Lucky something that will help ease him into sleep and then stop his heart from beating. Don't worry, it won't hurt him."

Mom put her hand on my shoulder. It felt heavy. "I know this is a shock and it's not what any of us want, but it's time to say goodbye to Lucky, Christa."

My chest convulsed. *Time to say goodbye?* The weight of her words sank into my ears, but their meaning was lost to me. It didn't make any sense. I thought I'd have an endless supply of time to spend with Lucky. I stroked the tender skin around Lucky's eyes just the way he liked it. He lifted his head and met my gaze. His expression seemed to hold all the love in the whole world. "Not much longer now, you brave pony," I finally said. "The pain will be gone soon." Thick tears rolled down my cheeks. "You're my best friend ever. You'll always be the best."

Sara kneeled next to me and stroked his neck. A sob escaped her lips. "Goodbye, sweet Lucky."

Mom and Dad crowded in, whispering their final words.

The vet waited until we were done and then injected Lucky with the sleeping medicine. I bit my tongue to keep from screaming. Lucky raised his head one last time and I thought I caught a fleeting expression of surprise followed by relief flash across his face. He lowered his head back to the ground and exhaled.

The wind changed and a slight breeze picked up his mane. Odd, how it didn't even seem like Lucky's mane anymore. It was just hair, belonging to no one. I can't explain how I knew he was gone, but I did. Sara began sobbing in earnest. I focused on a spot just over Lucky's neck. White dots danced behind my eyes and a sharp pain seared through my head. *There is no way he's gone.* Not knowing what else to do, I draped my body over his neck. I'd wait for him to come back.

* * *

Later that morning Mom and Dad put a blue tarp over Lucky. They said it was to keep the flies away. Mom dragged me inside for breakfast. I ate nothing. I went to the bathroom and looked in the mirror. The skin on my cheeks was taut with dried tears. I splashed my face with water and dried it with the guest towel. I didn't recognize the girl in the mirror. Mom shadowed me, following me from room to room. She wanted to talk, to hug, to make everything okay, but she couldn't. Her worry sent the panic I felt inside into overdrive. I returned to Lucky's body. The dogs kept vigil with me, curled up by my side. I sat, staring at nothing. Occasionally I stole a glance under the tarp. The body still looked like Lucky. Maybe he was just sleeping. I rested my head in my knees and wept.

I'm not sure how much time had passed when I felt Dad's hand on my back. He pulled me away from Lucky, lifting me in his arms. "Time to take a break and head inside."

Dazed, I wrapped my arms around Dad's neck and let him pick me up. The sun hung low in the western sky. I guess I'd fallen asleep. When I saw Lucky's body lying there, I wished I'd never woken up.

The sound of a large motor caught my attention. At the top of the pasture near the oak tree, a tractor labored, scooping great shovelfuls of earth out of the ground. Against the setting sun, I could see the silhouette of a man sitting behind the wheel. Only one person in the world wore a hat that big. Our neighbor, Mr. Lattimer. What was he doing up there? The tractor had a backhoe attached. The kind you use to drag a dead horse into a hole. Like the one he was digging.

I gasped. Lucky's grave. I struggled in Dad's arms. "I need more time to say goodbye, Dad! I'm not ready."

"Let's go inside for a while, Christa," he said in a voice he tried unsuccessfully to keep steady. He walked quickly toward the house. For one second, I leaned into his shoulder, inhaling the smell of coffee and cigarettes embedded in his flannel shirt. Then I began to fight against his hold on me. He walked faster. Sara and Mom ran to Dad's side, flanking us. They reached out for my hands. I swatted them away. "Let go!" I said harshly because this was upsetting me and I didn't want to cry. Why wouldn't they let me go back to Lucky's side? What was the rush?

I glanced desperately over my shoulder. Mom said something I couldn't quite make out. Dad tightened his grip and carried me up the stairs of the front porch. I kicked my legs frantically and writhed against the circle of his arms. "Please, Dad. Put me down. I need more time with him…" I gestured uselessly over my shoulder toward Lucky's body.

My words turned into wails. Even if he never took another breath, I couldn't leave Lucky—couldn't let them put his body in that hole. As soon as we entered the house, I lost sight of my pony. The sound of the tractor sputtering down the hill rang in my ears. Dad closed the front door and Mom closed the windows. Sara grabbed both my hands and squeezed hard. Louder now, the tractor's engine roared. It came closer. And closer. Right to the pasture gate where Lucky lay under the blue tarp. A realization sparked deep inside me, one I fought against with all my strength. I could wait forever, but he wasn't coming back. I would never see Lucky again.

CHAPTER 11

I TRIED TO PIECE the events of Lucky's death together, but nothing made sense no matter how many times I went over it. Maybe I didn't drop the pin all the way into the hole that locked Lucky's stall or he jiggled it open and got out. It wouldn't be the first time. Lucky had always been a clever pony with a million tricks up his sleeve. Maybe the wind loosened the broken lock on the old door to the grain shed and blew it open. Or maybe I'd left it open. Wouldn't be the first time for that, either. But no matter which way I figured it, it always came back to the fact that Lucky was gone. Once I arrived there, I sank down into a dark hole a mile wide and at least as deep.

Days passed, with one blurring into the next. My normally white skin looked blotched, and my red hair frizzed hopelessly into curls I didn't even try to brush. My blue eyes washed out to a dull gray. On the worst days, it felt like there were holes in my heart, as if one of the arrowheads I'd found on the trail with Lucky had lodged itself into the tissue and worked its way deep.

Lucky had touched every part of my life. Everyone at school knew me as the girl with the pony. Everyone at home knew me as the girl with the pony. Now I was the girl with nothing, who deserved nothing. I realized just how painfully alone I was.

I guess it was safe to say I wasn't exactly a barrel of laughs.

Family dinners passed in strained silence. Dad lost his patience with my sullen moods and crying jags and ordered me to get over it. As if I could control my feelings through sheer willpower. When Mom was up and about, she tried to get me to talk about it, which only made me feel worse. Sara regarded me with a mixture of pity and suspicion. She looked over my shoulder when I fed Star and Eastwood, waiting to catch me in the smallest error. She ordered me around like an army general. Because I had screwed up so badly, I had no choice but to do whatever she asked. Going to the barn became unbearable.

One day after school, Mom knocked on the door to my room. She handed me a package and told me to open it.

I tore the paper away, revealing a green, leather-bound journal. I turned it over in my hands.

"Even if you can't talk to us, maybe you can write," she said gently.

"Write what?" The only thing I'd been writing was my letters and emails to Bob Downs. Somehow I'd kept that up. My link to the Lost Herd was like a thin thread tying me to the world.

She smiled and sought my eyes. "Anything. What you're feeling…or things you want to have happen. Your life isn't over."

But my life was over. A life without Lucky didn't make sense. It was as if the path below my feet had dropped away. "Thanks."

"Christa, you need to know there's a difference between taking responsibility for your mistakes and beating yourself up," Mom said.

I nodded grimly, but I had no idea what she meant. They seemed like the same thing to me.

She sat next to me on my bed and held my hand. "Your father thinks you need to get another horse and move on. Give yourself a second chance."

My eyes filled with tears. "No."

"What happened with Lucky was an accident. We all know that." My hands felt clammy enfolded in her warm ones.

"Sometimes the best way to make up for a mistake is to prove to yourself that you can do better and try again."

I felt myself shrink inside. I sat like a rag-doll, completely limp. Everything in my room was just as I had kept it before he died. The sounds in the air were the same, and yet nothing would ever be normal again.

She crushed me in a hug. It felt a bit awkward. Her stomach had gotten bigger. "Your father feels he played a part in this for not fixing the door to the grain shed. I wish I had insisted he replace the lock on Lucky's stall door sooner."

The late afternoon sun slanted past me down the hall. I could see the little dust particles floating in it. "Not his fault," I mumbled. "Not your fault, either." I wished I could say what she wanted to hear, but my thoughts became disjointed. I wanted to curl in on myself, to hide from everything that had happened. I said nothing. Talking wouldn't bring Lucky back or change what I had done.

When Mom went downstairs, I gathered my souvenirs from trail rides–the arrowhead, some Native American pottery bits, a dead scorpion, a shiny stone, and a rattlesnake skin– along with some show ribbons and pictures of Lucky and put them into a box. I buried the journal at the very bottom. I couldn't risk keeping a journal with Sara around. Besides, I had nothing to say. I closed the lid firmly on top and shoved it under my bed next to forgotten board games and discarded toys. Then I grabbed my laptop. I dragged all the documents I'd saved regarding the Lost herd into a folder and closed it.

I was done with horses.

CHAPTER 12

A COUPLE OF MONTHS later, Dad hooked the horse trailer to the truck and gathered the whole family outside. Saturday, June first, happened to be my fourteenth birthday, so I knew something was up. Sure enough, Dad announced we were going to the horse auction in Albright to find a certain birthday girl a new mount.

I put my sunglasses on. All I wanted to do was sleep. "Thanks, but I don't want a horse."

"You don't seem to want anything these days," Dad said, kissing the top of my head. "Your mother's worried about you."

Mom seemed fragile, her hand on her belly. Dark circles ringed her eyes, and I could see the worry lines on her face. She ran a hand through her auburn hair, her freckles sharp in the bright sunlight. "We don't expect a new horse to replace Lucky, but it's time to start over."

I hesitated. All three of them were staring at me. If I could get out of this, maybe I could crawl back into my warm bed. "I don't deserve a horse," I said.

Sara exhaled in exasperation. "Oh, for crying out loud! I'm so tired of your moping around." She stalked toward the house.

"Sara, get back here," Mom said.

Sara glanced back over her shoulder. "I can't take anymore of her."

Mom motioned for her to get back like she'd do with wayward school kids. Sara stomped back and stood beside Mom and Dad. She stared at me with her hands on her hips.

All three of them turned toward me now. I felt my face flush. I didn't want to back down, but with all of them ganging up on me, I couldn't see a way out of this. "If it makes you happy, I'll look for a horse today... on one condition. If I don't see one I like, we'll come home with an empty trailer."

"Deal!" Sara said without waiting for Mom and Dad's reply. "Now let's go."

I met Dad's eye. He was the one who bought Lucky. He was the one who taught me how to ride, who logged miles riding with me on the trail. "I'm doing it for you, not me," I told him.

"That's a start," Dad said, giving my shoulder a quick squeeze. He held the truck door open, and I slid into the back seat beside Sara without another word.

Mom leaned in through the passenger side door. I thought my decision would make her feel better, but her brow furrowed. "I need to stay home and rest, but I promise you this will be a great day," she said.

"You're not coming?"

She reached for my hand. "Just a headache. I'll be fine."

"Okay, whatever," I mumbled. I guess it didn't matter if she came.

"Remember the good things," Mom said, squeezing my hand gently. "School is out and Grandma is coming for your birthday dinner."

Thank God Grandma was coming. She always made me feel better. The truck engine roared to life and we took off.

As we drove down County Road 7, Dad talked at length about

how a good horse could help me in every area of my life. I sure wished Dad didn't feel so chatty. I got the picture. My life could use some improvement.

The school year had ended on a sour note. I wasn't looking forward to Mom seeing my report card. My grades had dropped to C's, even in English and Spanish, and I had stopped texting Amy Whitehorse. I felt like a clunky, redheaded, messy-haired outsider.

I stole a glance at Sara. She was in her happy place listening to her iPod. She took one earphone off and the music bled into the car…probably the smash #1 pop single of the week, but I didn't recognize it and I didn't care.

Sara nudged my leg with her boot. "What are you thinking about? Aren't you excited?"

I shrugged. All I could think about was Lucky. My only birthday wish was that he would somehow, impossibly come back to me.

Sara kicked me again, harder this time. "You're getting a new horse, stupid. Can't that even put a smile on your face?"

"Not yet."

"One depressed person per family is the new rule," Sara whispered. "Pull it together for Mom, Christa."

"Yeah, okay." I managed a weak smile. Mom had been spending lots of time in her room. When she'd come down to dinner, she seemed distracted, as if her mind was on other things besides us. I thought she was just tired. "I didn't know Mom was depressed."

"She's concerned about the baby. She's been cramping."

My stomach rolled and clenched. Mom could not lose this baby! If Mom lost the baby, she'd never recover. I prayed losing Lucky hadn't somehow ruined my mother's luck, too.

But Sara didn't look concerned. She tapped her boot in rhythm to the music. Her hair was silky and shiny even as it blew in the wind, and the sunlight caught the graceful curve of her cheekbone. I absolutely hated her for being so perfect.

"Aren't you worried?"

She shrugged. "You're a bigger mess right now than Mom."

A sweat broke out on my palms and I rubbed my hands on my loose-fitting jeans. I was growing so fast they were already way too short.

Of course, Sara noticed. "Where's the flood?" she asked, glancing at my ankles and shaking her head in disgust. "Get Mom to take you shopping."

I crossed my legs. "She's too depressed."

Sara scowled. "What's up with you?"

"Nothing's up with me!" I turned away and leaned against the car door, pressing my cheek to the cool window. I could feel her staring at me.

"Nothing, huh?" When I met her gaze, her eyes softened. "You can talk to me, you know."

I gritted my teeth. "I don't need you or anybody else feeling sorry for me."

"Whatever. You'll get over Lucky someday." She put her earphones back on, drowning me out with her lousy music.

I groaned. She was as bad as Dad. I wish everyone would just get off my back. Suddenly, I felt the strangest sense of dread. Something bad was going to happen today; I just knew it.

We passed through a large entrance gate. Dad pulled up and parked next to a rusty red Ford in a giant lot scattered with cars, trucks and trailers. We all piled out. "I'm gonna take a look around, be right back," Dad said.

I walked to a corral behind Sara where a group of twenty or so horses stood quietly. There were lots of older and injured horses, and I felt like one of them. All washed up at fourteen.

Sara bent over her cell as she texted back and forth with someone. She glanced up and waved happily. "There's Kim!"

"Oh my God, it's Kim!" I mimicked her tone.

Sara made a face at me and motioned Kim over. I stood up a

little straighter because Cisco was walking right beside her. I tried to smooth my hair, but strands of curls flew in every direction. I crushed the fly-aways under my pink baseball cap and straightened my Ramones t-shirt. By the time they reached us, my confidence level had dropped from one to zero.

Cisco nodded ever so slightly at me, but before I even had time to say hello, he dropped his eyes and hid behind his Stetson hat. My stomach lurched.

Kim wasn't so shy. "I am so sorry about your pony!" she said. "Sara said you've been a wreck."

"I did not!" Sara said.

"You did, too!" Kim said.

This was awkward. Hoping for a subject change, I motioned toward the corrals. "Check out all these horses for sale."

"I know," Kim said. "I want one so badly, but we don't have the money right now."

Cisco strode over. His worn jeans hung on his hips. "You could try getting a job," he said. "I've heard that's how people make money." The sarcastic smile on his face twisted my gut in a crazy way, leaving me slightly breathless. What was my problem?

"I'll keep that in mind," Kim said dryly. "I sure wish I was the one getting a horse today." She looked me right in the eye with so much conviction I almost cried. I knew she wasn't faking.

"Well, how about you come ride with us sometime, Kim?" Sara asked. Her smile was irresistible, inching up on one side of her mouth and deepening her dimples. "Dad's got a horse you could ride."

Kim's eyes widened. "Really? That would be great."

"Yeah, well don't get too excited." Sara jerked her thumb in my direction. "Christa might try to follow us."

"On what?" I snapped. "Our dog?"

Sara giggled.

Cisco snuck a glance at me. I thought I saw understanding in his eyes. Maybe he got the same little-kid treatment from Kim.

Kim feigned disappointment. "Ahhh, the little sister tag-along thing. I get it."

Suddenly, I wanted to kill both of them. I had a fleeting vision of running away with Cisco to a ranch of our own where we raised horses and were admired by everyone for being such a talented couple.

Kim put her arm around me again. "Can I tell you a secret?"

I nodded mutely. I didn't have the strength to fight, and I couldn't think of anything clever to say.

"I've always wanted a little sister," she whispered. "I'm so tired of my bonehead brother over there," I glanced over to see Cisco kicking a stone on the ground with a bored expression, his hands jammed into his pockets, "I'd love to go riding with you."

I couldn't help but smile a little. "Okay."

"Well, we better find her a horse today then because I'm not riding double." Sara said.

We wandered the property, looking for that special horse, but nothing caught my eye. Cisco drifted off by himself into the corrals. I watched him size up a bay mare with nice conformation, stroking her withers and talking to the auctioneer. He had a nice way with horses.

Sara and Kim walked a few steps ahead of me, deep in conversation. I eavesdropped ruthlessly. "Cisco knows his way around a horse," Kim said to Sara. "You should see him work with the Miller's new mustang."

Cisco trained mustangs? Oh, that wasn't fair. I hated him for being so cool. So that's how Amy knew Cisco. He must be training her new mustang. But he was still probably madly in love with her, with all that time he was spending at her ranch.

"Did they adopt it from the BLM?" Sara asked.

"Yup. The Millers try to find good homes for them," Kim said.

Sara's face brightened as she leaned against the pipe corral. "The Millers are your neighbors?" she asked casually. "Any chance I can go over there with you?"

Sara's obsession with James Miller was easier to spot than his biceps.

"Don't see why not," Kim said with a smile.

"That would be great." Sara glanced down at her fingernails. "I heard he's home from college for the summer."

I groaned. As if she didn't care. Gah! "She's boy-crazy, not horse-crazy anymore."

Kim laughed. "He is pretty cute." She stood a minute, face to face with an old paint. I wondered if she was talking about the boy or the horse.

Kim turned and nudged me with her elbow. "So, what was it like seeing the Lost Herd?"

"It was unbelievable," I said. For an instant I was filled with longing, remembering Mesteño's grace and raw beauty. The spirit of those horses seemed to live in my bones. They were a secret breath of power inside me.

"You're lucky you saw them. The way things are going, they may not be around much longer," Kim said. "You know, with the roundups."

I tried to speak, swallowed, and tried once more. The Lost Herd could never end up in a holding pen. I coughed like a cat with a hairball in its throat.

Kim patted me on the back and I took a deep breath.

"Maybe there's something we can do to trip up the BLM," I blurted out.

"Maybe."

I found myself thinking of Corazón, her nose inches from

my face while I lay on the grass, and sweet little Echo. My heart thumped more solidly in my chest.

"Isn't your Dad on the city council?" Sara asked Kim. She seemed to know everything about everyone.

The breeze blew Kim's dark hair into her eyes. She turned into the wind. "Yep."

I was impressed. "He must know some important people. Like Bob Downs."

"Yeah, but Bob's in the back pocket of the corporate ranchers. Did you know the BLM used to be the Cattleman's Association?" Kim laughed bitterly. "The government agency that's supposed to be taking care of our wild horses and burros are into cows, not horses." She hooked her boot into the pipe corral and pulled herself up on the fence.

A ball of anger knotted in my stomach. "That's like a coyote looking after the chickens."

Kim nodded. "The deck is stacked against the wild horses, and they have no way of defending themselves," she said.

"Well, then we have to help them," I said." I bet with your connections we could get in to see Bob Downs. Tell him to stop the roundups,"

"Christa, stop pressuring her!" Sara looked mortified by my blunt questions.

A spark of steel ignited in Kim's eyes. "It's okay. I feel the same as she does."

"Bob Downs is more like Bob Downer," Sara said. She seemed to be coming around now that Kim was interested. "Christa sends him emails and texts all the time. She even snail mails him, but he never responds," Sara said.

"All the more reason to see him in person," Kim said, tossing me a crooked smile.

I grinned back. With Kim on my side, maybe we could get his attention.

Cisco ambled up, his boots scuffling the gravel as he walked. "We gotta go, sis. I'm late for work." He checked his watch. "I gotta be at the Whitehorse's Ranch by noon."

Of course he did. I bet he was dying to see Amy.

Kim hesitated.

Cisco gazed steadily at her. "Like you care; all you plan on doing is giggling with your girlfriends all summer." He spat on the ground.

Kim punched him in the shoulder. "FYI, I just got a job, you jerk!"

"Oh yeah, I forgot. Big career move. Pizza Hut." Cisco dodged Kim's swinging fist. I laughed and he glanced over at me. "Some nice horses here. Hope you find one you like." He shifted his cowboy hat on his head and turned away.

I twisted my hair in my hand. "Thanks." I watched Cisco's back as he walked away.

CHAPTER 13

SHIELDING MY EYES from the harsh rays of the sun, I scanned the auction grounds for Dad. Sara said she'd go look for him. I stood and looked about awkwardly, feeling overwhelmed. The overpowering smell of horse manure mixed with dirt and diesel fuel stung my nose. Little kids ran by, kicking up dust that seemed to stretch all the way to the low hills on the horizon. Horses stood listlessly in corrals, swatting flies with their tails. I wished it would rain. I wished a soft gray storm would wash over this place and make everything clean, fresh and cool again.

I turned away and drifted over to the main corral. An auctioneer spoke into a scratchy sounding microphone, announcing the first horse to a sparse crowd in the bleachers. A young girl led a gray pony into the corral. I did a double take and gripped the fence. He walked with a springy stride that was familiar, but when the girl turned him around I saw brown markings on his side. This wasn't the pony I had in mind. He wasn't Lucky. As if I'd find him here. What was I thinking? I had to get used to the simple fact that Lucky was never coming back and start looking for a real horse, not a ghost.

Dad and Sara slipped up behind me. "Follow me, Christa," Dad said. "Think you might wanna see this one." He was all keyed up, whistling and fiddling with the keys in his pocket. "There's a smaller corral in back where they keep the new arrivals."

"Okay," I said to his back. He and Sara paced ahead so fast I could barely keep up with them.

Sara swung a look over her shoulder. "Hurry!"

I followed them to a round pen tucked under some tall trees, and my heart started beating like a crazy drum.

There stood the biggest, most brilliant red horse I'd ever seen. He had a white blaze running down his face and three white socks. His neck arched and all his muscles rippled in the sun as he trotted, his tail a thick red plume streaming out from behind. Maybe it was his beauty, or his pride, but I felt an opening in the fog that seemed to swirl around me, and everything came into focus.

If I had him, I could ride out to see the Lost Herd again. That thought made my heart beat even faster.

The whole family gathered at the fence. I swear that horse knew he had an audience and started showing off for us. We all laughed, watching him toss his long red mane and move the other horses around the corral as if he was a wild stallion. He pranced right past us on his strong legs, and I whistled to him. He didn't turn his head, but one ear swiveled and locked on me as he passed by.

Sara broke the silence. "That is one incredible horse. Why would anyone sell him?" She pulled her sunglasses off and stared.

"That's what we need to find out," Dad said. "Let's take a closer look at him."

We watched the auctioneer approach the giant red horse, which stood politely for the halter and walked respectfully behind the man to the fence where we were standing. The horse had a spark of mischief in his eye and a beautifully defined face all the way down to his dark red muzzle. His long forelock fell perfectly between his eyes. He was so cute. I realized I was grinning, but then I wiped the smile off my face. It was too early to get excited. There had to be a fatal flaw with this horse. I stepped back and let everyone else get close to him.

Dad asked the auctioneer a bunch of questions while he ran his hands carefully down the tendons to the pastern and the hoof of each leg of the horse. After he finished his examination, he glanced at me and raised his eyebrows encouragingly. Hope licked at my insides like a fire. I didn't trust the feeling. I kicked the dirt with my boot.

"He's okay." I said.

Sara stuck her face next to mine and glared at me. "Earth to Christa!" She grabbed me and pushed me up right into the horse's nose. "You have no idea how lucky you are, you spoiled brat," she hissed into my ear. "I'd give anything to have a horse like this. You can at least pretend to be grateful."

I was trying to think of something I could say back to her when she gave me a little shove and pushed me even closer. The big red horse's head shot up in alarm as I stumbled toward him, but he turned one eye to me and held my gaze. I saw kindness there and sadness, too. At first I saw my reflection in his eye, my face shadowed by a pink baseball cap. Then he tossed his head and I disappeared.

The horse stepped closer. I felt his warm breath on my head as he snuffed my hair. He dropped his forehead right onto the center of my chest and left it there, like we were old buddies. My stomach stopped aching for the first time since Lucky died. I breathed in his warmth. "What's his name?" I asked.

"Jenner," the man working the auction answered. "This one came with a name, and we've got papers for him, too. Apparently he's got Man O' War a few generations back. That's what gives him that fancy shade of red. It's called Red Dunn."

"Uh-huh," Dad said with no expression. "Guess that would be quite a few generations back."

The auctioneer smiled as if he understood Dad's sarcasm. I knew Dad didn't believe a word.

Dad pulled me off to the side. His voice carried an undercurrent of tension. "Here's what we've got so far on this horse. He's seven years old and seventeen hands. According to the auctioneer, he's had lots of training and he's bombproof. But the auctioneer's a man selling a horse, and if his lips are moving, he's probably lying."

"Yeah, but the horse looks pretty good," I said.

"He's a little bigger than I'd like, but you're already tall and still growing."

I couldn't stand to see Dad all twisted up. This horse was special. Getting him at an auction seemed like the opportunity of a lifetime, but what was the catch? "Why don't we see how it goes?" I offered. "We can always sell him if he's got some big problem. He's cheap, right?"

"Yeah, that's what's got me worried. This horse should be worth a lot more. Maybe the owners need cash more than they need a horse." He looked off into the horizon, his face a sun-weathered mask of lines. His unruly brown hair stuck up in places it shouldn't, and his worn flannel plaid shirt hung loose on his tall body.

I loved him for trying to make this right, even though I knew he never could.

"You said his feet were good?" I asked, trying to be sensible. He nodded. "Well, then," I said, thinking of finding the Lost Herd, "how bad can it be?"

Dad chuckled. "Okay, Christa," he said, kissing me on the top of my head. "Why don't you ride him and see how he feels?"

Within minutes, Jenner was saddled and bridled. I swung onto him and enjoyed the view. This was the tallest horse I'd ever sat. I could feel the muscles rippling through his body and the strength that lay just below the surface. Dad and Sara watched from the fence. Well, Sara was on her cell phone, but Dad watched me like I was a movie.

I stroked the proud arch of Jenner's neck and signaled him to walk. He sneezed and snorted and looked around him at any sound or flash of movement, but I talked to him and he calmed right down.

With light leg pressure and almost no rein, I guided Jenner in circles and figure eights. He had the softest touch and was happy to go wherever I asked. At least the man selling Jenner wasn't lying about his training.

It felt so good to ride again that I began daydreaming. I saw myself riding Jenner into the hills and finding Mesteño's band. Maybe Cisco could come along on one of those mustangs he was training.

Dad smiled at me and waved. He loved watching me ride 'cause I sat up so straight and tall on a horse. I had a habit of slumping when I wasn't riding. At least, that's what he said. Mom was always telling me to stand up straight or to sit up like I was running for Miss America or something. Well, riding this horse made me feel beautiful. With each giant step, my chest opened wide and my shoulders relaxed so much it was like the weight of Lucky was sliding right off my back.

Even Sara nodded in approval as I rode Jenner up to the fence and pulled him to a halt. "You look great together," she said, helping me down. "Dad says you can have him. You want him, don't you?"

It scared me how much I wanted him. "Yep," I said.

I glanced at Jenner's face. He slid his eye back to meet mine. I noticed he had a little bit of white in the corner of his eye and it made him look almost human, like he was thinking. "But first I have to ask Jenner," I said, stepping in front of him.

Sara looked up at the sky. "Seriously?"

"Jenner, " I whispered, looking into his eyes, "do you want to be my horse?" It may sound silly, but I was nervous. It was important that he wanted to come home with me. He was going to be my partner and that was a big commitment, especially seeing as I wasn't exactly easy on horses. Jenner dropped his lovely nose to my cheek and gently nudged my face. That felt like a yes, for sure. Just when I reached up to give his ears a tug, he caught the bill of my pink baseball cap with his upper lip and flipped it right off my head.

Dad handed my hat back to me, brushing the dust off. "Well, if nothing else he's got a sense of humor. He'll need one of those if he's going to be your horse." He roughed up my hair. "Happy fourteenth birthday, Christa."

We bought Jenner right out from under that auction, and before the first bid was placed on any horse, he was loaded in the trailer and on his way home to our ranch. For better or for worse, Jenner was my horse. And I'd get to show him to Grandma tonight.

CHAPTER 14

BRINGING JENNER HOME set my mind racing in circles. There were two parts of me at war with each other. One side thought Jenner might be the answer to all my problems. The other side insisted Lucky was the only horse in the world worth having. Well, one thing was for sure—Jenner trailered like an angel. I could see the edge of his red muzzle hanging out the window, sampling all the new smells.

When we turned off the highway at the wooden sign that said Cassidy Ranch, I felt my stomach do a flip-flop. I had a big, strong new horse. It was my responsibility to ride him, train him and keep him safe. I couldn't screw up again. I was more than a little scared, and not just because of all the mistakes I could make... I was afraid of Jenner. He seemed too perfect. We'd got him for almost nothing. What was his story?

We drove the quarter-mile gravel drive lined with cedar and fields of grass waving in the wind. I could see the familiar trail leading to Walden Pond, the spring-fed swimming hole on our property. We pulled to a stop in the turnaround and the dogs ran out to greet us. Our yellow farmhouse sat across from the old red barn. Dad had fenced and cross-fenced the whole five-acre property, including our big pasture on the hill overlooking the barn where we let the horses graze during the day.

On top of the hill under the giant oak tree, a mound of earth marked Lucky's grave. "I hope you don't mind my getting a new horse, Lucky," I said under my breath. "Don't worry. I'll always love you best…"

When I led Jenner out of the trailer, Dad snapped a few pictures. I made an effort to look as good as I could, standing up tall and trying not to squint in the bright Nevada sun. I didn't want to waste Dad's talent as a photographer. Neither did Sara. She stood beside me for every photo.

Jenner worked the camera like an old pro during the photo shoot. He tilted his ears forward and swung his head to look right into the lens. If a horse could smile, I swear he would've flashed us a big one. Mom walked across the lawn and made a fuss over Jenner, but she made sure to stand back from him, one hand on her stomach. After a few minutes, she gave me a quick hug and went inside.

Star and Eastwood acted more eager to meet Jenner. They ran the fence line, whinnying.

Dad motioned toward the barn. "We'll keep them separated for a while until they get used to each other."

"Sounds good, Dad." I took Jenner's lead rope and walked him toward the barn.

"Jenner sure doesn't look like he needs protecting," Sara said, falling into step beside me. "He's big enough to look after himself."

"Good thing you have long legs or you'd never be able to sit him."

"I know. I hope he's as sweet as he seems. If I come off him, it's a long way to the ground."

Sara and I led Jenner down the wide barn aisle to his stall. Lucky's old stall. A bale of hay with a plaid blanket thrown over it served as our barn couch. Sara sank into it with a sigh, watching while I threw Jenner some hay. He buried his head into the flake of grass and did what horses do best. He ate.

"I hope Jenner makes you happy, Christa. You've been such a drag since Lucky died," she said. "You used to be so sweet. Now you're moody...really moody."

I let that one go. You had to pick your battles.

"This family is such a bummer." She pushed her lips into a pout and ran a hand through her silky long hair. "I deserve better. Like, I should be surrounded by happy people."

I felt a stab of jealousy. "Happy, beautiful people like Kim?"

"Exactly," she said brightly, crossing her long legs. "And James Miller."

Jenner caught a scent and threw his head over the stall door, his nostrils quivering. He looked regal.

"It's fate that James Miller happens to live right next door to Kim and Cisco," she said.

Cisco. For a second, I felt a tiny flutter in my heart.

The corner of Sara's mouth twitched into a grin. "Well, it wouldn't do any harm, my running into James this summer."

"Just don't jump into his arms before you've introduced yourself," I said and then I thought about Cisco. I hoped I wasn't morphing into a younger version of Sara. Cisco would never like me anyway. I pulled my thoughts back into orbit. Suddenly an idea came to me. "Why don't you go over to the Miller's with Kim?" I asked. "That'd be fun."

She perked up. "I couldn't go to see James, he doesn't even know me," she said, blushing.

"No, not to see James or anything, just to talk to his parents. See if they've heard anything about the Lost Herd." Sometimes she didn't think things through.

She grinned. "Not a bad idea."

"And get Kim to set up an appointment with Bob Downs. I'm tired of sending him emails with no reply."

Sara regarded me with a mixture of horror and respect. "You never give up, do you?"

"Nope."

Jenner was giving me confidence. I pulled out my phone and texted Amy for the first time since Lucky died. Maybe she knew something. She texted right back. She didn't have any info. Her grimacing emoticon face made me smile. I'd ask her about her and Cisco another time. No big deal.

I wrapped my fingers in Jenner's mane and leaned close. Warmth rose from his skin. He smelled good, like warm earth. A horse this strong could cover a lot of ground on the trail. "I'm riding Jenner up to Crow's Nest tomorrow to look for the Lost Herd."

Sara's face fell. "It's too soon to take him out alone. You could get hurt."

I let go of Jenner's mane and crossed my arms over my chest. "He's my horse. I'll ride him where and when I want."

She brushed the hay off her jeans. "You'd think after what happened with Lucky you'd be more cautious."

After what happened with Lucky… she hadn't spoken a word to me about it until now, but she was always watching over me around the horses. Of course she blamed me for Lucky's death. It was obvious it was my fault.

I turned away from Sara, my heart aching. Suddenly the barn seemed unbearably small. "Leave me alone!" I growled, pushing past her.

"Hey, don't be like that!" she said. "C'mon, don't go! Grandma will be here any minute."

Tears pooled in my eyes. I blinked them away and ran. The pain of losing Lucky slashed through my body. I felt like a cloud split apart by lightning. For the whole afternoon, I had managed to set it aside, like something I would think about later. Now, all of a sudden here it was, like a monster popping out from under the bed. A metallic taste flooded my mouth. I ran faster, blowing past the round pen. Strands of Lucky's tail hung from a deep crack in the wooden fencing around the arena where he used to scratch his back. I couldn't believe they were still there. I yanked them out and stuffed the long, coarse hairs in my pocket as I raced down the path through the trees.

Then it came to me in one sick flash: Lucky, turning an eye to me as he died. Lucky, writhing in pain. A crushing weight seemed to settle on my shoulders, and I ran until my lungs hurt. I could never hope to grasp that Lucky was gone. Dead. Forever.

I crossed the meadow and turned sharply into the woods. Branches whipped my bare arms, lashing my skin. I rounded the last curve in the trail and burst into the clearing, greeted by cheery birdsong, filtered light and beautiful blue water. I slowed to a walk, holding my sides. I bent over, trying to catch my breath. My knees were shaking. Calm down. My heart was beating so hard I thought it might come clear through the skin. I dropped my head and willed myself not to cry. Then thankfully, my heart slowed and the world came back into focus.

Walden Pond sparkled in the sun, and the long, graceful branches of the willow tree drifted in the water. A warm breeze teased the trembling leaves of the tall cottonwoods.

I leaned against the willow and slid all the way to the ground, my back scratching against the grainy bark. The dogs raced to my side, snuffling my shirt and tickling me with their breath as they tried to lick my face. I swear they tried to make me laugh, rolling on their backs and grinning at me with their tongues hanging out the sides of their mouths. Finally I gave in. I sat cross-legged and patted my knee. Elvis pushed his nose under my palm and Chico curled up beside me, resting his muzzle on my leg. I stroked his sand-colored fur and thought of Jenner. My new horse was beautiful. And it was my birthday. Everything would be okay.

I pulled the strands of Lucky's tail out of my pocket and braided them into a long plait. Mom had some ribbon in her sewing box that I could tie onto the ends. For now I used the hair ties I always wore around my wrist.

A voice sounded in the woods. The dogs exploded down the trail, barking furiously. "Hello! Christa, are you there?"

I knew whose voice that was. I scrambled to my feet. "Grandma!"

She burst into the clearing, waving wildly with one hand while she appeased the dogs with the other. She took big strides. Her long, gray hair fell gracefully around her shoulders. She wore a white, button-down with a black t-shirt underneath and a pair of dark jeans. "Sara told me I might find you here." She held her arms wide.

I ran into them. Grandma was the best hugger in the whole world. She was solid and sturdy, not willowy and thin like Mom. I leaned into her with all my weight.

"Now, let me get a good look at you." Her Irish accent was so cute. She stepped back, keeping her hands on my shoulders.

I must've grown a lot, I realized with a sudden shock, as her blue eyes came level with mine.

A stray curl hung in my eyes and she brushed it back. "You've gotten taller and even prettier, if that's possible."

I shrugged. "I may be taller, but prettier is really stretching it...even for you."

She laughed. "Still waiting for the smarts to go with the looks, I'm afraid. Silly girl. Someday you'll realize you're lovely." She reached out to touch my cheek. "But you look sad."

I glanced away. "I'm fine."

"Yes, you are. Fine enough to deserve to be happy on your birthday." She winked and unzipped her backpack. "Now sit, so I can give you your birthday presents."

It struck me that Grandma was one of my favorite people in the entire world. "Did you see my new horse?"

Her eyes widened. "He's as big as a racehorse. "

"He's seventeen hands!"

"Well, he is just gorgeous. Can't wait to see you ride him."

"How long are you staying?"

"Long enough to be of some help to your mother. Maybe a few weeks or so."

I laughed and clapped my hands. "A few weeks or so! That's awesome." Then my smile faded. "Does Mom need that much help?"

"We're going to get her feeling better in no time. Bless you, dear. I know it's been hard for you," she said, melting my worry. I could never stay upset when she started talking. She grew up in Galway and Mom was born years later in the states. How many years later, we didn't know. Grandma wouldn't tell us how old she was. She pulled her long, gray hair back in a ponytail and sat beside me under the tree.

"I've missed you, Christa." Her voice was so warm it took me off guard.

I swallowed hard. My throat felt dry. "I've missed you, too."

"Of course you have." She grinned and handed me a box wrapped in white paper and a shimmering gold bow. "Open this first."

I tore the paper off the box and lifted the lid. It was a model horse. The tag said it was a mustang. I held it up to see it better. It looked just like Mesteño.

"I hope you're not too old for a toy horse," Grandma leaned into me with her shoulder. "After all, you're a teenager now. But I saw this and thought of your adventures with the Lost Herd. He looks just like the stallion you described. Mesteño, right?"

I smiled, thinking of Mesteño and his flowing mane, the way

he seemed to dance around his mares. Oh, how I missed him! It figured Grandma would know exactly what to get me.

"He's perfect."

As I placed the horse back in the box, I saw a small blue velvet case. I opened it and pulled out a silver heart locket on a long chain.

The heart opened with a tiny clasp. There was nothing inside. How perfect…a hollow heart, just like mine. There was a gift tag in the box that read, *"Happy Fourteen, Christa. We love you, Your Grandma Gillian and Grandpa Dave."*

"Did Grandpa make this?" He crafted jewelry for their store in Reno. Grandma preferred painting and had huge cheery canvases of modern art hung all over her house. She was into circles. For years, that was all she'd painted.

"Yes, dear." Grandma helped me with the clasp. "He engraved it before he put it together."

I examined the locket again more closely. On the back of the heart, there was a letter "C" in sweeping cursive. "So Sara can't try and wear it all the time."

Grandma grinned. "Exactly."

"Thank you so much." I hugged her again.

Grandma reached for my hand. "I'm going to go back to the house and help Claire with dinner." She laughed uneasily. "You know, your father called me to come and help make life easier for all of you, but my cooking skills have never been too impressive."

"No worries. It's you we want, not your cooking." I let go of her hand, picked up her backpack and slung it over my shoulder.

As we walked back to the house, my hand flew to the silver locket. I liked the cool feel of the silver against my skin.

"Happy Birthday!" Dad and Sara shouted when we opened the front door. On the table stood bowls of popcorn, pizza cut into squares, and unopened bottles of soda. A plate of Mom's fudge brownies rested on the counter next to a huge chocolate cake with vanilla frosting. My favorite.

Grandma put her arm around my shoulder. "They told me to keep you busy out there so they could set all this up."

My jaw dangled open. "Well, it worked." I glanced around the room. "Where's Mom?"

Dad cleared his throat. "She's lying down."

"Is she okay?" I asked.

"She'll be fine, dear. She just needs her rest," Grandma said.

It wasn't like Mom to be resting on my birthday. What was going on with her? I hoped the baby was going to be okay.

Sara lit the fourteen candles and carried the cake to the table. "I say you make your wish before we eat," she said. "Shake it up a little bit."

"Fine with me."

I closed my eyes. I thought of Mom and the baby, Lucky, Jenner, and the Lost Herd. Okay, I'll admit it–Cisco flashed through my mind. With a lungful of air big enough to blow the barn down, I snuffed those candles out, one by one. I wasn't taking any chances. All my wishes had to come true.

CHAPTER 15

THE NEXT MORNING I leapt out of bed, saddled Jenner and rode him into the arena. We quickly gathered a crowd of admirers.

"Turn him to the left and canter," Grandma called from the fence as Jenner and I flew around the ring. He transitioned effortlessly from a trot into a smooth lope, and a smile broke over my face as big as the sunrise.

"Gorgeous!" Grandma clapped enthusiastically. We slid to a stop in front of her and Dad.

"He's perfect," I said, patting his neck.

Dad shook his head. "No such thing as a perfect horse."

"Or the perfect anything," Grandma said.

"Just go slow with him, Christa," Dad said.

The last thing I wanted was to go slow. "Can I take him out on the trail, Dad?"

"Not without me or your sister. Not this soon." His face darkened with concern. "We need to get to know this guy's tricks," he said, holding out a carrot. Jenner took it politely, as if he had all the time in the world.

"Well, this is one of them," I said proudly. "Someone taught him how to spin. I mean, at least they started to teach him." I swung my leg to his shoulder and set my weight just right. Jenner jumped in the opposite direction. After a few repeats, we lurched around in a complete circle.

"Well, that's a great start!" Grandma exclaimed.

As I showed Jenner off, Dad's expression never changed. "We got him for a song, " I heard him said quietly to Grandma. "Kind of wonder what the catch is with this one."

"Maybe it's just a good thing happening to a great girl." Grandma clapped for us again as we spun in the other direction. "Don't worry so much, Harrison."

I walked Jenner up to the gate. He stood calmly and I leaned forward to circle my arms around his neck. "Is Mom up yet?" I hoped to show her some of Jenner's moves.

Dad cleared his throat. "Not yet."

I straightened up in the saddle and fiddled with Jenner's mane. "Oh." I took a deep breath. "I hope she's feeling okay."

Grandma exchanged glances with Dad. "I'll go check on her. Meet you inside for breakfast," she said to me.

"Sure." I eased Jenner through the gate. I'd turned him out with Star and Eastwood for a few hours the night before. At first, Star did her best to pick a fight, pinning her ears back and striking at him with her front legs, but Jenner would just amble out of her way and go back to grazing.

After our ride, I turned Jenner out again. He was a piece of work, that was for sure, because after watching for a few minutes, I could see he was the new leader in the pasture. He was first to the best grass, and Star, who'd been chasing and squealing at him the previous night, stood like an angel by his side. It was pure magic watching her turn from a bossy, tough mare to pure sweetness. The three of them stood peacefully together in the morning sun, head to tail, Eastwood touching noses with Jenner briefly from time to time like they'd been best buddies for a lifetime. Red, black and yellow…they were beautiful together.

Sara was quiet at breakfast. I think she was a little jealous because she didn't even mention Jenner. Still no word from Kim about the Lost Herd, but Sara said she was going over to Kim's today and would hopefully talk to the Millers. I noticed she was wearing skinny jeans and her fancy cowboy boots. James didn't stand a chance.

We were finished eating by the time Mom joined us. She sat heavily in her chair at the head of the table and rubbed her eyes. Sleep lines etched her face. She wore the same wrinkled gray t-shirt and capri pants she'd worn the day before. Grandma bustled around the kitchen, making coffee and toasting bread while Dad read the paper.

"How are you this morning, Claire?' Grandma asked cheerily.

"Fine," Mom said, her eyes staring at nothing.

"You sound less than fine from your tone," Grandma said, clipping her syllables as the Irish do. She slid a piece of paper under Mom's cup. "That's our to-do list for the day. Acupuncture, the doctor, and then a bit of rest."

Mom shot Grandma a disgusted look and scanned the list. "I'm not helpless, you know."

"Far from it," Grandma concurred.

I couldn't stand to see Mom upset. "This time it will be different, Mom," I said. "Little Hazel will be just fine."

Mom set her jaw. "I'm not going to have it any other way. If I have to lie in this house for months, then that's what I'll do."

Dad took a sip of his coffee. He spoke slowly. "I thought the doctor said you were out of danger."

"Well, excuse me if I don't trust the doctors!" Mom slammed her hand down on the table so hard it rattled our plates. All of us froze.

Grandma nodded sagely. "Sometimes that's what it takes for a man. A gesture loud enough to be heard."

"I heard," Dad said. "She's upset."

Grandma smiled. "See how observant he is!"

Sara giggled.

Mom crumpled her napkin up and threw it at Grandma. "You're as bad as he is, if not worse, and you know it," she said.

Grandma patted Mom on the shoulder lovingly. "Use that anger. It's motivating. It'll help you get through the quality time we're going to spend together."

I hid a smile with my napkin.

Mom pushed her chair back and her eyes traded their dullness for a flash of her old fire. "Well, let's get going on those errands, then, since I won't get any peace around here."

Grandma drained her cup of tea. "I'll start the truck."

Dad folded the paper and winked at Sara and me. "I'm off to work. Meeting with a client." He kissed Mom, who grudgingly offered her cheek and grabbed his keys.

We sat, stuck to our seats, as Mom picked up her purse and followed Grandma and Dad out to the driveway. It had been awhile since Mom had left the house. I guess having Grandma around was going to be different. A lot different.

Sara whistled. "That was cool." She jumped up and hustled out the door. "Let me drive, Mom. I need the practice. Just to Kim's house. She can give me a ride home." Car doors slammed and the motor started.

Silence. Golden, delicious silence. The clock above the kitchen sink ticked. I cleared my plate and contemplated the long day ahead. This would be a perfect opportunity to take Jenner up to Crows Nest. After all, he was warmed up after our short ride that morning and if we left right away, no one would have to know. I wouldn't give Dad anything to worry about; I'd be really careful with Jenner.

I just wanted things to be like they'd been with Lucky, the two of us on the trail. With the thought of seeing the Lost Herd again, a burst of adrenaline flooded my veins. I gathered the bridle and saddle from the tack room, and called to Jenner from the pasture gate.

He lifted his head and looked right at me.

This was my horse and my chance to take.

CHAPTER 16

WE RODE EAST toward the sun. Jenner's big walk ate up the miles; and while he walked, I talked, filling him in on the Lost Herd. I told him about Corazón and her little filly, Echo, and the peaceful old roan, Grandfather. And, of course, I warned Jenner to stay out of Mesteño's way. He listened closely to the story of Mesteño's victory against the red bachelor. I could tell he was interested because he'd flick an ear back in my direction for the more exciting parts. Before I knew it, we were almost there. Just one more hill between Crows Nest and us.

We stopped and stared up the daunting trail that wound up the mountain. As hard as this climb had been for Lucky, I sensed it would be easy for Jenner. There was only one way to find out. I pointed his nose straight and let him go. He sprang into a gallop. The wind ripped through my hair and stung my eyes as we raced upward.

I checked his reins to help balance him for the next curve. He did a flying lead change, hit it perfectly and leapt into an even higher gear for the last stretch up the mountain. Dirt flew from his hooves and his red mane flamed out behind him. He lengthened his stride and reached his neck forward hungrily. I felt the thrill of power singing through my body. As we reached the top of the hill, I pulled him up with all my strength. "Whoa, Jenner. Good boy!"

Jenner danced in place, straining at the bit. I swear he could have leapt straight off the cliff into the air and kept on running if I hadn't held him back. He was panting from the sprint, his sides heaving and wet, so I walked him in circles until his breathing steadied. Jumping down from his back, I landed with both boots in the red dirt. Jenner dropped his muzzle to the scant patches of desert grass, chewing noisily around the bit.

We had the perfect view of Gold Canyon from up here. I longed to see Mesteño prancing out of the brush with his mares in a cloud of dust, but all I saw was a hawk gliding low over the canyon floor. I scanned the wash for any movement while Jenner grazed, unconcerned with my problems. I looked until my eyes were strained with trying, but there was no sign of them. Nothing. *Nada.* It was an empty world without the Lost Herd… and Lucky.

Lucky would've done anything for me. Jenner was magnificent, but all he cared about was the grass. We were as good as strangers. I kicked a stone with my boot and tried to swallow the bitter taste of regret choking my throat. I missed Lucky with a hollow ache in every bone of my body.

Jenner stepped closer to me, busily chewing. I stepped away from him. He stopped eating and came to me with a kind look in his eye. He nudged my arm and exhaled with a long sigh. My heart softened. Maybe I just needed to relax. After all, I couldn't expect him to understand how I felt about Lucky—or the Lost Herd for that matter. He'd never even seen them.

I ran my fingers through Jenner's long mane and tried to make my voice sound cheerful. "Not bad for our first day out on the trail together, is it, boy?"

He swiveled an ear to my voice. I stroked his shoulder, running my hand down to his pastern. It was cool and firm with no swelling. His hooves were massive and heavy as I lifted them to check for stones. So far, so good. Jenner was perfectly sound.

"Let's head back. No wild horses for us today."

I led him to a boulder I could stand on and shoved my left boot in the stirrup, swinging my right leg over him into the old, creaky western saddle. I'd grown a few inches this year, but I still needed practice getting on him. Jenner's head jerked up into the wind, his nostrils working. I felt a stab of panic, as if something bad was blowing in on the wind. Jenner danced forward before I was settled, and I slipped in the saddle. I shifted my weight back and checked him hard with the reins. He stopped, but I realized my hands were shaking. *Stop being such a baby. Nothing bad is going to happen.*

I rewarded him with a loose rein and a pat on the neck. See, no problem. Everything was okay. I rubbed my shoulder, remembering how I'd fallen off Lucky and broken my collarbone a few years before. It had taken six weeks to heal. When Lucky bucked me off, even though he was such a small pony, it was a long way to the ground. Grandma said when a horse wanted you off, you came off. And the rest of the time, when they let you ride them, well, that was a privilege.

Jenner seemed calm enough now, so I settled into the ride. We wound down the hill and I took the Carn River Trail home, flushing jackrabbits from the brush and sending them zigzagging across our path. We entered the forest and stillness descended. So quiet. The soft earth was a deep, rich brown. Sparrows stirred in the gnarled cedar branches, charming us with little snatches of their chirping songs. Leaves filtered the light above us, drenching us in dancing shadows.

As we emerged from the forest into a sunny meadow, Jenner lifted his head. I could tell he'd caught a scent. His ears rotated forward, and his muscles tensed. A slight breeze sent a hushed trill through the tops of the taller trees. Then, the golden grasses parted slightly to reveal a bobcat stalking his prey. The bobcat was the same color as the grass, but he moved like a shadow flattened to the ground. My heart lodged in my throat. "Good boy, easy now." I tensed, waiting for Jenner to bolt. He strode forward, swinging his head to look, but didn't spook. I tightened the reins in my hands, still waiting for him to break into a run, but he kept his steady pace. I let out my breath in a long sigh. The bobcat disappeared into the tall grass and Jenner snorted, relaxed and happy. What a horse!

A hawk hung above us, catching an updraft and shooting straight up into the sky. Then he swooped low and coasted right over us. The smell of sagebrush drifted on the wind, and I breathed deeply. Jenner's huge hooves made a muffled sound on the packed dirt of the trail, and I turned in the saddle to put a hand on his rump. He exhaled, dropping his head lower, appearing to be as relaxed as I was.

I guided him down the winding trail to where it crossed the river. The water smelled dank and muddy. Cottonwoods grew near the shore. I could see the little river leaping over and around the stones in its path. I loved the gurgling sound it made as it rushed over the smooth rocks.

We were about twenty feet from the water when Jenner snorted and planted his feet. I squeezed my legs as hard as I could and kicked the heel of my boots against his sides, but he refused to budge. I talked to him in a low voice, encouraging him, but he danced in place and tossed his head. He was afraid of the water, even this little stream.

He took big gulps of air and his skin twitched under the saddle. I tensed. *I'm losing control of him.* He jumped sideways and tried to whirl around, but I blocked him with the rein and my opposite leg, turning him back toward the river. "No, Jenner, it's okay. Easy, now. It's just water."

There was no logic to what might frighten a horse. He wasn't afraid of a bobcat, but water spooked him. I thought if I let him stand a while, maybe he would get used to the river and see it was only a few feet deep. But every time I tried to move him forward, he'd get worked up, his nostrils pumping air and his neck a steel arch of muscle pushing back against my command. Just when I was about to give up, he flicked an ear to the sound of my voice. "Jenner, you can do this. Just try," I crooned. Both his ears swiveled forward. The wind picked up and a branch broke from a tree just behind us.

Suddenly, he bolted straight into the river. His front feet slipped on the slick rocks and he stumbled, almost falling. When he regained his footing, he reared straight up into the air. I grabbed Jenner's mane and leaned into his neck, hoping he wouldn't go over backward and crush me under his body. I could see his left eye, white with terror. When he came back down, I dug my heels into him again, trying to keep him moving. I had to get control of him!

With a snort, he charged through the water and then halted. He stopped so fast I flew out of the saddle and slammed into his neck. Jenner shuddered and I could feel his big muscles, pent up and ready to explode. I pulled on the reins with all my strength, trying to direct him to the other side of the river. But he reared again and my foot lost purchase on the leather, slick with water. Jenner rose like a mountain and while my boot searched blindly for the stirrup, I slid backwards almost out of the saddle. Quickly, I grabbed a chunk of mane and held on. He leapt to the side, and I found myself dangling off the side of his neck, looking down at the cold water swirling around the boulders. I pulled myself back on top of him and jammed my feet into the stirrups.

Finally, I sat firmly astride my horse in an almost upright position. *The worst is over*, I told myself. But then the strangest thing happened. Fear overtook me. The reins dropped like a feather through my trembling fingers. I commanded my left hand to pick up the reins, but my limbs would not move. With a start, I realized my other hand was gripping the saddle horn as if I was a young frightened child, just learning to ride.

Nothing could stop Jenner now. He spun away from the river and galloped wildly through the brush. I screamed as he charged back up the trail, racing for home.

CHAPTER 17

WHEN WE PASSED through the gate onto our property, Jenner finally slowed to a walk. Somehow I had stayed on. I hoped the blood would stop hammering in my ears. My stomach churned with nervous energy, but the familiar sight of the dogs racing to greet us slowed my breathing down. They trotted ahead of us toward the barn, glancing over their shoulders to make sure we were following.

When we reached the hitching post in front of the barn, I slipped off Jenner's back and ran my hands over the scratches on my arms. He'd swerved into the brush on the way out of the river and galloped all the way home at warp speed. Now I knew why this magnificent red horse had landed at the auction. No one in Nevada wanted a horse that ran a mile in the wrong direction when you asked him to cross a stream.

After bathing Jenner and walking him until he cooled down, I put him back in his stall. I brought Star and Eastwood in from the pasture, put them in their stalls, and threw them hay. It was a little early but I was still feeling shaky and wanted them here with me and Jenner.

I crooned to them, telling them how beautiful they were. Star and Eastwood, my old and trusted friends. They reached their heads over their stall doors, brown eyes watching me while they chewed their alfalfa. Star nickered softly and shoved her muzzle into my hand. Her breath was warm. I rubbed the dainty white star in the center of her forehead and ran my hand down her perfectly sculpted face. Oddly enough, her easy confidence in me slowed down my ragged pulse, but I still felt an ache in my belly. "My first ride on the trail with Jenner was a complete failure," I said. I felt like I'd fallen at the first hurdle. Star just gazed peacefully at me. "That's a sweet girl," I whispered, tugging on her forelock. "Thank you for not judging me."

Eastwood stamped impatiently in his stall and nipped at Star, hoping to be the first in line to get a carrot. Star put her small ears back and nipped back at him. "Easy, boy. Your turn will come, Eastwood." I held out a carrot to him only after I'd given one to Star. He dropped his pink lips to my hand and lifted the carrot gingerly, barely brushing my fingers, like a perfect gentleman. "Eastwood, you're a charmer, but I've got your number. You're all about the carrots." I stroked his long forelock and ran my hand down his golden neck.

He shook his head and nickered.

I had two more carrots ready when I reached Jenner. My horse. My responsibility. My problem. He brushed my face with his muzzle and craned his neck over the stall door to smell my pockets for treats. His upper lip tickled my skin. He seemed calm enough now. I took a shaky breath as I watched him inhale the carrots, crunching noisily. A horse that's afraid of water is a dangerous horse, especially when the rains fell and flooded the washes, creating rivers and streams everywhere. My thoughts raced. I felt like a scared hamster running on a wheel, looking over her little hamster shoulder at an imposing shadow approaching.

How was I going to search for the Lost Herd on a horse this unpredictable? Although, to be honest I didn't know what riding out to see the Lost Herd would solve. Still, I had the strangest feeling that Jenner held the key to coming up with a plan to help them. Maybe it was the regal curve of his neck, or the way I'd felt when I'd ridden him the first time. There was something about Jenner that stirred a long-ing in my heart to do something important–something that mattered. Besides, it might take months to convince Sara and Kim to go see Bob Downs. I was still writing Mr. Downs emails and sending snail mail letters with no reply. Ugh. Patience was not my strong suit.

Jenner snuffed my chest. When he pulled his head up, I stroked the white blaze running down his face. "You need to get over this water thing. Oh my God, not a small glitch."

Jenner's eyes slid away from mine, as if he knew what I was talking about. If Mom and Dad knew what had happened, we'd both be in a different kind of water. Hot water. Thankfully, they weren't home yet.

I sat in the barn all afternoon, cleaning saddles and bridles and trying to keep my mind blank. I hoped Grandma was taking good care of Mom. The setting sun filtered through the cracks in the barn walls with a warm, red-tinted hue, sending a shaft of golden light through the open window in the hayloft. I heard Mom's car, and then Dad's truck, pull into the driveway. Doors slammed. Voices murmured.

Somehow, everything will be okay, I told myself. But it felt like time was running out for the wild mustangs. Jenner and I needed to find the Lost Herd as soon as possible and come up with a plan to save them. My hamster brain began running again, spinning the wheel faster and faster.

And then a horrible thought wormed its way into my head. Jenner's violent aversion to rivers could be a bigger problem than I'd imagined. A problem so big it could stop us from ever seeing the Lost Herd: When you were looking for wild horses, you always found them near water.

CHAPTER 18

BEFORE I ENTERED the house for dinner, I stood and watched Mom through the kitchen window. It was an odd feeling, knowing she couldn't see me in the growing darkness. It was kind of like watching someone in a movie, framed in that glass square. Her hair was still cut in short layers around her face, showing off her high cheekbones. For a moment, I wished I had her grace. Even as she did her mundane chores at the sink, her long slender neck made her look like a ballerina. When she glanced out the window, I could see she was gaunt—too pale and too thin—and her eyes appeared hollow in the shadows cast by the fading light.

I sighed. She needed to put on more weight for the baby. She was almost as moody as me; she went from being dreamy and distant to angry, annoyed, and cross. All that lying in bed didn't agree with her. I hoped Grandma could help bring the old Mom back.

When I entered the house, the table was already set for dinner. At the kitchen island, Mom stirred a large pot of homemade soup. My stomach growled with hunger.

"Did you feed the horses, Christa?" Mom asked.

The tension under her calm tone made me angry. I could feel my chest tighten. Didn't anyone trust me anymore? "Of course I fed the horses!"

"How about the dogs?"

"Not yet...I just got here!" I glared at her. "I was doing my chores in the barn."

Mom's blue eyes met mine. "Just checking." Her eyes drifted back to the soup and got that faraway look that I hated. First, she didn't trust me. Then she ignored me.

"Dinner almost ready?" I asked. I knew it was. I poured dog food into the bowls for Elvis and Chico.

"Yes."

"Just checking."

I turned and ran upstairs. I wanted to be alone, but Sara was in our bedroom combing her hair and singing along to a thumping dance remix. Why couldn't I have my own room?

As soon as Sara saw me, she held the hairbrush to her lips like a microphone and lip-synched her heart out. She danced on the worn, shaggy blue carpeting in her bare feet, past my horse posters on the wall. Her long dark hair swung as she moved her hips. *What a girl wants, what a girl needs...*she danced past our white desks, which sat side by side, and all the model horses and books lined up in a row on the shelf. The bulletin board over my desk was pretty bare. Hers was bursting with pictures and cards. Posters of boy bands hung on her side of the room. She held her hand out as if displaying these things, as if they were part of the song. *Whatever makes you happy sets me free...*her brown eyes locked on me, exuding love. Apparently, I was her one and only desire. She dropped to her knees in front of me. *And I'm thanking you for being there for me....*

I stifled a laugh. I couldn't give her a sliver of encouragement or she'd never stop. Now she was dancing to some Latino song, looking over her shoulder so she could see herself from behind in the mirror. It was embarrassing. I turned the music down. She dropped the brush on the dresser with a clatter and sized me up in one glance: dirty jeans, alfalfa clinging to my shirt, hair uncombed and frizzy. "How's life at the barn?" she asked.

"How's life with your butt?"

She giggled and flopped down on the bed. "What's up?"

"Not much." I wasn't going to tell her about Jenner. Not yet. "How was Kim?"

She sat up and a dreamy look came over her face. "I saw James Miller mowing the lawn without a shirt on."

I rolled my eyes. "And?"

"He was gorgeous…blonde curly hair, green eyes, perfect body. He had his old Spartans football jersey slung over the handle of the lawnmower. He was using it as a rag." She sank back into the pillows again, frowning. "A rag! What a waste. If I had that number twenty-two jersey of his, I'd frame it."

I groaned. "Did you talk to Mr. and Mrs. Miller? The ones who might know about the Lost Herd?"

Sara laced her hands behind her head. "He's got this space between his two front teeth that is so cute—"

"Sara!" I snapped my fingers in front of her face. "James' parents. Did you talk to them?"

"Okay, okay." She sat up and swung her legs over the bed. Her face brightened. "Hey, Sweet Potato," she said in her most condescending voice. "I've got a big surprise for you…it's going to make you really happy, I promise."

I doubted that, but still my heart beat faster.

"We did just happen to run into Mr. and Mrs. Miller…and guess what?"

"What?" I held my breath.

"They saw the Lost Herd last week."

All my sadness melted away in a flash and rainbows exploded out of my chest. "Oh my God, where? Where, Sara?"

"You know, that preserve where all the birds are. In the Twin River Valley."

I gulped. The Twin Rivers? I mentally tracked the way to the preserve; we wouldn't have to cross any water to get there. But once we got there...well, they didn't call it Twin Rivers for nothing. I forced back my fear. Jenner would be all right. Today had been a fluke. First ride jitters. Besides, he had to be okay because we were going.

Sara disappeared into our bathroom and started to wash up for dinner. I followed her. "We have to go tomorrow. It's only a couple hours' ride." I jumped up and sat on the bathroom counter, blocking Sara's view in the mirror in a desperate attempt to distract her from her own reflection. I knew Dad wouldn't let me go alone on a new horse. She knew it too. She held all the aces in the deck.

Sara put her hands in the prayer position and closed her eyes. "Dear Lord, if we deliver Christa to the Lost Herd, will You, in all Your wisdom, please bring back the sweet, innocent little sister I used to know?"

I danced out into the room. The thought of seeing the Lost Herd again made me feel giddy. Maybe my luck was about to change after all. "I'll be sweet. I promise," I said.

"Good, because Kim's coming with us on Eastwood, and I don't want you to ruin all the fun by being Little Miss Moody," Sara called from the bathroom. "I want to be happy tomorrow!"

"I'm a sweet, sweet potato!" I spun around the room like a crazy person. "Always!"

Sara peeked out from the door and told me in her most adult voice to grow up, but I saw her grin before she turned back to the mirror.

CHAPTER 19

I STARED OUT AT Lucky's grave from my bedroom window. The branches of the oak tree on the hill appeared as shadowy arms against the crimson sky. "We're going to see the Lost Herd again, Lucky. Wherever you are, please come with us," I said.

I dressed quickly, throwing on whatever was handy in the drawer. Jeans and a t-shirt. My usual stunning wardrobe. All fashion, all the time. I knelt and pulled Lucky's box out from under the bed. Rummaging around in the dark, I found the braid of his tail and slipped it into my pocket.

All through breakfast, I said yes to anything Mom or Dad asked. Yes, we'd be back in time for dinner. Yes, we'd pack a lunch and lots of water. Yes, we'd bring sunblock. Yes, we'd be careful. Yes, I'd listen to Sara. I was a little angel, the model daughter. The last thing I wanted to do was cause trouble today.

Sara and I managed to slip out of the kitchen and race to the barn in record time. Before the rising sun topped the highest ridge, we'd groomed all three horses within an inch of their lives.

"You wanna see the Lost Herd?" I whispered to Jenner. He snorted and stomped his big hooves. "I guess that's a yes!"

Jenner chewed on the bit, shaking his head and jangling the bridle. "Okay, boy! We're going!"

I tied back my unruly curls and stuffed my hair into my

favorite pink baseball cap, pulling my ponytail through the back. I squeezed the heart pendant necklace Grandma and Grandpa had given me for good luck, and tried to smooth the folds of Dad's old Rolling Stones t-shirt. It was so big it looked kind of lumpy when I tucked it into my jeans. I usually wore it as a sleeping shirt, but it had been so dark when I got dressed, I'd put it on by accident. Sara raised an eyebrow and shook her head in disapproval when she saw me in it, but she let it go without a word.

We packed our saddlebags with lunch on one side, and a rain slicker and a first-aid kit on the other. Sarah carried horseshoe nails, rope string, wire, and a wrench. We both carried a halter and lead. I threw Jenner's saddle on his back. That old saddle glowed as copper red as his coat, and even the tarnished silver accents embedded in the leather sparkled like I'd spent all night polishing them. With his heavily muscled chest and hindquarters, Jenner looked strong and ready for the ride.

"Jenner is a beauty," Sara said, tightening the cinch on Star's saddle.

"Did you hear that?" I ran my hand down his white blaze. "You just got a compliment from Miss Perfect."

"You promised you'd be sweet."

I mounted Jenner. "It's still early. I'll get there."

"Be careful."

I knew what that meant. It meant I'd better be nice sooner rather than later. Kind of a friendly warning. I decided I'd warm Jenner up in the round pen and wait for the sweetness to come to me.

A plume of dust rose in the drive as Kim arrived in a beat-up, white Dodge truck. I wished Cisco had come with her.

"Hey, girl!" Kim called to Sara as she jumped out of the truck. "Nice place you have here." She gestured at the barn. "Reminds me of the ranch where I grew up."

"Where was that?" I asked, hating how young my voice sounded. Kim wore a beat-up cowboy hat, her jean jacket and a neon-pink t-shirt.

"Austin, Texas." She stopped short when she saw Jenner.

"Well, well, well, that is a fine horse you got yourself there, Christa."

"Thanks."

Sara handed Kim Eastwood's reins. "Let's get going. My sister's dying to see those horses…and whatever Christa wants, Christa gets."

"Yeah, like the biggest horse in the world." Kim whistled appreciatively. "That auction was sure good to you. Sara said he was kinda fancy. Is it true he can spin?"

"If I ask him just right." I felt a grin break out on my face. The truth was I couldn't wait to show Jenner off. In that moment everything felt so rosy and nice, I almost forgot that he'd run off with me. Jenner spun to the left, smoother and a little further this time than he had for Grandma and Dad yesterday.

Sara clapped. "That's great. He's already improved."

"Someday we'll actually go in a full circle," I said, laughing and patting Jenner. I was so proud of him.

Kim gave me two thumbs up. "You two look great together. "

Sara swung up on Star. "So, let's ride."

Kim eased into the saddle and stroked Eastwood's neck. "We've got wild horses to see." But then her smile faded. "But I'll tell you one thing that's been weighing on my mind. Just between us—"

Sara brought Star alongside Eastwood. "What?"

Kim straightened her cowboy hat and took a deep breath. "I'm not happy they're in the Twin River Valley. It's too exposed. A helicopter could spot them easily. The BLM's round-ups have taken their toll. The rumor around town is that there's more horses in holding pens than there are left in the wild."

I couldn't believe it had come to this. It seemed impossible.

Where did they keep all of them? How did they feed them? And how could we save the Lost Herd from that fate? I searched Kim's face. "What should we do?"

She met my eyes. "I thought about it all night. Someone could try to drive them someplace where there's more cover."

"Like us?" I asked.

Sara laughed. "Who are you, John Wayne? How are we going to drive a herd of wild horses anywhere?"

I got the feeling Kim didn't appreciate Sara's sarcasm. Her eyes narrowed. "I figure if we get behind them, they'll run away."

"Shouldn't be hard to get them running," I said. "The trick will be getting them to run someplace safe."

Sara shook her head. "Yeah, and where's that exactly?"

"You against checking it out?" Kim snapped.

Sara looked down. "Nope."

Kim kicked Eastwood into a trot. "So, let's get going. We're burnin' daylight."

"Well, lead on then, Texas." Sara fell in behind Eastwood.

Jenner fought against the bit, wanting to take the lead. I held him back. We swung through the gate and urged the horses onto the trail leading into the foothills. It felt like the most beautiful bird was captured in my heart, singing at the top of its lungs. The Lost Herd had returned to the Sage Mountains, and we were going to find them. But then, the truth of Kim's words sunk in and my mouth fell into a hard line. It might be dangerous, even impossible, to keep the Lost Herd safe from capture.

CHAPTER 20

WE RODE HARD through the piñon pine and climbed over the first foothills of the range. As the piñon gave way to a stand of ponderosa, taller and softer, the ground became a bed of pine needles and smelled sweet. We rode three across into the forest, weaving in and out of those trees, refreshed by the cool shade and good footing. The horses wanted to gallop, but we held them to a brisk trot. When the trees thickened, we slowed the horses and moved back into a single line. One by one, we emptied out onto an open ridge with a wide trail leading down.

We descended onto the desert floor and rode through the sandy flats of the Little Grande Basin. The rock walls around us gave me the shivers in a good way, like magic was alive in the land. If I listened just right, I could hear a melody in the wind as it swept through the basin.

Out of nowhere, the wind gusted fiercely, driving sand into our faces. I pulled my bandana up over my mouth and set my teeth. This was what I called dirty weather. Across the wide expanse of brown desert, I could just make out the distinctive rock formation of Two Brothers mesa. Our goal was to climb that steep slope–the last butte standing between the Twin River Valley and us. But first we had to get there.

With the sun pummeling down on us in the flat basin, it took us longer than I thought possible to close the gap to the butte. We finally reached the base of Two Brothers mesa and climbed out of the worst of the dust into the sagebrush. Now that we had some cover, Sara insisted we stop and rest the horses. We slugged water from our canteens and kneeled in the shelter of a juniper tree. Restless and wind-battered, we mounted again.

Under the long shadows cast by the Two Brothers, we labored up a narrow trail that led to the top of the mesa. With every step, the basin floor dropped further and further away beneath us. I gazed out over the surrounding foothills and said nice things to Jenner. He was the one doing the heavy work. Still, my back ached and my feet cramped from being jammed in the stirrups for so long.

I was more than relieved when we climbed the last switchback and emptied out on top of the Mesa. Gnarled branches of piñon and juniper, twisted by the never-ending wind, brushed our legs as we passed. I spotted animal droppings that looked like coyote. The horses' hooves echoed on the sandstone as they snorted and pranced, happy to be on level ground. I stroked Jenner's sweaty neck, grateful to him for making the difficult climb.

We pulled the horses to a stop at the base of the two spires. The Two Brothers stretched high above us, silent except for the endless wind moaning through the barren landscape. I shivered, kind of creeped out; but as we rode cautiously to the other side of the mesa, we were stunned by what lay before us.

Down below in a sheer drop lay the most verdant, gorgeous river valley I'd ever seen. Rolling mountains thick with fir trees gave way to canyon walls that encircled half the basin. Layered in thick stripes of yellow and white, the red rock rose like an amphitheater above the flats. There was only one trail down, and it looked like a slender ribbon winding its way through the rock. My stomach lurched, but Kim wasn't afraid. She took off her cowboy hat and waved it in the air like we'd discovered the New World.

Dad said wherever two rivers meet is a sacred place. Seeing this valley, as beautiful as a song, I thought he might have a point. From this height the rivers looked like two giant serpents made of sparkling green water, dancing together.

Then I pumped my hands in the air. On our side of the river, grazing the rich grasslands stood the Lost Herd! I whooped for joy. Prettier than a painting, they dotted the landscape with color, and we gazed over that valley with a sense of awe. It was clear this was still the biggest herd left in Nevada, and they were as strong and beautiful as ever.

Sara rode up right beside me. "Now that might be the biggest smile I've ever seen on your face, Christa!"

"Well, look at them," I whispered.

Kim's friendship with the Millers had helped us find the most important wild mustangs in the whole world. I wanted to have a million dollars so I could give it to her. I started to say so, but she was so wide-eyed and speechless that the words faded on my lips.

I scanned the herd, hoping to find Mesteño or Corazón, but we were too far away to see anything but a broad expanse of grazing mustangs. There was something so thrilling about watching horses without fences and without humans. They really could live without us, which made it even more amazing that they would work so hard for us and be our friends.

With a nod from Kim, Jenner and I moved to the steep rocky trail leading down to the valley. Sara's voice was in my ear. "Be careful. You could fall."

It would be easy to slip on a trail like this, but Jenner was surefooted. I gave him his head so he could find his way and leaned back in the saddle, helping him to balance on the steep slope. Shale and loose rocks skittered beneath his hooves. We seemed awfully close to the edge, but I told Sara in my most confident voice to stop worrying about me.

Kim gave Eastwood plenty of rein as she picked her way through the rocks and the divots in the trail a few steps behind me. I stayed as close as possible to the rock face because the other side of the trail was a sheer drop off that would surely send Jenner and me plummeting to our deaths. My hands shook just holding the reins. I kept my eyes straight ahead and talked in a low, sweet voice the whole way down, hoping I could trust those big hooves to get us to the bottom.

And then the very rock we stood on began to tremble. At first I thought Jenner had stumbled, or worse, gone lame. But then I heard it: the staccato drumming of a propeller shattered the silence. A helicopter whirled up over the rock wall directly above our heads. It was so close, I swear I could've reached out and touched the runners.

The horses whinnied in terror and Sara screamed. Before I had time to react, the silver chopper shot high into the sky, as if a puppeteer had it by a string and yanked it straight up. Then the chopper sped away. My relief was short-lived. It was heading straight for the Twin Rivers and the Lost Herd.

CHAPTER 21

THAT HELICOPTER BURSTING out of nowhere right over our heads could've sent any of our three horses off the edge of the cliff, but they all stayed on course. I chanced a quick look over my shoulder. Sara was pale. Kim cursed the helicopter like an angry cowboy. "It's the BLM," she growled. "Who else would be out here?"

I slowed Jenner and watched the helicopter fly toward the Lost Herd, my heart pounding. If they got caught, they could end up going to slaughter. How could it be these horses were like outlaws, worth more dead than alive?

My mind raced ahead of the chopper, and I wanted to warn the herd to run. But the truth was, they couldn't outrun or outsmart that helicopter and neither could I. If the BLM wanted to capture the Lost Herd, they'd be caught and never run free again.

Jenner and I worked our way painstakingly down the switchbacks until we finally reached the valley floor. Sara and Kim joined us, all of our eyes fixed on the helicopter, all our faces strained to stiffness.

The metal bird flew higher than it would have if it was going to give chase, and that gave me an ounce of hope. But I knew it had to be a BLM helicopter. What other chopper would hover above wild horses? I reached out, clutching Sara's sleeve as the chopper circled higher and higher over the herd. My breath came faster. As one, the wild horses stopped grazing. In a blur of motion and a flash of flying manes and tails, they charged across the river. Just as the last band plunged into the water, the helicopter circled and veered south following the Twin Rivers. Within seconds, it disappeared from sight.

Slowly I let go of Sara's arm and let myself breathe again. Tears stung my eyes. If anything ever happened to them...*please, God, not one more thing...not one more bad thing....*

But then my lips tightened and I felt like I was going to be sick. The Lost Herd was now on the wrong side of the Twin Rivers. If we were going to drive them to a safer place, I'd need to cross the river. On Jenner. I stroked Jenner's trembling neck and tried to gather my wits.

To my relief, Sara insisted we stop to regroup and have lunch. The horses were tired and we needed time to think. We dismounted and pulled our packs down off the horses, turning them loose to graze. At the base of the cliff under a rock overhang, we sat cross-legged in the hard-packed brown dirt. Sara passed water and sandwiches around, but I couldn't eat. The sun was directly overhead now and so bright my temples throbbed, even in the shade. I pulled my baseball cap low over my eyes.

Kim leaned back, stretching her long legs. She kicked a loose rock with her boot and swore quietly. "That was too close."

"Way too close," I agreed. "Why did it fly away?"

"Maybe it was just scouting for the July round-up," Kim grumbled.

Blood pounded in my ears. "What July round-up?"

"My dad heard about it from Jack Marshall. I'm guessing the Lost Herd will be on the list."

I felt a new kind of dread. "The BLM is breaking their own rules! They're supposed to wait six weeks after foaling season. The babies are way too young to be chased for miles by a helicopter."

"With the sharp rocks and the heat, it could be a massacre," Kim said.

Sara sucked her breath in hard.

I couldn't hear another word. Overcome with worry, I went to check the horses. I loosened their cinches and rubbed their sweaty bellies with my thick leather gloves. Jenner, Star and Eastwood grazed as if nothing had happened, busily nosing their way through the sage. How did horses do that? How did they recover so quickly? I picked the pebbles and rocks from their hooves and looked out to the Lost Herd. Even from this distance I could see their necks stretched down to the grass. As far as they were concerned, there was no problem and that calmed me a bit.

Regardless of whatever danger might be lurking for the wild horses in July, we'd survived the cliff and the Lost Herd was okay for now. I rejoined Sara and Kim and sat with my back against the cool rock, nibbling half-heartedly on a granola bar.

Kim spat on the ground. "Why do they have to destroy everything that's beautiful and free in this world?"

"Don't know. At least the chopper flew away." Sara took a bite of her turkey sandwich and dabbed at the corners of her mouth with a paper napkin.

The smell of the sandwich roiled my stomach. I slipped the granola bar in my pocket and glanced at Kim. "How are we going to keep the BLM from going after the Lost Herd in July?"

She finished the last bite of her sandwich and crumpled the foil wrap into a tiny ball. "Dunno. Go talk to Bob Downs and make sure they don't, I guess."

"Well, I'll go with you, that's for sure." I said. Although, what I was thinking was, it's about dang time! Just last night I'd barraged Mr. Downs with emails and even called and left voicemails for him, which I was sure he'd never return.

Kim narrowed her eyes and twisted her hat in her hand. "How 'bout you, Sara…you in?"

Sara riffled through her pack, pulling out her lip gloss and a hairbrush. "What am I agreeing to, exactly?" With her legs tucked under her at an angle, she looked more like a model than a girl sitting in the dirt.

Kim nudged Sara's leg with her boot. "You coming with us to pay a visit to Mr. Downs?" She had a little smile on her face, but the question was more serious than playful.

"Yeah, sure," Sara said.

"Good. Then let's have a look at this valley and figure out what we're gonna do," I said.

We all stood up and studied the landscape. Kim pointed. "We could try and drive them into that slot canyon."

Across the water and beyond the meadow where the mustangs were grazing, the dark mouth of the canyon beckoned. It looked like a mere crack in the massive red wall. Boulders tumbled down from the sheer cliff on either side, choked by brush. It was hard to believe a river had carved its way so handily through all that rock however many hundreds of years ago. For now, it was dry. Scrub oaks grew all along the narrow canyon walls, providing cover that could hide the mustangs and make them harder to see from the air.

"How are we gonna get them in there?" My throat was so dry, my voice came out in a squeak. I gulped water from the canteen.

A welcome breeze gusted, circling under the rock overhang where we sat and lifting Kim's dark hair off her face. "Ride across the river. And then fan out to put pressure on them from all sides."

I picked up a flat stone and tossed it out into the sagebrush, my heart sinking. "Cross the river?" If Jenner couldn't enter a stream yesterday, he'd never swim across the Twin Rivers. A hard seed of doubt took root in my stomach. "Maybe we can come back with Cisco and some other riders. We may need more people."

Sara tapped the toe of her worn boot on the hard ground. "I don't like it. No way I'm going through with this. It's too dangerous.

We don't know how our horses will react to the mustangs or how they'll react to us."

"I'm not sure you get it," Kim said. Her eyes burned with a fierce light. "Now that the BLM knows where the Lost Herd is, how long do you think they'll wait to round them up? This could be their last day of freedom."

"Okay, I get it," Sara snapped. "I'm listening."

Kim kneeled in the dirt and drew a picture in the sand with a stick. "The slot canyon winds up into the mountains for a few miles and then opens into the foothills near the Hondo River. They'll have water and tree cover."

"Then, even if it's not the best idea in the world, we've got to try and herd them into that slot canyon," I said. "Today."

Kim nodded. "My thoughts exactly."

"Okay, okay, I'm in." Sara said, not moving. "Just wait a second." She stared at the herd for a long minute. "Seems like a lot of horses to get into a small space."

Kim strode out through the tall grass to where Eastwood grazed. "True, but if we can get the lead mare to go, they'll follow her. Which one is she, Christa?"

"Too far away to tell."

"Well, let's go find her," Kim said, tying her pack to the back of the saddle with so much force I thought she was going to break the leather straps. She glanced darkly across the river. Without another word, she swung up onto Eastwood, tipped her hat and eased him into a smooth canter, leaving us in the dust. For a full second, Sara and I stood watching her ride away.

"Nice," Sara said, shaking her head. "Guess we're going now."

"Guess we are."

CHAPTER 22

I TIGHTENED JENNER'S CINCH and hauled myself onto his back. Sara mounted Star with her usual grace, and soon we were chasing after Kim, letting the wind whip through our hair as we gained speed. Eastwood appeared as a golden blur. The horses made their own zigzagging trails through the sagebrush, easily closing the distance. We caught up with Kim as the sagebrush gave way to grassland about fifty yards from the river. She'd already pulled Eastwood to a halt and was casually leaning on the saddle-horn, chewing another piece of grass. "Did you girls stop for coffee?"

Sara shot Kim a withering look.

I turned my face so Sara couldn't see my smile. I couldn't help but enjoy any sarcasm at Sara's expense, even if it was directed at me, too. And then my smile faded. The river looked awfully wide from here. The water ran high from snowmelt in the mountains and once it hit the plain, it broadened and meandered until it seemed to cover half the valley.

The rich smell of the muddy riverbed reminded me of the Carn River. Yesterday, Jenner had spooked at the mere sight of the water. I rubbed his withers, watching for the first sign of trouble. Jenner's nostril's curled, but he stood steady. *Maybe he'd be a good sport today*, I thought. But my hand tightened on the reins.

"It's like an oasis in the middle of the desert," Sara whispered, still gazing dreamily at the river.

Kim spat on the ground. "The drought may have brought them here, but they won't get to stay long. Park Rangers don't want wild horses hanging around."

"Great. Another strike against them," Sara said, her voice rising in a crescendo of frustration. "They're like weeds that everyone wants to get rid of."

"Shhh, we don't want to spook them," I cautioned.

Across a stretch of water about one hundred feet wide, interrupted by a crescent-shaped sandbar, the wild horses grazed. I guessed they were tolerating our presence as long as we stayed on the other side of the river. They tore at grasses turned golden by the sun, devouring the tassels swinging at the top of each stalk, snuffing in and out with pleasure as they chewed.

A dusty black horse watched us as we came closer. I grabbed Sara's sleeve and pointed. "There's the lead mare! I call her Corazón." Corazón stood at attention, ears pointing straight up, body tensed and ready to run. She looked like she'd had a rough time of it. Two long scars marked her left flank, and a chunk of her right ear was missing. I wanted to throw my arms around her neck and run my hands through her thick mane. I wanted to promise her I'd always protect her and the herd.

Her black eyes locked onto mine and I felt a thrill run through my heart. Then the mare dropped her head and went back to grazing, her thick black tail swishing flies. Nearby I caught sight of Echo. She skittered along beside another colt, her mohawk mane bristling.

Then I spotted a paint stallion. It was Mesteño! His tail swept into a tapered point, his white markings looked like clouds on his deep red body, and his long white forelock covered his eyes.

I wondered what it would feel like to jump on his wide, painted back and race across the rolling grasslands.

The wind came up and Mesteño pranced, his white mane and tail flying out behind him. He took off running, a red and white blur against the grass, so powerful, so graceful. He stopped as suddenly as he had started, threw his head high in the air and trumpeted as only a stallion could. I laughed at his wildness, watching him paw the ground and toss his head.

"That's Mesteño, the lead stallion," I said.

Kim whistled through her teeth. "He's crazy beautiful. Looks like we pledged ourselves to one hell of a bunch of mustangs."

"Looks like he won another mare," I said, noticing a pretty blue roan mare next to Corazón.

I pointed out the members of the Lost Herd as if they belonged to me. Sara let me show off without a word. She smiled as she studied the herd through her field glasses. "They're all so amazing," she said. "And the lead mare reminds me of Star."

I let that one pass. Besides the fact they were both black, Star looked nothing like Corazón. But if Sara needed to think Star was the spitting image of Corazón in order to love this herd, then I'd go right along with it. I reached forward and gave Jenner a hug. "Aren't they something?" He touched his nose to my boot and faced forward again, smelling the wind. Jenner's ears locked on the herd, and his body trembled. I rubbed his neck. Eastwood and Star were jittery, and Star whinnied to the herd.

"I can't believe how cute the foals are," Sara said.

I pointed. "That black one is Corazón's filly, Echo."

Echo pawed the ground with her tiny hoof and a bay colt danced by her side.

"So cute! Who's the bay colt? He's like glued to her," Sara said.

Kim grinned. "Kind of like Dylan is to you."

Sara blushed and laughed.

"Oh my God," I said. "Let's call him Dylan."

As if someone had waved a flag, the foals took off at a dead run, each daring the other to go faster. They ran side by side on knobby knees, their short flappy tails flying. Dylan took an early lead, but then Echo stretched her neck forward and won the contest in a final burst of speed. We all cheered. They were so unbelievably cute. I sighed happily. Wild Horse perfection. The only thing more perfect would've been a bowl of popcorn and a coke to go with the Lost Herd TV channel, but I settled for a swig of water.

"There's Grandfather–the old red roan stallion, grazing near Corazón," I said. They stood side-by-side, nose to tail, their long tails swatting flies for each other. Grandfather's back swayed and his hipbones jutted with age, but I thought he was magnificent.

"There's something special about him," Kim said. "Old guy. I bet he's seen it all."

Grandfather shook his head from side to side to get rid of flies and lowered himself to the ground for a good roll.

Meanwhile, a band of bachelors played and roughhoused together, rearing and biting each other's necks or swinging their rumps into each other and kicking hard with both back feet. It was a wonder they didn't break bones every day with the strength of their play, but they didn't seem to have a care in the world.

With no warning, Jenner pawed the ground and shook his head. His back coiled like a spring beneath me. Was it the wild horses that had him on edge? I had a feeling if I jumped off him and removed his saddle and bridle, he'd be running with the mustangs in a hot second. It was most likely the river that had him trembling. Still, I clung to the slim hope that Jenner's fear yesterday had been a one-time affair. I gritted my teeth. There was only one way to find out.

Sara interrupted my thoughts. "So let's spread out before we cross the river and see if we can put enough pressure on Corazón to get her to move into the canyon."

Kim nodded. "I'll go right, you go left, and Christa, you can cross in the middle."

"Sounds good," I said, trying to sound brave. I urged Jenner forward and said a silent prayer.

CHAPTER 23

JENNER SNORTED AND hopped to the side, refusing to budge another inch forward. As his feet danced on the riverbank, my last hope for him sank.

Sara pulled Star up alongside us. "What's up with Jenner?" she asked, frowning.

"Not sure," I mumbled. "Maybe he doesn't like the river."

Kim threw in her two cents. "That's no big deal. Lots of horses are spooky around water, especially when they can't see the bottom."

"True," Sara said, but her radar locked onto Jenner. She knew something was wrong. "How about we walk Star and Eastwood into the river, so Jenner can see it's okay?"

"Well, okay, I guess." I scanned the river. I estimated the distance to be about fifty feet to reach the sandbar. We could make it if Jenner followed the other horses. "Just don't go too far in… you'll spook the Lost Herd." A thick knot formed in my stomach.

Sara guided Star alongside Jenner and me. "Are you sure about this?" She stared at me with that worried look in her eyes I'd seen so often since Lucky died.

I hated that expression. I was not weak. "Of course I'm sure!"

"What up?" Kim laughed, shaking her head. "I'm not feelin' the love."

"I'm not feeling it, either," I snapped, swinging Jenner in a circle.

"I'm older than you are," Sara said, twisting in her saddle to search my face. Her brown eyes were earnest with no trace of anger. "And if anything happens to you, I'm the one who gets blamed."

"I get it, I get it. Just go!" I wanted this to be over, to get into the water without Jenner freaking out so we could get the Lost Herd safely into the slot canyon.

Sara nodded to Kim, and they both clucked to the horses. Star and Eastwood plunged into the water, kicking up a spray of water like a fountain. They made getting in look like a day at the beach, but I don't think Jenner saw it that way. He circled and backed up with a shudder. I looked across the river to the Lost Herd.

All their heads came up as one and Corazón exploded into a gallop, leading the herd back toward the slot canyon at a dead run. Maybe the plan could work after all.

Jenner pawed the ground near the black, silted bottom of the river. He put one foot in. It sunk. He whirled and stepped back to the shore. I swore under my breath. I had to get him to cross! I tried every riding trick I knew. We backed up, turned in circles and leapt sideways. I pleaded, threatened, and soothed with my voice. I blocked him with my right leg, then my left, trying to get him to go straight and then dug my heels into his trembling sides, but he wouldn't go one step closer to the river.

I watched Sara and Kim make their way across. The Lost Herd continued to run across the wide meadow behind Corazón, heading toward the slot canyon. Could the plan work without us? "Get it done," I whispered, willing Kim and Sara to continue.

Meanwhile, Jenner was melting down. He whinnied to Eastwood and Star so loudly his back expanded like a bellows with each ringing cry. He tossed his head. The bit jarred in his mouth. He jerked the reins out of my hands and a tingle vibrated up my arms. I took a firmer hold. I could feel his every muscle charged and ready to explode. His sides heaved between my legs as his breath came faster and faster.

I looked up in time to see Corazón gallop closer and closer to the slot canyon. I held my breath.

Sara circled Star around. "We're coming back," she shouted. "Don't worry, Jenner, we're not going to leave you."

"No! Don't turn back," I yelled. But it was too late. Corazón ran past the opening to slot canyon. The herd followed her up and over a ridge. We could never get them in the slot canyon now.

The sinking sense of failure I'd been resisting all day grabbed hold of me. If only Jenner had crossed the river, the plan might have worked. But before I could follow that train of thought any further, a large flock of ducks startled and took flight, wings beating frantically. They blasted right at Jenner in formation, quacking and honking. To Jenner, those ducks might as well have been fighter planes with bombs strapped to their wings. He lurched back and whirled away from the riverbank, his ears flat on his head.

I pulled on the reins as hard as I could, but he fought harder, almost yanking me out of the saddle. The wide, sage-covered plain opened up in front of us. He wrestled the reins out of my grasp and charged forward, gaining speed with each monstrous stride.

My eyes stung and blurred in the wind. I grabbed his mane, digging my fingers in deep. He stretched out in longer and longer strides, his hooves tearing chunks out of the ground. Faster and faster he ran. He stretched out low to the ground, his neck extended like a racehorse just out of the gate. Sharp rocks and hard ground blurred beneath us. The speed jarred my body. *I can't fall.*

I chanced a look over my shoulder. Star and Eastwood charged after us, Sara and Kim bent low over their backs. The grassy valley rippled below Jenner's hooves. When we reached the higher ground strewn with rocks and sagebrush, the sound of the wind screamed in my ears. Jenner's breath rasped, ragged and uneven as his hooves ground the rocks to dust beneath us. The strength in my arms bled away. I collapsed forward like a rag-doll onto Jenner's neck. This wasn't riding, this was praying. I begged Jenner to stop. My voice ripped away to nothing in the wind. Had he forgotten I was on his back?

I grabbed clumsily for one rein and jerked back hard. Jenner charged on with the power of a hundred horses. So much for the one rein stop. I thrust my hands into Jenner's mane again and held on with a death grip. When I looked over my shoulder, I saw Star gaining on us like a dark angel. Sara screamed my name. Jenner flicked an ear back, and I could hear Star's hooves approaching. As they neared us, I felt Jenner shudder. His muscles relaxed ever so slightly under my thighs. He slowed to a lope and then a trot. His sides heaved. Flecks of sweat dripped from his neck.

Jenner came to a halt, but it felt like the world was still moving in fast forward. We had covered the whole valley in like five seconds. Sara ran to my side and eased me down from the saddle, prying my hands loose from Jenner's mane. "Are you okay?" Her eyes scanned my body.

I stared blankly into her pale face. "I think so." My knees buckled.

Sara caught me and lowered me to the ground. "I've got you, I've got you, I've got you," she whispered in my ear. The wind roared around us. Jenner stood nearby with his head low, breathing. The whole world was breathing, trying to right itself. I closed my eyes against the harsh sun. My eyelids burned. For a second, I fought the spinning exhaustion snaking its way through my gut. Then with a stab of regret, I thought of the Lost Herd and how I'd failed them. I let go into darkness.

CHAPTER 24

WHEN I CAME to, Sara helped me back up into the saddle. On the long ride home, she kept Jenner in the middle with Star right behind us, and Eastwood in front. No one said a word. We kept the horses to a walk the whole way. What normally would've taken two hours, took three. When we finally arrived and climbed off the horses, my back was so sore, I couldn't straighten up.

We rubbed the horses down and fed them their dinner. I snuck Star a bunch of extra carrots for being so fast and brave. Her soft breath in my ear was like a thank you.

Sara held my arm to steady me as we walked back to the house, and Kim put a reassuring hand on my shoulder. I felt silly being that helpless, but I was almost too tired to care.

We must've been quite a sight when we stumbled into the house. My hair stood on end in a giant red tangle. I took in Sara and Kim's sunburned faces, chapped lips, and weary stance; but I knew I looked the worst. Both Mom and Grandma's faces blanched with one look at me. Before I could say a word, Dad swept me into his arms in a big hug. I flinched and pulled away. I couldn't look him in the eye. "I'm okay, Dad," I said.

"What happened?" Dad asked.

Sara bit her lower lip and glanced at me. We hadn't talked

about what we were going to say. The silence ticked on. A rare event with Sara.

I swallowed my pride. There wasn't much left of it anyway. "He ran away with me at the river," I said. "He's afraid of water. Sara and Star rescued me."

Sara's jaw dropped open. "That was brutally honest."

Mom rushed to my side. "Were you hurt, Sweet Potato?" She stroked my cheek with her soft hands. I didn't deserve comfort or sympathy, but feeling her touch calmed me a bit. Sara watched Mom fuss over me. She thought I got all the attention, but that was only because I was the one always screwing up.

"I'm fine." I grabbed Sara's sleeve. "She's the hero."

In an unusual show of sisterly love, Sara hooked her arm in mine. "Jenner runs faster than any horse I've ever seen and he doesn't stop once he starts. Christa stayed on this time, but if she'd fallen…"

Mom put one hand on her belly and sank into a chair.

Grandma took my hands and had me sit next to her at the table. She felt my forehead, kissed my cheeks, and said I looked all right to her. I could see her way of thinking. At least I was alive.

Dad ran a hand down his whiskered cheeks. "I thought this horse might be too good to be true."

"Well, let's talk about it over dinner," Grandma suggested. "Kim, why don't you join us?"

"After you call your parents and tell them you're okay," Mom ordered.

Grandma placed a big bowl of spaghetti on the table and Dad set another place for Kim. Within seconds, we were all seated. My stomach twisted and turned with the smell of the food. I was famished, but still too nervous to eat.

We told them every detail of our ride. Or, I should say, Sara told them almost every detail of our ride. She kindly skipped the slot canyon plan. There are some things grownups are better off not knowing. While Sara talked, Mom nibbled on a breadstick, her eyes glancing from my face to Sara's. "Can we trade Jenner in for another horse?" she asked.

She didn't even care about the Lost Herd or the helicopter. She just zoned in on Jenner. "He's not a car." I said.

Dad shifted in his chair. "It doesn't work like that, Claire."

Mom locked eyes with me. "Do you want to keep him?"

I thought back to the day we got him and the indescribable joy I felt sitting on his back. I'd hoped that together with Jenner I could do something worthwhile.

"Yeah, I do. I want to give him a second chance."

Mom's fork froze in midair. "That horse is too much for you, Christa. That seems obvious now," she said. "If you've got a horse that big running off with you, you've got a problem."

"I can work it out, Mom."

"Like you did today?"

Something snapped inside me and anger rose up from my belly like fire. "I stayed on him, didn't I?"

"Not good enough," she said quietly, but with the force of a mountain.

Grandma shot me a look of sympathy. Kim whispered something to Sara. I found myself wishing Sara would start talking again. This would qualify as attention I didn't want to be getting.

Dad rolled the spaghetti around his fork and took a bite. He chewed with rolling motions of his jaw. I waited for him to break the silence. All my fear from the ride had turned to fear I would lose Jenner.

"Jenner deserves a chance," he said. "But not at the risk of your safety. Sounds like we need a trainer."

A ray of hope emerged. I crossed my fingers.

He glanced at me. "And until we get some training into that horse, you're not to ride him."

"But Dad!"

Mom shot me a withering glance. She carefully returned her silverware to either side of her plate and leaned forward, meeting Dad's gaze. "We're not spending one more penny on that horse. He's already more trouble than he's worth."

"Not true!" My voice rang out into the room, which I obviously had no more control of than I did of Jenner. All eyes turned to me. I stabbed a meatball with my fork, and shoved it into my mouth.

Sara kicked me under the table and cleared her throat. "Um. I know a trainer who works for free."

My food lodged in my throat. "Who?"

Thankfully, all eyes turned from me to Sara. I was wilting.

Sara and Kim exchanged glances. "Kim's brother, Cisco."

Dad took a big bite of bread, Mom pursed her lips, and Grandma nodded sagely, as if she knew Cisco's reputation.

"Cisco! That's a great idea," I said. He was pretty easy on the eyes, too. But they didn't need to know that part.

"He's got a way with horses," Kim said.

Dad cleared his throat. "I'm listening."

Sara sat up straighter. "He's only fifteen, but he gets results. And he's too young to charge a big fee."

Mom shook her head. "No one's come out and said it, but I'm guessing Jenner could be dangerous. You're suggesting we let a fifteen-year-old boy in with that horse?"

The way she said "that horse" made Jenner sound like a convicted felon. I couldn't stand hearing one more word. "May I please be excused?" I mumbled through clenched teeth. Not waiting for a reply, I ran up to my room and paced. How could Mom be so lame? Even the sound of her voice annoyed me. But I still needed to hear what they were saying. I crept back into the hallway. The dogs flanked me on either side, panting and looking up at me, hoping this was a new game. I sank to my knees and wrapped my arms around them. "Shhh," I whispered.

Sara's clear voice floated up from the kitchen. "Cisco's been training a wild mustang the Millers adopted."

"Cisco's already come so far with Doc that he's gonna run barrels on him at the Albright rodeo this summer," Kim said. "If he can work with wild horses, he should be okay with Jenner, Mrs. Cassidy."

I heard the sound of plates being stacked into the sink and the water running.

Dad's voice echoed up the stairs. "Well, I'll call the kid and see what he can do."

When Sara came to bed, I pretended I was asleep, closing my eyes tight.

"How's my little Sweet Potato?" She turned her lamp on. Her sarcasm wasn't lost on me. Sure, she'd saved my life and stood up for Jenner and me tonight, but that didn't give her the right to treat me like a little kid. The light stung. I turned over dramatically, whipping the sheets up to cover my head. I could see Sara's outline through the sheet as she brushed her hair vigorously, each long silky strand falling into perfect place.

"So restless tonight," she taunted. "And so quiet."

I popped up from under the covers and glared at her. "You talk enough for the both of us. Can't you just shut it?"

She covered her mouth with one hand in mock astonishment. "Naughty little girl!" She pointed her brush at me. "Yeah, I can 'shut it,' but then you won't hear Kim's latest brainstorm..." She pulled her knees up to her chin, waiting for me to cave.

I did. "What's she got in mind?"

Sara sat back in the bed, folding her long legs underneath her. "She's a fast thinker. She's moved on to plan B."

I propped myself up on one elbow. "Plan B?"

Sara studied her fingernails. "I always thought the slot canyon was a bad idea. That could've been a disaster. I mean, just the three of us trying to move a huge wild herd—"

"Sara! What's plan B?"

"Kim wants to go visit Bob Downs this week and insist he stop the July round-ups and leave the Lost Herd alone." She sighed. "And she wants you to come for some reason."

My mind jumped into action. "Let's get right in his face," I said, gulping a great lungful of air, "and tell him to burn up their list of roundups starting with the Lost Herd! Because he doesn't know anything about wild horses if he thinks they need to zeroed out." I sat up and slammed my head against the wooden head-board, but that didn't slow me down. My breath came faster. "They're such a strong herd, and they're not competing with the cattle—"

"Christa! Chill. I'm not the one that needs convincing." Sara looked at me hard. "Bob Downs hasn't replied to any of your texts, emails or voicemails. Don't go getting your hopes up." She switched the light off and settled under the covers. "If you ask me, this is another bad idea."

I couldn't help but grin. "But not as bad as the slot canyon plan."

"Nope. Not as bad as that."

Plan B could be even harder than trying to herd the wild horses into a canyon. This time when I stood face to face with Bob Downs, I had to say the right words to stop the roundups. I just didn't know what those words were yet.

"Christa, I can hear you thinking. Go to sleep," Sara said.

My body ached with exhaustion, but my mind was attached to a zip-line, shooting through the Amazon Forest of Worries.

I slipped out of bed, tiptoed to my desk and opened my laptop. I typed, 'wild mustangs', 'Nevada', 'public land', and 'BLM' into my search engine. One of the top articles I found was a story about a very rich couple from New York. They were negotiating to buy enough acreage to start a sanctuary for the wild horses in Nevada. It would be an eco-tourism park that families could visit. The idea was to have a big enough place for all the horses that were trapped in holding pens to live as families in bands and roam. The next best thing to being free.

If that actually went through, I think I'd die and go to heaven, but I knew none of this could happen fast enough to save the herds already slated for capture. Still, I found their website and emailed Sara and Kim the link. Next, I composed an email to Elizabeth Levine, the woman starting the sanctuary, and told her I was willing to help in any way possible. I closed the computer. I still didn't know what to say to Bob Downs, but the idea of the sanctuary gave me hope for the future. Could there be a world where ranchers, cattle, mustangs, and the BLM all co-existed happily together?

I climbed back into bed.

An owl hooted outside our window. "Night, Christa."

"Night, Sara."

CHAPTER 25

I SENSED A PRESENCE in the deep abyss. Then something moved—a silver flash in the pitch black—and I knew I was not alone. Strong currents swirled through the nothingness, pulling me down. I was sinking in an ocean of water, a pulse of flesh beneath me. My legs were wrapped around a big shuddering animal, a blood-red horse. Oh my God, it was Jenner. We were both sinking into the bottomless darkness. Shadows flitted around us and took form. To my horror, I saw horses falling around us with their mouths open in a silent scream, eyes rolled back into their heads. I called for help, but no sound escaped. I couldn't let my horse die. Couldn't let all these horses die.

"Christa!" Sara's voice summoned me from the dream.

"The horses, we gotta save them," I mumbled, still half asleep.

Sara's hands gripped my shoulders. "Wake up!"

I opened my eyes into the bright glare of the morning light. Sara was dressed, her bed made, pillows neatly arranged. I sat up, clutching my blankets. "They were drowning."

She opened the curtains and a wave of heat blew in from the window. "No one's drowning today. It's hot as Daytona Beach during spring break." She sighed, staring wistfully into space. "But without the cute guys, the beer, or the ocean."

I rubbed my eyes. "I had another bad dream."

"You okay? Good," she said, without waiting for an answer and breezed out of the room.

I sat transfixed with the curtain billowing in the wind. Jenner and me and all those horses drowning…creepy! I reached for the glass of water on the nightstand and tried to clear my head.

Every muscle ached. Even my bones felt hollow and tired. I had a horse hangover. Too much horse, too fast. The sun hurt my eyes, and the birds sang way too loud. I rolled back under the covers with a groan and put the pillow right over my head. I needed more sleep, like a hundred years' worth. I'd ruined our chance to get the Lost Herd into the slot canyon. I wanted to wake up next year sometime when this sorry thing called my life was sorted out. But as it happened, I dragged my bones out of bed in time for breakfast.

After we ate, Mom and I went to Safeway. I was now her teen-slave and would do her bidding with no complaints. While Mom sipped a cup of tea at Starbucks, I filled the cart with items from her list. Just as I flung the last box of cereal on top of the heap and turned to go, I collided with a tall woman, nearly knocking her over. I mumbled my apologies before I recognized her. "Mrs. Miller!" I said.

She wrapped me in a quick hug. "Christa. Good I ran into you today. I've heard something very disturbing…it's about the wild mustangs."

What she told me made my blood run cold.

When we returned home, Grandma took Mom to her acupuncture appointment and Dad left for work. The temperature shot to ninety degrees. Elvis and Chico passed out on the front porch panting, their tongues lolling out of the sides of their mouths. I'd been given the honor of turning our dirty house into a sparkling gem by the time everyone returned. When the doorbell rang, I was only too happy to hide the dust rag and pretend like I had a life. Sara thundered down the stairs, beating me to the door.

"Hey there!" Sara held the door open with a big smile.

Kim high-fived me as she walked in. "Cool website. When I grow up to be a millionaire, I want to be just like Elizabeth Levine. Let's start a wild horse sanctuary."

She breezed past me, not waiting for a response. Cisco stood behind her. I attempted to run a hand through my hair, but my fingers lodged in a tangle. Had I even brushed it yet today? I held the door open for him, trying to look casual.

Cisco was wearing boots, jeans, and a faded blue Nike t-shirt that barely came to his waist. He took off his cowboy hat and ran his fingers through his dark hair. "Hot out there."

I assumed he was talking to me, 'cause Kim and Sara were locked in their own conversation, talking a mile a minute in the kitchen. Probably about clothes.

"Yeah." I led him toward the kitchen. I had a way with words.

Sara gave Cisco a Coke. He popped the lid and drank a big swig of it in one gulp. He glanced at me for one half of a second. "So, I hear you got a horse who might need some training?"

"Here's the deal with that." Kim stepped in front of Cisco like she was his manager. She pressed her Coke can up to her forehead. Her gold necklace shone against her brown skin. She fanned her t-shirt out to get some air.

"Cisco will work with Jenner for free if you guys will let him start alone. No people watching him." She crossed her arms over her chest to emphasize that this was not negotiable.

Cisco cleared his throat. "It's just that I—"

Kim held up her hand, interrupting him. "If Jenner isn't better after three sessions, then you can fire him, but give him one session alone with the horse." Her eyes locked on me briefly to make sure I got the point. "If Jenner shows improvement after the three sessions, and you want Cisco to continue working with Jenner, then we'll talk about money."

Cisco tried to speak again. "All I want to do with Jenner is—"

Kim stopped him again with a look. She sighed and shook her head. "I think it's fairly obvious that Cisco's good with horses."

"Well—" Cisco tried to get a word in.

"He can start today." Kim acted as if she hadn't heard him.

I giggled. It could really suck being the youngest. Cisco had shrunk almost an inch and had tipped his cowboy hat down over his eyes. But I really, really hoped he could make Jenner better. Even a little bit.

"So, we're good, then?" Kim asked.

"I agree to those terms," Sara said, like we were striking a major deal and as if Jenner was her horse instead of mine.

"I'm in," I added. It was fine with me if I wasn't there.

Cisco strode to the door. "Thanks for the Coke," he mumbled. "Now that you've talked this to death, maybe I'll go get something done."

"His halter is the blue one hanging on the pasture gate," Sara called after him. "Good luck!"

I followed him quickly to the front porch. "Cisco!"

He turned and waited for me to say something. I paused, distracted by his brown eyes framed by incredibly thick lashes. "He's afraid of water and he ran off with me." I rubbed my aching shoulder. "Can you fix him?"

He shrugged. "I don't fix horses." He glanced back at the house. "Look, Christa, it's not like Kim's making it sound in there. She gets going on these crazy tangents sometimes."

I grinned. "It's not like you're making the big bucks doing this anyways."

"Good point." He stuck his hands in the back pockets of his

faded jeans and rocked back on his heels. "Anyways, your dad called last night. He gave me the okay to do some basic stuff with Jenner. Just to get his confidence back." Cisco adjusted his cowboy hat. "And I'll be checking in with your dad later this afternoon. He's giving me a ride home."

"Okay."

"So, no worries." He turned to go.

"And Cisco?"

He paused. His eyes were so brown they almost looked black.

"Just in case you were wondering, he's the big red horse."

"Got it." He held my gaze for a second. I thought I caught the hint of a smile on his face before he headed toward the pasture.

I wandered back into the kitchen, my fingers crossed for Cisco. Kim whistled softly and watched him admiringly through the window. "That kid's a real talent. Gotta hand it to him."

"You've done a great job bringing him along," Sara agreed.

Sara and Kim chuckled like this was some private joke. You could tell they were both getting a big kick out of each other. I didn't see what was so funny. If this were one of their horses, they'd be dead serious.

Sara leaned against the counter and laced her hands behind her head. "Does Cisco ever run into James Miller when he's training over there?" she asked casually.

Kim collapsed with laughter. "You are so obvious!"

Sara flushed pink. "Well, I'm just checking. It's not like I'm in love with the guy or anything."

"Everyone with a pulse is in love with James Miller. He's like the cutest guy ever," Kim said.

Sara squirmed. "Okay, subject change."

I clapped my hands together. "So, here's what I want to do while Cisco's frying in the sun out there with Jenner."

"What's up?" Sara seemed annoyed. "Me and Kim are going swimming."

I swung up on the counter and wriggled my toes. "Instead of swimming, I thought we could pay that visit to Mr. Bob Downs."

Kim leaned forward, her green eyes sparkling. "No better time than today."

"Oh, you mean Bob Downer?" Sara rustled around in the fridge. "He's just gonna ignore us like he does Christa."

"We have to try. We pledged we'd help the mustangs," I said.

Kim jumped up on the counter beside me and crossed her legs. I'd never seen her in shorts and sandals before. Her toenails were painted blue. "The Lost Herd in the Twin River Valley worries me. A lot."

I twisted a strand of hair in my fingers. "Because the helicopters can see them so easily?"

"Yeah, that's part of it. The valley makes them an easy target, and I don't think the BLM will be able to resist that. God knows they're ruthlessly chasing down and capturing every herd they can get their hands on. The park rangers are only going to encourage the BLM to round the herd up."

Finally it seemed like the right time to share the news I'd been bursting with all morning. "There's something else," I said. This morning I ran into Mrs. Miller. She told me the BLM is planning a total lockdown of roundup activities. They're closing all the public roads around the area for the July roundups. I guess they want to do the whole thing behind closed doors."

Sara grimaced. "Ouch. But what do you think we can do about it?" She emerged from the fridge with a bowl of red grapes.

I felt my cheeks getting hot. How could she be so flip? I was so tired of people not caring. "We can make it harder for Bob to do anything sneaky," I said, trying to keep my voice steady. "Like, if he knows we're watching him, he might be less inclined to try and go under the radar."

"Yeah," Kim spoke in a conspiratorial whisper. "And I know from some of my"—she made quotation marks with her fingers—"sources that he's not in the field on Saturdays, so we'll have a good chance of catching him in the office."

I could feel the hairs on the back of my neck tingle. "Maybe we can find out what herds they're going after in July."

Sara jerked her thumb toward me. "Check her out. Thinks she's a P.I."

I glared at her as she popped a grape into her mouth.

Kim hopped down from the counter. "The ranchers want to wipe out all the competition. Like, all the herds. Dad told me. They joke around about it."

Sara frowned. "They're just trying to feed their families."

"Yeah, like the steak we eat comes from them, right?" I asked.

"Well, that's the thing," Kim said, taking the bowl from Sara. "Dad says they only raise two percent of all the beef in the whole USA here on the range." She tossed a grape in the air and caught it in her mouth.

That made me mad. "So they really don't have the right to push the wild horses off the range."

Sara raised an eyebrow at me. "Easy there, little girl. The ranchers pay to graze their cattle on that land."

Kim laughed bitterly. "They hardly pay anything!"

I felt my jaw tighten just thinking about it. The ranchers and the BLM were acting like big bullies. How could anyone think the wild horses were pests? To me, they were the jewels of the Sage Mountains. "Then they shouldn't be chasing the mustangs out of there, like they own the entire earth. That's public land!"

Kim flashed me a dark look. "You're right."

Sara put a hand on her hip. "Yeah, but it doesn't add up. I can see culling some of the herds, but wiping all of them out? "

"So…you wanna talk to Bob about it?" I raised my eyebrows encouragingly.

"No, I don't wanna to talk to Bob about it," Sara mimicked my tone. She put the bowl of grapes back in the fridge and wiped her hands on her jeans. Then she smiled the smile of a princess. "But seeing as you've ruined any chances I might've had for having fun today, I guess I'll go along for the ride."

I held myself back from saying anything snarky. I couldn't give Sara any chance to back out now.

She glanced at me like I was a pest. "But does she have to come?"

Sara could make it very hard not to be snarky, but I held my tongue.

Kim jumped down from the counter and fished the keys out of her purse. "Absolutely. If there's any dirty work involved, we'll get Christa to do it!"

I pushed Kim out the door. They could say anything they wanted. We were going to see Bob Downs and speak up for the wild horses. I finally knew what I was going to say to get his attention.

CHAPTER 26

KIM TUNED THE radio to an oldies country station and sang along to all the songs. I'd be the first to admit she was not headed for stardom. What she lacked in talent, she made up for in confidence. As Kim drove, singing at the top of her lungs, Sara reached over and cranked the air conditioning up so high I began shivering, and when she joined in singing, "Save a horse, ride a cowboy," I covered my ears. It sounded like coyotes howling.

A half hour later, we arrived in Albright, which was bigger than our town, had more stores, some newer pick-up trucks, and more people hanging out in the park. Other than that, it pretty much looked the same as Spring Hills.

We found Bob Downs' office in an ugly brown two-story building just outside of town. Kim pulled into the lot and shut off the engine. I ran my fingers over my slightly chapped lips. My mouth felt dry.

Sara offered Kim a stick of gum, passing me by as if I didn't exist. "So, do we have a plan?"

Kim folded the gum into her mouth. "I think we should have Christa ask him about the Lost Herd and if they're planning to round them up this summer. She's sent him all those snail mail letters, so he's got to know her."

Sara waited. "That's it?"

Kim frowned. "Yep. Unless you come up with something better."

"How about making something up, like that we have a lot of people who don't want to see the Lost Herd rounded up, and we can prove it," Sara said.

I'd had that same idea like a hundred years ago, but if she wanted to think it was hers that was fine with me. It was about dang time. "Great idea," I said.

"If it came down to it, you know we could get people to sign a petition or something," Sara said.

Was she finally ready to do something? "Yeah, like all your friends for starters…and fans." I added that part to butter her up.

She blushed and poked me in the shoulder. "Shut up!"

It was time for me to share my big idea. "I think we should threaten to film Bob Downer's secret roundup and post the whole thing on YouTube."

"Nice thinking. That'll put some pressure on him," Kim said.

Sara studied her fingernails like she does when she's thinking. "Not bad."

"Maybe I was worth bringing after all," I whispered in her ear.

She rolled her eyes.

Kim opened the door. "So, any questions before we head in?"

I glanced out the window. "Why is there a black limo with tinted windows in the BLM parking lot?"

Kim leaned over to take a look. She whistled, "And a Texas license plate with just the number three on it."

Sara peered at the plate. "Dude's got pull, whoever he is."

We entered the lobby. Gray linoleum floors and gray walls. I'd go crazy if I worked in here. The receptionist looked like she was gray, too, and half dead with boredom. "I need you to sign in." She had a half-eaten bag of chips on the counter and was pretending to be busy on her computer, her long fake nails clicking and clacking. She was probably typing out her grocery list.

"We're here to see Bob Downs," Kim announced, standing tall and sounding really polite.

The receptionist didn't look up from her computer screen. "Do you have an appointment?"

"No, but maybe you could tell him I'm Kim Rodriguez, Ruben's daughter."

"Ruben Rodriguez?" The receptionist glanced up from her computer sharply.

Kim folded her hands behind her back. "Yup."

The receptionist's eyes fluttered like a startled bird. "Oh, I'll tell him right away." She picked up the phone and quickly dialed an extension she knew by heart. I guess being on the city council held some sway around here.

"Mr. Downs will see you in just a few minutes if you'll have a seat." The receptionist motioned to the chairs near the door.

We barely sat down when a couple of ranchers walked past us, talking in hushed tones. They were so deep in their conversation that they didn't even notice us. I recognized the big man as Jack Marshall. He was a friend of Dad's, but everybody knew Jack. He could run for mayor and win. He stood around six feet tall, but seemed more like seven feet in his cowboy boots and Stetson hat. Right now he looked as mad as I'd ever seen him, glaring at Greg Nichols, the wealthiest rancher in the area. As they reached the door, Greg grabbed Jack's arm and said something I couldn't hear.

Jack ripped his arm away. "This is wrong and I'm not going to pretend to like it." His face grew red as he stepped nose to nose with Greg. "Or you!" He stormed out the door with Greg Nichols right on his heels.

"Whoa." Kim watched Jack through the window as he got into

his truck and roared out of the lot. "Never seen him act like that. Wonder what's got him all stirred up?"

"Can't be anything good." Sara shook her head. "Jack's an okay guy, and Greg Nichols is…"

"Not so nice," Kim finished for her. "My dad says he's smart, but ruthless. He's put a lot of pressure on the BLM to get the mustangs off the range."

My toes curled in my boots. "What are they doing here? Were they talking to Bob?"

Kim and Sara shrugged.

By the time the receptionist led us back to Bob's office, I had a bad feeling eating at me. And it didn't get any better when we got there. Bob sat behind a big desk, talking heatedly with a tall, lean guy stretched out comfortably on a leather couch. The man was dressed in jeans, brand new snakeskin cowboy boots and a sports coat. As we paused in the hallway, he met my gaze with a haughty, smug expression.

I hesitated at the door, but Kim walked right in and stuck out her hand across the desk, interrupting their conversation. "Thanks for seeing us, Mr. Downs. My dad says hello."

Bob stood up and shook her hand. "You tell him hello for me." The window air-conditioning unit buzzed loudly and I could feel the cold air, but I noticed beads of sweat running down Bob's forehead. As a matter of fact, the Bureau of Land Management's top dog wasn't looking too good. Even his breathing sounded labored, and a few extra pounds hung like a tire around his middle.

"I'm Christa. I met you with my Dad awhile ago at the Towhee Ridge Roundup." I held out my hand.

"Nice to see you," he answered with a stiff smile. "What can I do for you ladies?" He remained standing. I got the feeling he wanted us out of there as fast as possible.

The man with the snakeskin boots stood up, too, as if he were leaving. Before he could make a move for the door, Kim thrust her hand out to him. "I'm Kim Rodriguez, and this is Sara and Christa Cassidy," she said quickly.

When he heard my name, his eyebrows shot up in a sign of recognition. "You the girl writin' all the letters?" he asked me, his Texas drawl as thick as fog. He towered over me.

"Yeah."

Bob laughed uneasily. "Yep, if her name is Christa Cassidy, she's the one."

I couldn't believe my ears. Why would this guy know about my letters? Or care? A guy from Texas with fancy clothes… my mind flashed on the black limo parked in the lot. This must be the man who belonged to that car. "I didn't get your name."

Snakeskin Boot's answering smile was insincere. I thought I saw a threat in his eyes. "That's 'cause I didn't give it to you."

Sara moved in front of me protectively. He took a step toward the door. "Well, it was nice almost meeting you," I said, sarcasm dripping in my voice.

He tipped his cowboy hat. "Y'all have a good day now." He dropped a red file folder on Bob's desk, nodded at Bob, and was gone.

Kim drew a sharp breath. "Creepy," she whispered.

Sara sat down in a chair facing Bob and exhaled angrily. "And rude!"

Bob sat, too, and busied himself organizing papers.

"So, who was that guy?" Kim asked, her hand resting casually on Bob's desk.

He became interested in a stapler that wasn't working. "Just an old friend."

"Didn't seem very friendly," Sara said.

"No, he sure didn't," Kim agreed.

I shivered. That guy gave me the willies, but we had come

here to help the horses, not get sidetracked by some stranger. "Mr. Downs, is it true there are more mustangs in the holding pens than there are on the range?"

He sat back and chuckled to himself, like it would take all his patience to answer such a silly question. "Christa, everything is status quo with the mustangs."

I had no idea what "status quo" meant. The three of us stared at him.

He smiled and took on a patronizing tone. "Now, what you girls might not realize is that those wild horses would starve to death on the range if the BLM didn't gather them up and take care of them."

He was lying through his teeth with every word! I could feel the blood rushing to my face. "Well, the Lost Herd isn't starving to death!"

A door slammed down the hall, and Bob jumped like a startled colt. "Christa, you've got nothing to worry about with that herd." His eyes danced away from mine.

"Is that a promise?" Sara folded her arms over her chest. "Because we've got a lot of folks who don't want to see the Lost Herd standing in a holding pen, and we can prove it."

Bob clicked the stapler, discharging staples onto his desk. "Yeah, sure, it's a promise," he mumbled, not looking up.

A sense of hopelessness swept over me. I tried one last time to say something that would get his attention. "And none of those people want to see any foals being run to death. Mr. Downs, please promise us you won't go rounding up herds in July. Because we'll sneak in and film the whole thing. And then we'll post it on YouTube."

The phone rang, and he answered. "Yes, this is Bob Downs." He held his hand over the bottom of the phone. "Excuse me, I need to take this." He swirled his desk chair away from us. Kim and I exchanged glances. So much for my big plan.

I racked my brain. There had to be some information that could help us right here in this office. Every decision made regarding the wild horses and burros on the Nevada range went through Bob. I scanned his desk and saw the red folder the big Texan had left. It was labeled Prospective Gathers, Summer. My heart slammed into overdrive.

Bob kept his back to us and chatted on the phone. "Well, I was hoping for the BLT, but if you're out of bacon, you're out of bacon," he said. "Okay, I'll take a ham and cheese." He stood up and stared out the window.

My eyes flashed to Sara and Kim and back to the folder. I watched the blood drain from Sara's face as she read the front cover. I had to do something! Willing myself to move, I made a grab for the folder, but just as I reached my hand out, Bob Downs ended his call and turned around. I snapped my hand back. Had he seen me?

Bob adjusted the waistline of his pants, attempting to pull them up over his considerable gut. "Well, ladies…"

I exhaled in relief. So he hadn't seen me, then. But we needed to buy more time. I looked to Kim for help. She cleared her throat. "Mr. Downs, do you have any pictures of you and the horses? We'd sure love to see you in action, and I know my dad thinks highly of all the hard work you're doing to keep the range in such good shape."

Bob grew at least two inches taller. "I think I could find something you girls might like." He ducked into the back room of his office, and suddenly, I knew what I had to do. Quick as a cobra, I opened the red folder, grabbed the cover page and hid it behind my back.

Bob re-entered the main room, holding a glossy five-by-seven photo. It was a picture of the mustangs taken from the air. "I was riding shotgun in the 'copter when we took this one. One of the pilots is a good friend of mine." He handed it to Kim proudly. "So, as I was saying, it was great seeing you girls. Give my best to your father, Kim."

"Oh, I sure will, Mr. Downs. You take care, now." Kim held the photograph to her heart. "And thank you so much!"

Both Kim and Sara took care to stand between Bob and me as we backed out of the office. Kim waved one more time and closed the door.

We all took a deep breath and started walking. Fast. "Told you she'd do all the dirty work," Kim whispered. "Little Miss Sticky Fingers."

"What about you, Kim?" I did my best imitation of her voice and fluttered my eyelashes. "Bob, do you have any pictures of you and the horses?"

Kim grinned like the cat that ate the canary.

"I would expect that from her." Sara said. "But I cannot believe you swiped that document, Christa."

"Me neither!"

"I'll deal with Bob if he comes after us." Kim glanced over her shoulder.

We walked down the hall, trying not to break into a run. I was doing my best to look sweet and innocent, and not like someone who would steal an important BLM document.

I folded the memo and slipped it into my back pocket. I had a feeling it just might provide us with some of the information Bob Downs had so carefully held back. This could be the clue we'd been waiting for.

When we finally reached the truck and locked the door, I looked into Sara and Kim's wide eyes and then, with shaking hands, unfolded the memo.

CHAPTER 27

I SAT BETWEEN THEM and clutched the page in both hands. Sara and Kim leaned in to get a better view of the document. What a document it was. My eyes grew bigger and bigger with each word I read:

BLM's Wild Horse and Burro Program
Budget for the year: 76 million dollars
Proposed budget increase next year: 15 million dollars
Goal for total horses gathered by the end of the year in Nevada: 810
Horses already gathered: 15,000
Remaining horses in Nevada: 1000

Prospective Gathers:
Lost Herd: 200 head
Calico Herd: 100 head
Eagle Herd: 140 head
Owyhee Herd: 130 head
Little Humboldt Herd: 150 head
Rock Creek Herd: 90 head

A sticky note was attached for Bob Downs: "Bob, These numbers look sufficient. As discussed, sign off on heading up the Wild

Horse Relocation Program. You'll find the paperwork enclosed. We need to have this well under way by July." There was an illegible signature, followed by the corporate logo of a spiral.

I didn't know what the spiral stood for, but I had a hunch the mysterious man from Texas in Bob's office was behind this.

Kim put the keys in the ignition and the truck roared to life. We sat in stunned silence, the document resting on my lap. I knew Bob Downs hadn't been straight with us, but this was beyond anything I could have imagined. My whole body shook in anger.

Kim backed the truck out of the lot. As soon as we turned onto the main road out of town, we all started talking at once.

"Well, of all the things you could steal, Christa...guess we hit the jackpot." Kim said.

"Only a thousand horses left running free in Nevada. There used to be fifteen thousand." I said, tears starting in my eyes.

"Why? Why round them all up?" Sara spoke like she was in a trance.

The only conclusion I could come to blinded me with rage. "The BLM must want to zero them out."

"That doesn't make sense. How can they afford to feed the thousands of horses they already have in holding pens?" Sara asked.

Kim looked like she was going to rip the steering wheel apart. "Looks like they've got enough of the taxpayers' money in their budget to deal with that... seventy-six million dollars and counting just for one year!"

"What's the Wild Horse Relocation Program?" I asked.

Sara shivered. "Dunno. They're already relocating all the wild horses from the range to corrals." She pushed the AC vent away from her, and I felt the blast of cold air.

Kim ran her fingers through her hair. "Maybe they plan on moving the horses in the holding pens somewhere else?"

A bolt of fear shot down my back. "Where would they take them?"

"Could be slaughterhouses in Mexico or Canada," Sara said sadly.

"Oh my God, no." I dug my fingernails into my palms. "Would they kill all of them?"

Sara shrugged. "It's just a guess. They could get a lot of money for so many horses."

I stared out the window, lost in my thoughts. "So what are we gonna do?"

Kim looked in the rear view mirror as she changed lanes. "I can talk to my dad and see what he can find out. Maybe he can come up with something."

"That's a good start. I can do some research on the Internet tomorrow and see what company that spiral logo might belong to," Sara said. "But I'm not going to think about it anymore today. It's too horrible."

I bit my lip until I tasted blood. "The Lost Herd is next on the roundup list."

"It's our worst fear come true," Kim said.

Sara stared blankly. "Let's talk about something else." She flipped her hair over her shoulder and a spark came back to her eyes. "Kim and I are going to a party at Dylan's tonight."

"Great," I mumbled.

"What should I wear?" She asked. Not waiting for a reply, she dove into an endless stream of meaningless banter about the pros and cons of her various pairs of jeans.

Kim drove on in silence and I slumped down low in the seat. There was no stopping Sara when she got like this.

Later that night after Sara left, I sat at the computer fruitlessly looking for the company with the spiral logo. I'd never felt so alone. The Lost Herd could already be captured and standing in a holding pen right now... slated to be sent to a slaughterhouse. I shut down my computer and paced the room like a caged tiger. I couldn't let the legendary herd end up as dog food!

Laughter drifted up from downstairs. Mom, Dad, and Grandma were watching TV. I wanted to tell them about the document, I really did, but I would get in big trouble for stealing it. And how many times had they told me there was nothing they could do about the roundups?

The two people in the whole world that I could talk to were out partying. All Sara cared about was having fun, and Kim wasn't really my friend, she was Sara's friend.

I was on my own.

I went out to the barn to see the horses. They were the only friends I had. Jenner was a ball of pent up energy, pacing his stall. I knew it was against the rules, but anyone could see that a ride would do him good.

"Hey, Jenner," I said. He stopped pacing and stuck his head over the stall door. "How would you like to get out for awhile?"

He banged the stall door with his front hoof.

That's when I hatched my daring plan.

CHAPTER 28

AFTER MOM, DAD, and Grandma went to bed, I stuffed some pillows under my sheets and left a note for Sara on the nightstand telling her not to wake me up no matter what. Then, I snuck out of the house. Under the light of the full moon I entered the barn. It didn't escape my attention that Jenner and I had some problems. Secretly, I clung to the hope that Cisco had smoothed out my horse's rough edges in one training session. But when I approached Jenner with his halter, he darted to the back of his stall and pawed the ground nervously. Something I couldn't name flickered across his white-rimmed eyes.

I should've turned back then, should've thought things through, but my will to see the Lost Herd outweighed the risk of riding Jenner. Besides, only a horse with Jenner's power and stamina could get me to the Twin River Valley and back by dawn.

"Jenner, the Lost Herd is in danger," I said, hoping he'd understand. "They could be captured by the BLM any second now. We need to find them." He seemed to settle as I talked, so I kept up a stream of chatter as I slipped his halter on and brushed him. He accepted the saddle and bridle without as much as a head shake. So, I cinched up the saddle and led him outside. But he didn't stay steady for long. The wind came up and sent him prancing and snorting. "It's our first night ride, but you don't need to be scared.

If you're like most horses you can see pretty good in the dark." I patted his neck. "And we've got the light of the moon on our side."

I checked the cinch one last time. Panic fluttered in my heart and tears threatened. I tried to stay calm, but I was furious and heartbroken at the same time. "If there's a roundup tonight, at least we'll see it happen. We can track them down and break them out under cover of darkness, if we have to. That's our mission."

By the stroke of midnight, we set out for the Twin River Valley, the trail awash with moonlight. Jenner's skin rippled with muscle and nerves. The last two times Jenner had taken off with me, I'd been frightened to death. Now, I didn't even try to hold him back. I pointed him straight and let him go. I told him if he wanted to run, that was fine with me–I wanted to run, too. The faster we got there, the better.

The wind nearly ripped holes in my chest as Jenner tore through the pine forest. We slowed to follow narrow trails that wound down to the desert, and then Jenner shifted into high gear again, raising a trail of dust behind us on the Little Grande Basin floor. I held on tight to the reins and tried not to look down. There were poisonous snakes and rodents and God knows what other creatures slithering around out here at night. I prayed Jenner wouldn't step on a sidewinder or into a burrowing animal's hole. He veered to avoid a prickly pear cactus, his head low and nostrils working as he took in all the night smells.

The moon had risen high enough to cast shadows in the deep crevices of the Sage Mountains and illuminate a fine mist rising from the ground. I ducked under a branch of a lightning-killed ponderosa, startling a raven up from the tree. The flapping of his wings echoed off the rocks.

Jenner's breath grew louder. Sweat sprang from his skin like rivers. At least he could run. At least he wasn't in a holding pen or being shipped off to a slaughterhouse. My anger at the BLM drove me on, but underneath the fire, exhaustion threatened. All I have to do is get to the top of two Brother's Mesa. If the Lost Herd is still in the valley, then we can go home...then I can sleep.

Jenner and I raced through the basin, blue with the pale light of the moon. The rock spires of Two Brother's Mesa came into view on the horizon. As we raced closer, they loomed over us like two giant fingers made of bone pointing to the sky. Jenner labored up the rocky path, foamy sweat lathering his shoulders. When we'd climbed half way up Two Brothers Trail, I pulled Jenner to a stop and let him rest in the cover of a scrub oak. I got off him, my head pounding like a jackhammer. I kept telling myself I'd be okay when we got there, though I knew that wasn't entirely true no matter what I found. At least I'd be able to see the entire river valley from the top of the mesa. Maybe I'd see the Lost Herd grazing happily, and maybe I wouldn't. Steeling myself for the worst, I squatted in the dirt and listened to the eerie howling of coyotes and the steady chirping of crickets.

Jenner sank his head to the ground, catching his breath. I cupped my hands and filled them from my canteen, holding them out to Jenner. He sniffed and then jerked away, his nostrils working. A tight, hard place in my chest grew tighter. "When are you gonna come around?" I asked under my breath. "You'll never trust me. You'll never be like Lucky."

As if to prove my point, Jenner jerked his head sharply, reacting to every smell that downloaded into his huge nostrils. He'd forgotten I was there, lost in his own drama.

I remounted and held on tight as Jenner planted one giant hoof in front of the other up the steep trail. He seemed as fresh as when we'd left the barn. I wondered what magical substance was in his bones to make him so strong. I prayed for that kind of strength. I'd need it.

My senses sharpened and everything around me appeared

hyper-real. I could smell the pungent sage, wet with night dew. The spires of the Two Brothers drew us on. Almost there. Just a few more steps. Jenner's tail snagged on the branches of the gnarled piñon as we climbed the narrow trail higher and higher.

When we reached the top of the mesa, the wind blasted through the spires of the two Brothers and groaned through the rock hollows. I pulled my shirt collar over my neck and shivered. Jenner danced and spooked at every shadow, his hooves pounding on the ragged rock. With a firm hand on the rein I guided him to the lookout point. He snorted and shook his head, fighting me with every step.

The moon hung over the valley like a white pumpkin, fat and heavy. I was thankful for its light as I scanned the acres of land stretching out below. Nothing. No movement. No sign of the Lost Herd. My eyes raced to the Twin Rivers, almost dry with the lack of rain.

Maybe the BLM has already captured them.

Jenner tried to turn back the way we came. I reined him in a circle, looking desperately out to the valley. Squinting through the dusky dawn, my eyes swept all the way to the south end of the valley. Using my field glasses, I thought I saw something. A blurry wisp of a tail, a group of bodies walking slowly, breaking from the cover of a stand of trees. Were my eyes playing tricks on me? Maybe they were just shadows cast by the branches, bending in the breeze. No. Those weren't shadows; they were horses!

From this distance, they looked like small dots on the misty fields with graceful tails flowing out behind. Slowly, band after band stood up and made their way to the river to drink. I counted close to two hundred horses. They're still here. Still free. Love that lived somewhere in my chest surged and ignited, melting the hatred. Tears of relief started in my eyes.

I had a fleeting sensation of pure joy watching them in the

blue distance. The horizon was already lightening. Time to go. I had to get back before the sun rose, before Dad got up and noticed Jenner and I were missing. Jenner was only too eager to turn when I pointed his nose toward home.

Just as we began our descent of Two Brothers Mesa, I heard a grating noise echo from somewhere across the valley. It sounded like an engine. Quickly, I checked the view through my field glasses. A glow of headlights flashed to the north. What the lights revealed sent my heartbeat into overdrive. Miles of chain-link fencing stretched across the desert, running along the north border of Twin Rivers National Park. Several tractors pulled something behind them and men in white hard hats scuttled around, looking like ants in the distance. What was a construction crew doing out here at night? I had to get closer.

Jenner and I broke a trail down to the valley and blasted toward the lights. With his huge stride it seemed like only seconds before we were upon them. Those men must've thought they'd seen a ghost as Jenner galloped out of a cloud of dust, and charged right past them. Aside from the shock on their faces, I saw the corporate logo of the spiral printed on their hardhats. We galloped into the mist and looped back to the main trail.

My mind reeled, trying to connect the dots. The spiral belonged to Snakeskin Boot's company. It's the logo on the sticky note for Bob Downs. What were they building and what did it have to do with the BLM?

The dull ache that throbbed in my temples grew worse as I pulled Jenner to a halt. He danced in place long enough for me to dribble the last bit of water from the canteen into my mouth. I willed my head to stop pounding. As urgently as I wanted to get home, I needed to rest more. We both needed to. But I couldn't stop him. I was like a feather sitting on him, for all he listened to me. So I tucked the canteen back under my shirt, gave him his head and let him go. He flew down the trail.

As we ran, guilt settled on my shoulder like a dark angel. I couldn't let Jenner run himself to death. I had to try and slow him down.

Tugging on the reins with all my strength, I sat back and cried, "Whoa!" at the top of my lungs.

Jenner didn't seem too interested in what I wanted. He tossed his head high above the bit and kept running. I could barely stay in the saddle with the way he fought me. As the ride wore on, my shoulders spasmed from the strain.

To my relief, Jenner's pace gradually slowed to a trot. Maybe he was finally tiring. "Walk, please, just walk," I pleaded. I'd lost the brakes a long time ago with this horse, but still I tried to soothe him with my voice. "I know you're all keyed up inside, but please walk. You can do it." I rubbed his neck in a way I hoped he liked. "It's not good for you to run, boy. Easy, now."

We slipped into the Basin at a trot. With this long of a ride, I figured Jenner would eventually tire enough to slow down of his own accord; and sure enough, as soon as I quit bugging him, he settled into a walk. I was relieved when Jenner's breathing came back to normal. We inched across the wide expanse of desert, one step at a time. I found myself counting Jenner's footsteps just to stay awake. *One hundred and one, one hundred and two....*

Finally, we climbed up into the piñon and juniper, leaving the Little Grande Basin below. The sun touched the tops of the trees on the far side of the foothills, flooding the world with an amber light. This had been the longest four hours of my life.

I began drifting in and out of a dream-state, my head nodding forward and back. Images of me and Jenner as friends, magically bonded from our difficult ride, swam in front of my eyes. "How nice," I thought, wrapping my arms around Jenner's neck. "This is all I ever wanted."

I woke to Jenner throwing his head, and realized I'd fallen forward onto his neck. We weren't exactly living the dream. I sat up and checked the landmarks. We'd covered at least a mile since I lost consciousness. Like all horses Jenner had an incredible sense of direction. He knew the way home, but if I drifted off again, I'd be sure to fall. I wrapped one hand in Jenner's mane and clung to the saddle-horn with the other. We're so close to home. *Don't let go*, I chanted. But eventually I gave into the rocking motion of Jenner's stride, and my body slumped forward again. He veered sharply to avoid the low branches of a spruce and I slipped from the saddle. I landed on my shoulder and rolled, groaning. While I lay there in pain, Jenner galloped up the trail for home, the stirrups flapping at his sides as if a ghost rider was spurring him on.

CHAPTER 29

D AD AND SARA appeared on horseback and found me stumbling down the trail at sunrise. Dad's mouth was set in such a grim line, I could hardly meet his eyes as he galloped up to me. "Jenner! Where is he?" was all I could croak out.

"He's back at the barn. When we saw him saddled up without you–" Sara said, her face ashen. Her voice trailed off. She dismounted and rushed to my side. I took the bottle of water she held out to me and gulped it down greedily. "Did he buck you off?" She asked.

"Nope. I fell asleep in the saddle," I answered, lamely. "On the way back from Two Brothers."

Dad jumped down off of Eastwood and swept me into a brief hug. "Are you okay?"

"I'm okay. I'm not hurt." I stood motionless as Sara brushed pine needles and dirt off my back. Seeing the worried expression on their faces tore me up inside. "Sorry."

Dad rested his calloused hand on my shoulder. "We had an agreement you weren't to ride him. That agreement was for your own good." He pointed toward the barn. "Not only did you ride him, Jenner is half dead with exhaustion. What were you thinking?"

"I guess I wasn't."

Sara cleared her throat. "Dad, there's some stuff we found out yesterday about the Lost Herd that you should know."

Dad ignored Sara's comment and squeezed my shoulder. I wasn't sure whether he wanted to hug me or kill me. He looked out to the hills. "I'd hate to think what could've happened to you if you'd fallen off out there somewhere." He mounted Eastwood and pulled me up behind him. "We've got some talking to do later."

When we got home, I dragged my bones upstairs to the bedroom and collapsed. Sara followed and closed the door behind her. "I probably already know the answer to this, but are you crazy?"

"I had to see them. I had to know they were okay."

She paced the room. "Dude. You're grounded. Why couldn't you just wait until morning? Dad could've driven you out there." She looked hurt. "How could you just sneak out and not tell me?"

I rolled over into a ball with my back to her. "How could you just go to a party?"

She groaned. "Okay. I get it. You're hopeless. So did you see them?"

"The Lost Herd's still in the Twin River Valley," I croaked into the pillow.

"Thank God. But I still can't believe you rode two hours out and two hours back, by yourself...on Jenner."

I sat up, remembering. "It all seems like a dream now, but I saw something weird out there, just outside of the park. There were guys working in the middle of the night. They had hardhats with the spiral on them."

Sara frowned. "I did a quick search. There are only a million companies that have a spiral logo."

"Well, it looks like they're building something out there. They were erecting miles of chain link fencing near the north boundary of the park. On the range, Sara. Maybe that's why they want the horses removed."

"I was thinking that, too."

Mom stuck her head in the room. "Get cleaned up, Christa," she snapped. "And take care of the horses. Now."

Sara shook her head like I was doomed. "You are in such deep trouble."

My stomach did a flip-flop of dread. "Yep," I said.

I dragged my feet down the stairs. Mom was emptying the dishwasher, slamming plates together. Dad nodded toward the door, barely looking up from his coffee. "Make sure Jenner's cooled down before you feed him. Stalls need cleaning. Then get yourself back in here. Your mother and I need to talk to you."

Mom didn't bother to turn around. Her voice was deadly and low, like the hiss of air going out of a tire. "You've got some explaining to do, Christa Ann."

"Fine." I bolted from the house. Adrenaline flowed through my veins, hopping me up as if I'd had ten cups of coffee.

Relieved to be in the barn, I tried to work off my new blast of energy, throwing hay to Star and Eastwood and mucking their stalls in record time. It figured Mom and Dad wouldn't understand. They had no idea what was going on with the wild horses and they didn't care. But to be fair, they didn't know what Sara and I knew about the BLM; they didn't know because I hadn't had the guts to show them the document.

I sighed in resignation. No matter what I did I got in trouble. But I had to admit that what had seemed like such a good idea last night, sure looked stupid this morning. I shouldn't have ridden Jenner so hard. "It's just that Jenner is so strong, I didn't think anything I did could hurt him," I said to Eastwood. He buried his nose in the alfalfa, ripped off a huge bite and chewed. Even to me, the words sounded hollow. The truth was, I'd been only too happy to risk my own safety and I'd put Jenner at risk in the process.

I didn't trust myself. Why did I keep hurting the things I loved? Star gazed at me with a soft eye, making me feel even more guilty. "I told Dad I didn't deserve a horse," I muttered under my breath, trying to blame it on him. But it wasn't working.

My head felt like a jar full of old keys and rusty pennies and my collarbone ached in the hollow near my shoulder. I missed Lucky. I missed Lucky every minute of every day. The way he smelled, his whinny of greeting in the morning, the way he ran to me from the pasture when I whistled, all came flooding back in an instant. There was no chance I could bring him back by remembering, so I'd been doing my best to shut the memories out. Until now.

I approached Jenner. He paced and snorted. I slipped into his stall long enough to run a hand down his flank before he spun away. His skin twitched uncomfortably under my fingers, but at least he felt cool. Well, I'd throw him some food and maybe he'd calm down. Then maybe I'd calm down.

"Easy now. I'm gonna try and make it up to you, boy," I said, summoning up my courage. I needed to be strong. I could do better.

A ray of sun pierced through a chink in the barn wall, flooding Jenner's stall with light. Did all that happen just last night? The ride seemed like years ago. I dragged a couple of flakes out of the wheelbarrow in the main aisle. My arms ached as I tossed the grass hay into Jenner's stall. Instead of rushing to grab a mouthful, he backed up and regarded me with a sullen eye.

I watched him in disbelief. "What's up with you? Aren't you going to eat?"

His ears darted forward and back, and the red lining of his nostrils blazed with each breath. I had a feeling as long as I was standing there, he wouldn't eat. He began pacing in his stall, whirling in circles. Nothing I could do would bring him comfort. As a matter of fact, my being there seemed to make everything worse. I always made everything worse.

Something dark and mean rose up in me. Suddenly, I couldn't

stand the sight of Jenner. Why couldn't he be more like Lucky? Why couldn't he be Lucky? "I hate you, you stupid horse!"

He halted and stared at me from the shadows, not moving an inch. I kicked the stall door with my boot as hard as I could and ran out of the barn.

After five minutes of scrubbing my face and hands in the downstairs bathroom, I slipped into my chair at the kitchen table next to Sara. Thankfully, she was texting. I didn't want to talk, didn't want to fight. I wished I could disappear.

Dad looked up from his iPad. He poured cream in his coffee and stirred noisily, his spoon clinking against the mug. "It seems no matter what rule we set to keep you safe, you break it."

I bowed my head. "I'm sorry."

Mom slammed a bowl of Cheerios down in front of me. That was ironic. Wasn't too cheery around here. "We grounded you from riding for a reason. It's that horse. You could've been killed!"

I bristled. I could be mad at Jenner, but no one else was allowed. "I rode Jenner across half the range in the middle of the night. I can handle him!"

Dad pierced me with his gaze. "Were you in control of him?"

I paused. Caught. I kept my mouth shut.

Sara prodded. "Were you running the whole time?"

I hid my bruised hands under the table. "Well, you know Jenner. He was pretty keyed up."

"Uh-huh," Mom said dryly, as if she'd spent her whole life being right and wasn't about to be wrong now.

Dad drummed his fingers on the table. "That's not horsemanship. Running a horse down isn't a partnership and it can break a horse."

I took a deep breath. Now I had to tell them. Even if they grounded me for the rest of my life. "Maybe what I did was wrong, but...there's something you need to know." I pulled the crumpled document from my pocket. The sticky note was still attached. "We went to see Bob Downs yesterday. And we found this."

Mom snatched the paper from my hand. "He called today to see if either of you girls had found a document he was missing. Why do you have it?"

"Um…well, it's complicated. Sara can explain."

Sara shot me a glance, guilt written all over her face. For once, she was speechless.

Dad was expressionless, which was worse.

I pushed my bowl of cereal away. "That document proves that everything I've been saying is true."

Mom barely glanced at the paper. Suddenly she looked old and tired again. I had that special effect on people. "I'm guessing you took this from Bob's office." She held the letter up in the air like an accusation.

Sara's eyes widened. "I didn't take it, Christa did!"

Apparently, my big sister wasn't in the mood to protect me now. "Did you read it, Mom?" I tried to keep my voice steady. "It says the BLM's gonna round up the Lost Herd next!"

"The Lost Herd?" Dad reached for the document.

Mom's face fell. "Oh," she said. "But that doesn't excuse your behavior."

Dad scowled when he read the document. "This is what you've been worried about all along, Christa."

"Yep." I sat up straighter.

Dad pulled his reading glasses off and rubbed the bridge of his nose. "I don't want you girls thinking you can run around taking things that don't belong to you."

I met Dad's eyes directly. Rage is not a strong enough word for what I felt. "Taking things that don't belong to me?" I said, measuring each word. "How about the BLM capturing thousands of mustangs that don't belong to them! Maybe Bob Downs is the one who needs to learn that lesson."

Dad stood up and began pacing. "Maybe that's true, Christa, but the BLM is a separate issue." But when he looked down at the letter again his face blanched. "Only a thousand mustangs left on the range? This is criminal! The last BLM report estimated there were ten thousand horses still running free in Nevada." He shook his head. "I'm going to let Bob know how I feel about this."

I breathed a sigh of relief. Dad was as mad about this as we were! Now if we could only get Mom on our side.

Grandma padded down the stairs and into the kitchen. "You're all up early," she said, cheerfully. Her smile faded when she saw my face. I must've looked awful. "What's going on?"

All our voices tumbled over each other as we told her. She bent close to me and spoke in a low voice meant only for me to hear. "I know you're worried about the Lost Herd, but putting yourself in danger isn't going to help those horses," she scolded. "And why do you feel you have to do everything yourself? We could've helped you. We still can."

"She feels like she has to do it alone, because we've never been willing to help her," Mom said, clearly having overheard.

"Until now," Grandma said. She stared Mom down. The tea kettle boiled.

Mom sighed, as if all the wind was going out of her sails. "We've been trying to protect you, Christa," Mom said. "But now I know we need to do something to stop the BLM." She met my eyes. "They can't round up the Lost Herd."

"No, we can't let them do that," Sara said, kicking me under the table. She was probably relieved the subject had changed from us stealing the document.

I thanked all the angels in heaven that Mom was coming around and that I had such an ally in Grandma. As she joined us at the table with a cup of tea I realized that I wasn't alone in this anymore. Now we had a team.

"Isn't there a law that protects wild horses?" Grandma asked.

"Wild horse Annie got one passed," I said. "She got a bill passed in 1971, and the mustangs were declared to be 'living symbols of the historic and pioneer spirit of the West.' "

Dad's voice was heavy with sarcasm. "I guess they've forgotten that."

"So, how did Wild Horse Annie do the impossible?" Grandma asked. "Because we can't lose all of our wild horses."

Mom set a basket of cinnamon rolls down on the table and sat, the old wooden chair creaking unhappily. "Christa knows."

I could remember my speech almost word for word. "She fought Congress for ten years, but she couldn't get the law passed that would protect the wild horses. Then she wrote letters to kids and told them what was happening, and word spread all across the world. The kids wrote so many letters that they filled the halls of Congress."

Grandma's eyes lit with a spark of understanding. "So it was the kids who got that law passed."

"Kids can get a lot more done when they have their family behind them," I said, smiling at Grandma. Now that I finally had everyone's ear, I had to tell the rest of the story. "On my ride last night I saw men working," I said. "On public land."

Mom fixed me with a laser-like stare. "You saw them out there?"

I nodded. "And they had a spiral on their hardhats, just like the logo at the bottom of the note for Bob Downs."

She peered over Dad's shoulder at the document. "They're out there on public land in the middle of the night?" She asked. "Who would be out there working at that hour?"

"I have a feeling it's a mining or power company," Dad said.

My heart pounded ferociously now. "How can they do this without asking or telling anyone?"

"That's a good question," Dad said. "People in this town sure wouldn't be happy about a company using land they don't own." He paused and glanced at the document again. "Or the wild horses being zeroed out."

Grandma stood up and popped a slice of bread into the toaster. "You girls could change the way the BLM is doing business if you got the word out to enough people around here. I think you should do it in person. That way you can explain what's going on face to face."

I grimaced. "Going out and talking to people isn't my strong suit. I'll write the letters. Sara can do the meet and greet."

Dad stared at me and shook his head. He grinned at Grandma. "She got all that charm from me, Gillian."

"I can see that," Grandma said, nodding in agreement. "I can only imagine what you were like when you were fourteen. I can tell you Claire was quite a handful."

For just a moment, I felt the tension ease in the room. Even Mom fought back a smile. "I wasn't that bad," Mom said.

"No one could be as bad as Christa," Sara said and then everyone laughed.

"The joys of being a teenager," Mom said.

"Ha, ha, ha. Very funny," I grumbled. They made being fourteen sound like a disease.

Mom slid into the chair beside me. "Let me remind you of a few things"

The room grew still. Grandma was the only person moving, humming as she buttered her toast. Sara drew her finger across her throat in one quick motion.

"It seems you have a good reason to be upset. This is a noble cause and we are on your side. But there will be a consequence for what you did." She met my gaze. "We haven't made up our mind yet, what that will be. So I would advise you to be very careful. You are still grounded from riding."

I nodded solemnly. Then a horrible thought struck me. "But we're not going to get rid of Jenner, right?" I asked.

Mom and Dad exchanged glances.

"We need to give Jenner a chance. None of this is his fault. I promise I won't ride him. And Cisco can still work with him, right?"

"We'll see," Dad said. By the tone of his voice I knew the conversation was over.

CHAPTER 30

THE STORM BROKE right over our heads and within seconds, Jenner and I were soaked to the skin. We ran deep into a forest. The sky was so dark I could barely see. I dismounted from Jenner and peered into the rain. I thought I saw Lucky—a stark white form against the black trees—but he faded into the mist. I chased after him, pulling Jenner behind me until Jenner planted all four feet and would go no further. We took shelter under a giant oak. I saw the words "Lucky + Christa," carved into the tree trunk. My body filled with an aching sadness so heavy I could not move. A shaft of lightning zigzagged out of the heavens and struck the tree with a huge crack! I screamed. Jenner reared, pawing the air with his hooves. The tree was falling. Huge branches hit the ground all around us. The trunk stood bare and smoking. Jenner wheeled and ran, pulling the reins from my hands. "Jenner!" I yelled into the storm. His hooves became the rumbling of thunder getting further and further away.

"Christa, wake up!" Sara commanded, propping herself up on one elbow. "What's wrong?"

I shivered under the sheets. A cool breeze blew in through the window. Somewhere in the hills, a coyote barked. "Had a nightmare," I mumbled, switching the bedside lamp on.

"Turn that thing off." Sara squinted sleepily in the light.

"Jenner galloped off. I couldn't stop him."

She hid her head under her pillow. "Go to sleep."

I looked at the clock. Three a.m. Within seconds Sara began snoring, peaceful as an angel.

Just a dream, just a dream, just a dream, I said to myself over and over. I watched her until my breathing slowed and my head grew heavy.

I woke to loud voices in the kitchen and doors slamming. Light streamed through the curtains. It was late morning. We'd overslept.

Dad's heavy footsteps came pounding up the stairs and his voice boomed forcefully. "Girls!"

We both shot out of bed and met him in the hallway. Light flooded the house.

Sara rubbed her eyes. "Dad, what is it?"

He glanced toward the window and back at us again.

I followed his gaze, panic rising. "What happened?"

"Jenner ran away."

I grabbed his arm. "No!" Goosebumps raised down my neck. Leftover traces of the nightmare played at the edge of my awareness, blurring reality.

"How'd he get out?" Sara asked, fully awake now.

Dad looked pale. "I put all the horses out to pasture at dawn. I just went to check on them and noticed he was missing. Looks like he jumped the fence. He left some skin there. I don't know how bad he's hurt."

Sara inhaled sharply. "Is that his blood on your gloves?"

He glanced down at his fingers, smeared with dabs of blood. He nodded. "Just where I touched the fence. Like I said, he didn't jump it clean."

"I'll be dressed in two seconds. We can track him if we get going right now." I spun and raced back to my room.

Dad blocked me with his arms. "Sara and I are going after

him. You're staying here. We've only got two horses." I knew there was no arguing with him when he looked like that. He turned to go.

I sank to the floor. "You have to find him, Sara!"

Sara threw some clothes on and grabbed my hand. "We will."

"You promise?" I held onto her hand with both of mine.

"I promise, Christa." Her hand slipped through my fingers. The floor shook as she raced down the stairs and out the door.

CHAPTER 31

THE DAY DAWNED with a dry heat that baked the earth and dried the grasses from green to yellow right before my eyes. A northeast gale blew in from the desert, blasting heat into my face and threatening to snatch my hat off my head as I ran out to the pasture. Blood stained the top cross rail of the fence and hoof prints marked the ground where Jenner had jumped. The tracks looked fresh enough. Maybe Dad and Sara could catch up with him, but only if Jenner wanted to be caught. He could outrun the wind. I shielded my eyes from the gale and scurried back to the house.

And then I waited.

I paced the front porch and ducked inside to check the clock over the kitchen sink again and again. One hour, then two. Without the horses here, the whole property seemed empty. Jenner was gone and it was my fault.

Mom came out with a tray of iced tea and sandwiches. My stomach clenched. I couldn't eat anything. "Did you hear from Dad?"

"Not since the last call."

"What did he say?"

"I already told you."

"Well, tell me again."

She sighed and ran the back of her hand over her forehead. "It was hard to understand him. His cell was cutting in and out. But he said they'd tracked Jenner across Michael and Cecilia's ranch."

"Then they'll catch him soon, right?"

"Sure they will," Mom sank into a wicker chair and took a deep gulp of lemonade.

I stared at Mom's cell phone sitting quietly on the table near her chair, willing it to ring. Time slowed to the pace of sap dripping from a tree.

Grandma joined us on the porch and sat in the wicker rocking chair next to Mom. She was quiet, deep in her own thoughts.

My eyes filled with tears as I leaned against the porch railing. "I don't think there's any hope for Jenner," I said. "He was fine when we brought him home. Maybe I ruined him." I resumed my pacing.

"Nonsense." Grandma's voice was sharp.

It was just a word, but it stopped me in my tracks. I sighed and collapsed onto the porch swing. I didn't think losing two horses was nonsense, but I was silent.

Grandma had a wild look about her. Her hair was blowing loose in the wind; she had all her silver jewelry on, and the green silk scarf was tied neatly around her neck.

"I think I know why he ran off. " My voice sounded small.

Grandma's eyes clouded. "It could've been coyotes, a sound, or the wind."

"Horses run when they're scared. Everyone knows that," Mom said. "That horse has been running since the day we got him."

"He has not! It's just around water that he spooks, Mom," I said.

"What about your ride last night?" Mom snapped.

A dust devil rose from the dirt in the driveway and spun itself out over the pasture.

Of course Mom would never understand. I crossed my arms over my chest and stared her down. "You never really cared for Jenner anyway, did you Mom?"

Her face looked strained. "That's not true."

"Makes it easier for you with him gone. Now we don't have to get rid of him," I said.

"Christa Ann, that is not fair and you know it." She stood slowly, holding her stomach and walked inside.

I am so lame, I thought, following her into the kitchen. She was leaning against the counter with her back to me, staring out the window. "Mom?"

She turned.

"Are you feeling okay? Do you have cramps?"

She smiled a tired smile. "No, honey. I haven't had cramps for quite a while now."

"Oh. Well, that's good."

She shooed me away with her hand. "I'm fine. Get back out there. You don't want to miss the call."

A blast of wind struck the property with such force, the windows of the house rattled and groaned.

I paused. I didn't know what to do. "Okay," I said, bolting back to the porch. I pressed my face against the screen of the front door, smelling the musty scent before pushing through it back to the wicker chairs, back to pacing.

When a shrill ringtone burst from Mom's cell phone, both Grandma and I jumped like long-tailed cats in a room full of rocking chairs. Mom ran back to the porch and for a second we all stared at the phone. It sat on the table, ringing and vibrating, turning itself around. I snatched it up and pressed the talk button. My hand shook. "Dad? It's me, Christa."

"Christa! We got him!" I drew a deep breath and nodded at

Mom and Grandma. Relief flooded from the top of my head down to my feet. "Is he okay?

"He's been hurt," Dad continued. "Can't tell how bad. Call the vet and tell him to meet us at the Whitehorse Ranch."

The Whitehorse Ranch–that was where Amy lived! "Okay. Should we meet you over there?"

He hesitated. "Not until I talk to the vet." I knew that meant Jenner didn't look good.

"Okay," I lied. I was getting over there as fast as I could. I needed to see Jenner. Dad hung up.

I handed the phone to Mom. "Dad says to call the vet and meet him at the Whitehorse Ranch with the trailer."

"Got it." Mom slipped back into the house with the phone.

Grandma had a slight smile playing on her lips. "Interesting the way you handled that, dear."

I froze. How did she know I lied? Before I could say a word, she patted me warmly on the back and took my hand in hers.

"You've got to see your horse. And the sooner, the better." Grandma was becoming more of a mystery to me every day. "You go on ahead with your mother."

I paused. I wanted her to come. "Are you sure?"

She nodded at Mom who was walking toward the car. "Your mother will take care of you."

"Yeah, right," I said under my breath. "I mean, is she strong enough with the baby?"

Grandma cupped my cheek. "She may surprise you."

I let go of her hand and took the porch stairs in one giant leap. My heart was pounding so loud in my ears, I could hear it over the wind.

CHAPTER 32

WE PULLED INTO the Whitehorse's driveway, and I burst out of the truck. Mr. Whitehorse stood on the front porch, his old cowboy hat pulled low. He walked quickly to meet me. He had black hair tied back in a ponytail and kind brown eyes.

"Mr. Whitehorse, where's Jenner?" I asked frantically. Mom was right behind me.

He pointed to a path that led past the house. "He's down in the round pen. Go on, I'll wait here for the vet."

"Okay, thank you," I called over my shoulder.

I ran as fast as I could past the house and the corrals filled with a few horses, pigs, and sheep. Down the hill was a smaller pipe corral with a water trough, sheltered by a huge cottonwood tree. And there, lying on the ground was Jenner. Sara, Dad, Amy, and Mrs. Whitehorse stood around him in the corral. My breath came faster.

"Jenner!"

I tore down the hill, tears stinging my eyes. He had to be okay; he just had to be alive and breathing.

Dad ran up the path to meet me. "Christa!"

"Dad! Is he okay?"

Dad reached me and held my arm tightly. "I'm not sure, Christa."

My heart almost stopped.

Dad's voice was calm and low, but his hands shook as they held onto to each of my arms.

Mom came up behind me and put her arm around my shoulder, as if bracing me for a strong wind. "Tell us."

"He's lost a lot of blood." Dad glanced down the hill at Jenner's still form. "He needs to be stitched up."

I couldn't wait another minute to see Jenner. "The vet's on his way, Dad." I wrenched away from their grasp and raced down the hill to the corral.

Jenner lay on his side, his breathing labored. Sara sat beside him, stroking his neck. She glanced up at me with tears streaming from her eyes. I could hardly breathe. They had covered his stomach and leg with towels that were stained with blood.

Jenner turned his head to look at me. His eyes were glazed with pain, but I saw a spark of recognition flicker before he dropped his head back to the ground. I slid down on my knees beside Sara. I moved Jenner's forelock out of his eyes. My whole body ached with the shock of seeing him so bloody. "I'm so sorry, Jenner," I said.

Mrs. Whitehorse nodded at me and then turned to her daughter. "Amy, we need more towels." Amy cast me a glance full of sympathy and then took off running toward the house.

I traced the curve of Jenner's cheekbone. "Can you ever forgive me?" His ear twitched. "You're not a stupid horse...you're a great horse, and I've been so horrible." I lay my head down on his neck. "I'll make it up to you."

For a long minute, the world shrank to the sound of Jenner's breathing and my heartbeat, both fast and ragged. Tears fell from my eyes onto his neck.

Sara watched us, her expression grim. I reached out and clasped her hand. I couldn't believe she'd tracked him down. "How did you find him?"

She tipped her cowboy hat back and wiped her tears away with the back of her hand. "We were lucky. He left an easy trail to follow, and Dad was, like, possessed. Star and Eastwood were strong, but it took hours to catch up with that red horse of yours." She gripped my hand harder. Her skin felt electric and her eyes were wide as they met mine. "Christa, it's so weird. That dream you had…"

Chills raised the hair on the back of my neck. I shrugged. "I know it's weird. But what good did it do? It didn't keep Jenner from running away and getting hurt." Jenner swished his tail weakly. I ran a hand down his back, trying to keep the flies off him. "Stay with me, boy." For just a second, his eyes tracked with my voice and he met my gaze. "Oh, Sara…Jenner has to live!"

"Well, here's what you're up against." Sara reached over and removed the bloody towels from Jenner's belly. I gasped when I saw the deep cut. I had no idea it was that bad.

Jenner's sides were heaving with every breath. He didn't even lift his head. "We cleaned him up as best we could," she continued. "He jumped a few fences and some of them were barbed wire."

I nodded, my heart breaking. He'd wanted to get away that bad. I knew only too well how far and how fast he could run. Blood oozed out of the cut in his stomach and a deep gash on his hind leg, soaking the ground a dark crimson. Sara replaced the towels over Jenner's stomach. "I'll be right back. I need to take a break," she said.

I glanced over at Mom and Dad standing behind me near the fence. Mom stepped forward and put a hand on my shoulder. "I'm here." I felt a softness from her words flow into me, warm and comforting.

Amy returned with fresh towels for the cut on Jenner's right hind leg and pressed them to his wound. It was weird seeing her outside of school. Her bangs were highlighted orange now, but she was the same Amy, always so kind to me. Our eyes locked. "Thank you," I said. She nodded.

Jenner groaned. "Oh, Jenner. Please hang in there," I pleaded, pulling on his forelock. "Please stay with me."

Mom kneeled next to me. "Please get well for my little girl," she whispered to my horse, running her hands through his thick mane. "She needs you." Jenner's eye rolled open at the sound of Mom's voice. He stared straight ahead, seeing nothing, his eyes clouded in pain. Mom's shoulders shook. With a start, I realized she was crying. "We all want you to stay with us for a long time, Jenner."

She held her arms out to me and I fell into them, loving her, needing her. When I pulled away, she kissed the top of my head. "I'll be right here," she said.

Dad was at her side in an instant. A wave of love swept over me for him, too. I thought he'd only wanted to get rid of Jenner, and instead he'd tracked him halfway across Spring Hills.

"So, how did Jenner wind up here?" I asked.

"I'm not sure," Dad said. "Amy's the one who caught him."

"He was running across the field when I spotted him," Amy said. Her hand looked as small as a child's as she pointed off into the distance.

I nodded at her to continue.

"He took our fence like it was nothing. It's four feet high and solid wood! He was calling out to our horses and they were whinnying back, making a big racket. That's when I texted your dad. He'd already left a message with us and half the other ranchers nearby to be on the lookout."

Dad was my hero. He'd done all this to save Jenner.

"I texted you, too, Christa," she said quickly.

I checked my pocket. "I don't even know where my phone is."

Amy looked at Jenner in admiration. "It's not every day we see a huge red horse jump our tall fence and come galloping across our land. It felt like a vision, seeing Jenner eat up that field with his big stride."

The way she talked about Jenner made me love her. I couldn't believe I'd ever stopped texting her, she was so cool. "Thank you for helping us," I said. "How did you stop him?"

"The fight—or the fear—had gone out of him. He let me and my mom walk right up and put a rope on him," Amy said.

Sara came back and sat beside me. Her tears were gone. "He's a big horse, with a big heart," she said, stroking his neck.

Just then we heard Mr. Whitehorse's voice calling out from the top of the hill. "Doc Ferguson's here!"

CHAPTER 33

DOC FERGUSON STEPPED softly to Jenner's side. His eyes narrowed in thought as he looked him over. "We gotta get him on his feet."

Jenner lay flat out on the ground, his breath coming fast. In a flash, I was beside him. I caressed his face and the soft skin around his nostrils. "Jenner, you gotta get back on your feet," I pleaded. Jenner groaned and slanted an ear toward me. I leaned down close to his nose. "C'mon. Get up!" He was covered in blood. "I know how bad you must hurt, but you gotta get up!"

Doc Ferguson clapped his hands encouragingly and hollered, and then one by one all our voices joined together, rising in a desperate chorus. Jenner raised his head and looked around wide-eyed, like he'd been woken from a long nap.

Star and Eastwood called to him from the field where they'd been turned out, their ears pinned on us. Jenner called weakly back to them and rocked his body until he gained enough momentum to swing onto his belly and get a leg under him. We kept cheering him on and he struggled, one front leg out, then another until he raised himself to standing on three legs, holding up his back right leg. He shook his body and turned his face toward me. His brown eyes were soft and so trusting. My eyes locked with his and then, almost against my will, slid down to the patch of skin hanging from his stomach and his blood-streaked legs.

Doc Ferguson whistled through his teeth. "Hurt yourself pretty good, didn't ya, big guy?" He ran a gentle hand down Jenner's hindquarters to the hoof. "Looks like the hock's been scraped up, and he may have strained the tendon, but it's intact. And the ligaments appear to be okay."

Dad and I released a long breath. If he'd crushed the tendon or ligaments in his hock, there'd be nothing we could do.

"Think he can ever be ridden again?" Dad asked in quiet voice—as if it wasn't the most important question in the world.

"Hard to say." Doc bent to examine Jenner's belly. "Now this we can stitch up no problem, although it might leave a scar." He straightened and glanced at me. "The hock is more complicated. If you can ever ride him again, this injury may limit what kind of riding you do."

I nodded. I didn't care what kind of riding I did, as long as it wasn't the kind of riding I'd been doing.

"Even if I can't ride you, I'll still be your friend, Jenner." He turned his eye to me. I felt my heart go out to him in a rush, and I kissed his white blaze.

Doc Ferguson moved forward with a syringe. "We'll give him enough to take the sting out while we put the stitches in." He nodded curtly. "Christa, you stay right there at his head and keep him calm."

I felt Jenner's breath on my face. He nuzzled my chest with his upper lip, right over my heart where it hurt the most. My skin was stained with sweat and tears, but he didn't care one bit. "It's gonna be okay," I crooned. "Doc's gonna fix you up."

Amy stepped up beside me. "He's going to be okay, Christa," she said. She ran her hand down Jenner's nose and spoke to him in a hopeful voice. "This won't hurt a bit. It'll be over before you know it."

I was relieved the vet didn't make a liar out of her. He worked fast, clipping Jenner's coat around the wounds and washing the cuts. He stitched the wounds clean and neat. The swelling was ugly, but both cuts looked less dangerous now that none of Jenner's insides were showing. The vet gave him fluids and something to help with the swelling and infection. He told me if he rested for a week or so, he should be strong enough to turn out to pasture, but no riding for a few weeks.

When he said we could take Jenner home with us, my whole body slackened with relief. While my family gathered with the Whitehorses to talk, Doc pulled me aside. "Christa, these cuts are deep and can get infected. He needs to be kept in his stall for a week."

I nodded. "Then can I walk him outside?" I wondered how I was going to keep a big horse like Jenner in his stall all week.

"Slowly and carefully and for very short distances," he answered sternly. "I'll be giving your dad explicit instructions. He'll be checking to see you keep those cuts clean."

CHAPTER 34

I SLID THE BARN door open and peeked inside. Star and Eastwood nickered, eager for breakfast, but Jenner stood quietly in the dim light. His big sad eyes stared back at me a moment, and then his lids closed halfway. My breath caught in my throat as I slipped into his stall.

Jenner stood with his feet planted, his eyes staring at nothing. It was hard to explain how I knew he was feeling bad. He didn't have the proud, faraway look he got when he was outside sniffing the air and he didn't have the gleam of terror of a frightened horse, or the sullen eye of a bored or resentful horse. What he did have was an eye clouded with pain, as if he was fighting a private battle inside of himself. Gently, I wrapped my arms around his neck. "Oh, Jenner," I sighed. Star nickered and I pulled away. "Time for breakfast."

I threw the horses their hay and Star and Eastwood dug into their breakfast with gusto. Jenner just nibbled. "You can wait until you're feeling better to eat, but you have to drink right now," I said.

I filled his water bucket and while he drank, I studied him as if I were seeing him for the first time. Since I'd had Jenner, I was either comparing him to Lucky or thinking of him as a ride out to see the Lost Herd; as if he existed solely for the purpose of shuttling me from the barn to the range. I felt rotten. It was time for us to just hang out.

The sound of voices drifted in through the open barn door. "We've got company, Jenner," I said and slipped out of the stall.

"Knock, knock," Kim called. She strode into the barn in cowboy boots, hip-hugger jeans, and a lime-green t-shirt. Cool as ever. Star and Eastwood nickered and popped their heads over their doors, campaigning for a carrot, but Jenner stood quietly.

"Who's there?" I asked, grinning.

"None of your business," Kim answered with her usual sass. Her expression softened when she saw Jenner. "Big Red's back." She stared at him, wide-eyed.

"Yeah, thanks to Sara and Dad," I said.

Sara came in and stopped short. She looked at Jenner with a calculating expression. She was probably planning his whole healing regimen. I pushed my tangled hair out of my eyes. I was truly grateful to her, but I was over Sara being my savior. I wanted to be the kind of girl who didn't need saving.

I glanced up to see Cisco hovering near the door, as if still deciding whether to come in. My pulse sped up. Stupidly, I waved. He nodded and shuffled toward us. He wore a baseball hat on backwards and a navy blue t-shirt. His eyes met mine. "Hey," I said. My heart thudded softly.

"Hey," he said back.

Our usual stunning repertoire.

We all gathered outside Jenner's stall.

"So I guess Sara told you I rode Jenner out to Twin Rivers in the middle of the night," I said, breaking the silence.

"Yep," Cisco said, his expression unreadable.

"Of course I told them," Sara said as she stroked Star's nose.

Kim jerked her thumb toward Sara. "As if she wouldn't tell us! Yeah, we heard and I don't blame you one bit. After seeing that document…I mean, if I had a horse like Jenner I probably would've pulled a Paul Revere, too."

Cisco muttered. "Was Paul Revere a jockey?"

Kim shot him a withering look. Cisco shrugged.

I realized I hadn't talked to Cisco since he'd trained Jenner the other day. Felt more like a hundred years ago. "Well, what did you think, Cisco? About Jenner, I mean? Was he okay when you worked with him?"

"He's good. He seemed a little jumpy, but okay. When a horse gets worked up like he did," He shook his head, "they don't come back down for awhile."

I twisted my fingers in my hair. "Do you think that's why he ran away, because he was worked up?"

Cisco held his hands up in the air, as if to fend me off. "I have no idea why," he said, as if only a girl would ask that.

"It's just that I don't want him to run away again," I said.

Kim put a hand on Cisco's shoulder. "When Jenner gets better, Cisco can help you train him. Isn't that right, Cisco?"

Cisco's eyes flickered over Jenner's beat up body. His expression looked doubtful. "Yep," he said.

We were back to one word.

I unlatched Jenner's stall and swung the door open. "C'mon in and take a look at him." Jenner briefly touched his nose to Cisco's arm, then faced forward again with a sigh. "Everything's gonna be okay, Jenner. You'll see," I whispered in his ear.

Kim and Cisco bent down with me to examine the wound on Jenner's belly. His stitches ran in a clean line.

"Whoa," Kim whispered. "He cut himself good."

Cisco remained stoic. "Stitches are holding. He's not tearing at them or anything. That's good. What we don't wanna see is yellow or green puss."

"I really don't wanna see that," I said, gripping my stomach.

Sara crowded into the stall with us. "Clean the stomach and re-wrap the leg, Christa," she ordered. I pulled off the standing wrap.

Kim leaned back against the stall door and watched silently. When Cisco saw the deep cut, his brow furrowed. "What?" I asked. The sight of the blood made me gag.

"Nothing," he said. "No big deal."

"Go ahead and clean it, Christa. You have to learn this," Sara said from behind me.

"Okay." My stomach churned. I knelt down with the cloth the vet had given us, but when I got closer to the wound, I hesitated. Cisco kneeled next to me. Without a word, I handed him the cloth.

"Here, like this," he said. He wiped the wound with a firm hand. Jenner swished his tail once, and held his leg up in the air like a dog with an injured paw. "The antiseptic stings for a minute, but he's all right."

"Okay. I can do it now." As I reached in with a fresh cloth my forearm brushed Cisco's and the hair on my arms tingled. Being this close to him was distracting. I refocused and remembered to breathe.

I began to wrap Jenner's hock with the clean bandage. Sara stood over me directing my every move. "Not too tight, and not too loose...here, use your arm to hold it in place."

Cisco glanced up at Sara and Kim. "Hey, why don't you two go do your nails or something?"

I stifled a laugh.

"Not a bad idea," Kim said, glancing down at her chipped polish.

Sara crossed her arms over her chest. "Not till this is finished."

Cisco paid no attention to them. Instead, he encouraged me, reaching in to help once in a while, but mostly watching. His eyes were impossibly dark and kind. He sure seemed to know what to do with his hands. He had strong arms, I noticed. Now my stomach was flip-flopping about that. I had to get a grip!

After three tries, my task met with Sara's approval. Neon pink vet wrap was the final touch to hold everything in place. Poor Jenner, the final insult. We couldn't even use a manly color. Cisco winced when he saw it. "We'll bring some black vet-wrap next time."

"Sure. Anytime," I said, trying not to sound too eager.

Kim stretched her arms over her head. "Nothing works up an appetite like seeing blood and guts. I'm hungry. Let's get some breakfast." Before I could answer, she took my arm and steered me out of the stall. "We've got things to discuss."

"Like?"

"Like wild mustangs."

CHAPTER 35

I NEVER REALIZED HOW popular McDonald's was with toddlers. The bright red and blue plastic playground swam with little bodies. Exhausted parents looked on, sipping coffee and gossiping together. They ran to pick up the fallen, the scraped, or the emotionally wounded. Some kids squealed with joy, while others screamed in outrage. Humans. We were complicated from day one.

All four of us slid into a booth with our paper-wrapped breakfast sandwiches. Kim glanced at the playground. "You think you have problems with your horse? Wait till you have one of those."

Sara giggled. "I want one. They're so cute."

I took a bite of my Egg McMuffin. "Probably won't have to wait long the way you're going."

Sara raised her eyebrow threateningly. "Well, I've got my hands full with you. You have the emotional maturity of a toddler." She waved a chunk of hash brown at me for emphasis.

"Maybe your skinny jeans are cutting off the blood flow to your brain," I said.

Kim almost choked on her coffee.

Cisco shook his head. "Think I'll hitch a ride home." He shoved the last half of the sandwich into his mouth and stood up. "It's been nice."

"Take me with you!" I said, holding my arm out dramatically. "Don't leave me with the evil ones."

Cisco managed a crooked smile. "You're on your own." He clasped my hand for just a second, long enough for me to get a swimming feeling in my chest, like my heart was made of jelly. Then he let go. I felt a flush creep up my cheeks. He was out the door. When I came back to reality, Sara was talking. Big shock.

She snapped her fingers in front of my face. "Hey. Are you listening, Christa?"

"Yeah, er. Sort of," I answered.

Kim watched me with a glitter in her eyes. Did she know? "Now that Elvis has left the building, maybe we can talk mustangs."

"Elvis?" I said innocently, as if I didn't know.

Sara almost spit the coke out of her mouth as she laughed. "I think it's cute to see Christa around boys. She doesn't get out much."

I breathed a sigh of relief. So Sara didn't know.

Kim grew serious. "I don't want to see the Lost Herd rounded up."

That brought me back to full attention.

She leaned forward on her elbows. "I can't believe what you saw out there in the desert. Guys sneaking around at night building things on public land. It's creepy."

"I know. What are we gonna do about it?"

Sara brushed her hair back from her face. "James Miller has agreed to help us circulate petitions to stop the round-ups. Wherever he shows up, a million girls are bound to follow."

"James Miller?" I said, incredulous.

Sara grinned devilishly. "He's the new face of the Save the Mustang movement."

"How did you manage that?" I asked.

"I got a hold of him last night," Sara said nonchalantly, as if this was an everyday occurrence.

"Whoa…you work fast," Kim said. "Hold of him how?"

"On Facebook," Sara said and laughed. "Such a dirty mind, Kimberly."

"Okay, enough about boys!" I blurted out. "We've got work to do."

The hamster wheel in my brain spun wildly. "The petitions will put some pressure on Bob Downs, but we need to hit the BLM hard enough to stop the summer round-ups."

Sara and Kim nodded in agreement.

All three of my brain cells were firing now. "That means we need to do more than get petitions signed…maybe we can stage a protest outside of the BLM office."

"We can make signs that say SAVE THE LOST HERD!" Kim said.

"Yeah," I said. "And SAVE THE FOALS, KEEP OUR WILD MUSTANGS FREE, that kind of stuff."

Sara raised an eyebrow appreciatively. "Okay. We'll focus on the foals, too, for the protest. That's a good angle."

"And, it's the Year of the Horse," I said.

"Yeah, let's catch that wave," Kim said. "We could make t-shirts."

"That would be cool," I said. Then I thought of Jenner standing alone in his stall and my smile faded. "I think I need to get back to Jenner."

Kim swallowed the last bit of her coffee. "You rehab your horse. We're on the protest."

"Not without me. I can do two things at once!" I said.

Sara met my eyes. "Try doing one thing without messing it up."

"Thanks for that vote of confidence." I stared right back at her until she blinked.

Kim held her hands between us like a referee at a boxing match. "Break it up, girls. This round is over." Her eyes sparkled with steely determination. "Save that energy for the real fight, Christa. You're gonna need it."

CHAPTER 36

I REMEMBERED LOVING A pony once. I remembered spending hours with that pony, braiding his mane, brushing him, and laying on his back while he grazed in the pasture. Lately, I could barely picture Lucky, as if he were a black-and-white photograph faded to yellow. So I took those memories of Lucky and channeled them into new ones with Jenner. I iced Jenner's hock, took him for short walks down the barn aisle, changed his bandages, and kept an eye on his stitches. I found things to keep me busy in the barn so I could be close to him. Sometimes I'd just stand in his stall and breathe with him. He'd blink his long lashes and stare at me with a shy eye. In those moments, my heart melted like ice cream left out in the sun.

Amazing what you could learn about a horse by just watching. He slept standing up in the afternoon and laid flat out in his turnout in the late morning sun. He napped at eight o'clock for about a half hour right after he ate. Eastwood and Star rested then, too. As far as horses went, he was tidy. When I mucked stalls, Star and Eastwood's stall looked like a bomb went off, but Jenner's was clean. He pooped in one corner in a neat pile. When I turned the other horses out to pasture, he'd call out to them, especially Star. After I brought them back in, he'd touch noses with them and murmur.

Jenner began to meet me at the stall door with a soft nicker and a sparkle in his eye each morning. He ate more and more every day and took long pulls of water from the trough. I braided his mane and searched out itchy patches of skin. I found the magic place to scratch him halfway down his neck. When I hit it just right, he'd stretch his head forward and wiggle his upper lip in ecstasy. I scratched his withers, and he'd swing his head around so he could nuzzle my back. His upper lip moved in circles over my shoulders with the perfect amount of pressure.

I'd seen the Lost Herd grooming each other this way, but they used their teeth and really chomped on each other. Maybe that's why I'd never wanted a massage from a horse before. But Jenner avoided using his teeth and it felt nice. With his giant neck wrapped around me, I all but disappeared in his warmth.

I brought my laptop to the barn and while Jenner rested, I signed every online petition I could find to save the mustangs. Sara surfed the Internet and put us on the mailing list for all the Wild Horse advocates in Nevada. Before I knew it, I was writing letters to congressmen, senators and even the President of the United States. What a step up from writing Bob Downs! I hunted for information on the Wild Horse Relocation Program, but came up empty.

At night, Kim, Sara and I hit up coffee houses, libraries and restaurants armed with pens, clipboards and signs that read: SAVE THE LOST HERD! PROTECT OUR WILD MUSTANGS! Sara's video from the Towhee Roundup went viral and we blew up pictures Dad had taken of the foal with the injured leg and passed them around. When we told them how young the foals were and how the BLM was planning to do the July roundups in secret, most people got angry enough to sign our petitions.

Kim and Sara used their charm and James Miller's star status to draw the locals. He rarely showed up in person, but I got to meet him at Red's Diner one night. Even though I wasn't the boy predator that Sara was, I had to admit he was freaking gorgeous.

His broad shoulders, green eyes, and curly blonde hair nearly knocked me out. But his easy smile and concern for the mustangs are what really impressed me.

Unfortunately for Sara, when James did make an appearance, he always had an entourage. Girls flocked to James like he was a rock star. Sara didn't let that sidetrack her from our purpose. While James oozed charisma, Sara shoved the petition to stop the round-ups in the girls' awed faces and they signed.

Red's Diner became our hangout. Red, a big guy with a beer belly, was all for us bringing in customers. He even gave us cokes and french fries for free once in a while. We printed and posted newsletters stating the BLM's plans to zero out the last of the wild mustang herds in Nevada, and stories of how thousands of horses stood in holding pens. We hooked the old-timers in town when we explained that it was our money–taxpayers' money– that was going to feed all the wild horses in captivity. More and more people turned up to sign our petitions. They said they thought there were millions of wild horses running around on the range and it was all the BLM could do to keep the herd population in check. "Yeah," we said, "that's what the BLM wants everybody to think."

Meanwhile, back at home, Dad dropped in regularly to assess Jenner's progress. By the end of week two when we stripped off the bandages, the wounds looked clean. "You've done a good job here, Christa." He patted my shoulder. "I think you can take him out today. Might do him some good to walk now." He caught my arm in a firm grip as I went in to halter Jenner. "It's important you understand something. He can't run yet, or even trot."

"Okay, Dad!" I said, wriggling out of his grasp.

"His hock still needs time to heal, and the stitches could still come out in his stomach if you're not careful."

"Got it," I said. I couldn't blame him for being worried. "I'll be really careful, Dad."

Jenner nudged my arm playfully and bumped the stall door with his nose. Dad laughed. "Looks like you're getting your old horse back."

"Sure does," I said, putting Jenner's halter on him and stroking his neck. I leaned into Jenner and buried my face in his mane. A strange thing was happening. As long as I was standing near him, I could think of Lucky without breaking into pieces. I still missed Lucky something terrible. There was a hole he'd left in my heart as big as Nevada, but the least I could do for Jenner was to try and live with it.

"Any news on the Lost Herd, Dad?"

"We got word from the Millers this morning that the herd disappeared again. No one's seen them for a week now."

Maybe they had slipped into the slot canyon after all. "Wouldn't it be awesome if the legend were true and we could never ever catch them?"

Dad scuffed the heel of his boot along the barn floor. "This might not have a happy ending, you know."

Suddenly everything went very quiet. "I know."

Dad scratched his whiskered cheeks. "Went to see Bob Downs this morning with Kim's father," he said. "Bob didn't have much to say."

"I bet you had Mr. Downs sweating behind that big desk of his."

Dad nodded. "Don't know if it will change anything, but we said our piece."

I leaned on the stall door. "Better than doing nothing."

"Doing nothing is not an option anymore," Dad said over his shoulder as he walked back to the house. He managed not to look back to check if I was handling Jenner right.

Jenner and I walked slowly outside. I gazed out to the pasture and watched Star chase Eastwood up the hill. She galloped in long graceful strides, tossing her head, and Eastwood bucked playfully, his golden tail a sunny contrast to Star's black mane as she caught up to him. They paused at the top, touched noses, and dropped their heads to graze under the big oak tree. Lucky's grave. With a start, I realized I hadn't been to visit his grave or even bring him flowers since we buried him. Maybe it was time I did.

CHAPTER 37

I WALKED WITH JENNER to the top of the hill and kneeled down at a mound of dirt where small white stones spelled "Lucky." I pulled the sparse weeds that had sprung up around the stones, yanking them up by the roots until I'd cleaned it up. Then I placed some wildflowers I'd picked on top of the stones.

I love you, Lucky. You were so beautiful.

Jenner nudged my arm. Star and Eastwood stopped grazing and stood quietly. The wind rattled the dry oak leaves above our heads and whispered through my skin. *I wish I could call you now and you could come, but I don't know where you are.*

A crow landed in the tree and cawed down at us. I sighed and drew the plait of Lucky's hair out of my pocket. I squeezed it close to my heart as the wind groaned through the arching branches above us. The ever-present ache lifted enough for me to take a deep breath.

I turned and saw Grandma making her way up the hill. "Hey, Grandma," I said, as I stood up.

"I've got something I want to give you," she announced, waving. When she reached us, she removed the green scarf from around her neck. "I suppose I should've given this to you a long time ago, but it never occurred to me until now."

It was the silk scarf she always wore, the one with the horses. "Grandma, you can't give me that scarf. It's so...*you.*"

"Then it's mine to give." She patted me on the shoulder. Grandma spread the scarf on the ground. I'd never seen it laid out before. Three horses ran together, encircled by an intricate braid. Jenner sniffed it. "Remember when you were little and I told you stories from Ireland?" she asked.

I'd loved escaping into the worlds Grandma had created with her words. "Yeah. Faery folk and castles and curses and goddesses..."

Grandma chuckled. "Well, this scarf represents a Celtic Horse goddess known as Epona. Her magic is horse magic."

I leaned in to take a closer look. "Horse magic?"

Grandma traced the design in the scarf. The breeze billowed, sending the horses running with the wind under them, and suddenly, Star and Eastwood took off at a gallop. A shiver ran down my spine. Jenner's head shot up and he tensed. I tugged on his lead rope. "Don't even think about it," I said. He nudged my arm with his muzzle and settled. "So who is this Epona?"

"Epona is a protectress of horses."

"She protects horses?" I asked, my mouth dropping open. "Where was she when I needed her?"

Jenner stuck his head between Grandma and me. She ran her hand down his nose. "Well, that's part of the mystery. She might have shown up for you without you knowing it was her...it's said she can appear in the form of a horse."

I smoothed the wrinkles in the scarf and traced the twisting knot design that surrounded the horses. "What's this?"

Grandma lifted the scarf from the ground and held it up. "See how it never ends? It's the infinite path we're on of life and death, faith, and loyalty. We're all connected by our loves, our losses, even our mistakes…woven together in a giant tapestry. You, the horses, your family, and all of nature."

I liked that idea. I'd never heard things described that way before.

Grandma wrapped the scarf loosely around my neck and tied it. "My mother gave it to me when I was a girl. Now it belongs to you."

I didn't know what to say. My skin felt good where the silk rested, and my cheeks flushed with sudden shyness. "Sure you don't want it?" I asked.

She fussed with my hair and adjusted the scarf. "It's all yours."

Grandma had given me something so nice, and I didn't have anything I could give in return. Or did I? "I want you to have this." I held Lucky's braid out to Grandma.

Grandma took it from me and kissed my cheek. "I'd be honored to hold onto this for you," she said softly, her eyes glistening with tears. "Let's get off this hill before I get all emotional."

"Don't cry, Grandma," I said and took her hand.

Together, we walked back to the house.

CHAPTER 38

AS JENNER HEALED, we weaned him off the painkillers, and his energy came back strong as ever. Each day during our walks he tested me, and this morning was no exception. Our first step out of the barn he tried to jig ahead of me, but I sent him back with a flick of the lead rope. "I'm in charge now. We aren't having it any other way," I said firmly. He raised his head high and stared me down. I stood at my full height and stared back. "You can't trot and that's that," I said.

He took a step forward. I flicked the end of the lead rope toward him. "Not until I say so, Jenner." He pawed his front leg. I cocked my hip and held his gaze. "I can wait here all day for you to settle down. If you can't behave, you'll be going back to your stall."

After a minute, his eyes slid away from mine and he lowered his head. "That's better," I said softly, handing him a carrot. He chewed with relish. "There's a lot more of these in your future if you mind your manners," I said. "C'mon, I'll show you."

I led him around to the side of the barn. He walked calmly at my shoulder, his ears pricked forward and a sparkle in his eye. When I stopped and pointed to the ground, he sniffed out an apple I'd hidden in the tall grass. His eyes were so wide with wonder I nearly laughed out loud.

I hid treats for Jenner all throughout the property. Each day we walked a little further on our treasure hunts, until one day we walked right out the gates. When Jenner let me lead him along the shoulder of County Road 7 on a loose line, I knew we were making big progress.

Of course, I'd played the treasure hunt game with Lucky, along with anything else I could make up. Why hadn't I done any of that with Jenner until now? I guess I'd been in too much of a hurry. Or I'd forgotten how to play like a little girl.

When Dad let me ride Jenner, we started in the ring, and slowly, we edged out onto the trail. Dad suggested I start working with Cisco and Jenner once a week. I didn't think that would be a big hardship for me to see a little more of Cisco. But suddenly, the thought of riding with him made me nervous.

On the morning of our first ride together, I paced in front of the bedroom window, obsessively scanning down to the driveway for his truck. My hair was misbehaving as always.

I was so over myself and my stupid hair.

Sara was getting ready to go out with some friends. While she gazed at herself in the mirror, running a brush through her silken hair, she rambled on about Dylan's latest crushes.

Sara was never over herself.

"Why don't you just marry him and get it over with?" I asked.

She blushed. "We're just friends!"

"Well then stop talking about him all the time," I said, wishing in the same breath that I could stop thinking about Cisco all the time—who was just a friend. Gah! And then I had an idea. I changed tack. "Sara, can you do something with my hair?" I asked in my Sweet Potato voice.

She sprang up from her chair and made me sit down. "I thought you'd never ask." Using some spray she had on the dresser, she tamed my snake's nest hair into gentle waves of red.

"Cool, thanks," I said, sweeping it back into a ponytail with a hair tie on my wrist.

"Christa! Don't ruin it."

I slipped the hair tie out." Okay. But I'm going riding."

She looked me over, hand on her hip. "Hmmm…let's braid it, then," she said. Quickly, she wove my thick mane into one braid on the side. I couldn't believe my eyes. It actually looked good. "Sara, you're a magician!" I said, awed.

"I'm not finished yet." She rifled through her closet and emerged with her old cowboy hat and placed it on my head. I almost didn't recognize myself.

"It's better than that pink baseball cap," she said, adjusting the hat and pulling the braid in front of my shoulder. "Now for some lip gloss and a little color on your cheeks–" She stopped and fixed me with a stare. "So what's the occasion? You've never let me do this before."

"I'm just going riding," I said.

Her radar locked in on me. "With who?"

I felt a flush stain my cheeks. I hesitated one second too long, and she honed in on me like a missile with a tracking device. "My little sister's got a crush on Cisco!" she taunted, dancing around me. She grabbed my hands and dragged me to the bed. "You're going riding with Cisco!"

I ripped away from her grasp and spun toward the wall. Panic rose from some dark corner of my mind, flooding my whole body. "Sara! You don't get it."

She grew quiet. "What don't I get?"

I turned my face to hers. "He likes Amy Whitehorse."

She sighed. "Ah, young love. So painful."

I scowled. Her sarcasm drove me to the door. "Just don't ever mention him again."

Her eyes softened. "But you look adorable."

"Yeah, right."

"Especially when you're grouchy," she called after me as I left the room.

I scuffled out to the barn. By the time the white Dodge rumbled down the drive, I had my thoughts in order and my heart carefully subdued. There was nothing between Cisco and me except a big red horse named Jenner. And we had lots of work to do to get that horse safe and sound.

Cisco cut the engine and hopped out of the truck. Faded jeans, beat up t-shirt and a cowboy hat low over his face. I swear he was even taller than the last time I saw him. "Hey, Christa."

"Hey. Driving alone? Did you turn sixteen or something?"

He reached into the front seat for his wallet. "I've got my permit. You wanna see it?"

I grinned. "A permit means you have to drive with someone else to be legal, right?"

He glanced back at the horse trailer he was hauling. "Oh, I've got Doc with me in the trailer," he said, a slow smile spreading across his face.

"Doc?"

Cisco nodded and circled back to the trailer. "He's the little mustang I've been working with at the Miller's. Feel like going for a trail ride?"

Out came Doc, the cutest buckskin I'd ever seen. He was a little shy at first, but he warmed up to me in no time. It only took about three carrots and a nose rub for him to see I was okay. He had the most soulful eyes I'd ever seen.

We saddled up and hit the trail. Cisco wanted to see me cross the Carn River on Jenner. I told him that might be shooting a little high for our first day. While we walked down the trail, Cisco rode behind us and studied Jenner's gait. He said he was moving sound, even uphill. That was the best news I'd had in a long time.

Wispy clouds drifted lazily across a sun blazing so hot, it raised streams of sweat down my back. I wiped the dampness from my face with my sleeve. Cisco brought Doc alongside us, and I snuck a glance at him. "Do you think Doc misses the wild?"

"I don't know. Sometimes I catch him looking out to the hills, but I guess it's better than standing in a holding pen or being sold for slaughter."

"Is he hard to train?"

"I have to move real slow around him. He's got a good kick in him when he's startled. Besides that he's curious and really smart.

Cisco sure seemed smart. "Are you good at school?" I asked, lamely.

He shook his head. "I'm good at being bored at school. You?"

Saddles creaked. Doc bumped Jenner with his nose and Jenner sneezed. "My grades kind of dropped this year. I mean, like, they slid to the bottom of a C."

"Just don't get used to it down there."

"Well, I got an A on my essay about the Lost Herd," I said, defensively. Grandma had helped me write it, but he didn't need to know that.

He adjusted his hat and looked straight ahead. "Grades go up, grades go down. The tide goes in and out, things live and die. It's just the world breathing." I tried to wipe the shocked expression off my face. Who is this guy?

"Wow. That was pretty deep."

He shrugged. "Just basic stuff."

I laughed. "Maybe so, but I have no idea what you're talking about."

"We don't have to talk."

I squirmed and cleared my throat. "So, what do you want to do in this big world?"

"I want to go to Spain, Portugal and France. Live over there for a while."

He sure wasn't who I imagined him to be, and who he was made my pulse race and my mind spin. "I've only been to Disneyland," I managed to say. "I can't think of anything besides horses that I want to do."

He simply nodded. We rode on in silence until we reached Carn River. At the sight of the water, Jenner started acting up, dancing in place and snorting.

Stabs of fear prickled my skin. "You go first," I said, turning Jenner in a wide circle.

"Nope. Today, you're going to be the leader."

"But—"

"Just do what I say, and you'll be fine."

Butterflies were fist-fighting in my stomach, but I nodded.

Cisco pulled Doc to a stop and leaned back casually in the saddle. "Back him up to where he's not so excited, and get off of him."

"What?"

"You heard me."

I walked Jenner a few paces back from the river until he settled. "But if I get off him, he's just getting the best of me!"

Cisco pushed his hat back and scratched his head. "If you can't cross a stream on your own horse, isn't he kind of getting the best of you already?"

I had to admit he had a point. I sighed in defeat and dismounted.

"Good. Now lead him across the stream."

That was the most ridiculous thing I'd ever heard. As if I could lead Jenner across the stream. I knew for a fact Jenner and water didn't mix. A demented vision of Jenner taking off and pulling me behind him like a waterskier flashed through my mind. Maybe we could make a YouTube video of me zooming past the camera trying to hold onto my hat while drowning. I bent over and laughed until my eyes teared up.

"When you're done laughing," he added.

That made me laugh more. Jenner took a step away from the river toward Doc. It was time to stop laughing and start leading. After all, what did I have to lose?

I walked as confidently as I could to the river's edge and stepped into the cold water, gripping the reins. They tightened in my hand for just an instant as Jenner pulled back against me, and then to my amazement I felt them go slack. I turned to see Jenner following me, his head craned down to try and see through the water to the bottom.

"Look where you're going, don't look down," he said.

I kept walking through the cold water, slipping on rocks and soaking my jeans up to my waist. But I was smiling, all the way to the other side.

Cisco called from the shore. "Good, now bring him back."

We slogged back across the river, docile as two lambs. Jenner stopped a couple of times, but started moving again with a tug or two on the reins. Cisco had us do that over and over until Jenner could have cared less about that little stream.

We returned to Cisco, dripping wet. "How can leading a horse across the water cure them of their fear?" I asked.

He shook his head. "There's this old trainer named Bill Dodge I've been learning from. He said this trick doesn't work all the time, but it's worth a try."

"Because I'm leading him, and he doesn't have to go first?"

Cisco nodded. "Maybe."

We took a lunch break, and then with strict instructions from Cisco, I got on Jenner and rode him all the way across the river without stopping. And that was just our first day!

After that, Cisco came by every few days with Doc. He said we needed practice, so we located all the water we could find in the Sage Mountains and got down to the business of crossing rivers. Some were deep, some were shallow. Some moved fast, and some were more like lakes, but Jenner and I got across every single one.

There was one day I'll never forget. It was our fifth ride together, and everything that could spook a horse was out there on the trail. We had high winds, tree branches down, plastic bags fluttering wildly from low branches and birds exploding out of thickets inches from Jenner's nose. Doc was spooking like the devil was on his shoulder, and Cisco had his hands full. When Jenner crossed the Little Humboldt without so much as a head toss, Cisco met us on the shore with a rare grin. "You're ready," he said.

"For what?"

He shrugged. "Anything."

CHAPTER 39

IN SPITE OF the shadow of dread hanging over me about the wild horses, the month of July had a few happy surprises. Cisco invited our whole family to see his big blue-ribbon win in the barrels competition at the Albright rodeo. The Millers were ecstatic and Sara had never clapped louder. Of course, when I followed her gaze she was looking at James Miller sitting in the bleachers, and not at Doc, who was down running his butt off in the arena, but that was to be expected.

The Lost Herd was rumored to be back in the Twin River Valley again, but I resisted any urges I had to race out to see them. I wanted Jenner one hundred percent before I pushed him that far or fast ever again and I could do more for the wild horses right in Spring Hills.

We organized a protest to stop all the July roundups. We printed up 'Year of the Horse' t-shirts and sold them to cover our costs. People began marching with signs in front of the BLM building. Because of all the protesting, petitions, and letters, we got the roundups delayed. It felt like a big victory and fired us up even more, but we knew August would come soon enough. At least the foals had one more month of growing to gain strength in their legs before the sound of a rotor would blast over their heads, but it wasn't much consolation. I shuddered, thinking of the Lost Herd on the top of the BLM's round-up list.

The wild horse sanctuary had hit a roadblock. The BLM was stalling in the negotiations. I continued to sign all of Elizabeth Levine's petitions, and she even emailed me back, but she said this could take time. Although it stood at the top of the mountain of the most exciting things to happen to the wild mustangs, it would only benefit some of the horses standing in holding pens. I was more determined than ever to keep the Lost Herd free, racking my brain every day for a way to protect them.

While I dreamed and lived horses, Grandma kept Mom busy. They transformed the tiny room down the hall from ours into a baby sanctuary. Grandma painted Hazel's room a spring green, and Mom added a forest decal to one wall. With the angels floating over the crib and the sun streaming through the imaginary tree branches, it looked like something out of a fairy tale.

I wished Grandma would stay with us forever, but Mom was stronger now, and Grandma said she'd probably be going home in a few weeks. I couldn't bear to think of her leaving. I decided I'd put off worrying about that until her suitcases were packed.

The last week of July was an oven, and we baked under a cloudless sky. The sun burned so hot, I feared it would melt our clothes right onto our skin. Sara, Kim and I spent hours at the swimming hole with the horses grazing lazily in the shade along the shore. We all got tan. Well, actually, I turned red and more freckled than usual, while Sara and Kim turned copper and dark brown and looked like movie stars.

I invited Cisco to join us at Walden Pond, but I guess he was too cool to get into the water. He watched us from the shore in the shade of the big cottonwood, his cowboy hat pulled down low over his big brown eyes. Elvis and Chico panted by his side.

From his perspective, we must have been quite a sight—the three of us girls wading with our horses, having water fights and laughing at almost anything any of us said. It felt like all four of us and our faithful horses were wrapped in a magical cocoon... one I wanted to last forever.

CHAPTER 40

AFTER WEEKS OF blue skies and punishing sun, the clouds gathering over the Sage Mountains were a welcoming sight. Sara and I sat on the front porch, swatting at flies and drinking iced tea. It was so hot we were sweating more than the glasses. When the wind came up, we sighed and held our shirts out from our bodies, hoping for some relief.

"Oh great Rain Gods, please bless us with your sacred water," Sara called dramatically to the mountains.

Elvis and Chico emerged from under the front porch. Elvis stretched.

"Not exactly what I had in mind," Sara said.

I shrugged. "Dog is God spelled backward." Chico began digging in Mom's vegetable garden. "Hey, Chico," I called half-heartedly, "don't make a mess. Be a good boy."

Chico didn't look up. His paws churned furiously as a pile of dirt flew out behind him.

"He's obsessed," Sara said.

"He's gotta dig deep for those carrots." No sooner did the words leave my mouth than an idea blasted into my heat-addled brain. I clapped my hands over my head. "I can't believe I didn't think of this earlier."

Sara crunched an ice cube and fanned her face with a Teen Vogue magazine. "What now?"

"Remember when Dad said he thought it was probably a mining company building something on the range?"

Sara nodded.

"Well, if that's true, then it's either somebody digging for gold, silver, copper, or gas...but regardless, somebody's making a big mess."

"If there was precious metal out there, they would've probably dug it up by now." A light dawned in Sara's eyes. "I'm thinking we should do some research on what kind of a mess you can make when you dig around for gas."

Sara typed furiously on her cell phone. "They either get the gas by importing it from somewhere else like the Rocky Mountains through a pipeline, or they dig it up doing something called fracking. There's a long list of bad stuff that can happen when they frack. Water pollution, air pollution, and danger to livestock to mention a few." She rubbed her eyes. "I can't believe what I'm reading. They blast tons of water and toxic chemicals down into the shale to break it up so they can get the gas out. The chemicals don't get cleaned up. They stay in the ground and poison everything."

"Oh my God," I said, horrified. "That could kill the horses."

"Christa, this isn't just about the wild mustangs anymore. Once those chemicals and gas get into our water, they'll poison us, too."

"How would they get into our water?"

"We drill wells because there's water deep under the ground, stupid."

I groaned. "Let's print everything out we can find and email it to Bob Downs."

"You don't expect Bob Downs to do anything, do you?"

"Nope." I swigged the last of my iced tea and picked up my phone. "I've got another idea." I tapped 411 and asked for the

BLM office in Albright. They connected me and the phone rang. I put my phone on speaker and placed it between Sara and me on the side table. When the receptionist answered, I spoke with a drawl and tried to make my voice sound older. "Is Bob Downs there, sweetie?"

Sara's eyebrow shot up.

"No, I'm sorry. He's stepped out. Can I take a message?"

"I'm callin' from that company you know and love with the spiral logo…"

"Abbot Oil & Gas?"

Sara typed the letters into her phone and held it up. Abbot Oil & Gas had a website. Beside it was their logo… a spiral.

I cleared my throat. "That's the one, honey. My boss has got some good news for Bob. He'd like to fly in and take him out to dinner tonight if he's available."

Sara smirked.

"Bob's schedule is free tonight."

"Does six p.m. at Red's Diner sound okay? Good. Now, there's only one detail I've left out." I waited a beat and then spoke in a hushed voice. "My boss wants to keep this visit a surprise till the last minute."

"Oh, don't worry," the receptionist gushed. "You can trust me. I'll have him there by six p.m. tonight and he won't know a thing." She laughed. "He eats at Red's seven nights out of the week as it is."

"I can't thank you enough for your cooperation Miss…"

"It's Miss Kristin Reed. And you tell Mr. Simmons hello for me."

"I sure will. Y'all take care." I hit end.

Sara giggled and slumped back in her chair. "That was awesome! You're killing me over here, Christa." Then the smile faded from her face. "So, Simmons is the name of the creepy guy with the limo and the snake-skin boots."

"And Abbot Oil and Gas is the name of the company he runs."

She scanned their website. "It says here that Abbot Oil and Gas extracts gas using hydraulic fracturing." She looked up at me. "That's what fracking is."

I nodded impatiently.

She went back to reading. "And then they export it with a pipeline. Oh no. That means they'll have to put a pipeline in on the range."

"Yeah, after they blast the range to bits and poison everything." I shuddered. Gas meant everything to us humans...the power to heat our homes and run our machines. We'd tear the heart right out of the wilderness for that kind of power. "Email me a list of articles on gas pipelines and fracking," I said. "Let's write an email to Bob right now."

> *Dear Mr. Bob Downs,*
>
> *I have reason to suspect that a certain gas company, known as Abbot Oil & Gas is surveying out on public land. I saw a crew of men working out there at night a few weeks ago. I know what they're doing and you know, too. That's public land and nobody asked the public if it was okay to put a gas pipeline in. Weren't you supposed to be protecting the horses and the land? Don't you care about this community?*
>
> *Please see the attached list of articles on how the air and water are affected by fracking. Spoiler alert: gas poisons the air and the water. Oh, and did you know the chemicals they use for fracking cause cancer? It doesn't take a genius to figure out that it's bad for everybody.*

We'll be marching outside your office all summer protesting the roundups and the Abbot Oil & Gas company.

I don't think Mr. Simmons is going to like it.

Sincerely,

Christa and Sara Cassidy

Within minutes, we'd written and sent the email. Now that I knew what Abbot Oil and Gas were doing I felt worse than ever. This fight kept getting bigger.

The clouds that had been gathering over the mountains blew in and rain began to fall in small delicate drops, spattering the driveway and making little puddles in the sun-baked ground. A rush of cooler air mingled with the scorching heat, soothing my skin.

We ran out into the front yard and spun in circles with our chins pointed up to the sky, letting the water run down our faces and soak our hair. "Oh, thank you Rain Gods!" Sara cried.

I held my arms out and let the rain wash over me. We splashed in the water with our bare feet and sighed with relief. The sun was still fighting for center stage, but the wind smeared the monstrous, billowing cloud bank around the sky until it blotted out every last ray of light. It was only two o'clock in the afternoon, but the day grew still. The birds stopped singing.

"This might be more than a friendly little rainstorm," I said, looking out to the Sage Mountains. Clouds sat over the ridges like a giant serpent, growing darker and more ominous by the minute.

Sara splashed out of a puddle. "It did get awfully quiet."

We paused. The air had an electric charge to it that made me bold and alert. The sky took on an eerie green glow.

The wind came up out of nowhere and gusted with such force it toppled the chairs on the front porch and sent them skidding into the rails. The rain pelted down harder and harder and turned to hail. We ran back to the shelter of the front porch, cowering. A bolt of lightning sizzled out of the sky and struck the ground only inches from where we'd been standing with a crack that sounded like a bomb exploding. We heard a shrill whinny from Star across the pasture.

"Oh my God, the horses!" Sara said.

"The horses!" We pulled on our boots and raced to the pasture where they were pacing anxiously at the gate. Mom's voice carried across the yard screaming at us to get back inside this instant.

As soon as Star, Eastwood, and Jenner were safely in the barn, we made a run for the house. Fingers of lightning flickered and lit up the yard like a strobe light. Thunder rumbled and rolled, an angry dragon ready to blow us down. We screamed as we raced through the rivers forming on the ground and flew across the gravel driveway to the front porch, hoping the whole while that lightning wouldn't strike us as we ran. The rain streamed down in such a thick spray, we couldn't see an inch in front of our faces. I could barely hear Mom over the howling of the wind.

"You two are soaking wet! Both of you get upstairs and get your clothes changed. I don't want you catching colds."

Sara slipped out of her boots. "You're the boss." We were both crackling with energy. I bumped her with my shoulder, knocking her off balance. She pushed me back.

"Girls, settle down," Mom commanded. "Did you see that lightning?" She shook her head at us. "I want you both right here under this roof where I can see you. This is the kind of storm that can split trees in half and blow cars off the road."

She switched the TV to KGBA news.

A reporter excitedly pointed to a map darkened by storm

radar. "We've got breaking news. A major front is moving through Albright County, and we're issuing severe storm warnings for tonight and tomorrow."

"Maybe the Rain God is mad because you woke him up," I whispered to Sara.

She punched my arm.

Mom shook her head. "Get outta those wet clothes. NOW!"

Sara headed for the stairs. "Okay, okay!"

"When's Dad getting home?" I asked Mom.

"Any minute. He went to town to run some errands with Grandma." Mom's eyes were fixed on the TV.

Sara nudged me with her elbow. "Come on, Christa, race you up the stairs!"

"Not fair, you had a head start!" I tried to reach out and trip her with my hand, but she slipped out of my grasp with her wet legs.

By the time we got downstairs in dry clothes, Dad and Grandma were coming through the door with bags of groceries filling their arms. They looked like they'd gone swimming in their clothes. It was dark as night outside. Wind and rain battered the windows. Grandma nodded a hello without so much as a smile and walked straight up the stairs to her room.

"Some storm, huh?" I moved to help Dad with the soggy bags. His jaw was set, and there was no sign of the usual good humor in his eyes. "Dad, we found out that Abbot Oil & Gas is the company I saw working that night on the range."

"Is that so?" He leaned against the counter and rubbed the back of his neck.

"Dad, what's up?" I asked.

He shook his head. "It's not good news…"

Sara grabbed a bag of pretzels and sat at the table. "Who died?"

Dad hesitated. Mom looked up from unloading groceries. The

rain came down so hard it sounded like we were in a kettledrum being played by giant hammers. "The rain started at dawn today in the Sage Mountains," Dad said, "and parts of the Twin River refuge have flooded."

"That's where the Lost Herd was," I whispered.

"There are reports that they're still there." Dad met my eyes. "Jack Marshall told me the horses are clustered on the highest ground they could find, but they're running out of time. The rains are raising the rivers and flooding the valley. Water is rushing in from the slot canyon. The Twin Rivers are as big as a lake." Dad stepped closer, his voice soft now. "Horses are drowning trying to cross."

"Drowning," I said. A horrible picture formed in my mind, a picture of wild horses swimming and drowning...like the nightmare I'd had where Jenner had sunk underneath me. "But the horses should've been able to sense the storm coming," I said. Why didn't they leave the valley?"

Dad sat down at the table next to Sara. "Jack suspected that the fencing from your gas company along the north boundary of the park could've stopped them. And there are rumors that the BLM was trying to round up the herd with a helicopter just before the storm broke. You know the parks don't want wild horses on their land."

"Nobody does." I clenched my teeth and swallowed my anger. "The horses have enemies everywhere." I refused to even think of the gas issue. You can only concentrate on so many disasters at once. "Well, we have to do something!"

"Yes, of course we do," Mom said.

"There's going to be a meeting tomorrow to discuss a rescue." Dad struggled with his wet boots, finally kicking them off. "Most of the ranchers could care less about the wild horses, but some of them are concerned. And a lot of other folks care. They've contacted the BLM. Together we can coordinate a rescue effort with the park rangers."

I tried to picture saving two hundred horses from a flood. We hadn't even been able to get them into a slot canyon.

Dad must've read my face. "A rescue is not going to be easy," he said. "If this storm doesn't let up, it may be impossible."

I tried to force my heartbeats and breaths to follow some sort of order. "We have to save them!" The rain, which had been so welcome an hour ago, was now the enemy, a power so great it could destroy the lives of the Lost Herd. I felt my spirit would drown with them.

I collapsed into a chair. How could this be happening? Grandma entered the room with dry clothes on. "Let's try and stay calm, everyone," she said, glancing at me, but she looked worried, too. She put the kettle on for tea and started a pot of coffee. "This storm is just getting started, Harrison. What can we do?"

Dad glanced briefly at Grandma. "That's what we're going to discuss tomorrow. We can take small boats out to them, and at least throw them some hay. We can also try to help them cross the river, which according to Jack is more like an ocean now. The BLM may have some ideas."

"That'll be the day," I grumbled.

"They're bringing Bob Downs in from Albright tomorrow to discuss the rescue."

"Bob!" Sara groaned. "All he does is lie to us."

I felt a wild flutter of panic. "The BLM doesn't care about saving wild horses. As far as they're concerned, this storm can save them a helicopter run." A bitter thought pushed its way into my mind and out of my mouth. "They can reduce the wild herds by another two hundred horses without lifting a finger."

"Christa, that's enough!" Mom admonished. "They aren't bad people."

"Do you really believe that?" I asked.

Sara turned on Mom. "Well, how do we know what kind of people they are?"

"Exactly my point," Mom said. "We don't know any of them."

I bit my nails with furious zeal. "Bob hasn't given me the chance to get to know him. He's avoided me at every turn. I don't trust him. Even if he can coordinate this rescue, who knows whether he'll let the horses go free again or keep them in holding pens!" I said.

The teakettle whistled, and we all jumped. Mom rushed to turn off the stove. Grandma stood next to her, silently pouring the steaming water into mugs. The smell of chamomile with lemon and honey filled the kitchen.

"The girls are right," Dad said firmly. "We just don't know where the chips are going to fall." He looked from Sara to me, his eyes full of compassion. "I'll find out more tomorrow."

"I'm going with you to that meeting tomorrow," I said.

Sara tossed her silky hair back out of her face. "I'm going, too."

Dad managed a wry smile. "The meeting is at eight a.m. The truck leaves at seven."

Sara was already on the phone to Kim. Of course she was coming. The three of us had made a promise that if anything ever threatened this herd, we would do everything in our power to help them. I knew I had to or die trying.

CHAPTER 41

AS NIGHT FELL, lightning shocked the sky and lit the bedroom. I climbed into bed, gathering the covers around me. The rain lashed at the windows and pelted the roof. The Lost Herd was out there in that storm. I pulled the scarf Grandma had given me out of the nightstand drawer, holding it above my head with both hands. I stretched it taut so I could see the design of the three horses running in a circle. If Epona was truly a protector of horses, now was the time to ask her for a favor.

"Dear Epona, " I whispered into the green scarf, glancing over to make sure Sara was asleep. "Please help the wild horses survive this storm." I swallowed hard, thinking of Corazón, her eyes locked on mine, her long tangled mane whipping in the wind. Thunder rumbled outside. I really hoped it wasn't the goddess trying to answer me. "Epona, who are you?"

I still couldn't quite picture her in my mind. At first I imagined her as a tall woman in a dark blue gown standing on the curve of the green, green earth, surrounded by water and mountains, her long dark hair swirling around her and hands at her sides.

Then I saw the horses.

Millions of horses of every color and shape milled around her, like in a dream. I wanted to be standing in their midst. Suddenly Epona's hair color changed to red and her skin became very pale with freckles…she looked like me! Then she morphed into a gorgeous black woman, black as night, black as Corazón. She continued to shape-shift from one skin color to another until finally, she became a black mare and melted into the sea of horses. The horses began running, their hooves the thunder of the storm, shaking the foundation of my house, tearing me from the vision. My body trembled from the power of the storm, and I knew I had to finish my appeal to Epona, whoever–whatever–she was.

"I know I made some bad mistakes," I whispered, my heart aching. "And it's too late to save Lucky. But if there's anything I can do to help the Lost Herd, anything at all, big or small, I'm up for it."

The thunder crashed so loud I thought it was going to crack the sky into little pieces. Maybe Epona didn't like me.

"Get some sleep, Christa," Sara grumbled, half asleep. "Who are you talking to anyway?" She rolled over and pulled the covers over her head.

I lay very still and pretended to snore. The last thing I needed was for Sara to find out I was talking to a Horse Goddess. As much as she drove me crazy, I needed her now more than ever.

For the first time in a long time, I didn't feel alone. I had Sara, Kim, Mom and Dad. I had Grandma and Grandpa. I had Jenner, Star and Eastwood. I was a part of them, and they were a part of me, even on the worst day, even when everything seemed hopeless, impossible and unfair.

I placed the scarf over my racing heart and tried to calm my thoughts. Tomorrow would come soon enough. And maybe we could come up with a plan to rescue the horses and set them free. I prayed the Lost Herd could survive the night in this storm. I hoped it wasn't already too late.

CHAPTER 42

T HE RAIN FELL steadily as Dad pulled into the parking lot of Red's Diner. We were glad we had our boots on when we jumped out of the car; the streets were a muddy river.

The energy in Red's was electric. Families of ranchers, miners and cattlemen, along with some artists and hippies, all crowded into the big room, filling at least twenty tables and ten u-shaped booths. I recognized Mrs. Myrtle, my speech teacher and some familiar faces from school.

Several waitresses ran from table to table, pouring coffee and frantically scribbling orders on little white pads of paper. A couple of cooks in white aprons worked behind a tall counter, slamming eggs, bacon and pancakes onto plate after plate, and spinning a metal wheel cluttered with ticket orders. The smell of strong coffee mingled with the food. Two waitresses who'd been there forever, Dolly and Lorraine, hustled the plates to the tables.

We were barely inside the door when Mrs. Miller wrapped me in one of her hugs, and then pointed to her "Year of the Horse" t-shirt.

"You keep up the good work, Christa. I've signed your petitions and seen the protests on TV. You're getting quite a following." The corners of her eyes crinkled when she smiled.

"Thank you, Mrs. Miller."

"We adults are too busy to stay on top of the wild horse issue. You kids are the future," she said.

The future! I was just hoping to get through today. "Keep your fingers crossed for the Lost Herd," I said.

Kim waved us over to her booth and introduced us to her parents, Ruben and Maria Rodriguez. Maria held my hands in her warm ones, her long dark hair swinging as she bent over to kiss my cheek. Ruben was distinguished-looking with his graying hair at the temples and perfect posture. He shook my hand formally.

We shrugged out of our rain slickers and milled through the crowd. Everyone was animated, talking, and gesturing. The Whitehorses saw us and jostled their way through the crowd. We all exchanged hugs like old friends.

"Hey, Christa," Amy said, her smile warm. "How's Jenner?"

"He's so much better thanks to you," I said. "He must have a Ph.D. in running away 'cause he was smart enough to end up at your ranch. Thanks so much for all you did for him."

"Now we're onto a whole other challenge," she said, chewing on her lip.

I nodded and swallowed hard. "We have to save them."

"I know." Her brown eyes looked like still pools of water. "They don't deserve to die like this." Amy gestured to a table in the middle of the room where she was sitting. "Looks like they're about to start the meeting."

Several men were gathering at the front of the room near the fireplace, setting up metal folding chairs for the speakers. "Okay, cool, Amy. Talk to you after," I said, then slipped into our booth next to Dad.

Sara sat on my other side. "Hey. I'm sittin' next to you and your uppity big sister," Kim said, sliding into the booth next to Sara. "We've gotta stick together today."

Several boys from school stared at Sara with stars in their eyes, but she didn't seem to notice. I guess she was used to it by now.

Kim leaned over and tapped my arm. "My brother's trying to say something to you."

Cisco stood across the table. He tipped his cowboy hat sarcastically. I hadn't even seen him there. I reached up and gave him a high five.

"This is crazy," he said, glancing over his shoulder. "Bummer about the flood, but great turnout for the Lost Herd."

"I know, right?" I sounded stupid.

"Better grab a chair," Cisco said. "Later."

Cisco made his way to an empty chair in the center of the room…next to Amy. Of course they were sitting together. Ouch.

A big man in jeans, cowboy boots and a Levi's shirt stood in the front of the room and banged on a cowbell with a sturdy stick. He looked older than Dad, his face was weathered and lined, but he stood taller than ever in his boots and Stetson hat. It was Jack Marshall. I hadn't seen him since we overheard him fighting with Greg Nichols in the lobby of the BLM office. Jack banged the bell one more time, and everyone got really quiet.

"Let's settle down and get on to the business at hand," he said, authoritatively. He held the cowbell high in the air. "Well, it worked, didn't it?" he said, laughing. "Now don't any of you go getting any smart ideas. I'm not gonna wear the damn thing, I'm just using it to test your hearing."

"How'd we do, Jack?" Dad bellowed.

"You all passed with flying colors!" He leaned against the big rock fireplace. He actually looked comfortable talking to this crowd. "I want to thank all of you for coming out today. As many of you know, I'm Jack Marshall of Marshall Ranch. We have a challenging situation facing us, and we're gonna have to work together to come up with a solution. I'm real glad to see that we all care about the wild horses. What happens to them matters to me, and I hate to see those beautiful animals suffer. Speaking for myself, I owe a lot to horses for what they've brought to my life, not only in helping me move my cattle, but in the friendship and loyalty they've brought me, my children and grandchildren."

Jack studied the faces in the room, an easy smile on his face, but I knew he was waiting for a challenge from some of the other cattle ranchers who might be against this rescue. We all knew the rescue was a charged issue, and I worried about the position the BLM would take. I didn't trust them one bit.

Gary Nichols, son of Greg Nichols and one of the most vocal opponents of the mustangs, rose from one of the booths in the back. He was thin and wiry with a young, handsome face. He kept adjusting his cowboy hat on his head. All eyes turned to him. "We've got a big story here, one of the biggest we've had in years," he began. "Right now, there are five news stations covering a speech the Mayor is giving about the wild horses at City Hall." Gary took a thick wallet out of his back pocket and lifted it high over his head, "I'd be willing to help fund this wild horse rescue as long as Nichols Farms gets a little bit of advertising." He held his hands out to the crowd dramatically and then placed them over his heart. "After all, it wouldn't look good if our community stood by and let these symbols of the American West drown."

There was a spattering of applause from a few ranchers. Gary waved and exchanged high-fives with his buddies as if he was at a baseball game and his team was winning. He didn't care about the mustangs.

"What a snake in the grass!" Kim hissed in my ear. "And I thought Bob Downs was bad."

"Son of a buck," Dad said, leaning back in his chair. His good cheer was gone. I guess none of us had any warm feelings for Gary Nichols. But at least Gary wasn't opposing the rescue. Yet.

Jack held up his hand. "Thank you, Gary," he said dryly. "If there are no other questions or comments, we'll continue. Let me be clear. No one's getting any advertising from this, so keep your money in your wallet."

Gary looked like he took a punch in the gut he didn't know was coming. His face turned a deep shade of red. I wanted to hug Jack for putting Gary in his place.

With that unpleasant exchange behind him, the easy smile returned to Jack's face. "I'd like to introduce the head ranger from the Twin Rivers National Wildlife Refuge, Rick Jensen."

"Oh my God, it's Ranger Rick!" Sara whispered as a slight man in a green uniform stood eagerly beside Jack, a plastic clipboard tucked under his arm.

"Who's Ranger Rick?" I asked.

She looked at me with disgust. "He is. He's a ranger, and his name is Rick."

Kim stifled a laugh. "Whaddaya think of Ranger Rick's uniform?" she asked.

His collar was perfectly starched and decorated with brass pins.

"He's no boy scout," Sara said, "as you can see from his medals, won in the foothills of Spring Hills." Sara and Kim giggled.

I wanted to laugh, but I was too worried about the Lost Herd. "Hey, knock it off!" I whispered. "If he's into his job, that could mean good things for the horses."

"He's our man," Kim continued, undeterred. "We need someone who knows the lay of the land." She glanced down at his legs, and I followed her gaze. Rick wore tall rubber mucking boots that stretched all the way up to his knees. "Someone who's not afraid of a little water," she added.

Sara laughed out loud. Dad glared at all three of us.

"Thanks, Jack," the ranger began. "I'll get right down to it for you folks. This is the worst flood we've seen in the park in two hundred years. I've never seen water rise so fast or so far. We've got more snowmelt from the mountains than ever due to the storms last winter. And the river valley is prone to flooding as it is, being a marsh habitat. In addition to the Twin Rivers flooding, water has been pouring in from the slot canyon. In short, we've got our hands full." He paused. "The thing that makes this situation especially tricky is the terrain. In this part of the park, we've basically got wet meadows and grassland that are now submerged in water."

Gary Nichols stood up. "Hey, aren't we gonna vote on this or anything?"

"You voted when you walked in the door, Gary," Jack Marshall said. "Everyone in this room wants to help or they shouldn't be here."

Gary grinned. "From what I heard, Rick here was organizing a roundup to get the horses out of his park a few days ago. Now, he's point-man for the rescue?"

Jack still seemed relaxed, but there was something dangerous under the surface. "We don't have time for this. Sit down and shut up, and let Rick finish what he wants to say," Jack ordered.

"Yessir." Gary gave Jack a mock salute. A few of Gary's buddies walked out, but not Gary. He stayed in his chair, sitting his butt down and hiding behind his hat.

"Go on," Jack said to the ranger. "You're doing just fine."

The air was thick with nerves. People began talking and whispering. What Gary said was probably true, but Jack was right. We had to focus on saving the horses. Ranger Rick was on our side now. He tapped his pen against his clipboard, waiting for the noise to die down.

Finally, the room was quiet. Ranger Rick glanced at his watch with a precision that suggested he was a guy who didn't like to waste time. "Listen up, folks. The horses are marooned on a lowland knoll. It's the highest patch of ground left on the south side of the Twin Rivers, and it sits like an island in the middle of the water. This herd's about two hundred strong crowded on a tiny bit of land. The water has risen so high and so fast, it has completely surrounded the horses." He glanced around the room. "I'm talking three hundred sixty degrees, folks. It's standing room only for the herd. It's cold, wet, and they can't lie down to rest."

"Oh my God," Sara whispered. She wasn't laughing anymore.

A serious chill filled Red's diner. Nobody stirred. I tried to picture the Lost Herd completely surrounded by water on all sides. It was impossible, horrible. Sara grabbed my hand. Kim clasped her hands in her lap.

"Now, there's good news and bad news." Ranger Rick held up a finger, as if he didn't already have our undivided attention. "Good news first. The water's not that deep. The horses would only have to swim in some sections. And there's not much of a current. The bad news is, the floor of the river is completely unpredictable." He stroked his sandy-brown mustache. "That's what's killing the horses that have tried to cross."

I felt like screaming, "What horses, and how many?" But I kept my mouth shut.

"With the soil kicked up from the rain, we've got muddy water with some sink holes and bogs," Ranger Rick continued. "And to make matters worse, there are reports of some submerged barbed wire from when this area used to be ranch land."

There was a collective moan from the crowd. Sara's hand gripped mine so hard, my fingers were going numb.

"So how can we get them across?" Dad asked, loud and clear.

"Good question," Ranger Rick said, glancing down at the notes on his clipboard. "I think what we need to do is map out the safest escape route for the wild horses, and mark that route with stakes long enough to be seen above the waterline."

"How much water we got to cross?" Jack Marshall asked.

Rick scratched the back of his head and looked up at the ceiling. "You have to see it to believe it, but let me try and give you an idea." He held his hands as far apart as he could. "It's approximately seven hundred yards wide, and depending on the rains that can change considerably. We just don't know. Could get worse, could get better, but here's where it stands now. We're lookin' at a length of about five football fields, or almost half a mile from the shore to that island those horses are standing on."

Kim whistled. The crowd murmured. I couldn't believe it, couldn't even imagine how this had happened. How could we ever get them to cross that much water during this storm? And how could the horses navigate through bogs and sinkholes littered with treacherous barbed wire?

Kim pointed out the window. The rain was still falling. The wind rattled the windows as if emphasizing what we were up against. This was going from bad to worse.

CHAPTER 43

"I'M ASKING FOR volunteers to man the boats we'll be using to help mark the safest route," Rick called out forcefully.

We raised our hands high in the air and waved enthusiastically, but Rick's eyes were drawn to the center of the room where Cisco and Amy sat. They were picked right away. Gary Nichols was sitting behind them and raised his hand ever so slightly. "I guess you can include me," Gary said.

"That was unexpected," Sara whispered.

"He probably just wants to be in the news," I said to Dad. "He doesn't care about the herd."

Dad shrugged. "You can never really know why anyone does what they do."

"Well, that may be true, but I can't believe Gary was chosen to help the Lost Herd over us," I said.

Kim shifted anxiously in the booth. "There's got to be something else we can volunteer for."

"Or else we're taking our own boat out there," I said.

Rick finished counting the raised hands, but we were not among them. "Great, thanks for our new volunteers. We'll break into smaller groups later and discuss details. But for now, the only other thing I want to mention is safety while entering and exiting the park. Grant Pass is still open, but it's a steep, windy road that's muddy from the rains, so only four- wheel drive vehicles will be allowed into the park. We don't want to create more of a situation than we already have. Once you reach the valley floor, a ranger will instruct you where to park. Do not go past the ranger station without checking in with us. Well, that's about it," Rick said, nodding curtly to Jack Marshall. "Let's all work together and maybe we can rescue this herd."

I leaned over to Sara. "Maybe we can rescue them? That's not good enough!"

Rick stacked his notes neatly and placed them back in his clipboard. He shook hands with Jack and stepped briskly into the crowd.

"Okay, thanks, Rick," Jack said, readjusting his belt. "Next, we've got Bob Downs from the BLM in Albright, who will discuss options for the rescue."

Kim crossed her fingers and held them behind her back. "Let's hope Bob can be the man with a plan," she said.

"And one that sets them free," I said.

Sara shook her head. "I don't have a good feeling about this." Suddenly she jabbed me with her elbow right in the ribs. "There's the guy who was in Bob's office!"

I rubbed my aching side. I was going to be black and blue from her before the meeting was over. But she was right. I'd recognize that smug expression anywhere. Mr. Simmons pulled a folding chair off to the side near the rock fireplace in the designated area for the speakers, and exchanged a few words with Bob Downs. In this room of small town cowboys, farmers and ranchers with dirt still on their boots, he stuck out like a sore thumb. He wore a black-collared shirt with a bolero tie, a big silver and turquoise bracelet and shiny snake-skin cowboy boots. I'm sure he thought he looked his best, but I almost laughed. All hat and no cattle. This wasn't how the cowboys dressed around here.

When Jack introduced Bob as the next speaker, Bob stood up slowly before facing the crowd. He dabbed the sweat from his temples with a white bandana. I almost felt sorry for him with the way he stood there looking down at the floor, his cowboy hat held in front of him, his shirt untucked and hanging over his considerable belly. Was he ever going to speak?

People started murmuring. I turned to see the standing-room-only crowd, and the rows of folding chairs set up in the back, all taken.

"C'mon, Bob, bring it!" Kim whispered.

Finally, Bob lifted his gaze from the floor. "Lots of people gathered together in a small room makes me nervous," he said with a chuckle. "Lots of people waiting to hear what I have to say makes me even more nervous." He ran a hand over his unshaven face and surveyed the crowd. "Even with fifteen years working in this community, I still didn't know what to expect today at this meeting. It seems people are either pressuring me to reduce the number of wild horses or asking me to save them."

Jack Marshall laughed uneasily to cover the silence. I squirmed in the booth. Where was he going with this?

Gary Nichols looked up from the brim of his hat for the first time and grinned. "Speak up," Gary said. "You're the man."

Bob ignored the comment.

"While I understand the concerns of the ranchers and work hard to keep the wild herd population in check, my deeper alliance lies with the horses. Always has. And that gives me some nights without sleep, let me tell you."

Snakeskin Boots stiffened. I thought maybe my ears weren't working right. Maybe Bob had too much coffee this morning or something stronger. Kim leaned over to whisper in my ear. "His alliance is with the horses?"

"He sure doesn't act like he's on their side!" I whispered back.

"Bob's just lying again," Sara said.

Gary Nichols pushed his chair back and stood, arrogant as ever. "I have somethin' to say," he said.

Bob shook his head. He seemed annoyed. "Well, say it then."

Sara grabbed my sleeve. Trouble was on the way, for sure.

Gary took a cigarette out of his pocket and put it in his mouth, unlit. "As far as you saying your alliance is with the horses after working with us cattlemen for over fifteen years, all I can say is…" He threw his hands up in the air, "you coulda fooled me."

Raucous applause broke out from the ranchers in the room. Then silence.

Bob clamped his jaws together hard. He spoke through clenched teeth. "I don't owe you an explanation." His gaze gradually softened as he scanned the crowd. "But I can see how some of you out there might be curious as to my meaning."

"Well, I'm sure curious," Gary said, smirking.

"How 'bout you go ahead and sit down," Bob snapped. "Take a load off."

Gary looked bewildered. He sank slowly into his chair.

Bob paused and took a deep breath, as if gathering his courage. I may have been imagining it, but I thought his eyes rested on me for just a second before he spoke. "My father passed away last week. That got me remembering the role horses played in my life. When I was growing up, well, there were some problems at home. Some of you knew my father. He was a lot of fun and could sure raise hell, but let me just say that he could lose himself in a bottle. And when he did, I'd saddle up and ride for miles. I was a kid who needed a place to go and horses got me there."

One of the old-timers spoke up from the back of the room. "Right on, Bob. You're preachin' to the choir."

Bob ran a hand over his balding head. "I guess what I'm trying to say is that the BLM is going to support this rescue, and as their representative I'll do everything in my power to help in any way I can. I've outlined a plan—"

"What?" Mr. Simmons' voice cut through the rest of the crowd noise. He rose to his feet.

Was Bob going up against this guy? I couldn't believe it. It seemed too good to be true. But I couldn't let him off the hook. Before I even knew what I was doing, my hand shot into the air and I called out for Bob's attention. "Mr. Downs!"

Bob searched for the face that belonged to the voice. "Hey, Christa. What can I do for you?"

All heads turned in my direction. I swallowed. "If you love horses so much, why are you heading up roundups for the last thousand wild mustangs left in Nevada this year?"

Snakeskin Boots put his head in his hands.

A muscle in Bob's face tensed. He took his handkerchief out of his pocket and swept it across his glistening forehead. "Well, I can't say as I agree with those gathers myself." He cleared his throat. "You know times are hard, Christa. Everybody knows that." A murmur of agreement swept through the crowd. "And I had doctor bills for my father that were driving us into the poorhouse. I'm ashamed to say this, but I was afraid of losing my job."

The crowd went silent. "I've done a lot of things I'm not proud of." Bob wiped his hands with the handkerchief and stuffed it back in his pocket. When he spoke again, his face was flushed a dark red and his eyes burned with anger. "You might want to ask Mr. Steve Simmons here from Abbot Oil & Gas why so many mustangs are being gathered and relocated to Kansas."

"Kansas!" I hissed. Sara, Kim and I exchanged glances.

Mr. Simmons started to interrupt, but Bob waved him away and continued. "Because I don't understand it myself when people like Elizabeth Levine have offered thousands, even millions of acres where horses can run free in a wild horse sanctuary. I've been talking with her about this for a year."

Simmons scowled. "You know why, Bob."

Sara's eyes widened, and I felt like I'd stuck my fingers in a light socket. So this was what the relocation program was about. They were planning on moving the horses from the Nevada range to Kansas so the gas company could poison the air and water and not leave a trail of sick or dead four-legged bodies.

I stood up. "Who's going to pay to transport our wild horses to Kansas? Are you serious? There are thousands of them!"

Bob hesitated. "Honestly, Christa, I don't know what the BLM is gonna do. I can tell you one thing for sure, your protests and petitions have gotten our attention."

I heard several voices say, "Go Christa!" As if I needed any more encouragement.

Jack banged the gavel. "Let Christa finish her thoughts, folks."

"We've been able to stop the July roundups with everybody's help." I glanced at the crowd. "And thank you for that, but there's something bigger going on here. Abbot Oil and Gas is fracking on public land, all without asking the public. It's gas your after. Isn't that right, Mr. Simmons?"

He removed his hat and smoothed back his already slick hair. "Actually, it's oil we've found here in Nevada." He smiled broadly, revealing large white teeth. "And it's a good thing, too. It's going to bring a lot of cash into this town."

Anger flamed to a roar in my ears. Steve Simmons was such a smooth talker, he almost made it sound like he was doing us all a favor. "Well, Sara and I have been doing some research." There's lots of information on the Internet about fracking. I guess you need to use a lot of toxic chemicals and they stay in the ground and poison the water. People and animals can get really sick." I scanned the faces of the community. "We let them do what they want with our horses, our land, and now our water.

The crowd broke into a frenzy of confusion. Everyone seemed to be talking at once.

Steve Simmons pointed a long, shaking finger at me. "You can go ahead and stamp your feet all you want, young lady. That oil is too important to leave in the ground." His eyes bore into me. "And you'd better check your facts before you go around making accusations."

I felt the blood drain out of my cheeks. Dad stood up and put his arm around me. He met Steve's eyes. "Her facts check out just fine, Simmons," Dad said. He turned to the crowd and everyone quieted down. "I guess the ranchers who want to see the horses removed from the range must be thrilled. You think life will be easier. But let's slow down and really think about this. Just ask our friends in New Mexico and Colorado about the reality of energy development in the West. They'll tell you about the stench of sulfur, the fences cut, the stock run over, the trash, the new roads constructed, loss of livestock and poisoned water. Chances are, you'll be wishing for the easy company of the wild horses before long."

Dad sat down and pulled me down next to him. He squeezed my hand and I squeezed back.

Steve Simmons held his arms out to the crowd like a senator running for president. "This pipeline is going to bring jobs and opportunities this town has only dreamed of." He rubbed his fingers against his thumb. "I'm talking money, folks." Sections of the crowd clapped and cheered. He grinned and gestured to Gary Nichols like they were best friends. "We've got the support of Nichols Ranch. They're just some of the many locals who recognize that Abbot Oil and Gas spells progress for this town. If you don't seize this opportunity, you people don't know what you're doing."

"But I know what you're doing, and I don't want any part of it…not anymore," Bob said.

Steve grinned sarcastically. "I've never seen this side of you before, Bob. The people who pay your salary are going to want to hear about this."

"I'll save you the trouble. You can put your pipeline in right through the range and transport all the horses to Kansas on the taxpayers' dime, but it won't be on my watch. I'm gonna quit as soon as we've finished this rescue!"

Steve's face darkened ominously. "You may have trouble finding a new job," Steve said.

Jack Marshall stood and addressed Bob Downs casually, as if they were the only two guys in the room. "I'd hire you, Bob. I could use a good foreman."

Bob nodded respectfully. "Well I sure thank you, Jack. But why don't we take advantage of all the resources the BLM has to offer while I'm still working for them?"

"We can deal with the fracking and pipeline situation later. Now let's outline a plan for the rescue."

Everyone sat in stunned silence.

"Are you with me?" Bob asked.

The room exploded with applause. Almost everyone there had signed our petition or argued with us about it at some point, but seeing them all together added up to a lot more people than I realized. Sara's eyes filled with tears, and Kim threw both of her hands above her head and whooped with joy. It looked like this rescue was going to happen after all. And I could've never guessed the BLM would take the lead to save the Lost Herd.

Bob didn't seem like a bad guy now. His face was flushed as pink as the inside of a watermelon. He looked like he wanted to crawl right out of his skin while the crowd cheered.

Steve Simmons placed his cowboy hat firmly on his head and

whirled around before he walked out the door. "This isn't the last of this. You can't stop progress!"

Just as the glass doors slammed closed behind him, a loud roll of thunder boomed outside, and lightning flashed through the sky. The lights dimmed. With a groan, the electricity went out. A hush fell over the room.

A generator clicked on and then died. A baby wailed.

I glanced over my shoulder out the window. The trees thrashed with the force of the gale and rain streaked the glass.

The generator tried again and caught this time. The lights flickered back on.

Bob shuffled his notes. "Thanks, folks. Let's get back to the matter at hand. There's not much time left for this herd."

With no warning, the doors at the front entrance blasted open and a gust of wind sent the rain spraying into the room. The firefighters ran over to close the doors. I'd never seen a storm this powerful. The Lost Herd needed our help. Now.

CHAPTER 44

BOB CLUTCHED HIS papers and waited for people to stop talking. Finally, the room quieted down. "Now, back to the rescue. I've spoken with the mayor of Albright, and he's ruled out the use of helicopters for rounding up or transporting the animals. The noise may panic the horses and cause more to drown. These horses are packed pretty tight on this...this tiny island, and they're going to be stiff and cold, and want to stretch out and run once they get going. But I don't think they're gonna be easy to move. We've already lost about eleven horses from the herd due to drowning."

A collective gasp rose from the crowd. People started talking again. My stomach churned with fear for Mesteño's band. For all of the bands. I hugged myself, shivering.

Bob held up his hands in a calming gesture, and Jack Marshall struck the cowbell like a schoolteacher telling the kids to pay attention.

"I don't want anyone to panic. Nature has its own way of culling the herd. I want us to do all we can to prevent any suffering, but I don't want hysteria. Let's stay calm and work this out together. We'll be bringing several veterinarians with us to the scene who will care for any horses in need once we get them across."

Which ones had died? I buried my head in Sara's shoulder.

Bob started coughing, and Jack Marshall handed him a glass of water. "What's your plan for encouraging them to move across?"

Bob looked thoughtful. "Well, that's tricky. If the boats aren't able to navigate in the shallow spots Rick was talking about, then we can't use them. Horses tend to follow other horses. What I'm going to suggest is pretty radical." He paused and took a noisy gulp of water. "I think what we need are some volunteers to follow a safe route that's been marked across the water and ride out to the herd on horseback. I believe the horses will respond the most favorably to a horse escort."

When I heard Bob say those words, the butterflies gathered in my stomach and fluttered right up my spine. My hands tingled, and I felt lightheaded. Suddenly I was standing up and raising my hand high in the air. An image of Lucky flashed through my mind, his eyes warm and trusting. "I volunteer to ride."

I could feel Dad's gaze on me and could see his shocked expression out of the corner of my eye. I kept my focus on Bob.

"I appreciate your courage," Bob said. "But I'll need your parent's consent."

I decided to ignore his comment. If we got our parents' consent for everything, we'd never get anything done. I avoided Dad's gaze. "Everyone in this town knows I've been riding since before I could walk, and Sara and Kim and I would sure like to step forward and help out."

Sara stood up beside me, and so did Kim. I was shaking.

"I volunteer to ride with my sister," Sara said.

"I'm in," Kim said, her eyes flashing.

Bob shrugged, "Well, if it's okay with all your folks that would be ideal. Young girls tend to have a way with horses, and may be less likely to spook the herd than some of the big tough cowboys in this town." Laughter rippled through the room.

I felt like he was talking down to us. My cheeks burned hot. Was he mocking us? What if he didn't have the best interests of the

Lost Herd in mind? It wouldn't be the first time he'd said one thing and meant another.

I dug my nails into my sweaty palms and stood as straight as I could. "But first we need to know if you're planning on letting the herd go free after the rescue or if you're gonna put 'em in those holding pens and send them to Kansas," I said.

Dad tried to hide his smile, but I saw it.

Bob shook his head and sighed. "Christa, I could wallpaper my house with the emails you've sent over the last few months. Every one of them was about your concern for the Lost Herd, how you want them to stay free."

I nodded, waiting for his answer.

"As far as it stands now, if none of the horses are badly injured, the BLM's planning to release the herd back into the wild."

"Do we have your word on that? Is that a promise?" Amy Whitehorse stood up. Our eyes met across the room.

I couldn't believe it. There she stood in her forest green rain slicker, still dripping with water, her dark brown eyes solemn and her orange bangs hanging straight across her face. She seemed so small and shy. But at that moment she was a tower of strength, and the most beautiful girl I'd ever seen.

Bob Downs put both of his hands in the air where we could see them. "Cross my heart and hope to die," he said, grinning. Then, the smile faded from his face.

All the kids in the room were standing up now, one after another. And then all their parents stood up, too, until everyone in the room was standing, united in a common desire to free the horses. Cisco caught my eye and nodded. Dad took my hand and held it in his rough palm.

Bob's eyes flared for just a minute and his gaze flickered from face to face. "Let's get those horses off that knoll and onto dry ground," he said. "Volunteer riders, meet at the preserve at first light tomorrow."

"Tomorrow!" I searched the faces of the kids. Amy's worried expression matched how I felt. "Is there any way we can start the rescue today, Mr. Downs?" I asked.

Bob's brow furrowed. He pointed to the window. "It's way too stormy right now—it's not safe—for you or for your horses. And the forecast says it's going to remain a severe storm until midnight tonight." His gaze softened. "Besides, it will take me a day to get all the boats, fencing, hay, and the staff organized. Let's not rush into this. We'll serve the horses better if we do it right."

Sara squeezed my hand. "It's okay, Christa, we'll start the rescue tomorrow. The mustangs are strong."

The whole group looked to me, as if I were in charge. "Okay," I said. "We'll do it once and do it right."

CHAPTER 45

DAD TOOK MY hand and led me to the door. "We've got some talking to do, Christa," he said. All of a sudden, he didn't look too happy.

We took cover from the rain under the awning outside. The wind whipped furiously, blowing my hair into my face. I held it back with both hands.

Dad watched the trees bend in the wind and his eyes grew as dark as the storm. "You can ride in the rescue if you ride Eastwood, not Jenner. You're not allowed to ride him."

"But Dad—"

"This ride would be dangerous with any horse, under any circumstances." His voice rose. "But you've got a horse that's afraid of water."

"He's crossed all the streams in the Sage Mountains."

"Streams?" His tone was hard. "Did you hear Rick in there?" Dad pointed back inside. "He said you have to cross *five football fields* of water to even reach the herd." He scratched his head and gave a bitter laugh.

I studied my reflection in the window. It was blurred from the rain. The plastic awning shook in the wind and water sprayed down into my face. Suddenly, I felt hopeless.

"What are you trying to prove?" He was practically pulling his hair out.

"I'm not trying to prove anything," I mumbled under my breath.

Sara came out of the restaurant, saw us, and turned on her heels in one motion, her eyebrows raised. She walked right back inside.

I gathered my courage. "I know it seems impossible. It may be impossible, but I have to try. And I have to try with Jenner."

He sighed. "Look, this family has been through enough, and you've been through enough with Jenner. I can't let you risk your safety."

I felt like I was hitting a wall at one hundred miles an hour. My head hurt, but my stomach burned with a fire that kept me going. "Dad, you can't keep grounding me from Jenner forever." I met his eyes. "If he tries to run or won't cross the water, then we'll have our answer. And there'll be plenty of people to stop him and keep him from hurting himself or me...plenty of people to watch me fail. If I'm willing to risk that, then the least you can do is let me try."

He put his hand on my shoulder. "I admire your courage," He gazed out into the rain. I could almost feel the wheels turning in his brain, he was thinking so hard. "I need to talk about this with your mother." He patted his shirt pocket for a pack of cigarettes that wasn't there.

"That's fine. Just tell her to let me try." I thought of how much I loved Lucky. I thought of Mesteño tossing his long white mane and the dark wild eye of Corazón. And then I thought of Jenner, resting his head on my chest, right over my heart. "Please, let us try," I said.

CHAPTER 46

"CHRISTA, COME HERE," Mom said as she waddled carefully into the kitchen, holding her belly. She'd been talking with Dad. I was dying to know what they'd decided. All I wanted to hear was the word "yes."

She looked different. For so long she'd been sad and tired, and her eyes had been lifeless, staring off at something I couldn't see. Now they were clear and focused on me. That felt good.

"There's something I need to tell you," she said, pulling out a chair at the dining room table and motioning for me to do the same.

My heart sank. Here it comes. Talking was never good. They weren't going to let me ride Jenner.

She swept a stray crumb off the table. "First, I want to tell you how brave I think you are. You've impressed me with your courage. What you've volunteered to do is very dangerous, and how you've championed the wild horses is more than admirable." She exhaled. "But I don't trust Jenner. I don't trust that horse to keep you safe out there."

I noticed Mom's gold wedding ring shining on her hand as she interlaced her fingers, her elbows resting on the table.

"But Mom—he's a different horse now. There's going to be lots of people watching out for me in the water and everywhere."

She raised an eyebrow.

"You can ask Dad! He was at the meeting!"

She took my hands in hers. "I could ask him, but he already told me. And I've been talking with Grandma, too."

"Grandma?"

"Yep. She keeps bringing up Wild Horse Annie and saying how you kids may have an important role to play." She looked up at the ceiling and took a big breath. "Christa, no matter how many people are out there in boats, this is a dangerous ride. The most dangerous ride of your life."

"C'mon! There's gonna be tons of firefighters and rangers—"

Her blue eyes locked on mine until I looked away. I could feel her fear. Well, that was it. Even though Grandma had been putting in a good word for me, Mom would say no, and all of this would be for nothing.

"Mom, I need to ride Jenner. I can't explain why, I just have to. We've gotten so close, and he's the only horse I know that's strong enough to get across that water." I clenched my hands into fists, breaking her hold on me. "You may not trust him, but I do."

She sat back in her chair and pressed the heels of her hands against her eyes. "Maybe I haven't been there for you like I should," she sighed.

I tried to keep my face calm, but my thoughts were racing. "Mom you've been fine. You've needed to focus on the baby. I get that."

Mom reached across the table and took my face in her hands. I was almost bowled over by her intensity. Her eyes were lit with a blue fire. "The worst thing I've ever been through was losing a baby. I won't lose another one. But you're not a baby anymore." Her face crinkled into a worried smile. "Christa, if you feel safer on Jenner then Eastwood...then ride him."

Relief swept through me, followed by a rush of fear.

Suddenly she was up and pacing. "Now, if the conditions aren't just right out there tomorrow, if Jenner spooks, or the rescue gets canceled, or…well, something doesn't happen just the way you planned…" She struggled to continue as tears streamed from her eyes. "I couldn't stand it if you got hurt," she said, blowing her nose and blotting her eyes with a tissue. "What am I thinking? I'm sending my child into a flood." She waved the tissue in the air and looked skyward. "On a runaway horse who's afraid of water! This is the worst decision I've ever made for you."

"It's okay, Mom," I said. She put her arms around me and held me as close as she could. Her belly arched between us. It felt good to have her care so much, but it kind of scared me, too.

She stopped crying and whispered in my ear. "You don't have to be perfect. No one can, even if we try our hardest." She stroked my hair. "So promise me you'll go easy on yourself tomorrow. No matter what."

I met her eyes and nodded. The rescue could go the way I wanted it to go or it could be a complete, heart-crushing disaster. Either way, the Lost Herd deserved our best. For Lucky, I had to try.

CHAPTER 47

THAT NIGHT, MY mind buzzed with questions I couldn't answer. There were a million things that could go wrong. Even if Jenner entered the water with no hesitation, the water would be deep in places, filled with sinkholes and littered with old fencing. As if that wasn't enough, there was no telling how Jenner would react to the wild herd or how they'd react to us.

I stole down to the barn, hoping Jenner would calm my ragged nerves. The moon rose full and bright, darting in and out amongst the clouds like it was playing a game. Everything was washed in moonlight. I figured I'd take advantage of this break in the rain and go for a quick ride. I led Jenner to the fence and tied him off, running a brush over his sleek coat and slipping on his bridle. On a sudden impulse, I climbed the fence until I was standing on the second rung and jumped onto him, bareback.

"Do you realize how important this is?" I whispered, leaning forward into his neck. His right ear flicked back. "Saving those horses is really, really important. And we can't help them if we can't get into the water." I ran my hand down his neck to his withers. He licked his mouth and chewed, as if trying to digest something that was hard to swallow. "It's going to be really scary for me, too, but we have to be brave."

I steered Jenner into the field and he pranced, his hooves

dancing a hollow beat down the path I used to take with Lucky. I wrapped my legs around him and leaned into his deep red mane as he picked up speed through the meadow. Faster and faster he ran until we were flying. I glanced over at our combined shadow running beside us, my hair flying out behind me like his mane, my shoulders square, my legs melting into his body like a centaur. The moon rose over my shoulder, and the grasses in the field waved silver in the wind, swaying as we passed.

I pulled Jenner to a stop and slipped off his back, stroking the proud arch of his neck.

He dropped his head into my chest. I put my hands on either side of his face. For a second all I could hear was his exhale, his soft breath warm on my cheek. I became aware of my breathing, slower than his, but still in rhythm. We stood together in silence, lightning flickering on the horizon over the Sage Mountains. Suddenly, I knew what to say.

"Jenner, none of them think we can do this. Can we?"

He turned his huge head to me, his red lashes thick and beautiful. He looked at me as if he actually understood what I was saying.

"I can't describe what the Lost Herd means to me, running free, but I think you know. The horses and their families are in danger. The future of the entire herd is at stake."

Jenner stamped his front leg and shook his head, jangling the bridle. It seemed pretty obvious he didn't want anything bad to happen to this herd. Anyone could see that. He bumped my arm with his soft nose.

I could hear the night sounds around us, like the soggy crickets and the hoot of the great horned owl. The trees were dripping. Huge drops fell from rain-soaked leaves onto the leaves below. Every blade of grass in the field sighed in the wind that ruffled Jenner's mane.

Jenner's head jerked up. His nostrils worked, smelling the breeze. I was losing his attention. I held onto his bridle and forced him to look into my eyes. This was the most important part. He dropped his head again and rested it near my shoulder. "I need you to be my partner," I whispered. His ears flicked forward at the sound of my voice. He stared solemnly into my eyes. "I need you to take those big hooves and step out into that water with me on your back tomorrow, even if it's the scariest thing you've ever done."

Thick clouds raced across the moon, and I knew the next wave of the storm was approaching fast. Jenner did, too. He danced in place, snorting and tossing his head. There was no going back. It was like we were on the edge of a precipice and all we could do now was jump.

CHAPTER 48

THE CLOCK READ 4:30 a.m. No use trying to sleep. I got up and dressed quickly in the dark. Something caught my eye on the nightstand. When I turned on the light, Sara barely stirred. Three envelopes were propped against the lamp, two of them with my name on them. I opened the larger envelope to find Lucky's braid wrapped in a red velvet cloth and a note from Grandma.

> *Christa, So much love to you and Jenner, and all the wild things of this world…thought you might want Lucky's charm back for the ride today.*
>
> *May the road rise up to meet you.*
>
> *May the wind be always at your back.*
>
> *May the sun shine warm upon your face.*
>
> *And may the hand of a friend always be near.*
>
> *Best of luck in the rescue and always.*
>
> *Love, Grandma Gillian*

I held Lucky's charm, as Grandma had called it, to my cheek and kissed it. It was too late to back out now. I couldn't disappoint Lucky or the Lost Herd. I slipped the gray braid, still perfectly pleated, into the front pocket of my jeans.

There was a smaller blue envelope addressed to me in Mom's handwriting. My hands shook as I tore it open.

Dearest Christa,

Remember, you are not alone, and we love you. No matter what happens out there today, we will always believe in you. Even if you never forgive yourself for what happened with Lucky, I want you to know that we do.

We are so proud to have you as our daughter.

Love, Mom & Dad

I realized I was biting my nails down to the skin. I shoved my hands in my pockets and took a deep breath. *They still love me.* Even though I was always screwing up, always letting people and horses down. I just couldn't believe it…Mom and Dad forgave me and believed in me enough to let me do this ride.

I walked into the bathroom and splashed water on my face. Steam rose from the hot water, and I felt a tight place in my chest open.

I willed myself to look in the mirror. There was the green silk scarf, tied around my neck. There was the red hair, even frizzier from the humidity. There were the pale blue eyes, the sun-kissed cheeks spattered with freckles. But that's not what got my attention. There was something new in my reflection that I liked. I saw a bold, young girl, eyes clear. I saw a girl who had suffered and come through the other side. I saw a girl who had weighed her options this time… and was still willing to risk everything for the stranded mustangs.

CHAPTER 49

WE CRAWLED ALONG the highway in Dad's pickup truck, pulling the trailer with the horses behind us. Dad drove and Mom squeezed in between him and Grandma in the front seat. Sara and I sat in the back watching rain fall from low misty clouds, noses pressed to the glass.

My every thought was for the horses caught in the storm, and I pictured them in my mind as they used to be, strong, happy, and free. "Hang in there, Corazón," I whispered. I could imagine her black eyes fixed on me as she pawed the ground, willing us to hurry.

I'd thought about it from every angle and visualized Jenner entering the water a million times, but I just couldn't picture where we would go from there. How would we get the herd to follow us back?

Finally we wound down the steep curves of Grant Pass, Dad downshifting on the slick road and Grandma commenting on the rain and the beauty of the canyon walls. Mom glanced back at Sara and me. I put on a brave smile for her, but my boot tapped nervously on the front seat like it had a mind of its own.

Sara reached over and grabbed my foot until it stopped. "Chill, Christa."

Dad had the defrost cranked on its hottest setting because Mom was always cold. Now it was stifling. I struggled out of my yellow rain slicker and tried to ignore the drops of sweat dripping down my back. The heart pendant Grandma had given me swung gently against my chest with every curve in the road.

Every time Dad took a tight turn, I glanced behind us to check the trailer, hoping it would stay on the wet road and not swing out into the thick forest on either side of us. Star, Eastwood and Jenner were all in there. Precious cargo.

By the time we reached the entrance gate to the Twin Rivers National Park, I was ready to jump out of my skin. I sat up straight and tried not to let my thoughts run away with me. I had to stay calm.

Ranger Rick walked out to meet us. He wore regulation ranger rain gear from his hooded head to his rubber boots. He looked like he was ready for a moon launch.

He leaned into Dad's open window and handed him a pass. "I want you to be very careful as you continue down to the valley," he said. "And, well, I hate to say it, but we've lost more horses..." He looked at Sara and me with concern. "Bob Downs is waiting for you. He'll show you where it's safe to park and give you the latest information we have. Weather report says more rain's coming."

Grandma grimaced and leaned in close to Mom. They talked in low voices, their heads together. Dad gripped the steering wheel so hard I could see the blue veins in his hands.

Sara leaned in to whisper in my ear. "They're really nervous about us riding. I heard them talking this morning. Dad's basically got a SWAT team out there for us in case anything goes wrong. He had Bob make sure to put firefighters and paramedics in most of the boats. It's a miracle he let you ride."

"Me ride? More horses have died, and you're still thinking I'm the problem?" I bit my lip.

"Yes, I'm thinking about you, you ungrateful little brat!" she hissed. She shook her head in frustration. "Look, I don't think I can do this ride and still take care of you. It's going to take everything I have just to stay in the saddle myself. I have no idea what Jenner's gonna do out there." She sighed and sat back, staring out the window. "Or Star for that matter."

I wanted to stay mad at her, I really did. But it was Sara's job to worry about me— always had been, ever since we were little. She couldn't help it. "I get it. But you don't have to look after me anymore."

She laughed a bitter laugh. "Yeah, right! I'll believe that when I see it."

I crossed my arms over my chest.

She exhaled. "I'm sorry," she said. " That didn't come out right." She turned to me, her face earnest. "Look, the Lost Herd practically belongs to you. The only reason I'm sitting here is because of how much you love those horses. And even with all the things that can go wrong out there, I'm glad to be riding with you."

I didn't know what to say. Sara was on my side? That was hard to believe. I sighed.

Sara waved her hand in front of her face. "I love you, but your breath is, like, horrible right now."

My hand flew to my face. "It's that bad?"

She handed me an entire package of breath mints as an answer. I took two.

"I'm scared for them," I whispered. "The Lost Herd."

"Me, too," she whispered back and clasped my hand.

"We got them into this with our fences and helicopters. And our greed."

"Then, we'll have to get them out."

"I can't believe you carry breath mints into a disaster area."

Sara smiled like I was a child who would never understand the important things in life.

CHAPTER 50

A VOLUNTEER IN A rain slicker and rubber boots waved us off the road and onto a grassy slope where we parked next to several cars and trucks. Just down the hill, Bob Downs held a megaphone, shouting instructions to the men wading in the water carrying long stakes painted in orange Day-Glo. Dad said the Day-Glo would help the men in the boats and the riders to see the markers from a distance. The riders—that would be us. I thought my heart was going to thump through my chest.

The sky grew even darker with angry looking clouds roiling above us.

Sara and I leapt out of the truck and ran across the hill to join the small crowd of people gathered in yellow and orange ponchos. I followed their gaze. At first I didn't see anything at all. When I focused all the way to the horizon, I spotted them. Way out across a freaking huge expanse of water stood what must be the Lost Herd. All I could see was horse butts huddled on a rounded knoll so tiny it almost looked like a child's cartoon version of an island. This was the last bit of dry land left to them. I pulled out my field glasses.

They stood with their heads down, backs to the rain and wind, filthy with mud. From their dejected posture, it looked like they were soaked to the bone and miserable. There wasn't as much as a tree or a bush on that knoll, and the herd was packed so tightly there was no room to move. A gray mist obscured the canyon walls, the slot canyon and the mountains beyond.

I scanned for Mesteño or Corazón, but from this distance the herd was a blur of color.

"They can't eat or move," I said to Sara.

Sara's lips looked pale. I don't even think she'd applied lip gloss yet, which was a first for her. "I hate seeing them trapped. Let's hurry and get out there."

We pulled our horses out of the trailer and tied them. Quickly, we picked their hooves, brushed, and saddled them.

KGBA news pulled up in a big van and parked near our truck. The news crew set up their big camera and dragged thick cables along the grass back to the van. When the on-camera reporter, Sandy Lyons, stepped out of the van I recognized her immediately from Reno's Nightly News. She was black and pretty, even in a hooded blue slicker. She looked excited as she stared out to the Lost Herd, papers clutched in her hand.

Gary Nichols would be really happy she was here. He probably called KGBA news this morning just to make sure they'd get here on time. But he was right about one thing. This was the biggest story Albright had ever seen.

Someone in the crowd waved wildly to get Sandy's attention. "So word is out?"

She nodded her head and flashed a big reporter's smile. "This is going to make national news, folks."

Sara glanced at me nervously. "National news?"

"It's about time the mustangs got some attention," I said gruffly.

Sara and I mounted. Dad checked the cinches wordlessly,

avoiding eye contact. I didn't try talking to him when he was like this. He saddled Eastwood.

Just when I was starting to worry about Kim, she appeared out of the crowd and ran over, looking winded and flushed. "Hey, sorry I'm late. I got hung up helping Cisco and Amy Whitehorse get into their boat. They'll be out there." She motioned to the ocean of water. "Somewhere."

What a happy couple. They have their own boat to share, I thought bitterly.

Kim fixed me with a strange look. "By the way, he said to wish you luck."

I felt my cheeks burn. "He did?"

Kim gave me a curious glance. "He didn't wish me luck. I mean, the guy never talks to begin with."

"Who never talks?" Sara asked.

"Cisco," Kim said.

Sara's eyes grew wide. "Ohhh…"

I shushed her with a glance.

"I think Cisco likes you," Kim whispered.

Just hearing his name sent a little tingle through my body. "He's out there with Amy. He likes her!" I blurted.

Kim looked confused. "Cisco and Amy?"

"Never mind," I said. "Let's get going."

Kim mounted and we glanced at Sara, hunched miserably in her slicker.

"You can't show off your hair for the cameras with your hood up," I said to Sara.

"I'm trying to keep it dry. My hair doesn't look as good when it's wet," Sara said.

Kim threw her head back and laughed.

I gulped. "Those cameras are going to catch every move we make today."

"Well, then… failure is not an option." Kim shook the rain out of her short, dark hair and pulled her cowboy hat low on her head. She wore a blue bandana around her neck. "You girls feel like ridin'?"

CHAPTER 51

B OB DOWNS JOINED us at the trailer, carrying a clipboard, three red life vests and a walkie-talkie spitting static at his belt. He was breathing hard from all the walking, his belly a big mound heaving under his rain poncho.

"Morning, everyone," he nodded at each of us. Mom, Dad, and Grandma pressed in next to us. Bob waved us into a huddle like we were a football team. I guess it was time for pre-game strategy. I was hoping there would at least be some kind of plan. The horses snorted and stomped the ground, as if they knew how important and dangerous this was going to be.

"You girls are gonna follow the route we've marked out with the stakes. We've got boats stationed along the way to offer you any help you may need."

I gulped. I hoped we wouldn't need a thing from those boats. The orange Day-Glo stakes in the water marked a long, winding path out to the Lost Herd. It was a long road.

Bob handed each one of us a life vest, his face grim. "Your safety is the number one priority here. We need clear heads out there. If you feel you're not the right one for this job, tell me now."

I looked from Kim to Sara as we pulled the red vests over our shoulders. Kim nodded and Sara steadily returned Bob's gaze. "We're ready to do this," Sara said.

I adjusted Sara's old cowboy hat on my head. I'd never been more afraid in my life. "I'm ready," I said.

Mom caught my eye and nodded.

Kim spun Eastwood in a tight circle. "Hell yes, we're the right ones for this job, Mr. Downs! We've got a whole pile of horses waiting on us out there, so let's quit talking and get to it."

Leave it to Kim to settle this once and for all.

"Good," Bob Downs said, finally moving on—and not a moment too soon for me. "If your horse falters or you and your horse get separated, swim to the nearest boat. They're out there to assist you." Bob ran a hand over his balding head. He seemed to be talking more to himself than to us as he continued. "Lord knows the boats haven't been able to do much for the herd. Damn things keep getting stuck in the shallows. We got some hay out to the mustangs yesterday, but not today."

"Let's get going, then, Mr. Downs," I said.

Bob received a transmission from his walkie-talkie. "I don't know how to put this and there's no easy way to say it, so I'm going to talk straight to you girls. We've lost a total of eighteen horses in the last two days, and I don't want to lose any more." He motioned to a blue tarp covering a row of dead horses lying on the ground at the very top of the hill. "We dragged them up out of the water, but it wasn't easy."

My breathing seemed to stop cold. I couldn't exhale or inhale— the air was knocked clear out of me. The wind ruffled the edges of the tarp, sending ripples along the row of covered horses. As the tarp rose, I saw the shapes of their bodies and an exposed leg. Tears sprung from my eyes. All those wild, beautiful mustangs...dead.

"This ride is essential to the safety of this herd, " he continued, his voice low and filled with emotion. "They won't last another day. They haven't followed any of the boats we've tried to get out there, and if we send in a helicopter to move 'em, we're afraid they'll spook and scatter in all directions. You're our last hope. Somehow, you've got to convince them to follow you back to dry land. "

"How do we do that?" I asked.

Bob shook his head. "I have no idea."

Great. There was no plan, no strategy.

He must have seen the blood drain from my face. "You all right, Christa?" he asked.

"Don't worry," I said, sounding more confident than I felt. "We'll save the rest of them."

"Okay," he said. "Let's get started."

Bob walked in front of us with Dad, Mom and Grandma while I rode beside Sara and Kim.

"We got a plan?" I asked.

Kim answered without looking my way. "The plan is, we've been riding together all summer, and we'll figure out what to do when we get there."

She was right. This wasn't something you could plan for. Even Bob didn't know what to tell us.

"Remember what Ranger Rick said yesterday. We've got about five football fields of water to cross." Sara pulled her riding gloves on with her teeth.

Kim's eyes narrowed. "Well, then we better get going."

My eyes drifted back to the horses lying on the hill under the tarp. I said a prayer for them and hoped luck would be on our side. I held onto Lucky's braid for a brief moment and made a wish. Somehow, we had to bring back the rest of this herd without ropes, halters, helicopters or bridges. We would need more than luck—we'd need a miracle.

CHAPTER 52

DAD TOOK HOLD of Jenner's bridle. He was dressed in a thick fleece pullover and a baseball cap, his camera and a pair of binoculars swinging from his neck. He'd led the way on a million family rides and hikes in the mountains. Seeing him in front of me was so familiar, so comforting, so…Dad.

"Okay, this is where we part ways," he said, pulling Jenner to a halt.

My stomach turned over. We'd be on our own from here.

Dad gave me a terse smile. "Ride smart and get this done quickly."

Mom reached up to me, her blue eyes shining. "No matter what happens out there, we'll always be proud of you."

I squeezed her hand briefly and then let go.

"I'll watch out for her, Mom," Sara said.

'I know," Mom answered, clasping her hand tightly.

Dad snapped pictures as we started our walk down to the water. I turned to see Mom getting smaller and smaller, wiping tears from her eyes. Suddenly, I felt guilty. "We'll be okay!"

She waved.

I raised my hand to wave back. Jenner trotted along with his huge stride, snorting and blowing. My green silk scarf fluttered like the wings of a bird.

The crowd turned to watch us, and a few people reached out to touch our horses. Then the crowd faded, and my focus narrowed to the path ahead. Sara led the way. Kim rode behind me. I heard Eastwood snort loudly, and Kim soothed him with words I couldn't hear.

I studied the water as we climbed down the hill. With Jenner sensitive to my every move, I held myself steady in the saddle and tried to take deep breaths.

I pulled Jenner up next to Sara, and Kim joined us at the water's edge. For a moment we stood side by side, peering through the rain out to the Lost Herd.

Sara backed Star up a step. "So we're going? Now?"

"Now might be a good time," Kim said, turning to look up the hill at the crowd and the cameras. She leaned on her saddle horn, chewing a piece of grass.

"If I know Jenner, he'll want to go first," I said.

Sara looked down and bit her lip. "Right. You go ahead, I've got your back."

Kim tipped her hat at me. "Lead the way. Remember, failure is not an option."

Sara looked worried. Really worried. "And stay inside the path they marked with the stakes!"

I nodded.

"And watch out for barbed wire, Christa," Sara warned. Her face was a shade of gray I'd never seen before.

"I will."

"Be careful. And if Jenner spooks and you can't control him, jump off and get to a boat. He'll swim fine without you."

"Got it."

Jenner's head arched, looking down at the muddy shore. He snorted, pawing the ground. The rain fell harder, churning the surface of the water as thunder rumbled in the distance.

"We can do this, Jenner," I said. Sara and Kim flanked us on either side. I stayed calm. I pictured us swimming easily out to the island. Jenner settled. I ran my hand down his strong shoulder; he was with me now.

Before Sara could stop me, I pressed my legs against Jenner's side, and we plunged into the water. His nostrils flared with each breath. He strode deeper and deeper, his eyes wide, but his step sure. I stroked his giant neck. "What a brave horse you are, Jenner. What a great horse!"

Tiny particles of icy hail fell, prickling the skin on my face. Squinting through the driving rain, I guided Jenner through the first set of stakes and searched for the next set of markers. I would have to make a sharp left to stay on course. I could hardly see, but with a touch of my leg, Jenner veered left and then plunged forward, barely staying within the markers.

Through the haze of rain I saw one of the small red boats and a man waving. I guided Jenner toward the boat, stealing a quick glance behind me at Sara and Kim. Sara waved. Star blasted forward, her nose smelling the water. Kim was behind Sara, her eyes focused ahead and Eastwood steady beneath her.

The man in the boat waved again, and I realized it was Gary Nichols. Seeing Gary in a rowboat was one of the strangest things I'd seen yet that day. "Stay clear of the sand bar," he hollered. "It's a sinkhole!"

Just yesterday, Gary was the creepiest guy in the room. I wouldn't have bought anything he was selling. Today he was a welcome sight.

The water grew deeper. Jenner sank under me. The saddle dropped from between my legs. Where was his body? I felt like an astronaut trying to land on the moon with no gravity. I grabbed the saddle horn and hung on. My feet drifted behind me. As he swam, Jenner was pulling me like a tugboat. His legs churned. His sides heaved with effort.

Then he slowed. I lunged forward and hooked my leg back over the saddle. Cold water soaked my jeans, making my legs feel numb and heavy. I held on to his mane until he came back up underneath me. We'd hit a shallow spot.

I was tempted to rest here, but I remembered Gary Nichols' warning. This could be part of the sandbar. I set my sights on the next set of markers, thirty feet off to the right. We sank into deep water again. My legs flailed uselessly and Jenner could barely feel the reins on his cold neck. I had to devise a new strategy to steer him. If I waved my right hand to the side of his face he angled left. This was hardly the kind of riding that would win ribbons, but I didn't care if we looked pretty. Jenner followed my gestures.

I glanced behind me. Sara and Kim swam a few yards behind us.

We zigzagged through the course. I barely touched Jenner's reins, giving him plenty of room to stretch his head above the treacherous waters. All the time I talked to him softly. "Good boy, Jenner. You're swimming like a champ. We're gonna make it all the way to that island."

The remaining markers continued in a winding route stretching on for what seemed like forever. On either side of the stakes, red and white buoys floated, all connected by a plastic rope. It helped me stay in the safe part of the channel, but I hoped the bobbing buoys wouldn't spook the herd on the way back. *If we make it that far.*

My eyes strained to see through the falling rain. I could see a paint stallion standing at attention, watching our every move. His head was the only head raised.

Mesteño. I begged him to hold on, to try his best to trust us and not run into the unmarked waters.

With renewed determination, I urged Jenner toward the next set of markers. His breathing was getting louder. Did he have the strength to make it? My best guess was that we were little more than halfway to the island. If Ranger Rick was right, that left at least two more football fields' worth of water to cross.

"C'mon, Jenner," I said. My shoulder ached from holding onto the horn. My legs hung as numb as pegs. "Not much farther now," I lied. And he knew it. But he moved on anyway.

"Good boy, Jenner," I whispered. He tossed his head and dragged us up from the abyss into the shallows. The muddy river bottom came up underneath us. I sank into the saddle. My jeans sloshed against Jenner's sides and then we were wading again—not swimming—and the water level receded to below Jenner's knees.

"We're right behind you!" Sara called out.

Suddenly, Jenner leapt to the side, almost unseating me. I pulled myself back to center and scanned the water for what had spooked him. I saw something dragging from his right front hoof. At first it appeared to be a plant, dark and undulating under the water, but then I realized what it was. Barbed wire! Barbed wire coated in mud, with spines sharp enough to cut Jenner's foot to the bone.

CHAPTER 53

VEN AS I called for help, I knew it was hopeless. What could they do? The boats were getting stuck in the shallows and no one would risk walking in this bog.

"Christa, hold on, slow down!" Sara shrieked.

Dread filled me as I remembered. This used to be farmland with farm animals. That meant there were fences. Think! Don't panic! I pushed the fear out of my mind and focused on Jenner. With the pressure of those sharp points digging into Jenner's leg, his every instinct was to run. He fought me for his head, but I fought back. If Jenner ran, he would only further entangle the wire. I had no idea what that wire was attached to. Jenner had the strength of an ox. A horrible image of Jenner dragging an entire barbed wire fence behind him, wooden posts and all, with pools of blood filling the water, flashed through my mind. I had to stop him.

I yanked on the reins. Muscles strained along my forearms. I locked my shoulders and leaned back. He stopped. I pressed my legs against his sides and held tight to the reins, so he couldn't move from side to side. I leaned down and stared. The wire was in the shape of a loop. It was closing tighter around Jenner's front leg with each step we took.

Star splashed up behind us. Sara and Star, who had come to

my rescue time after time, who had chased Jenner down on this very stretch of ground now unrecognizable from the floodwater, were coming to our rescue again. But it wasn't going to play out that way this time. I had to do this alone.

"Sara, don't come!" I said firmly. "You'll only spook him." I didn't dare turn around. I didn't have the time to explain. The sound of Star's footsteps stopped. Miracle of miracles, Sara had listened to me.

"Okay, Christa," she said. "We're behind you."

I needed to keep Jenner calm. I stroked his neck. *Steady now, boy.* I shifted my weight back and squeezed my legs, signaling him to back up. Had the barbs cut him? Afraid of what might be behind him, Jenner resisted and tried to leap forward, but I held him. "Back up. You can do it. Trust me."

His ear flicked back to me. He backed one step, then two, his hind end sinking in the mud. With each step, the barbed wire loosened. He could step free of it now if he lifted his hoof at just the right angle.

I had to ask him to do something we'd barely practiced, an advanced move reserved mostly for cutting horses—spinning. We'd tried it for Kim when we first met her. We'd have to do it again now.

While pulling straight up on the rein, I touched my right foot to his right shoulder. He responded and swung hard to the left in a half rear, lifting both front hooves off the muddy ground and landing clumsily. I hastened to pull back on the reins and keep him halted. Then I leaned over to check his foot.

The barbed wire had slipped off. Jenner had done it! He was free of the trap. I turned and gave the thumbs up sign to Sara and Kim. Sara waved back with so much enthusiasm, I almost laughed.

"You did it!" Sara cried.

"That girl can ride!" Kim cheered. "Now you're just showin' off!"

I let my breath out with a sigh. *Thank you, Jenner. You are a great horse. But we still have a long way to go. Are you ready?* The rain swept down in a renewed torrent. We couldn't afford more delays. I glanced back at Sara. "Keep your distance from the barbed wire."

"We'll swing around it," Sara called.

Then Kim's voice carried over the pounding rain. "Let's ride!"

And ride we did. From deep to shallow water, we gained ground, gradually closing the gap between the island and us.

I gasped for breath, but Jenner seemed to get stronger with each stride. He navigated each transition of the river bottom. When his feet found solid ground, his powerful haunches drove us into a trot so big, I felt like we were flying. I couldn't believe this was the same horse that had bolted from the water's edge just four months ago. I sat tall and admired his raw power, the regal curve of his neck, and his red mane blowing in the wind.

Jenner was my dream horse. Even Lucky wouldn't have had the strength to cross this water. I closed my eyes and wished on Lucky like I was wishing on a star. I asked him to be with us in spirit, to ride with us. Some part of me knew he was already with us, bringing us the good fortune we'd needed to get this far.

Looking out to the tiny knoll and the rain-soaked mustangs, I made a promise to the Lost Herd. "We're not leaving without you," I whispered.

CHAPTER 54

WE DREW CLOSER and closer. I could see Mesteño clearly now. Ever the stallion, he turned away from the herd to face us, his white mane and tail swirling in the wind, his forelock swinging over his eyes. There were two things I'd heard about stallions. Never look them directly in the eye and never charge straight at them. Quickly, I steered Jenner so we approached at an angle to the island. Mesteño tossed his head and pawed the ground.

Easy, boy. My mind spun in a tangle as dangerous as barbed wire. I knew it was crucial not to spook the herd and yet, somehow, we needed to convince the herd to follow, to trust us—three humans on strange horses. It seemed impossible, but we had to try. This was the Lost Herd of legends. This was the herd I'd loved since I was a little girl, since the first time I'd seen them, their thick manes streaming in the wind and eyes as wild as fire. If we ever had the chance to rub shoulders with something magical, this was it.

I glanced back to see Sara and Kim fanned out behind us in formation. Good thinking. Maybe if we staggered our approach we could avoid sending them running in the wrong direction.

I searched for Corazón and Grandfather, but couldn't pick them out of the mass of bodies. Foals stood under their mother's legs with their heads drooped down, noses almost touching the ground. They leaned into each other, soaking wet and exhausted. Then I saw him. Grandfather leaned heavily against a sturdy bay mare near Mesteño. The mare nipped at him, but he did not so much as flick an ear in her direction. If we didn't hurry, Grandfather would go down.

With renewed commitment, Jenner and I inched close enough to see markings and ear positions. But the mustangs stood very still. Were they conserving energy? Did they have enough strength to make the swim across? Even if we could get them to follow us, would they drown for their efforts? Mesteño still had a glint of fire in his eyes. I prayed he would do what was right for the herd.

When we were close enough to see every last whisker on the stallion's face, I pulled Jenner up. Water poured off of us as rain fell in thick sheets. I held up my hand, and Sara and Kim fanned out behind us on their mounts, waiting for me to do something smart. The only problem was I had no idea what to do next.

Mesteño stood his ground, nostrils working. His eyes locked on Jenner. He threw his head back and trumpeted a challenge. I eased Jenner back a few paces. We didn't come all this way to start a fight. If we could give Mesteño some breathing room, the stallion might back off, too.

We stood still. The seconds ticked by. I looked back to the distant shore, our finish line. Every few minutes, I stole a glance at Mesteño. Gradually, the stallion's posture relaxed–his head lowered a fraction.

I rode back to Sara, nice and easy. Kim joined us.

"Will they follow us back?" Sara asked quietly.

"I'm not sure," I answered. I scanned the herd for Corazón. I knew the herd would follow the wise old mare, but I couldn't find her in the mass of bodies. Was she still alive?

I swiped the rain from my eyes and tried to clear my head. I had to come up with a plan. Mesteño followed Jenner's every movement, but at least he wasn't pawing the ground anymore. He seemed to be accepting our presence for now.

"I don't know what to do," I said.

Kim grimaced. "Doesn't matter what you do, just try something. You're the one who knows this herd. If they go for it, we'll be ready."

Sara nodded. "We'll stay near the markers on opposite sides. Hopefully they'll see us and stay in the middle of the channel."

"Okay," I said. I waited until they had faded back about fifteen feet. They stood in water up to their horses' shoulders. Kim hugged the marker on one side and Sara did the same on the other.

Jenner and I edged back to the herd. Mesteño's head shot up and his neck crested, but he didn't call out. We stopped about twenty feet from the island. Jenner and I were now in the center of the channel.

Like a general trying to come up with a speech to motivate the troops, I rode Jenner back and forth along the shore, my eyes drinking in every member of the herd. I saw the weariness in their eyes, their rain-soaked hides and mud-splattered bodies. The wind blew their thick manes as they watched us suspiciously. Mesteño's body tensed.

"We're here to lead you back to safety," I sang quietly to the herd. "Follow us!"

My mind flashed back to the wild horses lying on their sides under the blue tarp on the hill. Something pulsed through me. A spark, a strength I didn't know I had, grew until my whole body tingled, and I knew, I just knew we had to get these horses moving, now. As we turned to make another pass, I sensed a ripple of excitement pass through the herd. Mesteño whinnied and tossed his head.

"C'mon!" I thought of the day Mesteño fought off the red, challenging stallion. *You belong in a place with no fences. Let me help you get back there.* My eyes willed Mesteño to move. If he jumped, there was a good chance the rest of the herd would follow. I swore I could see the wheels turning in the stallion's brain as he weighed his options. Every muscle in his body tensed as he looked from the herd to the water and back again.

You can do it! You'll die out here if you don't try! Jenner and I moved back a few paces in knee-deep water, leaving clear a path for the stallion.

And then a black horse appeared in the rain-grey darkness. She jostled through the herd to the edge of the water and turned her gaze on me. I saw panic and rage in her liquid eyes. *I'm sorry, Corazón. Sorry about the fences, the helicopters, and all the horrible ways we've tried to capture you. We're hopeless, us humans...but please don't give up on us. Not today. If you follow me, I'll help you.*

She stamped a foot at me. Her skin twitched.

It's not a trick. We'll feed you, let you rest, and then set you free again. I held my breath and fingered the braid of Lucky's hair in my pocket.

Corazon snorted impatiently through her red-lined nostrils. Then she raised her head and stared at me from one eye. I found my bones tingling in the strange way they did when she looked at me. My heart throbbed with emotion.

Do you remember me? Do you remember that day Lucky and I broke a trail through Gold Canyon so we could find you? The day I woke from my dream to discover you watching me. When we shared... what? I'm not sure I even know.

Suddenly, I wanted to tell her everything. A wave of heat rose from my chest and tears swam in my eyes. *Lucky's gone. I've lost him like you've lost some of your herd. But I have Jenner now.*

And then, I swear, Corazon dipped her head like she was bowing at me. I bowed my head in reply. Then she poised herself, rocked back on her hind legs, and leapt from the island into the river. Mesteño followed close behind. Together, they hurtled through the knee-deep water.

I pleaded silently, *Yes! Yes! C'mon!*

An avalanche of horses followed. One after the other, the wild horses plunged into the water. Noses turned up to the sky and manes danced; they snorted, pushed, pulled, jostled, kicked, and neighed. The film of hopelessness lifted from their eyes. They charged like the force of nature they surely were and nearly swallowed us in their power.

We'd have to move fast if we hoped to stay ahead of them.

"Ride!" I cried, kicking Jenner into a gallop.

Kim waved her hat and leaned forward in the saddle as Eastwood took off. "We're riding!"

The water grew deeper with each step. The Lost Herd gained on us, firing up through the middle of the wide channel with Kim and Sara on either side. Jenner's hungry stride ate up the ground, the water, the sky, and everything in between. I could barely hold on. I tasted water, I smelled and breathed water. We kicked up a wall of the stuff. I couldn't see anything in front of me or behind me. The air shook with the neighing of horses.

Then Jenner began swimming, floating through the strange flooded landscape. My legs drifted and I hung onto the saddle horn with one hand and Jenner's mane with the other. Felt more like flying than riding.

Jenner passed Sara and Kim. His shoulders worked steadily, piston-like. His ears pointed forward, honing in on the shore. Jenner didn't need me to tell him where we were going, and he sure didn't need me to tell him to go faster.

We passed the volunteers in the boats. They stared with their jaws hanging open. Before the rescue, Bob had drilled it into their heads to stay quiet, so as not to spook the mustangs. Either they were following directions or they'd lost the gift of human speech. The volunteers didn't so much as wave at us; they just gawked.

I couldn't blame them. None of us had ever seen anything like this. Behind us in a seemingly endless procession, two hundred wild horses swam for their lives. The legendary Lost Herd–the mustangs that had inspired me for as far back as I could remember–filled the channel. Not one herd member remained on the island.

A wild joy rose in me.

CHAPTER 55

FTER RIDING THROUGH the winding route and trying to sit Jenner's ever-changing gaits, I nearly cried with relief as we neared our starting point. Boats flanked us on either side, and people waved and cheered from the hill. As if on cue, the rain subsided and a shaft of sunlight broke through the dark clouds. The sun danced through the rain, sending a rainbow arching across the sky.

I picked out Grandma, Mom, and Bob Downs from the crowd. They jumped up and down like school kids. Dad held his Nikon steady in front of his face. A news crew from Reno set up close to the water.

Jenner reached the shore in full gallop. The crowd roared as we passed. Star cantered behind us, her nostrils flaring, and Eastwood's golden coat glistened as he ran alongside her. Together we made a path across the hill, and pulled our horses up away from the crowd. The horses were breathing hard and dripping water. We were, too, as we turned back to watch the wild horses come ashore.

Mesteño reached land first and everyone cleared a wide path for the stallion. He pranced and snorted as other horses joined him, and his white mane blew back dramatically with each shake of his magnificent head. BLM men stood at intervals along the hill with flags to guide Mesteño and his herd into a giant holding pen located at the very top of the hill, filled with bales of hay and troughs of fresh drinking water.

"Can you believe it, Christa?" Sara asked as more horses reached dry land.

"No way! And there's Echo and Dylan running with the blue roan mare from Mesteño's band!" The foals were all legs, but keeping up somehow.

"Thank God they made it!" Sara said.

The cheers of the crowd swelled as wave after wave of horses came galloping onto the shore, strung out in a long line. We had a ways to go, though. Most of the herd still filled the channel, swimming hard.

A veterinarian rushed over to us and checked our horses from head to toe. I asked him a million questions when he got to Jenner's front foot and his rear hock, but all the horses received a clean bill of health. No tendon pulls, no lameness, nothing serious, just a few scratches. They had come through the rescue without injury.

Dad sprinted over to us and pulled us down from the horses, crushing us in huge bear hugs. He swung me around. "You're a true horsewoman," he whispered to me. I knew that was the biggest compliment he could give.

"Okay, Dad. Great. You can put me down now," I said, laughing. I peered over his shoulder trying to keep an eye on the wild mustangs.

He put me back on the ground, ruffling my hair before running down the hill. "Gotta get the action shots while I can!"

Grandma swept me up into her arms. "There are no words for what I saw today, love." She wiped the tears from her eyes. "That was pure magic. Pure and utter magic."

I hugged her back, relieved to have made it. "I'm just so glad the horses are okay. They deserve to be free."

Grandma kissed each of my cheeks. "We all deserve to be free," she said.

"Oh, but don't we, though?" Mom put her arms around me and hugged me so tightly I couldn't breathe. She smelled like home. Our wet hair clung together when she pulled away. "You were so brave out there...you've been so brave, Christa," she said, searching my face.

"Jenner was the brave one. I just had to stay on him!"

I glanced back at my horse. His breathing had returned to normal, and he nuzzled my arm with a soft nose and sparkling eye. I was so proud of him. Jenner had faced his biggest fear today and overcome that fear.

"Uh-oh," Mom said, slipping her arm in mine and turning quickly down the hill. "Don't look behind you."

But it was too late. KGBA news snuck up on us with a cameraman. Before I could run, Sandy Lyons shoved a microphone in my face and flashed me a winning smile. "Can I get a statement from you?"

"Sure," I said shyly.

Mom tried to smooth my curls and gave up. "I guess one miracle was enough for today," she muttered.

"All of you, please come here." Sandy gathered Sara, Kim and the horses near her in a tight circle. She singled me out first. "What's your name, young lady?"

I clutched Jenner's reins and stroked his neck. "I'm Christa and this is my horse, Jenner."

"Christa, can you tell us what happened out there?"

This could be my big moment. I flashed forward in my mind to a scene where I was telling this story to my grandkids. The day I, Christa Cassidy, stayed on Jenner long enough to do something memorable. But then I remembered the Lost Herd. I watched them coming through the floodwater in a long line, and I just couldn't imagine how anyone would want to waste their time hearing about me.

I pointed to the herd. "They're the story, not me," I said. "And I don't want to miss seeing one more horse come onshore."

I spun away from the camera, leading Jenner. So much for my public relations career. Kim and Sara followed right behind. I guess they felt the same way I did.

"Are you leaving all the air time for Gary Nichols?" Kim teased.

"Yep. He can have it."

Sandy Lyons wrapped up her segment. "The wild mustangs that were in danger of drowning are now safely on dry land. Three teenage girls from Spring Hills, Nevada, are largely responsible for their rescue."

I scanned the water for Corazón and Grandfather. Where were they? There was one last group of black horses, gray around their muzzles, struggling to navigate the final stretch of water. I nearly screamed watching them. They slipped, went under, scrambled back up, then stumbled and pitched forward.

Grandma joined us. Tears streamed down her face.

"I've never seen anything like it," she said. "These old ones…"

"I know," I whispered, my eyes locked on them.

Could one of those dark horses out there be Corazón? But she had been in the lead…had she dropped back?

And then I saw her. Of course, it was the beautiful mare. No other horse had that thick wavy mane and proud glint in her eye. She was the last one of the group and swimming strongly. She nipped at the older horses flanks', ears pinned back and eyes flashing. In that moment, if Grandma had told me Corazón was Epona herself coming to the aid of the herd, I would have believed her.

Corazón moved those horses in front of her like a stallion. Just when I thought I understood wild horses, they did something new. She stayed behind them, nipping and biting at their flanks until they clambered ashore. One by one, they climbed from the bloated river.

They shook the water from their thin bodies and walked slowly up the hill.

Corazón trotted through the shallows, tossing her head. Her battle-scarred flanks dripped water and her tail flew high. My heart raced at the sight of her.

"Corazón," I whispered as she galloped past, "You and your herd are safe now."

The crowd began slowly breaking up. I stretched my aching body. Mom shoved a bottle of water in my hand and a power bar and urged me to drink. I swallowed half the bottle in greedy gulps. Sara yanked on my arm.

"Look!" She pointed out to the water.

About a hundred yards out from the shore I spotted an old roan, barely moving. I looked again to be sure. Mostly gray muzzle, hipbones jutting out, and a long wispy tail. It was Grandfather! Several wranglers and firefighters gathered around him. What were they doing out there? Grandfather seemed not to notice, as if he was in a trance.

"It's like he's stuck," I said.

Grandfather stumbled and his hind end collapsed. Four firefighters rushed to his side and leaned their shoulders into him until he was steady enough to stand upright.

Kim spoke the obvious. "Those men are strong, but if that horse goes down, he's not getting back up."

"He can't die out there—that's Grandfather!" I said. Renewed strength pumped through my veins. "We can't lose him. We've got to help that horse!" I mounted up again. This wasn't over. Before anyone could stop me, I turned Jenner and galloped back down to the water.

CHAPTER 56

JENNER BLASTED INTO the water like a jet ski. Sara and Kim plunged into our wake on Star and Eastwood. Within seconds, we were close enough to see the whites of Grandfather's eyes. His body trembled. Two men stood on either side of the old horse, knee deep in water, while a boy stood behind. When he turned his face to me, I couldn't believe my eyes. *Cisco?* "What are you doing here?" I asked.

"I was in the neighborhood." Cisco's yellow rain slicker hung down to his knees. He was half the size of the firefighters next to him, but he exuded a quiet confidence. He studied Grandfather with a furrowed brow while the firefighters waited. I smiled to myself. These big tough guys were taking orders from a skinny fifteen-year-old.

I urged Jenner closer. "What's wrong with him?"

"I don't think he can lift his left hind leg. He's locked up at the hip."

"We're losing him," a firefighter said. Grandfather swayed dangerously to one side. The men strained to hold him up. They dug their heels in and pushed with all their might.

"We've got to save him!" I met Cisco's eyes. "We've got to!"

"You're the horse trainer. Figure something out, Cisco!" Kim ordered.

He shot her a dark glance. "I'm thinking as fast as I can." He pushed back the hood of the slicker and scratched his head. "If only we could get his weight off that bad hip." A light crossed his face. "Christa, hand me your rope."

I untied the rope from my saddle and threw it to him.

Cisco slipped the rope around the roans' hindquarters and tied a sailor's knot. I couldn't believe a wild mustang would let a boy get a rope around him without flinching, but Grandfather seemed to be in shock. He stood swaying, letting the men push and prod him, his eyes blank.

Cisco took the long end of the rope and threw it back to me. "Tie this to your saddle horn and take up the slack. If you can keep Jenner alongside this old guy walking slowly, I think we can get him back."

"I don't get it," I said, confused.

"We're going to use Jenner as a sort of tug-boat to lift the old guy's bad hip and pull him along. We need to get the weight off of that bad leg. He's got three legs he can still use."

I finished tying the rope to the saddle horn. "Okay. It's worth a try," I said.

Cisco motioned to Sara and Kim. "You two, get your horses behind him. We want to give him a good reason to keep moving."

"You got it," Sara said. Star gracefully waded behind Grandfather, sniffing at the strange horse.

Kim and Eastwood splashed into position beside Sara and Star. Eastwood ignored Grandfather completely. He sank his golden muzzle into the water and drank casually, like it was every day that he came this close to a wild mustang.

I moved Jenner to the wounded side of the old roan. Jenner towered over him. Hopefully, with Jenner's height, we could support the weight of Grandfather's bad hip by lifting it slightly up in the air and allowing the roan's three good legs to carry him. Cisco was a genius.

When the rope pulled tight, Cisco signaled to Kim and Sara. They pressed in on Grandfather from behind, gently encouraging him to move forward. The roan took a tentative step. I swore a look of relief passed over his face. It must've been much easier for him with his bad hip supported. He hobbled slowly along.

I could've kissed his old gray muzzle for not giving up. "Grandfather," I whispered. "One step at a time. All your friends are waiting on you and there's a big flake of orchard grass in your future."

I saw a glint of light in Grandfather's eye. Each step was agony for him, but every step brought him closer to his herd.

I made sure to keep Jenner moving at the perfect speed to keep the rope stretched tight.

"Stay slightly ahead of him, Christa," Cisco suggested.

Jenner slanted an ear back to me, obeying my cues. He eased forward a bit and it seemed to speed Grandfather's progress. Cisco's plan was working. We closed in on the shore.

Jenner snorted playfully and bumped Grandfather with his nose. The roan flattened his ears and nipped at Jenner with large, yellow teeth.

"There's a good boy," Cisco said to Grandfather. He grinned. "Looks like he's getting his spirit back."

"Jenner, you be nice!" I laughed.

After that, Grandfather kept his eyes and ears pinned on the shore as if we didn't exist. When we only had a few feet left to go, the firefighters began to cheer the old horse on. "C'mon, old man, you got what it takes."

We all counted down his last ten steps. "Ten, nine, eight, seven…" Grandfather's head shot up, smelling the wind, "six, five, four…" Mesteño screamed a call that blasted down the hill and

Grandfather whinnied back with all his strength. "Three, two, one–!"

With the last step we reached shore and I untied the rope from Jenner's saddle horn. A team of wranglers stepped in and surrounded Grandfather. "We'll take him from here. Easier for him to walk on dry land," Cisco said. I handed him the rope.

The old horse looked back at Jenner and me with a look I could only describe as grateful.

I heard a gasp from the gathered assembly of people and followed their gaze. Corazón stood a short distance up the hill. Her long, black mane blew in the wind. She whinnied to Grandfather, tossing her head and pawing the ground. Bob Downs sprang into action, clearing people out of her path.

Grandfather nickered back to the lead mare. She came to him slowly, her nose stretched out, suddenly looking like a young filly. She touched noses with him for a brief moment and exhaled forcefully.

She swung her head in my direction and I stared back at her, wordlessly caught in her spell, chills running down the back of my neck. Then she whirled and charged back up the hill to rejoin the herd. It seemed impossible after the long swim that she would have the energy for such a display of strength, but from the first day I'd saw her, Corazón had been full of surprises.

For a long minute, nobody moved. Then somebody began clapping. More people joined in until it swelled to a crescendo. I guess I wasn't the only one who found Corazón compelling. That mare was as dark and mysterious as death and as wild as the storm she had so narrowly survived.

Sara slapped me on the back, bringing me back to the moment. "Nice going out there."

I shrugged off my life vest and tossed it on the ground. "You, too."

Kim grinned. "Guess we girls did a good thing today."

I jumped down from Jenner. He looked at me with his soft brown eyes gleaming and nickered. "You're the bravest horse in the world!" First, I kissed his wet nose and stroked his white blaze. Then, I ran to congratulate Star and Eastwood. They stood, breathing hard, ears swiveling at every sound.

Kim leapt off of Eastwood and threw her arms around me and Sara. With our horses in tow, we made our way up the same hill we had come down hours before. It felt like a year had passed since then. I'd grown another inch taller. Okay, well, maybe two inches. Yep, at least two.

CHAPTER 57

THE TOP OF the hill swarmed with activity. Large bales of hay rose from the ground, stacked high and covered with plastic tarps. Vets administered care to the several horses that had collapsed. Foals ran in circles around their mothers, whinnying shrilly. Set back away from the people, the Lost Herd grazed in a huge grassy meadow, enclosed by temporary fencing.

Sara and Kim each threw an arm around my shoulder. "You and Jenner were awesome out there," Kim said.

"Well, we had some room for improvement." I laughed.

Sara looked into my eyes. "You never gave up," she said, a tinge of awe in her voice.

"None of us did," I said.

We brought our horses back to the trailer and pulled the heavy, waterlogged saddles off of their broad backs. We gave them well-earned flakes of alfalfa, orchard grass, and a little bit of grain for energy before rubbing them down until they were gleaming. All three horses dropped to their knees and rolled in the grass, grunting and groaning with happiness.

A pod of little kids descended on the horses like fireflies, climbing under their legs, pulling on their manes and tails, and stroking their soft muzzles. Jenner reached down and sniffed their faces. He looked like a giant next to them. His head stretched the entire length of one child's body. They giggled and crept close, then screamed and ran when Jenner sniffed their pockets. Star and Eastwood let the kids crawl all over them, their eyes gentle and kind. Finally, we shooed the kids off so the horses could get a moment's peace.

Once the horses were happily eating, we followed the sound of music to the celebration. Just above the parking lot under an awning, portable grills smoked with hot coals. The smell of hamburgers and hotdogs sent my stomach from a rumble to a growl.

Coolers stocked with soft drinks, juice, and bottled water lined one table. Chips, dips, and potato salad crowded a second table. Country music played from a portable stereo.

"Where did all this come from?" I asked.

Sara shrugged. "Mom packed a couple of coolers. I guess everybody else did, too."

"I don't think Bob would want to miss a meal. He probably keeps a grill in his truck," Kim said.

The food smelled good, but I couldn't think of eating yet. Sara grabbed a hotdog and chips and ate while standing up. Kim sipped a coke and nibbled on some grapes. She said she was still too keyed up to eat a full meal.

We spotted Cisco looking lean and animated, talking and eating with a group of wranglers. Several enormous firefighters patted him on the back, clinking beer bottles together in a toast.

Cisco's eyes caught mine as we passed. "Nice job out there. Thanks for the tow."

"No worries. That was a brilliant idea." I paused. "Hey. What you did for Jenner and me. All those rides on the trail. What you taught us. It made all the difference out there today."

A blush tinged his cheeks. "You would've found a way. Just might have taken you a little bit longer."

I laughed. "Yeah, like the rest of my life!" Without thinking, I stepped in and gave him a hug. He wrapped his arms around me and hugged me back with such warmth I melted into him.

"You're amazing," he whispered.

I pulled back. "Me? What about Amy?"

"What about Amy?"

"You're not like, with her?"

"Nope," he said, still holding onto me.

If he didn't like Amy, then maybe he liked...me. He pulled me closer. Oh my God! Was he going to kiss me? I panicked and my body stiffened. Instantly, he let go and shoved my shoulder playfully. "We'll have to ride again soon," he said.

"Yeah, of course!" I blushed.

The firefighters started whistling, teasing us. I spun away, waving awkwardly. My heart was beating faster than it should, and I actually felt a little dizzy. Way too confusing. Quickly, I caught up with Sara and Kim.

We ran into Amy Whitehorse, her brown eyes widening with excitement when she saw us. She wanted to hear every detail of the ride. We each blurted out our version of the rescue. People I didn't even know interrupted us to introduce themselves. I was lost in a blur of smiling faces for what felt like hours.

Bob Downs wandered over to our group. He looked ten years younger than he had that morning. He'd also gotten his appetite back—his plate sagged with a mountain of potato salad and a big cheeseburger. "We hadn't planned on having a party, but you girls made this a day worth celebrating! And what with the storm breaking and all, we just couldn't resist."

I glanced down at my feet, suddenly shy. Kim gave Bob a high-five and Sara shook his hand. "Thank you," she said.

"You wanted a rescue. We gave you one!" Kim cried jubilantly.

Bob laughed and pulled away from Sara, probably not wanting to be separated from his plate for too long. "And that old roan horse is going to recover." He took a huge bite of his burger and mayonnaise ran down his chin. "The horse is out with the rest of the herd." Bob winked at me. "They won't go to the BLM holding facility. We'll keep them here till they recover and then they'll all be set free."

"That's so great!" I said. "But this doesn't mean I'm going to stop writing you letters."

"Well, I'm relieved to hear that," Bob's eyes twinkled. "I'd hate to lose my pen pal after all these years."

"I know how hard that would be on you. Although we may be on the same side now."

He put an arm around me. "We always were, Christa, even though it took me awhile to realize it."

Just when it felt like my face was going to fall off if I smiled another minute, Bob Downs got serious. "I want to thank you young ladies from the bottom of my heart," he said, his voice warm. "That was a real stroke of luck out there, watching you turn that herd." He leaned in closer. "By the way, how did you get the herd to follow you, Christa?"

I thought about my silent communication with Corazón. And how even though I'd only seen her a handful of times, I felt that this horse knew me as well as any person ever could. How could I explain that to Bob Downs…or to anybody? My connection with the lead mare was a complete mystery. "It was just luck, I guess," I said.

He mulled over that, patted me on the arm, and walked away. "She has no idea how she did it," he said to a stranger. The stranger glanced at me and I smiled awkwardly. Bob chuckled as he wandered through the crowd. "She says it was just luck," he muttered. "Christa's luck."

And then all I heard was music blaring in my ears. The energy seemed to drain from me in an instant and I yearned for a hot shower and my soft pillow. I had to get out of here before I fell asleep standing up.

But I had one more thing left to do.

CHAPTER 58

I WALKED THROUGH THE soft grass to the trailer and untied Jenner. I led him across the hill to the blue tarp where eighteen horses lay dead. We stood there in silence, the wind rustling the tarp. I removed my green silk scarf and placed it over the tarp. Securing it with four stones in each corner, I said solemnly, "This blessing is for all of you. For every one of you." My eyes blurred with tears.

I knew how fortunate I was to have had the chance to see the Lost Herd again, let alone play a part in their rescue. But my heart ached for the horses under the blue tarp.

The silk scarf fluttered in the wind, revealing the three horses dancing through the Celtic knot design. "Epona, please care for all of the horses who died in this storm. And, er, set their spirits free. Or do whatever a horse goddess does," I added, wiping the tears away with my sleeve.

Dusk fell, tingeing the edges of the gray clouds with pink. I tipped my head back to the sky. For a minute, all the clouds seemed to take the shape of horses running—spirit horses dancing, rearing, and thundering through the sky. I searched for Lucky. I would never give up hope that I'd see him again.

"Epona, please tell Lucky that I love him." The image of Lucky staring at me with his sweet eyes flashed through my mind and then dissolved, leaving a feeling of warmth and peace in its place. "Until we meet again, Lucky…" I whispered.

Jenner stood patiently by my side, his head lowered respectfully. He nudged my arm and I laughed. I'd forgotten the most important part.

"And finally, Epona, please remember to protect Jenner, my big red horse." I turned to Jenner and threw my arms around his neck. "I promise I'll love you and care for you the best I can no matter what…always."

CHAPTER 59

A WEEK LATER, A crowd gathered on the same hill to watch the release of the mustangs. For the previous few days, the bright sun had triumphed over the clouds and the swollen waters had receded back into the familiar shape of the Twin Rivers.

I missed Grandma. She'd gone back to Reno. I managed to hug her goodbye without making a scene, but I'll admit I teared up as I watched her car disappear down the driveway. She was hanging out the window, dabbing at her eyes with a tissue and waving so hard I thought her arm might fall off. I wished she could see this with her own eyes, but a YouTube video would have to do.

Mom and Dad stood further up the hill with the Whitehorses and Mr. and Mrs. Rodriguez. Mom held a small bundle in her arms. Swathed in a white blanket, Hazel slept peacefully. She was the cutest baby ever born. She had the plumpest cheeks you could imagine and eyelashes that made me melt.

I had a cluster of pictures of Hazel on the bulletin board over my desk, along with pictures of Jenner, Sara, Kim, Cisco, and Amy. Dad's photos of the Lost Herd crossing the water went along the top. I'd retrieved the box under my bed and fished out my favorite pictures of Lucky and tacked them up, too. There were pictures from the shows we'd won, all our blue ribbons and the arrowhead, all woven in with the newer pictures of Jenner and me during the rescue. Grandma's green scarf hung proudly in one corner, waving like a flag. As for the journal Mom gave me? I'd get to it some day.

Amy Whitehorse waved from the top of the muddy slope.

I waved back and she scrambled a few steps down to where Kim, Sara, Cisco and I paced restlessly. "Looks like they're getting close to opening the gate," I said.

Bob Downs sat astride a black horse standing near the corral. He tipped his hat in our direction, and I nodded. The BLM employees swarmed around the large corral, waving long sticks with flags on top. The flags were intended to help them "manage" the herd, but I don't think they were working.

The horses seemed to sense something was about to happen and began crowding the gate. I caught sight of Mesteño and his band near the front. Corazón stood near Echo and Dylan, keeping the foals in line with gentle nudges. But too many horses were gathered in a small space and tensions were mounting. Mesteño flattened his ears and nipped at a black stallion from another band. The black stallion whirled and kicked, but Mesteno dodged the blow and the stallion smashed the fence with his hooves.

Sara started videotaping with her phone. "Is Bob going to open the gate?"

Kim kicked the ground with her boot and grimaced. "If he is, I wish he'd get to it already."

"Sooner would be better than later," Cisco grumbled from under his hat. He'd lost all patience and was lying on the ground with his cowboy hat over his face.

Finally, Bob walked the black horse to the gate and in one swift movement, undid the latch.

Mesteño exploded out of the gate with his band close behind him. They made for the river. A howl of joy swept through the crowd. Cisco leapt to his feet.

I clasped my hands over my mouth to keep from screaming. Band after band raced through the sagebrush-covered plain. Mesteño tossed his head and trumpeted when he reached the water. Corazón plunged into the river fearlessly, leading her band safely across. They took the far bank and kept running.

Everyone watched in silent admiration.

Another season would come and go for the Lost Herd. The grass would grow under their feet, foals would be born, and others would die. Their wild souls could return to nature. "Their legend lives on," I said.

Polite clapping from the crowd rose into a loud cheer as the last band of wild horses swept out of the corral and charged into the desert. I hoped they'd never see the inside of a fence again.

A woman walked up beside me. She had long brown hair and cradled a tiny dog in her arms. I recognized her from the Wild Mustang Sanctuary website. "Elizabeth Levine?" I asked.

She smiled and held her hand out. "Call me Liz."

"I'm Christa Cassidy," I sputtered.

"Well, Miss Cassidy, I saw what you did at the rescue. I want to take you up on your offer to help the Wild Mustang Sanctuary." She nodded at Sara. "Your sister and your friend's help would be great, too."

I exchanged an awed glance with Sara and Kim. "We're in. I mean, yes."

Elizabeth slipped me her card. "Call me. We've got a lot of work to do."

The Lost Herd ran well beyond the river. The outline of their flying manes and tails receded into the horizon. I imagined them galloping deep into the remote areas of the range where humans seldom traveled. Grandma's words echoed in my mind. *We all deserve to be free.*

Cisco caught my eye. My stomach did a little flip as he walked over.

"Hey," I said.

"Hey," he replied. He put an arm around my shoulders, and we looked out toward the mustangs. "You know what?" he asked.

I hoped Boy Wonder wasn't going to say something deep. "What?

"Now I can die happy," he said, grinning.

A smile spread across my face. For once, I knew exactly what he meant.

THE END

CHRISTA CASSIDY

MRS. THOMPSON, ENGLISH 2ND PERIOD

ESSAY

Great job Christa!

The Legend of the Lost Herd

MY GRANDMA GILLIAN was the first person to tell me the Legend of the Lost Herd. It was the kind of story old timers would tell around the fire with a wink and a nod. And yet, at any mention of the Lost Herd, my skin tingled and my heart beat faster. They were rumored to be the finest mustangs in Nevada, led by a stallion so fierce, he could go a week without eating and run all day without so much as a break in his stride. I think everybody must have dreamed of taming a wild mustang from the Lost Herd because they wanted to capture its wild spirit and have it for their very own. But the Lost Herd remained free.

During the Gold Rush, men poured into the West. Lured by riches, they ventured into territory belonging to the wild things. Like a small child turning a piggy bank upside down and shaking it in hopes of a single penny falling to the floor, the men all but turned the wilderness upside down, begging the earth to give up her secrets. They swarmed along the rivers and trashed the waterways. They dynamited holes in the ancient rock and sifted through the rubble. They shook, dug, blasted, mined, sorted, picked, and panned, all in a frantic effort to procure even an ounce of gold.

It was said that the Lost Herd disappeared deep into the Sage Mountains to escape from the men and their madness. But on certain nights when the moon was full, people swore they saw a herd of wild mustangs running along the high ridge of Gold Canyon. Echoes of a thousand hooves thundered and shadows flitted against the ochre walls. Some claimed they saw a black mare gallop right out of the sky! As rumors spread that the Lost Herd haunted Gold Canyon, people grew skittish about going anywhere near there. The miners shut down the mines, cleared out, and never returned. To this day, if you wait until the moon is full, you may hear the call of the wild stallion ring through the canyon or see a black mare vanish into the night.

Some say the Lost Herd never existed. Or if they did, they were wiped out years ago, scattered to the wind like gold dust. But I know they are alive and well because I saw them with my own eyes.

CPSIA information can be obtained at www.ICGtesting.com
Printed in the USA
LVOW10s2014070815

449270LV00006B/589/P